House

THE FOUNTAIN ARETHUSE

Academic Books

By Marian F. Sia and Santiago Sia

From Suffering to God: Exploring Our Images of God in the
Light of Suffering

By Santiago Sia

God in Process Thought
Process Theology and the Christian Doctrine of God (ed.)
Charles Hartshorne's Concept of God (ed.)

THE FOUNTAIN ARETHUSE

A Novel Set in the University Town of Leuven

M.S. Sia

The Book Guild Ltd
Sussex, England

The Book Guild Ltd
25 High Street,
Lewes, Sussex

First published 1997
© Marian F. Sia and Santiago Sia, 1997
Set in Bembo
Typesetting by Acorn Bookwork, Salisbury, Wiltshire

Printed in Great Britain by
Antony Rowe Ltd, Chippenham, Wiltshire

A catalogue record for this book is
available from the British Library

.

ISBN 1 85776 256 8

TO

our beloved parents

at whose fountains
we first drank
the water of life and wisdom

Begin then, Sisters of the sacred well,
That from beneath the seat of *Jove* doth spring,
Begin, and somewhat loudly sweep the string,
Hence with denial vain, and coy excuse,
So may some gentle Muse
With lucky words favour my destin'd Urn,
And as he passes turn,
And bid fair peace be to my sable shrowd.

. . .

O Fountain *Arethuse*, and thou honour'd flood,
Smooth-sliding *Mincius*, crown'd with vocall reeds,
That strain I heard was of a higher mood:

John Milton, 'Lycidas'

In the centre of Leuven stands the Fons Sapientiae, the symbol of the town's academic tradition. But like every other symbol, it means various things to those who see it and makes a different impact on all who visit the place.

It reminds Aisling O'Shea of the fountain Arethuse in ancient Greek mythology since Leuven draws scholars from all over the world for inspiration. To Richard Gutierrez, the difference between the refreshing sight of the scholar and the dullness of the same monument when the water is turned off represents his experience of the gap between life and academia. Just as the stone scholar in the fountain hides behind an opened book, Jennifer Sidney turns away from life and buries herself in her scholarly task – and learns the consequences of such a choice. Piotr Malachowski sees in the water flowing into the scholar's head the wrong source of wisdom. For him, it is within oneself, in the struggles of life, that one gains true wisdom. Fr. Miguel Fuentes learns to view the fountain from a new perspective, one that challenges his nationalistic sentiments.

The Fountain Arethuse highlights the vibrant play of tensions, personal and academic, that influence the modern university, yet it raises vital issues which extend beyond its campus into all walks of life.

I

Richard Gutierrez had just retrieved his mail from the mail center of his university. As he scrutinized the contents of his rather stuffed mailbox, he noticed among the usual flyers, book catalogues, internal mail, the particular letter he had been waiting for.

'I do hope it's good news,' he muttered with some anxiety as he hurriedly tore the side of the airmail envelope which bore the seal of Mercier University in Leuven, Belgium. Richard had lifted the envelope from the rest of his mail and there and then proceeded to read its contents, ignoring the young undergraduate whose path to her own mailbox he was thoughtlessly blocking.

He had applied for a research fellowship at the renowned university in Belgium in the belief that it would provide him with the opportunity to finish his manuscript on the problem of evil, a scholarly endeavor that he had been working on for three years. Unfortunately, it had become somewhat of a Damocles's sword. Every time he was asked about it he would reply that he was writing the last chapter. He found himself giving that answer repetitively. And it was starting to sound unconvincing even to himself.

As time sped by, he was also becoming painfully aware that his Dean was not really impressed. At his recent annual speech marking the beginning of the academic year, the Dean had remarked quite emphatically, 'When somebody tells me that he or she is working on something, that's fine.' Then with a rather serious countenance he had added, 'But a time should come when that same individual comes to me and says, it's finished. That's when I am really impressed.' Richard did not feel that the remark (or was it a veiled threat?) was directly

1

aimed at him since there were others in his college who were in the same boat, so to speak. Like him, his fellow academics were bumping into all sorts of obstacles. As they set out to sail in the sea of scholarship, prodded on by the administrators, they kept floundering and just could not land.

In Richard's case it was particularly crucial because this year he was required to apply for tenure, the prized academic achievement that would give him job security at his university. While he prepared the file which would serve as the basis for the important decision, he realized that his publication record was abysmal: only three reviews in six years. Would that be sufficient, he wondered as his stomach muscles tightened as if in warning to him? Indeed, he had good reason to be seriously concerned, because research and scholarship had begun to feature as the primary criterion for tenure and promotion at his university. Although his students regarded him as an excellent teacher ('the best ever', 'well worth the huge tuition fee we pay to this university' and other such comments in the students' evaluations) he had been informed on the occasion of his second year evaluation by the department, four years ago, that this was not enough. He had to publish.

The letter was now in his hands. There was no doubting its origin. From the practically endless correspondence he had carried on over the past few months with one of the professors there, he had become very familiar with the letterhead of Mercier University in Leuven, whose academic seal featured prominently on the right-hand side of the stationery.

'But it's in Dutch!' he groaned. Unlike the responses in English which he had been receiving from the professor in Leuven, the official notification was written in a language completely foreign to Richard. Involuntarily he turned to the bemused student behind him. 'How the hell am I supposed to know what it says?' Richard caught himself expressing his sentiments out loud.

The student's amusement turned into an embarrassed silence. Suddenly she decided that this was not the best time for her to

2

insist on opening her mailbox, so she smiled rather coyly and beat a hasty retreat. She would rather return when the coast was clear.

Richard's voice betrayed the frustration he felt. His knowledge of languages was embarrassing. Like so many others in the English-speaking world he believed that because English was almost universally spoken or at least understood there was no reason to learn another language. When he was accused of neglecting his Spanish origins, he defended himself saying that he belonged to the second generation. His parents, who were bilingual, insisted that he spoke only English so that he would get on in America. They did not want him to speak English with a foreign accent like they did. They wanted him to learn the American way and be American. In that way he would be assured of success, of a better life than his parents ever had.

With quick steps Richard cut across the lawn to his office, which was a short distance away. Normally the few extra seconds needed to walk on the concrete L-shaped path to his office, rather than on the grass, did not bother him. But today he wanted to telephone a colleague immediately. In no time at all he was in front of his office fumbling for his keys. After unlocking the door and dropping the rest of the mail on top of his oak desk, he reached for the telephone at the edge of the desk.

The newly installed telephones, equipped with Voicemail, as well as state-of-the-art personal computers, complete with indecipherable programs, were the brainchild of the Vice-President for Academic Affairs. 'The working environment of the faculty should be first-class. Then we can rightly expect more from them,' she had declared with that characteristic left-hand smile of hers. But the eager and highly motivated technicians of the Computing Central Office were always feeding new programs into the computers, confusing some of the less technologically inclined faculty, like Richard, who did not believe that it was right that technology should dominate their life. At least that was their excuse for not being able to master all the programs, never mind keeping up with the

3

computer programmers who seem to be regularly on the prowl.

As Richard rested the receiver against his right ear and heard his colleague's telephone ring, his eyes wandered around his office, a cozy working environment indeed. His books were properly shelved rather than stacked up, which is a more common sight in academic offices, eliciting comments on how neat and impressive his office was. Everything seemed in its proper place, he was told. Aquinas's *Summa Theologiae*, flanked by other volumes in medieval philosophy, occupied a prominent place. On one wall was his laminated diploma testifying to the award of a Ph.D. from Loyola University of Chicago. Richard was lucky that his office was in Bergman Hall, a one-story building built in the style of the Missions and one of the most aesthetically designed buildings on campus. More importantly, the offices here were spacious.

Colleagues in the English Department and the Theology Department never failed to remind him of the 'fortunate circumstances' under which Philosophy and the other Liberal Arts departments conducted their so-called affairs. In comparison, the offices of the two separated brethren departments, up on the top floor of the Ahimsa building, were rather 'compact and cozy' in the words of the Dean – 'minuscule' corrected the literary inhabitants and 'lofty' chimed in the contemplatives among the theologians. Their Ahimsa building was a more recent construction; it appeared on the campus when the university received a donation from a very generous Indian benefactor. As a gesture to that part of the world, the university being concerned about its international image, and in honor of (and possibly as an encouragement to) the newly found member of the circle of generous friends of the university, an attempt had been made to make the façade resemble the Taj Mahal. But somehow the designs did not exactly materialize as expected. Instead the result was a tall building whose black arches and white outer walls, with windows only at the very top, hid some faculty offices on the fourth floor. Definitely not the kind of architecture that would remind anyone of the famous landmark of India.

4

Inside the Ahimsa building the narrow passages separating the two rows of offices were just sufficient for the student, while waiting for a professor – particularly during conferencing time for English 110 courses – to sit on the floor, with his or her back against one wall. They would stretch their legs to the opposite wall (which is what most of the students did since they found that to be a more comfortable position). The more nimble of the faculty did not mind skipping over these sun-tanned outstretched legs, their owners usually clad only in shorts to accommodate the climate in southern California. But a senior member of the Theology Department who belonged to a well-known religious order resented 'having to see all those bare legs and having to make a darn good effort at avoiding them.' No, he assured everyone, they were not a threat to his vocation. It was his bad back that he was worried about!

Richard was relieved that he did not have any of those concerns. Rather abruptly, his musings were cut short when a voice came on the line:

'Hello, this is Jan Vergote.'

'Jan, can I check something with you?'

'Fire away. What's on your mind?'

'I received a letter from Leuven, but it's in Dutch. Can I read it to you over the phone?'

'Sure. Just hold on a minute while I close the door.' The corridor was rather noisy from the chatter of students who were visiting the office next door. 'That's better,' he said when he picked up the phone again. 'Go ahead. I'm listening.'

Richard made a valiant effort at reading the letter, but he could hear Jan laughing at the other end of the line. Richard's face colored.

'Whoa, that sounds like, well, double Dutch to me. Why not come around with the letter to my office?'

Originally from Belgium, Jan and his family had immigrated to the USA. Fluent in Dutch, French and English, Jan had been energetically fighting for the introduction of international studies at the university and of a foreign language in the core curriculum. Lamenting the fact that the

5

students were not being prepared for a global perspective, he carried, with the fervor and enthusiasm of a missionary, his message to his language and literature classes, to any committee of which he was a member, and to the Vice-President for Academic Affairs.

After rummaging through the contents of the top drawer of his desk, Richard picked out a small yellow note with a gummed edge, wrote 'Back in a minute' on it and stuck it on his door. It was his office hour and he did not want his students complaining on their evaluation sheets that he had been unavailable. Most of his students were aware that he was in the university most days, but one or the other student could come to see him in the office on that one occasion and miss him. The disgruntled student could louse up his percentages in question 1 of the evaluation which inquired whether the instructor was 'available during office hours.' Better not to be sorry, he thought, as he rubbed his thumb over the note to make sure it would stick, I don't have tenure yet.

Jan's office was located in the same building as Richard's. The shortest way between the two offices was down the corridor to the Department of Languages. On the walls of that corridor were noticeboards belonging to the Philosophy Department. One of these was constantly being updated since on it were the philosophy courses offered for the semester: Philosophy of Human Nature, Ethics, History of Philosophy. The first two were part of the university's core curriculum (the set meal, as somebody euphemistically described it), the third was a requirement for philosophy majors. This semester History was Ancient Philosophy and featured the popular, by-no-means-ancient, Dr. Lawrence Goodman as the instructor. The elective courses, printed on visually inescapable hot-pink paper in the hope of attracting more students to philosophy, were also on show. For the fall semester the *à la carte* included Postmodernism, Asian Philosophy, Metaphysics, Lonergan, Philosophy of Art, Philosophy of Science. The rather imaginative Chair would do a write-up of the philosophy courses every semester, which the fully supportive members of the department would distribute to their classes. 'Did you know that the highest scores in the GRE, LSAT, etc. were achieved by philosophy students? Are you thinking of Law School? Then *study* philosophy since statistics show that Law Schools favor philosophy students!' So students were finally beginning to see the relevance of philosophy and they started enrolling in droves in philosophy courses, much to the annoyance of the Political Science Department, which until such carefully thought out law-speak had been a firm favorite among students about to embark on a legal career.

But the most popular elective had been Philosophy of Death. It certainly was the talk of the university. The professor, who had unfortunately retired last semester, used to bring in a coffin to class. It was packed. The classroom, that is, not the coffin. The students loved it. Now the department was under pressure to offer such down-to-earth courses.

On the same side of the corridor was a huge bulletin board, also a prize possession of the Philosophy Department. Pictures of various philosophers, in different sizes and degrees of eminence, were pinned to this board. Plato, Aristotle, Aquinas, of course. But there was always a lively meaningful discussion on who should feature on that board. Some noticed that all the pictures were of philosophers who were dead. Does one have to be dead to be considered prominent? Why were there no female philosophers? What, no Asians, Africans, or Latin Americans? It was fast becoming known as the 'politically incorrect offering of the dead philosophy department.' That raised the hackles of the department, of course. It was not a dead department, the Chair was heard shouting in the corridor, as if to make people aware that the philosophers were after all a lively bunch.

The challenge was on to display more pictures. Iris Murdoch and Edith Stein found themselves staring at budding philosophy students. The different members of the department rescued pictures of their favorites: Lonergan, Scotus, Marx, etc. It was turning into a fierce competition. If one's favorite philosopher remained on the board, that meant he or she had gained the acceptance of the department. Someone surreptitiously tried to add to the display a resemblance of Confucius. It was removed overnight, much to the annoyance of the Asian member of the department although she denied any responsibility for featuring the Chinese philosopher in the first place. She was informed that the pencil sketch of Confucius did not harmonize with the rest of the pictures. The photograph of a controversial political figure appeared suddenly, causing some confusion. 'I thought this was a board for prominent *philosophers*, not for the idols of the present members of the department,' a present member of the department was being quoted. But the department was landed in a dilemma: to take it down was to pass judgement on the reputation of the individual and the philosophical judgement of his admirer, to leave it up was to create a sore point for the other members of the department.

Richard smiled as he passed by that board and once again got a glimpse of the controversial photograph. It was a real philosophical problem!

Jan had cleared a chair for Richard. Stacks of newspapers had been sitting on different chairs in the room since Jan was running out of space for his fast-growing collection. 'Forgive the mess. My student assistant was doing some work today – for a change. Anyway, did you bring the letter?'

'Is it good news? That's what I really want to know.' Richard's eyes were wide with expectation as he saw Jan skim over the letter.

'Yup. It says here that you have been awarded a research fellowship at Mercier Universiteit in Leuven...'

He could not finish for Richard was already up.

'I've got it! Leuven, here I come!' With those excited words, Richard bolted out of Jan's office.

*   *   *

Aisling O'Shea was picking up her son Philip at the parish primary school at Rathfarnham. She had just come from her university, where she had given a lecture on the metaphysical poets to the First Arts students. This morning she received a letter and now she was anxious to know her son's reaction to it.

Parking her rather battered, slimy-green Ford Escort at the schoolyard, she headed towards her son's classroom while glancing back at her car. She had baptized it Jiffy because she claimed that it would take her to wherever she wanted to be in a jiffy – provided she could get it started, of course, which was somewhat of a problem, especially during the cold early mornings in the winter. Aisling tried to remedy the situation by removing the battery practically every night and charging it. She often joked that her car ran on electricity! She also joined the Automobile Association of Ireland and certainly became a household name to the employees of that association, given the number of times she called for help with starting her car. Once when the same AA man answered her call for help twice on the same day, he duly informed her that satisfied customers of their service did not have to insist on using it so regularly. Rather sarcastic, Aisling thought, but she shrugged it off and instead offered him some hot tea to cure his poor humour. It was a mistake. As he sipped his mug of tea, he told her – without mincing his words – the story of 'this missus who had a similarly dilapidated car'. She became such a frequent caller that when she was finally persuaded to change her car, the AA, so this AA representative claimed, was able to let two crew members off for lack of work! 'Know what I mean, ma'am?' was his parting shot after he politely thanked her for the 'hot cuppa'.

Aisling also got some teasing on account of her Jiffy from her friends. They reprimanded her for parking her car beside theirs – just in case the rust in her car jumped into theirs! Another one remarked, winking in the direction of her not-so-new Jiffy, that some cars should carry a sign: 'If stolen, please do not return'. It was all banter, of course, and she got her own back when one cold morning one of those friends living nearby asked her for a lift. And the reason? Her own car would not start and she had an important appointment! To Aisling's surprise and undisguised pleasure, when she started the car, Jiffy, without any of the usual chugging,

9

roared – eager to go to the rescue of the damsel in distress, especially this particular damsel. When Aisling reached her friend's home, the distressed but now relieved friend had to admit that she saw Jiffy in a different light now. Beaming, Aisling patted her car, 'Hear that, Jiffy?'

In contrast, the school building Aisling was now approaching was without a doubt new since it was one of those prefabs. But there was a plan to build a more suitable building once a grant from the Department of Education came through. The school had been opened only last year to cater for the rapidly growing population in the parish. Several housing estates had been developed in the area in the last few years and now the number of children ready to start school was increasing. Fortunately, the request for a new school in the area had been approved. Philip belonged to the very first group of the parish schoolchildren. Next year there would be another class and a second teacher while Philip's class would move on to the next level. However, Aisling had her sights already set on the junior school of Carmel College for Philip since that was Sean's former school. Proud of his education in that school, both he and Aisling wanted their son also to be educated there. It had good academic standing, spacious grounds, and a long rugby and acting tradition, staging a Shakespearean play each year.

The narrow corridor of Philip's school was cheerfully decorated with large attractive posters by the young teacher, who worked hard to provide some kind of a learning environment for her very young charges. The feedback from the parents had been enthusiastic, a response that was good for the morale not only of the teacher but also of the parish community since they all wanted 'their school' to succeed.

Aisling joined the other parents in the relatively spacious classroom. It was their custom to go inside and wait at the back of the classroom so that once the children were dismissed by the teacher, the parents immediately assumed the responsibility for their child. Aisling gave a short wave to the other parents whom she had got to know through this daily routine. The children had been strictly instructed not to break ranks even when their parents arrived until the teacher said so.

So when Philip saw Aisling, he pretended to look at the ceiling and then at the wall. But Aisling knew he had seen her so she smiled at him. It was always a pleasure to see her son at lunchtime and unless her university commitments prevented her from collecting Philip at school, she always went home with him at this time of the day.

'Well, how was it today?' inquired Aisling as she and Philip slowly made their way towards the car. Ahead of them was a young mother with her daughter from Philip's class stepping down from the concrete steps just before the car park. The young girl turned around to wave to Philip. He hesitantly waved back. The two mothers smiled at each other.

'We drew pictures. This is what I did.' Philip showed his mother the sheet of paper he had been holding in his left hand. On it was a rather rough sketch of an Irish countryside, in the centre of which was something meant to resemble a thatched cottage. Bits of shaky lines were supposed to be smoke coming from the chimney.

'That's beautiful, Philip. Were you thinking of the cottage we stayed in during the holiday?' Aisling always tried to be encouraging, no matter what the outcome of Philip's attempts was.

During the summer she and Philip had spent a couple of weeks in one of the cottages in Connemara. It was a most wonderful time, free from the concerns of academic life, and a welcome opportunity to grow even closer to her son. It was not easy combining career and parenthood, but she wanted to succeed in both. Philip enjoyed the countryside enormously. It was a chance for him to roam around in the wilderness, chasing butterflies and experiencing another kind of life, so different from Dublin. Mother Nature had smiled at both of them and at all the inhabitants and visitors of Connemara for it was one of those warm, lazy summers, always to be hoped for but rarely granted in the west of Ireland.

She thought this was also an opportune time to break the news to Philip. 'How'd you like to go on a holiday?'

'Another one?' His face lit up; he had been at school only a couple of months so the summer was still fresh in his memory. But then he became pensive. 'What about school?' Philip liked going to school and now he was probably wondering how his mother's plans would fit in with his schooling.

Aisling had been relieved that Philip enjoyed school. She had dreaded the separation which it entailed, but luckily she had been spared the agonizing experience of the young child clinging to its mother on the first day of school and refusing to be left behind. Sometimes there would be that embarrassing moment when the parent dithers between running away with the yelling child or fleeing from the child. That did not happen with Philip and her. She had prepared him for that day, assuring him that he would meet many friends and do many new things at school. That seemed to have done the trick and he never liked missing even one day.

'Oh, we're not going immediately. After Christmas. And we'll bring your school things with us so you can continue having fun with your drawings, learning your words and so on. It'll be a different kind of holiday, I promise.' Aisling was not sure how to explain to Philip that they would be away for several months since she would be doing some research at Mercier University in Leuven.

'What about my friends at school?' asked Philip as he climbed into the back seat, having cheerfully greeted Jiffy.

'We'll think of something.' Aisling settled herself in her seat, put on her safety belt and checked her rear-view mirror to see that Philip was comfortably seated.

Philip would indeed miss his newly found friends at school. Clearly, it was not going to be easy since she realized the importance of peer interaction for her young son. How would her six-year-old Philip react to the scholarly world of Leuven?

*   *   *

'Did you hear about the research fellowship that Richard Gutierrez got from Mercier University in Leuven?' Jan turned to Raissa Dimitrovich, from the Department of Russian Studies, as he poured coffee into his rather fashionable mug

12

sporting the words 'I've had a hard day.' The two professors were in the Faculty Commons, taking a break from their academic work.

The Faculty Commons was a welcome meeting place for some of the faculty. As one of them rather tactlessly put it, it was some kind of haven 'to escape from the pressures of constantly being confronted by the students.' It was the one place that was specifically reserved for non-academic activities of academics, like drinking endless cups of coffee/decaf/tea of various flavors/drinking chocolate, reading newspapers, chatting, plotting various strategies for any kind of projects that only academics are capable of concocting, criticizing the administration (a favorite pastime for some of them) and so on. The complimentary refreshment was much appreciated and so were the subsidized donuts. Sometimes a kind-hearted individual would leave cakes to celebrate an event, or at times leftovers from a social (or from a sorority party, which usually occurred before finals, with the tag 'to our beloved professors') would be found on the counter.

Last year there had been a mini-crisis since fresh milk was no longer supplied. There was a mild protest from some disgruntled coffee-drinkers, but the Proctor announced that it was due to some faculty actually drinking the milk! The budget, it appeared, could not support such drinking habits. Alternatives were suggested: creamer? (but someone pointed out that it was a possible cause of cancer); small doses of the longed-for stuff like those supplied in restaurants? (It was argued that whoever was drinking the milk would have to open several of these and he/she might even be caught in the act.) One rather creative faculty decided that he would bring in his own supply. But since the refrigerator was in the common area, some mistook his carton of milk to be common property. Not surprisingly it kept disappearing, to the disgust of the creative-thinking faculty. But creativity did not stop here. The same individual decided to attach his name on the carton and added 'medicated milk'. Unfortunately, that ingenious idea did not stop the 'theft' either. In the end, pressure was put by the Faculty Senate on the Proctor to continue the milk supply –

with a strong reprimand to the faculty milk-drinker, whoever he/she was. 'We cannot have anyone milking the system,' proclaimed the President of the Faculty Senate.

There was also this curious incident about an elderly lady who had comfortably stretched out on the sofa right in the middle of the room. She was fast asleep with her head buried in one of the corners of the sofa. Since her face was hidden from view by a cushion, various individuals who, at first respectfully, passed by failed to recognize her. Her rather elegant clothes provoked even greater curiosity. When it was clear, however, that she would be there for quite some time, there had been some disquiet. 'She can't stay there. This is not a sleeping quarter!' someone insisted. 'Disgraceful!' another one added. And yet neither of the two professors approached the reclining mystery. When someone else finally summoned enough courage and was on the verge of waking her up, one of the two, as if enlightened Zen-like, lurched forward to stop the bold individual. 'She could be one of the trustees!' was the explanation for this sudden restraint. Indeed that morning there was a trustees' meeting, and an important item on the agenda was the proposed increase in the salaries of the faculty. So the sleeping elegantly attired lady, contrary to practice, was allowed her rest in the Faculty Commons – and no one found out her true identity.

'No, but when did he get the news?' Raissa was curious, her eyes now closely focused on Jan. She was personally interested in this bit of information because she too was feeling the pressure of having to apply for research grants.

'Just this morning. I had to translate the letter for him. From Dutch. Funny, how some people get the good news in a form they don't understand.' A swipe at the non-linguistic abilities of the monolingual members of academia. Having made his point, Jan stirred his coffee with the small red-and-white plastic strip left for that purpose.

'What's this all about?' piped in the Chair of the History Department.

Dr. Zimmermann, the new arrival, had overheard the conversation as he was passing through the Faculty Commons on his way to his office in Bergman Hall. To the utter annoyance of the students who were in charge of cleaning the place and of Seamus O'Brien, the Proctor of the Faculty Commons, some faculty used the door into the Faculty Commons as the entrance into Bergman Hall. If these people helped themselves to the coffee or tea and sat down, like decent lads and lassies, and chatted with the rest of us, that would not be too bad, complained the Proctor, who despite the 20 years in LA never lost his Irish perspective on things. Instead, they are wearing out this part of the carpet by the constant traffic, he complained. Sure enough, that part of the carpet between what was really a side door into the Faculty Commons and the kitchenette which had an exit into Bergman Hall had taken on a worn-out look.

Jan brought Maximilian Zimmermann up to date on this morning's event. Dr. Zimmermann's imposing figure towered above the counter.

'Hmm. That's interesting.' The history professor nodded his head gravely. Dr. Zimmermann was proud of his opinions – they were always taken seriously. He had also a special status in the university – he was a member of the prestigious Alpha Sigma Nu (although another professor proudly announced that he did not care that he was not in Alpha Sigma Nu – after all, he had been an esteemed member of Alpha Alpha Alpha for several years!)

Normally Dr. Zimmermann would just fill his cup with coffee and then disappear from the room without even a word of greeting. But this time he was staying for a longer chat. So he put his briefcase down beside him. He wanted to know more. And he wanted to be reminded of Europe.

'That is exactly what I want to know.' Raissa's personal interest was undisguised. 'How did he get it?' She knew that Richard was a neophyte in the scholars' world. 'Probably knows a professor there who pulled strings. That must be it.' Then with a shrug of her shoulders quickly followed by a dismissive sweep of her right hand, she declared, 'It's like this publishing business. It is not what you write but who you know that gets your article accepted by journals.' She had a

15

chip on her shoulder. And who could blame her? She was the unhappy recipient of several rejection slips from editors and publishers.

'I disagree,' Jan was quick to retort. He put down his mug on the counter so he could make his next statement with greater emphasis. 'Whenever I submit a manuscript to a scholarly journal, it's always done with my name on a separate sheet. Blind refereeing. Any respectable journal would do that.' He did not want the others to think that his article which was recently accepted, his first incidentally, was going to be published in suspicious circumstances. He was thinking of his merit pay this year, and the Vice-President for Academic Affairs had insisted that scholarly work should be 'evaluated by one's peers.'

'Oh, come on. This whole thing about peer evaluation is not really true.' Raissa did not want to give in. But she was not interested in providing examples in case the conversation turned in her direction.

'This damn business about scholarship and research again.' The three turned around to find out who the culprit was. John Peters had come in, unknown to the others, and had seated himself in one of the cozy armchairs in the Faculty Commons, seeking refuge from the day's activities.

Aside from the suite of furniture in the center where John Peters had settled himself, the Faculty Commons provided for different groupings. The various chairs were arranged so that two or three could have a corner to themselves.

Right now in one of those corners Dr. Lu was seated, minding his own business, with the front page of the *New York Times* covering his face, and his balding head, clearly visible above the paper, looking like a stage floor illuminated by the wall lamp. The few wisps of hair sticking out on top were vibrating like ballerinas. Dr. Lu was scanning the inside pages of the paper to catch up on the latest goings-on in the world.

Beside the door into the room a round table had been placed. This was the student's station. It was also a study desk. After all, one of the perks of the job of ensuring that nicely brewed coffee was always available for the hard-pressed

16

faculty members was being able to spend hours studying and be paid for it. It was a much sought-after work-study appointment, sometimes even better than being a TA since one was not landed with all those photocopying jobs and running back and forth to the library for the professors.

The most popular spot in the Faculty Commons, where the original trio had been standing, was the counter where the coffee machines were, particularly on Fridays when gourmet coffee was also served, probably to remind the hardworking faculty that it was almost the end of the week. But John Peters, of the Department of Business Studies, did not bother with coffee. His daily routine was to pick up the newspapers, skim through the pages while planting himself in one of the comfortable chairs in front of the fireplace. He had overheard the conversation of his colleagues and could not resist making the remark. Obviously, his colleagues expected him to defend his position. But they could come to him if they wanted more. So the trio took their coffee with them, obliging their colleague, as it were.

'What's bugging you, John?' Dr. Zimmermann asked, clearing the center table on which John Peters had laid his newspaper. The two had sat on various committees together, and he guessed what was on John's mind. He knew that John was not happy with the direction that the university was taking.

'This university was known as a teaching university. When I joined it twenty years ago, it was that. And we were expected to be excellent teachers, always available to our students. Now the faculty are reluctant to hold extra office hours, advise students, prepare new courses or offer independent studies. It's all going into research.'

John was obviously hurt. He was an exceptional teacher, but he was finding it difficult to engage in research. Somehow he had lost the discipline required for a protracted investigation of one topic. Or perhaps he realized that there were more important things to do, like giving his time to the students and to the community. As a result, he was not getting the salary increases he was used to because he could not produce article after article.

'But this *is* a university. No university worth its salt can exclude the commitment to scholarship. How can we be effective teachers if we're not up to date?' replied Jan, who had joined the university a mere two years ago. He hunched over in John's direction. 'In my case, what attracted me to this university was precisely the balance between teaching and research. I would not have liked to have gone into a high-flying research institution but I would not have been interested in an exclusively teaching college either.' With that he reclined back and took a small sip from his mug.

John did not respond. He had heard that argument several times before and he found it ill-informed because it assumed that professors like him did not update their knowledge of the subject.

But Dr. Zimmermann defended John's view. Although he was a noted scholar in German history between the two World Wars, he did not like the criterion being used for scholarship. Since merit pay was being tagged on to scholarship, he understood this to mean that a faculty member had to produce some published work every year.

'Well, what does scholarship really mean? Must I have an article, a paper and a review every year? But do you know what is happening? Faculty are now reluctant to write a book – now that is real scholarship for you.' There was no doubting the sarcasm in his voice. 'It appears that it is better to write an article once a year since one could get merit pay every year. A book could take one several years to write. It would be more solid research, of course, and yet one will benefit from merit pay only when it comes out.'

Raissa could not believe her ears. Dr. Zimmermann was one of the top scholars at this university, yet here he was, griping about the distribution of merit pay. Jan on the other hand was taking all this in. So there is a technique to this scholarship–merit pay situation after all, he thought to himself. There is method in this academic madness. Without his knowing it, Dr. Zimmermann had given Jan 'sound' advice: he should aim for articles rather than a book.

Dr. Zimmermann continued; he must have been giving this

a lot of his attention. 'What do I say to the editor who accepts my article? Do not publish it next year because I already have two lined up for that year? Could you wait for two years because I don't think I'll have one for that year?' Despite the sarcasm, the logic of his questions was evident. And there was no stopping Dr. Zimmermann either. 'Let me tell you this,' he said as he shifted the weight from one side of his buttocks to the other. 'Did you know about Joseph's experience?'

The others shook their heads. 'Well, five years ago he submitted an article to a university's journal somewhere in Turkey. Since it was regarded as important enough the plan was to translate it into Turkish. It was translated all right two years later. It was scheduled to appear that year. But the journal is so far back in its publication that it came out only this year.

'Well, what's the problem?' inquired Jan rather naively. Once more he took a sip, not wanting his coffee to get cold.

'The problem is...' stressed Dr. Zimmermann, 'that it came out this year but it was backdated! So he can't report it for merit pay this year nor include it in this year's faculty service report since technically, going by the printed publication date that is, it came out three years ago. *Now* do you see the problem?'

John butted in, breaking his silence now that he had a very competent supporter in Dr. Zimmermann but ignoring his latest narrative, 'In my field the difference between the material at undergraduate level and at the scholarly level is so great that I cannot use material from one for the other.'

'Isn't that true of all fields, John?' Jan asked, hoping to make a score.

'I can only speak for my field,' quipped John, more or less brushing aside Jan's point.

Raissa wanted to have her opinion heard on this matter. 'Are we not forgetting where our priorities lie? The students are paying very high tuition fees to this university. They expect to be taught. Otherwise, they could go to the state universities, where the fees are much lower. But then they claim that they do not get there the attention they need. Not only that.' With those words, she thrust her leg out front.

19

Poor Dr. Zimmermann did know what to expect. 'Have you noticed that the faculty are now spending more time chasing after grants and writing proposals?' Raissa continued. 'Look at the amount of time that goes into writing those proposals. How many are really successful? Would we not be better off making use of that valuable time to read more up-to-date material for the courses we teach?'

Jan was beginning to feel that he was on his own. He looked at the other three, who were much older than he. Did age have any bearing on one's position on this matter? he asked himself.

'But look at Adrian in the English Department,' he blurted out, oblivious of the significance of Raissa's last observation. 'He's close to retirement. But instead of complaining about the expectations of research, he seemed to have got a new lease of life. He gave a well-received paper at an international conference in Bogota last year. He's now finishing a book and received a fellowship to do that.' Jan was aware of the comment that had been made that if those who were complaining about having to engage in research applied their energies to doing it, their time would be better spent.

'What criteria do they use anyway for awarding these fellowships?' snapped Raissa. She had returned to her original question. Her own unsuccessful bid left her bitter because she thought she had a fair chance since she was completing the translation of an important book. Her friend informed her that perhaps it was because she did not have a track record in publishing. A sore point, and her friend should not have been so tactless. 'How do they determine who should get it or not?' the rather defiant Russian professor persisted.

No one in the group answered her, not wanting to provoke her further.

From behind came a new voice, however. It was Matthew Perry. He had been standing behind them eavesdropping.

'A free discussion, I presume?' He checked the faces of his colleagues for reactions to his intrusion.

'Sit down, Matthew,' suggested Dr. Zimmermann, moving so that Dr. Perry could take the space beside him. 'Give us the benefit of your wisdom.'

20

'Raissa, you've a reason to be annoyed. I myself feel very frustrated over these research awards. I was finishing a book a few years ago and I applied for a fellowship.' Instead of answering Raissa's question, however, he proceeded to air his own grievances. He angrily placed the blame on others, including the administration, for his failure. Dr. Perry's face looked flushed and his voice was increasing in volume. 'You know what I was really tempted to write? Instead of acknowledgements, a list of those who didn't deserve to be thanked! I can provide you with names.'

There were no takers. Instead there was a sudden hush in the room. The unobtrusive Dr. Lu gently lowered his paper and adjusted his spectacles to get a good look at the speaker. Oh yes, it was Dr. Perry; oh, well, he is tenured. So Dr. Lu resumed the reading of his paper. The student decided it was time to replace the decaffeinated coffee even though the container was still half full. She coughed a bit. But no one spoke, no one was prepared to add fuel to the Perry fire.

Clearly, research and scholarship was a hot issue. Richard's fellowship was forgotten in the lively conversation. But Jan knew that he had a suitable lunchtime conversation topic for his colleagues who munched with him here at the Faculty Commons.

He could not wait for lunchtime to arrive.

★   ★   ★

Richard, of course, had not forgotten his good news. And he was glad that Jan, who genuinely liked sharing the good news of his colleagues since he believed in collegiality, had been the first to hear of it as it saved Richard the trouble of telling others. It would appear in the university newsbulletin later on, but a couple of colleagues, who must have received the news from Jan, had already congratulated Richard. One of them had called him up to express her delight over the award. Not surprisingly it was Dr. Maribel Araya. When good news travels fast it is fantastic, but it is even better when a generous heart, like Dr. Araya's, responds to it.

Richard thought he better inform his Dean as soon as possible since he would have to discuss his plans with him. On his way to the Dean's office at Aloysius building, he passed by the Hideout, the university's cafeteria. Inside he could see through the glass wall a group of students, two of them from his class, huddled together, chatting, with books strategically opened in front of them. One of them was desperate to catch Richard's attention. When he succeeded, he pointed to the opened book – apparently evidence that he was keeping up with the reading. Richard merely smiled.

The day's outdoor culinary offerings were being prepared by one of the catering staff, who was lighting the barbecue. The tempting smell was making Richard hungry. But the aroma was actually coming from another part of the eating arena. Some students' clubs, competing with the university's officially appointed catering firm, were cooking ethnic food. Regularly, the Chinese Club, the Filipino Students Association, the Chicano/Latino Students, the Indonesian Club and others would showcase their ethnic origins in this way. It was also a practical way of raising funds for their clubs; since several students were unhappy with the alleged high prices of the catering firm, students were only too glad to avail of these offerings. Richard and some faculty did patronize these student efforts, not least because often the food was really more tasty than the pizzas and the hamburgers from the Hideout. There was a rumor that some students from Business Management were going to erect a stand on the side of the eating arena, selling gourmet coffee. Given the circumstances, Richard thought that an appropriate name would be 'Cup-out/Cop-out.' He wished them well and was looking forward to its opening.

'Hello, Dr. Gutierrez.' It was Cynthia Smith from his Philosophy of Human Nature class.

'Hi, how are you?' Richard greeted her back.

'I'm in your Philosophy 120, 11:00 AM MWF class.'

'I know, I see you're kept busy manning ... oh, sorry, womanning ... no, not that either ... whatever it is you are doing at this table.'

The outdoor eating place was also the setting for various student clubs and groups for their recruitment or sale activities. Sometimes outsiders, like the Bank of America or American Express, would also set up tables here and tempt students with their free gifts for joining.

'Yeah, we're trying to get sign-ups for the blood bank. A good cause, Dr. Gutierrez.'

'I can see that.'

'Will you sign this then?'

'You want to extract my blood?' Richard teased the student. 'Are you sure this has nothing to do with the mid-term grade I gave you?'

'Absolutely none,' swore Cynthia. She waited until Richard had signed on the dotted line. 'But no guarantees after the finals,' she added with a glint in her eyes.

Richard laughed.

He continued on his trip to the Dean's Office, arriving at the Square, a raised part of the grounds where commencement exercises took place in May. The Square was a lovely part of the campus, flanked by rows of tall palm trees acting like proud sentinels of the university's long academic traditions. The students had more prosaic views, however, since the trees were ideal for hanging their banners advertising the latest activities. From the Square one could also get a breathtaking view of the city. The only trouble was, given the smog in the city, that sometimes it was literally true. But today was a fabulous day: unclouded blue skies, typical of southern California, with just a slight breeze to temper the warm temperature and to force the smog to keep its distance.

A few steps away Betty Johnson, engrossed in conversation with Edmund Donne, barely managed to give a nod of recognition to Richard when he crossed their path. Usually, being of an exuberant nature, she would be profuse in her greeting as she had somehow taken Richard under her wing. Right now Betty was talking to Edmund, a visiting professor from England, about certain academic peculiarities.

'Here we like to be available to our students,' Betty was saying to Edmund. 'We make it inviting for the students to see us by leaving our office door wide open. Not just during our posted office hours. We want our students to feel that they can see us anytime. Unfortunately, that seems to be changing, compared to when I first came here about thirty years ago. More and more of the faculty prefer to work at home or if they're in they don't leave their doors open. Buried in their research, I suppose.'

'Well, in England we do keep our doors closed. All the student has to do is to knock. But you know, I was warned about that when I was coming here. I was told that I should remember to keep my office door open. Something about not being sued, I reckon,' laughed Edmund.

Betty gave Edmund a piercing look. 'That's being narrow-minded.'

'Do you think so? But one can't be too careful. However, this practice of leaving one's door wide open is too distracting.'

'You mean, you find it difficult to concentrate when there's a lot of traffic in the corridor? Oh, don't worry. You'll get used to that. Or you could simply turn your desk around.'

Edmund was chuckling hard.

'Oh no, no, it's not that at all. I mean, I find it distracting when I go around and see all those opened doors and the academic staff inside, some seated at their desks, others standing in front of their bookshelves or chatting with a student, still others rooting inside the drawers...' His words trailed off as he tried to suppress a burst of laughter.

'What's so distracting about that?' asked a puzzled Betty.

Edmund suddenly became evasive. 'Let's just call it a psychological barrier for me,' quickly adding, 'Shall we head for the Faculty Commons for some refreshment?'

Edmund Donne did not think it appropriate to divulge to Betty that this American academic custom of having the doors wide open with the professors inside waiting for possible callers ... well, somehow reminded him very much of the red light district of Amsterdam!

*   *   *

Aisling welcomed the chance to go to Leuven during the second term. A member of the English Department of Newman University in Dublin, she wanted to work on a journal article on Irish poets and Postmodernism. She had managed to secure funding from the Research Council of Mercier University since that university wanted to establish closer links with her own university. She had already done some work on modern Irish poetry, but she needed to do research on Postmodernism. Continental Europe, it seemed, was abuzz with this latest development. During her studies that word never featured whereas now almost every article she read referred to Postmodernism and the writers associated with that 'fashionable word', as the Professor of Irish Literature put it. Well, she wanted to know more about it, or as she put it in her application, she 'intended to investigate the varying reactions to this development in contemporary thought.' Secondly, she 'wished to trace any Postmodernist tendencies among Irish poets'. That seemed to have done wonders. She got her funding, and that was the important thing. It meant she could afford to take time off.

Right now there were so many details to be concerned about. But she was already looking forward to her stay in Leuven.

★   ★   ★

Richard was back at his office. The Dean, always available to the faculty despite a heavy daily schedule, had congratulated him, remarking that this would be a wonderful opportunity for Richard to finish his manuscript. So when Richard returned to his office, he immediately retrieved the bundle of papers inside the cabinet. On the very front page in large letters the words 'Manuscript for a Book' stared back at him mockingly.

He sat down in his swivel chair and leafed through the manuscript. He still had no title, but he had been consoled when a colleague of his, an author of five books, told him that sometimes one had to wait until the end to come up with the right one for one's work. He had also advised Richard to wait until the end before attempting the introduction. By then he would be a lot clearer about the real focus and the development of his topic. Richard thought this was solid advice. If that was good enough for the author of five books, it was good enough for him, the author of, well, an unfinished manuscript. He felt like an expectant mother, so to speak, whose delivery date was well overdue.

So his manuscript had no title, no introduction. It certainly had no last chapter. Obviously, there was no conclusion either. He had requested a couple of his former classmates at graduate school, one teaching in the philosophy department of one of the Ivy League universities on the East Coast, the other still looking for a tenure-track position and driving a taxicab in the meantime, to read his work. He respected their opinions (at graduate school in Chicago their professors thought very highly of those two.) They liked his work and had offered incisive, perceptive comments and constructive criticisms which he had incorporated. But he did not have the courage to get the opinion of published philosophers, believing that it would be an encroachment on their own valuable research time. In truth, he was afraid of what they would say. He certainly had no courage to submit any of his work for publication. The competition for publishing articles in scholarly journals in his field was particularly stiff. He had read somewhere that the average rate of acceptance by philosophical journals was only 30 percent. The 'publish or perish' syndrome, endemic to academia, meant that several others in his field were submitting their work to the same journals. The muscles in his stomach tightened again. If it was tough enough to get an article accepted, what chances did he have of getting a book-length scholarly manuscript published?

His departmental colleagues had urged him to present papers at professional conferences. A good opportunity, they told him, would be at the meetings of the American Philosophical Association, of which he was a member. But he had had a very nightmarish experience at the one meeting he had attended. It was during the Eastern Division meeting

26

which was held in one of the posh hotels in New York. He had gone to it for job-hunting, having sent his applications to about 30 departments of philosophy. Only one had invited him for a preliminary interview during the Eastern Division meeting. Not a very good sign, he thought. But he could not afford not to go. As it turned out, he had made the right decision since it was the only university that offered him a position, the one that he now held. His desperate search for job-openings which did not insist on prearranged interviews (he had brought about 20 copies of his resumé, just in case) yielded no results so he had plenty of time before and after that one preliminary interview.

So he decided to attend the session at which a friend of his, one of the lucky ones who got a tenure-track position the previous year, was going to present a scholarly paper. Richard was not even sure what the topic was, except that his friend was a member of a panel. So he had checked his friend's name on the program to find out where to go.

Richard found the large meeting room of the luxurious hotel. The decor was impressive, as is to be expected in these expensive hotels. At one end of the room was a long table covered in green cloth, on top of which were glasses and a pitcher of iced water ready for any speaker in need of refreshment. When Richard went in, his friend waved to him in recognition. But Richard sensed that it was more out of relief.

He was right: he was the only member of the audience! Already feeling very uncomfortable with his situation, he did not want to be addressed by four speakers. He was tempted to dash out of the room, but loyalty prevented him from doing so. So he kept shifting in his seat instead, hoping someone else would join them. Still no one came, despite the fact that it was already ten minutes past the scheduled time. The door did open once. Someone had looked in, noticed the four speakers, the chair and Richard all looking expectantly in her direction. She quickly changed her mind and pretended she was in the wrong room.

Finally, the chair had to start the session. He introduced

27

himself to Richard, the lone member of the crowd (well, it wasn't exactly a crowd), and to the four speakers. Richard checked his program and gasped: it was a three-hour session and the topic was something completely outside his field. He felt trapped. How could he remain here for three hours? He glanced at his friend. From the look on his face, however, he was begging Richard to stay.

So he had remained, but the experience gave him a bad start to presenting papers at professional meetings, particularly as an unknown and therefore ignored neophyte. It had not helped matters to see the chair of that panel nod off a few times while the papers were being given and then pretend to look extremely interested when he was awake. Talk of the chair's deep-seated interest in the subject! Richard shook his head as he recalled that event.

But he had to publish. He had to contribute to the developments in his field. He must help push the frontiers of his discipline .... He had to get tenure.

So he checked what he had accomplished. The topic was clear: it was the existence of evil as a philosophical problem. In fact, it was even more specific than that since he clearly wished to show that the Thomistic solution, despite its modern critics, was worth dusting up. He had already succeeded in enthusiastically developing his arguments in six rather lengthy chapters, complete with footnotes and references to primary sources.

But a year had elapsed since he had written those chapters. What was holding him up? The much dreaded writer's block? Surely, that was only for creative writing. This was a philosophical work and he had the skills to think and write philosophically. He had proved that with a Ph.D. dissertation comparing the notion of final end in Aristotle and Aquinas, and now with the manuscript in front of him. Yet why was he not getting the impulse to continue?

He thought long and hard as he swivelled towards the window, pulled up the venetian blinds and stared out of his office as if to get some kind of an answer. Outside he could hear a sorority group in the building across, conducting what looked like an initiation. The girls were chanting their sorority song. Like a well-rehearsed chorus line, the lavender-clad girls on top of the steps raised their arms in unison, shook their fingers deftly, and then lowered them gently as the initiands looked on in admiration. This was followed by cheers and clapping.

Richard wondered what all that meant. From where he was, the whole thing was strange and even weird. But to the group it must have meant something since communication had taken place. The ritual and the song established a bond between the old members and the new.

The group was beginning to leave the place now, each new member being linked by a veteran sister. They continued singing as they filed past his office.

Richard still had no answer to his dilemma. He had only a sorority ritual to reflect on.

II

Philip rubbed his sleepy eyes, forcing himself to wake up. It was only six in the morning, but Aisling wanted to have an early start. She intended to do a lot of reading today.

'Do we really have to get up now, Ma? I'm still very sleepy.' One eye was cocked open, but the other one was definitely shut. He wanted his mother to say no, to kiss his forehead and to allow him another half-hour in bed. This trick used to work when they were in Ireland. But it was different here in Leuven. Ever since they arrived in January, his mother was always up at daybreak. His six-year-old mind did not understand the change. Nor did he understand why, if they were on holiday, they were going to the office every weekday. A different sort of holiday, he had been told. It was all a big puzzle to him.

'I'm afraid so, son. We can't stay in bed. Will you have some orange juice today?' She rolled over to her side of the bed, sat up and put on her blue slippers. Then slipping into her dressing gown left at the foot of the bed and buttoning it fully to keep warm, she headed for the kitchenette.

Aisling was terribly disappointed with her accommodation. Her contact, a former student of hers now studying at the Irish College in Leuven, had managed to get Aisling only a studio apartment at Tervuursevest. She had hoped to be housed at the Begijnhof, where guests of the university had their accommodation, and she had been looking forward to living there. She had heard a lot about it from academics whom she met at various conferences and who had spent some time in Leuven. Instead here she was in this tiny studio. When they arrived, she was surprised to see no bed. One had to pull it down – it was propped up against the wall. Admittedly, once the bed was back in its place, the room

30

looked tidy. But she could just imagine the difficulties she would have with her son with such an arrangement. To add to her disappointment, she realized that, having invited her mother over for a short holiday, putting her up for two weeks would be a problem. There was no way the three of them could be holed up in this place. One could not swing a cat in this room. And, from her point of view, it was horribly expensive. The rent was BF18,500 a month plus utilities. When she inquired what exactly that meant, she was told that she had to pay extra for electricity, heating, rental for the electric meter, telephone calls and rental for the telephone.

Aisling had been sorely tempted to pack up again that afternoon when they arrived, so great was her disappointment. But when she looked at Philip, she saw that he was tired from the flight from Dublin since they had been up early that day. He had been good throughout the whole journey. It would have been cruel to start searching for alternative accommodation then, especially since she really had no idea where to go. But she had promised herself that she would find out about more comfortable lodging as soon as possible.

Philip was on his feet. 'Will I help you put up the bed, Ma?' He had got into the daily routine here.

Aisling had inquired about the Begijnhof the very next day but was told that there was no vacancy. So she had tried to make the best of the situation until she became more familiar with the place. Surprisingly, Philip found it fun, sleeping in the same double bed with her. He could cuddle up to her and fall asleep almost immediately. In Ireland he always wanted to sleep in his own bed in his bedroom. But here he seemed to be happy enough with the arrangement. Perhaps he sensed that there was no alternative.

'Ma, what day's today?'

'Tuesday. Why?'

'At home, I get to wear my tracksuit on Tuesdays and Thursdays. Remember? I suppose it's different here.'

'Rather cold for it today, I think. You can wear your nice warm blue jumper instead. You know, we have to walk to the office.'

31

Philip's face fell, but just for a few seconds. In Ireland he did not relish the thought of walking in the cold weather. He was always wondering why his eyes got watery when he was not crying. But maybe it won't happen today.

It was one of those crisp mornings. January had not been as cold as had been expected, but today seemed to forecast colder days ahead. Still, it was dry. So long as it is dry, the Irish would say, one can put up with the cold.

Philip looked cute in his blue winter cap and matching gloves. He had brought his backpack, a smaller version of those backpacks that youngsters all over the world seemed to have adopted as the 'in thing', one strap slung over one shoulder. Aisling could never make out why they used only one strap when the backpacks had two. Philip could not manage the fashionable look so he had his backpack carefully balanced between both shoulders – the proper thing to do, Aisling thought. Inside his bag were his crayons, a colouring book and a jigsaw puzzle. He also had his exercise book to learn his words and practise his spelling. Since he had been told that he could not bring all his toys to Belgium, he had suggested these articles.

As usual, Tervuursevest was a hive of activity; the early morning traffic was busy and noisy. Tervuursevest was part of the ring road of Leuven and therefore it was used by motorists into, out of and through Leuven. Aisling was relieved that at least their studio apartment was on the other side of the building away from the street. Since it was double-glazed, it was relatively quiet. In fact, when they were inside the studio, they could not hear the constant pounding of the street traffic.

Aisling and Philip made their way into Naamsestraat. She had come to like this road although the uphill walk towards the Centrum was too much of a forced exercise. Many college buildings, part of the famous Katholieke Universiteit Leuven, were situated on this street. Someone had described Naamsestraat to her as an 'outdoor museum' because the colleges here dated back several centuries and were marvellous architecturally. More than likely the hospital, which was also on this road, accounted for the several flower shops. Aisling could not help but admire the attractive flower arrangements. The colourful flowers had a way of dissipating the gloom of winter.

Philip also liked this road and somehow it compensated for the early morning rising. It had become a ritual for them to stop at the corner of Tervuursevest and Naamsestraat. The shopfront of the store there always had imaginative displays on specific themes. This time it was 'caring for the environment'. The window of Cover Story, another shop on Naamsestraat, was also a stop-point for them as Philip admired the latest display of toys and other colourful articles. Today the window carried a couple of trolls.

'Look, one of the trolls has got green hair!' he exclaimed in delight.

Ever since his cousin in America sent him a Santa Claus troll with green hair, he – and his mother, grandparents, aunt and uncle inevitably – was on a mission to find other obnoxious-looking (from the adult perspective) and loveable (the child's unfathomable value judgement) trolls with similarly coloured hair. Philip had been informed that there were families of trolls, and he wanted the green-haired family. His uncle, unable to comprehend this peculiar wish, thought trolls had been subjected to electric shocks, which accounted for the raised hair. But Philip had ignored his rather 'ignorant' remarks.

'We'd better get it before someone else buys it, Ma,' he suggested as he pulled his mother's hand towards the door of the shop.

Unfortunately, the trolls on display were not for sale. The shop assistant looked befuddled that it had to be a troll with green hair. Philip was disappointed but not discouraged.

'Oh well. I suppose we'll just have to continue looking for them, won't we?' Aisling could see that Philip had different expectations of Leuven.

Philip was trying hard to be brave as they resumed their walk.

After a few minutes they could see the Erasmus House,

33

where they would be spending the day, she buried in literature, Philip learning his words.

Aisling thought the name given to this building was fitting since Erasmus had been a great humanist whom Leuven claimed as its own. Erasmus placed great emphasis on the study of Greek and Hebrew, languages which in his view would enable scholars to dig out the original Bible and classical texts and shove aside the medieval verbiage of secondary commentaries. The intellectual climate of Leuven appealed to the great scholar; that was why he was intensely involved in this town. And yet he had not been a professor here although he had lived in Leuven from 1502 to 1504 and from 1517 to 1521. He enjoyed his freedom too much, however, to be permanently attached to this place. Aisling thought it was appropriate for his name to be used for the programme that encouraged academic exchanges within Europe and enabled scholars to appreciate what it meant to be European.

The Erasmus House was near the Stadhuis. In fact, on their first trek to this place Philip had noticed the ornate Stadhuis – twice.

'Are we lost, Ma?' he had inquired. 'We passed by that building already.'

Philip seems not to have thought much of the fifteenth-century late Gothic building. Aisling on the other hand regarded it as a marvellous piece of architecture, looking like lace or even a jewellery box.

Richly decorated, the building is definitely eye-catching. Aisling appreciated the informative books she had acquired on Leuven's buildings and history. In one of them, she learned that the builder Mathijs de Layens, unable to construct a tower because of poor subsoil, built into the building small towers which point up like oriels from the gables and connect to an openwork frieze along the rising roof edge. The building is decorated with niches for statues, a practice common to town halls in the Low Countries. These niches rest on consols which depict historical scenes, complemented by canopies with biblical scenes. For the keen observer the

34

building is indeed like an open bible. The statues in the niches had been placed there only after 1850 on the advice of Victor Hugo, who when he passed through Leuven told the town council to fill them because, as he put it, a town hall without statues is like blank pages. In his view statues are the letters with which history is written. It was sound advice, thought Aisling, although perhaps a little too complex to win Philip's approval.

Aisling did not want to admit to Philip that first day that they were going in a circle. 'The Erasmus House is quite far,' she had replied, without looking at him. But Philip was wondering why if they were going to what he was beginning to think was the next town, they had not got the bus. Aisling pretended not to hear him.

After that exchange, she had got hold of a town map and learned the short cuts very quickly. Now it took them only 15 minutes to walk the cobbled roads to the Erasmus House. And they did not even have to pass by the Stadhuis, about which mother and son had differed in their judgement.

One of the landmarks which both mother and son did like when they saw it on that first day was the Fons Sapientiae in the centre of Leuven. But for different reasons. Aisling admired the statue of the young scholar, whose left leg rested on a pedestal, reading a book and pouring water down into his head. She found it a most appropriate symbol of this academically charged town. Not even when she heard that sometimes beer flowed into the head, a result of student pranks, did her view change. She was reminded of the fountain Arethuse in Greek mythology, in whose waters the Muses played. Perhaps the university should adopt this name. It certainly drew scholars to drink, as it were, from its waters. To Philip, on the other hand, it was a cause for a giggle. The symbolism meant nothing to him. All he could see was a young boy pouring water into a hole in his head – there must have been nothing inside it!

'Remember our first day here, Ma? We walked and walked and walked – for hours, didn't we, Ma?' Philip was picking up very quickly the Irish fondness for hyperbole, thought Aisling. She could also see that she was not going to be allowed to forget the minor fiasco of their first trip.

Philip glanced up at her, his cheeks rosy from the cold. His nose, also taking on a rosy tinge, reminded her of his father, Sean. Every time Aisling caught Philip looking up at her, she would be reminded of Sean. Now as he waited for her reply, her mind drifted back to a few years ago.

She and Sean had been very happy together. They had met at postgraduate school, she studying English literature, he researching the classics. They spent a lot of their time researching together in the library. As their interest in academic work developed, so did their relationship, and so it was not unexpected when they announced that they were getting married. Everything seemed rosy then since both of them were lucky enough to get teaching jobs in the same university. Until she lost Sean when Philip was only one year old. Then her world suddenly collapsed and she was on the verge of giving up. What stopped her from losing her mind altogether was the gift of Philip. But even then she could not help but grieve over her loss. She kept asking: why did it have to happen?

As she looked at Philip now, she tried once again to forget the pain in her heart, just as she had been doing for the past five years.

★   ★   ★

Aisling was seated at her desk in Dr Bruggemann's office. Dr Bruggemann, a professor here at Leuven, was on her sabbatical and was spending it in Colorado, USA, so the Head of the Department of English and American Literature had given Aisling the use of the office. It was smaller than her own in Dublin, but she was grateful for it as it meant that Philip could join her. A few books in American literature had been left on the top shelf. But Dr Bruggemann had thoughtfully emptied the bottom shelf so that whoever was using her office in her absence could avail of that space.

36

Having such a room was indeed a benefit since Aisling had feared that she would have to have Philip in tow in the library. But the present arrangements meant that he could be contented with writing down 'his words'. And he was determined to learn them since he did not want to be behind his classmates when they returned to Ireland. His teacher had kicked up a fuss when she was told that Philip would be away for several months. 'Think of what he would be missing. You know, it will be difficult for him to catch up.' The young enthusiastic teacher prided herself in knowing her job and looking after the welfare of her charges.

But she did give in, even divulging to Aisling the spelling that her very young protégés would be learning during the next months. She also showed Aisling the planned activities for that time of the year. Aisling was confident that her Philip would learn his words during his absence from Miss Moore's class. After all, he was the brightest in the group. And that was not just her unbiased view as a mother. Her mother shared that view! Aisling's concern was more that he would not have peer contact. She was unsure what tutorial arrangements would be available in Leuven.

Philip settled himself on the floor. There was a nice rug in front of the professor's chair and it served as a cosy work-cum-play station for the young scholar. This morning he had the words 'books', 'pupil', 'fruit' and 'zebra' to learn. So he took out from the box the slips of paper on which these words had been written by Miss Moore.

'Can you read this one for me, Ma?' Philip had selected the slip with the word 'pupil'. Aisling obliged him, and Philip set out to copy the letters. Philip would be doing this for several minutes so Aisling thought she had better start with her reading.

But she could not concentrate. As she turned the pages of the book her mind kept flicking back the pages of her past. It took her back to the summer five years ago.

★   ★   ★

Richard kept thinking about his uncompleted manuscript. How could he credibly write on the problem of evil? He had been approaching this as a philosophical issue, and indeed it was, but whatever he had written was unconvincing in the arena of widespread human suffering. He could discuss various theories and the merits and weaknesses of each, but in the hard reality of suffering, whether it was the unexpected loss of a loved one, the sight of the malnourished and skeletal bodies of the children in the Sudan and Somalia, the victims of the violence in Bosnia or the long lines of the unemployed, every single one of these theories was bankrupt. Each one was shipwrecked on the hard rocks of reality.

As he tinkered with his pen, which he had lifted from its holder, he recalled with grief a talk he gave to a small group of educators. After his presentation on Aquinas's solution to the problem of evil, one member of the audience asked him how that would help her cope with the tragedy of her handicapped sister. Her vivid description of the agony and desperation both her sister and her family had been experiencing was sufficient to shake the foundation on which a theoretical answer, particularly the one he was defending, was built. Initially he consoled himself by saying that he was not writing a book intended to provide comfort to those who were suffering nor to offer solutions to remedy the situation. His notes for his introduction clearly stated that. He retrieved those notes. Sure enough, he had made those points. He was writing as a philosopher, not as a psychologist, nor a counselor nor a strategist. He could not be expected in this work to be all of those.

As a philosopher he was expected to focus on such issues as: what is meant by evil? why is there evil in the world? how can the reality of evil be reconciled with the belief in God? and so on. In his field he would be accused of skirting around the problem if he did not address these and similar questions. Philosophers investigate fundamental questions, and these were indeed fundamental. They were questions which a rational being sooner or later would ask. This was why great minds down through the ages and from different continents wrestled with this problem.

Richard leaned back in his chair, whose sturdy high back gave him comfortable support. That perhaps was *the real* problem, he surmised. If great minds had thought deeply about it, if they had provided theories which have been studied thoroughly by others, why did the problem of evil still exist? Why did one talk of 'yet another theodicy', often with sarcasm? Why was one left floundering about when confronted by the agony and misery of one individual or of millions?

It was a real problem, a very concrete one indeed. Richard continued his reflections as he put down the manuscript that he had been examining. How can he convince the Dean that there was a gap between what he had set out to do in this scholarly work and the experience of those exploited, oppressed, victimized, and in pain? What meaning could he provide to his work?

He seemed to be stuck. He wondered whether Leuven would provide an answer or even a hint of an answer. Would it be an answer that would inspire him to continue with his scholarly work?

★   ★   ★

It was a holiday that Aisling and Sean had been talking about excitedly for several months. Philip was one year old and they thought it was just the right age to take him on a two-week holiday on the Costa del Sol. Having heard so much about babies learning how to swim, they wondered whether Philip would take to the water. It would be nice if the pool were outdoors in glorious sunshine. The weather in Ireland, even in the summer, was not always the most reliable. Like so many of the Irish fated to live out their lives in a part of the world where it was 'either raining or threatening to rain', the young couple dreamt of the glorious sunshine of the Costa del Sol. Since they had no commitments to the university from the beginning of July, they thought they would go for the first two weeks of that month. In that way they hoped to miss most of the crowds, who seemed to consider the first two weeks of August as the best time to go. Then on their return they might still be lucky enough to avail of any warm days parcelled out by the Almighty to Ireland since these were occasionally in August.

They owned two timeshare weeks in Galway, described by one Irish cynic as the last stop before America. They were for the last week of December and the first week of January, the cheapest high-season weeks they could afford. But the weather in Galway at that time of the year was not particularly inviting (or as her mother bluntly put it, who in God's name would dream of spending a holiday there in the winter?) so they would exchange their weeks for other high-season weeks elsewhere through RCI, the worldwide exchange company. So Sean duly filled in the proper forms and requested an exchange for the first two weeks in July. He tried to be flexible and just asked for the Costa del Sol area.

The reply came almost by return post.

'We've got it! We've got it!' shouted Sean in undisguised glee. But he was in a teasing mood and would not say more.

'Where? Come on, Sean, don't be messing. The suspense is killing me.' Aisling was already thinking of the warm hazy days ahead. If one has ever looked out of the window during an Irish winter's day, one will readily understand. Even now, in March when it was officially springtime, there were only hints of sunshine here and there. From their bedroom window one could still see pockets of snow on the Dublin mountains.

Sean gave in. 'One week at the Doña Mona. A fully furnished two-bedroomed villa near the beach,' he announced. 'The second week at Las Farolas, also a fully furnished villa, accommodating six. And they're quite close to each other. So transferring will be no problem.'

'And do they have swimming pools?' Aisling was thinking of the baby.

'Yes, definitely.'

'Did you say, for six? Could we invite my mother and your parents?' Aisling's father had been dead for several years.

'Let's ask them. Wouldn't it be great if we could all go?'

So Sean and Aisling rang their respective parents. Aisling's mother was excited. Oh, yes, she could come, no problem there, her passport was in order and she could just tell the widows' association to go take a running jump at themselves since they were so slow in organizing anything. But Sean's parents could not make it. They had committed themselves to a couple of functions connected with his firm. Unfortunately, the dates coincided with the planned holiday. They wished they could come along, but Sean's father did not think the firm would like being dumped.

Sean suggested inviting Fiona and Tony, Aisling's sister and brother-in-law. Would they come? They'd be delighted, was their prompt answer. Fiona remarked that it would be a welcome break from their partially furnished house. She was tired of practically living in the sitting room since, aside from the kitchen, it was the only room they could afford to do up at the moment. Fiona and Tony had been married only a few months. Two weeks in fully furnished accommodation at the Costa del Sol would be like living in paradise.

The arrangements were quickly made: Sean and Aisling insisted that the accommodation was their treat, each one (except baby Philip, of course) was responsible for the airfare from Dublin to Malaga, and there would be a kitty for the meals. Sean volunteered to make the inquiries about fares. Make sure they are the cheapest available, his mother-in-law warned him.

And so the first Saturday of that July found Aisling, Sean and Philip O'Shea, Mrs Holohan, Fiona and Tony Burns winging their way to the sun on the Costa del Sol. Sean had managed to get five seats on the charter flights operated by Club Travel of Dublin to Malaga, a feat that endeared him not only to Mrs Holohan but also to the Burns.

'We'll bring the camera with us. This should be a good shot,' exclaimed Sean as the group prepared to go to the swimming pool on their very first morning. He was going to take baby Philip in the water and he had high hopes that all he had to do was to let the baby go and let nature take over – and the future Olympic swimmer would just glide in the water like a fish.

'Oh, no!' Aisling was very definite when she discovered Sean's unrealistic plan. 'We're all going to watch him. And you and Tony will be in the water with your arms under him. No fooling around, Sean, please.'

'I was only joking. Of course, we'll be very careful.'

'Don't worry, Aisling, we won't take our eyes off him,' Tony reassured her. But to Sean he gave a mischievous glance and whispered, 'But we'll take our arms off him.'

'What was that?' Tony's side remarks did not escape Mrs Holohan's ears. 'We'll have none of that, you hear? And you're not to stay too long in the sun either. The baby's skin's very delicate. Here, I bought this lotion at Quinnsworths. I was told that it's especially for babies. You are to put this on him every ten minutes.'

The last remark by the doting grandmother was really unnecessary since Aisling had already planned to do that. She had made a special trip to the Nutgrove Shopping Centre near where they lived. But it was good to know that her mother would also be keeping an eye on the lads.

Aisling, Sean, Fiona and Tony changed into their swimming togs. Fiona noticed that Mrs Holohan was not making any move.

'Are you not coming, Ma?'

'Of course I am. Did you think that I flew all this way to just sit here?'

'Will you get ready then?'

'I *am* ready.' Mrs Holohan was fully dressed in a new summer frock, short-sleeved, with splashes of pastel all over. It was a reluctant concession to the temptations of the Costa del Sol. 'I am not, definitely not, getting into one of those,' she said as she eyed the bikinis of her daughters. Aisling and Fiona had very shapely figures. They were quite stunning in their costumes, bought for the occasion.

'C'm on, the sun will be gone if we don't hurry.' Sean was getting a bit impatient.

'For goodness' sake, Sean. This is not Ireland. This is the Costa del Sol,' Fiona swayed her hips a bit, tilted her head upwards to the right and clicked her fingers as she swung her arms upwards, a would-be flamenco dancer in a bikini. 'This is where the sun is.' She thought Sean was rushing things.

Obviously, her words fell on deaf ears since Sean was already outside.

'Sean, the baby!' Aisling called frantically after him. Sean had to return to fetch the future Irish swimming champion.

The swimming pool was very close to their villa. Furnished in Andalucian style and equipped with everything they needed for comfort, the villa exceeded their expectations. It gave them a lot of privacy too, unlike the hotels in Torremolinos or Fuengirola. The usual crowds that throng these resorts were also absent, much to the relief of Sean and Aisling since after their first sun holiday they had tried to avoid places where often you could smell the lotion of the sun-worshippers all around you. On that holiday they coped with their disappointment by trying to guess which brand their fellow holiday-makers had applied. Not very academic work, but it brought on a few chuckles. Sean said that he was changing the subject matter of his research: from now on, no more the *Metamorphoses* of Ovid. The present field was more relevant and riveting. So long as you stop with the sun lotion, Aisling warned him. They also amused themselves by remarking on the latest arrivals, those with lily-white skins, and comparing them with those who had started to get a tan. From the degree of the tan, they tried to guess how long holiday-makers had been around.

In fact, there were two swimming pools here. The adult one had only one swimmer so far. The children's pool was quite shallow, obviously. Sean and Tony would have looked funny in the children's pool since the water was only up to their knees.

'You could sit down,' suggested Aisling. She was trying to be cautious and was getting cold feet over this whole thing of teaching Philip how to swim at such a tender age.

'We'll go to the adults' pool,' Sean decided. 'At the shallow end,' he added when he saw Aisling's concerned face.

Philip loved the water! He was kicking his legs vigorously. There was no fear in him, only cooing sounds of delight. Sean and Tony were quite responsible. They took turns holding Philip as the very young trainee splashed about. Mrs Holohan used up the 36 shots in her camera, photographing her grandson from every angle, except underwater, while Fiona and Aisling indulged in sunbathing, as if they could not get enough of the fabulous sunshine . . .

Aisling viewed the young pupil in front of her. He was on his stomach, stretched out on the rug. As he conscientiously wrote out the word 'pupil' for the fifth time, he was swinging his legs from the knees, almost like that first time he was in the water.

She couldn't believe that five years had sped by since that holiday. They all enjoyed it despite the fact that Philip did not become a true water-baby. But he did come to love the swimming pool and he was taking lessons at the Dundrum Recreation Centre, where there was a heated indoor pool. On the last three days of their holiday, they rented a car and went to Ronda, Malaga and Nerja. But the highlight was the last day when Mrs Holohan, to everyone's delight (Sean swore that he saw the baby take a second look at Granny and grin), slipped into a one-piece swimming suit when they went to the pool. She had brought this with her but did not have the courage to put it on. However, she explained, after seeing the other holiday-makers at the pool, she did not see why she should not use it. No one pressed her for a more elaborate justification of her action. Tony wanted to take a photograph, but she adamantly refused since she did not want to be blackmailed by the widows' association.

Yes, those were the pleasant memories, Aisling thought. But as her mind kept turning back to the past, tears started to form in her eyes

. . . They had just arrived back from their holiday, full of memories and, unfortunately, laden with dirty laundry. The

44

last bit, however, did not dampen their spirits and everyone in the group seemed bent on contributing to the conversation which seemed to have started at Malaga airport and continued throughout the flight to Dublin airport. Perhaps it was their way of prolonging the holiday since somehow even just talking about it postponed the inevitable end. They laughed at the various incidents during the two weeks, including the time when Aisling wanted to buy a Spanish veil and kept asking the confused shop assistant for 'mantequilla'.

Of course, there were moments of concern as when the baby got feverish. Fortunately, there was a nurse at the resort, and she attended to Philip immediately. It was a mild dose caused by the hot temperatures. He had to be 'grounded' – no swimming for a couple of days, the nurse told the parents.

As they neared their house, Aisling and Sean were wondering what had happened during their absence. They had all managed to squeeze into Tony's car, which he had conscientiously parked at the airport. The parking fees were still cheaper compared to hiring two taxis to drive them home, which was south of the Liffey.

Everything seemed fine, thank God. A neighbour of the O'Sheas had the key to their house and had looked after it while they were away. Every morning David had collected the post which the postman would throw into the hall through the letterbox. The letters, flyers, unsolicited newspapers were neatly stacked up on one of the stairs to the bedrooms.

When a quick look-around reassured Aisling and Sean that everything was indeed in order, they sighed with relief. The others brought in the O'Sheas' luggage but left their own in the car, since after a quick cup of tea they wanted to be on their way to Barrowtown, where Mrs Holohan and the Burns lived.

Suddenly, the phone rang.

'Hello, is Sean there?' asked the voice at the other end.

'It's for you, Sean. Could you hold the line, please.' Tony, being the nearest to the phone, had answered it. Sean came to the phone.

'Hello, this is Sean. Oh, it's you, Paddy. How's tricks?'

Patrick was a very close friend of his. They had grown up together in Dublin, had been classmates from Infants upwards and had gone to the same university, Trinity. 'Hold on, I'll be right there.' His tone of voice abruptly changed after Patrick told him why he had called.

'What's wrong, Sean?' Aisling sensed that it was quite serious.

'It's Siobhan.' Siobhan was Patrick's and Eileen's one-year-old daughter. 'There was an accident this morning, Siobhan's in the Mater, and she's not expected to make it through.'

'Oh, my God!' Mrs Holohan and Fiona said almost simultaneously as they sat down, a moment of weakness abruptly overcoming them. The kitchen where the group had settled themselves suddenly became deathly quiet. Aisling instinctively lifted Philip from his pram and cuddled him. 'You'd better go then right away. Please tell Patrick and Eileen I am very sorry indeed. I still hope the news will be better.' With tears in her eyes she kept kissing the baby.

Mrs Holohan, Fiona and Tony asked whether there was anything they could do. Nothing at the moment, Aisling said, and they'd better be on their way so as to get the journey over before the pubs closed.

Sean did not bother tidying himself up after the flight. Aisling could see that he was quite distressed and was struggling with himself. But he thanked the others for going on the holiday with them, which quickly became a distant past, and wished them a safe journey home.

At the door, he asked Aisling, 'Are you sure you'll be all right?' When Aisling allayed his fears, he added, 'You know, I love you a lot.' He then kissed her on the lips and kissed Philip's forehead. 'And you too, young fellow. I'm a lucky guy to have you both.'

The baby had gone to sleep in Aisling's arms.

It was almost 11.00 o'clock in the evening when Aisling heard a car pull up on the driveway. While waiting for Sean she had unpacked their suitcases, fed the baby and put him back to sleep. She had been restless throughout. Bad news like that always unsettled her. She breathed a sigh of relief. 'Thank

God, he's back,' she muttered.

The doorbell rang. Did he forget his keys? she wondered. Sean was so anxious to be of some comfort to their friends in their moment of pain that he must have forgotten them. She hurried down the stairs. The porch light was on. She opened the door.

It was the Gardaí.

'Mrs Aisling O'Shea? I'm afraid that we have some very bad news for you. Can we come in?' The two Gardaí removed their caps and followed Aisling, who had gone pale, to the sitting room.

There had been an accident, the Gardaí explained.

Sean was on his way home after spending a few hours with Patrick and Eileen in the hospital. There still had been no news about Siobhan. His presence, even when not much was said after Patrick gave Sean the details of the accident, helped the distressed parents tremendously. The wait was terribly long. Knowing that Aisling was alone with their baby, Patrick and Eileen had urged Sean to go home. He was driving on the Dundrum road when a drunken driver going in the opposite direction hit him head-on. Sean did not have a chance. He died instantly, while the other driver managed to pull himself out of the wreck . . .

Aisling was sobbing profusely. Like a shot, Philip was up at his mother's side.

'What's wrong, Ma?' he asked as he nestled into Aisling's outstretched arms.

'Nothing, son. It's just silly me.' She dabbed her eyes with tissue.

But Philip knew. 'It's Dad, isn't it?'

Philip had not known his father, but he had seen his portrait and countless photographs of Sean and Aisling together. He had also seen the pictures that had been taken during that holiday in Spain. Aisling had mentioned Sean innumerable times to Philip. She was determined to preserve his memory not only in photographs, in the journals that he used to keep for her whenever he was away ('so that we will never really

47

be apart,' he used to say), or in the various memorabilia around the house, but also in their son. So Philip grew up in Sean's continued presence.

'I miss him, too, Ma,' said Philip as tears welled up in his eyes. 'My friend and his father, they're always playing together,' he said wistfully. 'But I have you,' he added as he clung to her. 'We'll always be together. And I'll take care of you ...' He looked up at her. Those words sounded so much like Sean's. '... when I grow up.'

More tears flowed from Aisling's eyes as mother and son sought refuge, in their helplessness, in each other.

★   ★   ★

There was a lot to be done before Richard would be ready to go on his trip to Leuven. After all, he would be away for a whole semester. He was looking forward to it, but somehow he also felt apprehensive. Would he have things in order? What was Leuven like? He had never been there before. More correspondence ensued between him and his host professor as he tried to find out details of his fellowship, about accommodation, about Leuven. He also had to make arrangements with his landlady since his one-bedroomed apartment would be empty. Should he bring all his things? What about the few pieces of second-hand furniture that he had started collecting while still a graduate student in Chicago? His books, his files, his computer disks. Would he need them in Leuven? His manuscript and the disk on which it had to be stored, definitely. He was almost in a panic the more he thought of his trip.

But he did get most of his anxieties sorted out by the time he checked into the British Airways flight to Heathrow. He had packed his clothes into two suitcases which he was allowed to check in. In his hand-carried bag, he had a copy of his unfinished manuscript and the disk. But he had also, as a precautionary measure, made a copy of the manuscript and packed it with his clothes. He had heard too many tales, real or imaginary, of manuscripts being lost and of hopes and even longed-for academic degrees vanishing into thin air because their writers could not face the almost impossible task of getting their ideas together again. When his classmates and he were writing their dissertations, they heard of a Ph.D. student who used to keep a copy of his work in the refrigerator in case his room or the house went on fire. Of course, this was before personal computers became readily available and the present generation of students and academics could take advantage of its enormous benefits. But what if something did happen to his manuscript? He shuddered at the thought of it since there was no way he could reconstruct what he had done so far. It would be a total disaster as far as he was concerned.

He was staying in England for a few days. Friends of his had invited him over when they heard that he was going to Europe and he thought it would be a terrific opportunity to see them again and to enjoy the attractions of London. From there he would just take the train to Dover, transfer to the ferry for Oostende and finally get on the train which would bring him directly to Leuven via Brussels. His travel agent had been very helpful in making all the arrangements, particularly in securing a seat on the popular British Airways flight.

And so that January afternoon Richard Gutierrez, a tenure-track assistant professor of philosophy from Lonergan University in California, was at Los Angeles Bradley International Airport on his way to Leuven in search of some inspiration to complete his scholarly work.

★   ★   ★

Sean's death really shocked Aisling. After the Gardaí had left, she sobbed uncontrollably. No word came out of her mouth, just utter disbelief. She kept hoping it was just a nightmare. Only a few hours ago Sean had been with them – laughing and joking about the holiday, and then concerned about the plight of their friends. She remembered his last words to her and the child – and she shook with emotion.

It was not fair at all. Here he was on a mission of mercy and then struck down by an unconcerned drunk driver who survived the crash he had caused, while Sean died a violent death, leaving a young widow and a one-year-old son. Could you call that justice? It did not make any sense at all. What had they done to deserve this? Was she at fault and was she being punished in this way? Had they been having it too easy in life and needed to be brought down to earth, with a bang, as it were? Did it have to be this way?

She felt a real emptiness. A portrait of Sean, herself and Philip was in the sitting room. She grabbed hold of it and clasped it to her breast, as if by this action she could dispel the oncoming loneliness. She missed him a lot already and as it dawned on her that she would never see Sean again, the tears just kept flooding down her cheeks like an unchecked river. Their son would grow up without a father. What would he become? What kind of future would he have? How would she manage? The questions kept buzzing in her head.

The room was still warm. Although it was in the middle of summer, she had decided to light a fire to take the chill away, their house having been empty for two weeks. She had meant the fire to be a cosy welcome for Sean when he came back from the hospital. They were going to sit in front of it while Sean gave her the latest on Siobhan. Instead, there were only the dying embers for her to stare at. Soon they would be gone and the room would be cold. Even now she could feel a chill down her spine.

But it can't be. Sean is not gone, she kept telling herself. We were meant to have a future. A good husband and father like Sean had a proper place in this world. He deserved to be alive. Sean was a committed teacher too. He had worked hard at his studies so that he would land the job in which he thought he could do the most to make this world a better place to live in. For him, being a teacher was contributing to the task of lifting some of the darkness from this world. He had turned to classical literature because he was good at it, but he always considered the task of educating others and himself of greater significance. Any other academic discipline would have sufficed, if he excelled in it, so long as it enabled him to guide others to a better and more enlightened outlook in life.

Sean was fired with enthusiasm. So why was his future cut short? It couldn't be true, it just couldn't.

She and Sean used to go for long walks, hand in hand, at the nearby Marlay Park. They would converse endlessly on different topics, some of them profound, others trivial, as they followed the many delightful trails in that park, the longest of them ending up in Wicklow, the garden county of Ireland. At other times Sean would be silent and preoccupied, to enable her to yap along, he had teasingly told her. She used to tease him back by observing that whenever she had gone a bit silent, he would make intelligent grunts so that she could continue. Those long walks had brought them closer together and had made them keen admirers of the beauty of nature. They would recite lines of poetry to each other. Now all that was to be over. Why? Why?

Aisling got up and walked around in circles, not knowing what to do. She moved towards the bay window in the sitting room. It was here that Sean had put up a huge Christmas tree on their very first Christmas in the house. They had no curtains then and Sean had said with a grin that the huge tree helped to cover the emptiness of the room. They had no furniture, but they did have a genuine tree, he consoled her. What kind of Christmases lay ahead of her and her son? What would happen to all their dreams about the future?

Finally she dragged herself from the sitting room, unable to bear its emptiness, and went into the hall. But more memories flashed before her eyes as she saw the stairs. It was on this very step, she recalled, that Sean and she, practically penniless because they had used up their savings to put a deposit on this house, sat down drinking tea on their first day in their new house. The whole place was bare then − but they were celebrating because they had their roof above their head and their mug of tea.

Aisling steadied herself by holding on to the bannister and then tightly gripping it for support. Too weak to climb up the stairs, she sat down and placed her head between her hands.

Then her grief and loneliness turned to anger. We try hard, she said, so very hard to do a good job no matter what it is. Is this our reward? What is the point in doing that if it ends up this way? She could feel her muscles tense up. She was clenching her fists, as she wanted to strike hard, really hard, whoever was responsible for this. Not just the driver, but whoever allowed that situation to happen. Blast any community that does not prevent such things! Curse those barmen who keep selling drinks to those who are already too drunk to decide for themselves. Where are those parents who did not instil responsibility into this driver, even if they had to beat it into him? The pain he was causing her was unforgivable. Curse ...

'God, why did you let this happen?' Aisling cried out. 'We had always been taught to love you and trust in your goodness. This is not good, this is wrong. Then why, with all your power, did you not prevent the accident? Just a few minutes more and Sean would have missed the other driver.' She was angry with God, angry because, unlike Sean who had tried to take care of Philip, God was not caring enough for the likes of Sean and her. God seemed in fact to be toying with them, giving them a happy life, only to snatch it away now. 'God, how can you do this? Why do you do this?'

Suddenly, the phone broke the stillness of the night. It was her mother calling to let her know that they had arrived in Barrowtown safely. The irony of it all. God had waited until her folks were gone to let her suffer by herself. What kind of a God was this? Aisling wanted to strike God. After all, God had struck her and her family.

'Ma, it's ... it's Sean,' was all she could manage to say ...

Aisling continued to hold her son tightly, afraid that something or someone would separate them. Suddenly, Philip wriggled out of her grasp.

'Let's go have some drink, Ma,' he suggested.

Philip liked being taken to the cafeteria at Erasmus House. She would have coffee while he would have a glass of milk. It made him feel like an adult, sitting there with the university students who were enjoying a break from their studies. Here in Belgium he noticed that you got a biscuit or a sweet with your coffee or tea. His mother would pass her goodies to him.

'My head's getting all wet from your tears.' He shook his head as if to dry his hair.

Aisling had to laugh at his youthful innocence.

'So this is why you want to bring me on a date.' She took out more tissues to dry her eyes. 'We can't go yet, my eyes are all red. People will say that you have been bold and that's why poor me was crying.'

'But they'll say I've been good again. That's why we're going out.' Aisling could not refute the child's logic.

As they were making their way down the stairs, Philip whispered to her, 'You know, I like it better when you don't cry.' Aisling smiled as she ruffled his blond hair, wiping away the tears that had fallen on it.

III

It was the foundation day of Mercier University. Despite the cancellation of classes in celebration of this event, the students were not much in evidence in the town since this year the anniversary fell on a Tuesday. Officially or not, some of them had decided it was time for a long weekend away from their studies. As far as these students were concerned, Tuesday's free day surely meant their professors could not possibly expect them to be around on Monday!

Also absent from the streets of Leuven that day was the usual danger of being knocked down by cyclists, especially given the fact that almost everyone, including eminent and awesome-looking professors, travels here on a bicycle. On his first day in this university town Richard almost got hit by two cyclists since he did not know that the narrow lane he was trying to cross was actually a bicycle lane and cyclists, seemingly, could go in either direction. A bit fazed but grateful that nothing worse had occurred, Richard put it down as a harrowing experience in a foreign land while hoping that nothing similar would happen to him.

Richard and his host professor, Dr. van der Riet, had arranged to meet at the reception following the Mass to be celebrated for the academic community. Richard made his own way to Sint-Peters Kerk at the center of Leuven. He walked on the cobbled roads of the Groot Begijnhof where his accommodation was, crossed Schapenstraat and up into Naamsestraat and headed towards the Centrum.

Leuven looked a bit bleak since practically all the trees had shed their leaves and the sky was gray and cheerless. It was bitingly cold too, and despite his heavy coat he was still shivering. It seemed that the years of basking in the sunny

54

climate of Los Angeles had made him unaccustomed to such low temperatures. But the walk helped to keep him warm, and he enjoyed the change from being too dependent on a car as he was in California.

As he approached the Centrum, he noticed that the upper part of Naamsestraat had been closed to traffic. The Politie were diverting the cars to a side-street. Richard became curious. What could have happened? An accident perhaps? But he soon realized that the Centrum was closed to traffic because of the university festivities. Wow, he muttered to himself, isn't that something? He would soon discover that Leuven was one of those 'town and gown' cities in Europe, where whatever took place in academia affected the daily lives of the townsfolk.

Richard had spotted the Fons Sapientiae, prominently situated in the Centrum; it reminded him of the fountain near his office in Bergman Hall. He liked that fountain in the open courtyard, maybe because his Hispanic background made him appreciate such a gathering place. And it certainly was a gathering place – for student clubs which at times held their barbecues here, for photographers who endlessly clicked away at models doing various gyrations in front of the fountain, for friends who liked the open-air atmosphere for a chat. A couple of times film crews set up their equipment here, using the fountain and Bergman Hall as a backdrop. At times Richard would just look out from the window of his office and enjoy the sight of the water spurting upwards from a stone pineapple set at the very top and then trickling down into a small ornamental basin and down again into a larger one before finding its way into an even bigger round basin in a continuous cycle. On a number of occasions foam appeared – some students squirting washing-up liquid in good clean fraternity frolic. As Richard's wandering mind settled itself back on the Fons Sapientiae he wondered what kind of tricks the Leuven students played on this fountain.

Richard could see now why the traffic had to be diverted. There was a procession of the academic community, in all their finery, led by a formal-looking gentleman bearing what

55

looked to Richard like a golden rod. The line of impressive-looking professors and administrators had emerged from Universiteitshal on Naamsestraat.

He remembered reading that Universiteitshal was the former Cloth Hall built in 1317, part of which had been granted to the university of Leuven in 1432. When the entire building was handed over to that university in 1679, the university added a floor in Baroque style. The cloth trade had been pivotal in the development of the economy in this part of Belgium. In fact, Richard recalled that the thirteenth-century expansion of Leuven, the golden era, was based on the cloth trade. Edward Van Even, the nineteenth-century urban historian, had claimed that Leuven produced so much cloth that foreigners thought it was the name of the whole country! The prosperity it brought to the town had attracted the mendicant orders, the Franciscans, Dominicans and Augustinian friars, since they specialized in the care of the urban soul.

The academic procession, with all its regalia, wended its way to the church. As it entered the church, the organ sounded a triumphal note, a signal for everyone inside to stand up. Richard's eyes were on the gowns being worn by the different professors. Most of them had the same black-with-blue-striped academic gown of the university.

The sight of the gowned professors reminded Richard of the commencement ceremonies at his own university in Los Angeles. It was always a spectacle for the students, their families and friends to see the faculty in their academic costumes. The ones that really stood out were the faculty who had received their degrees in Europe, since their academic gowns were truly colorful and even ostentatious. One professor, a graduate of Salamanca, had a terrific cap and gown. It made him look like a character straight from the medieval ages. The Ph.D. graduates of English and Irish universities sported red gowns with yellow or blue stripes. Imagine – red! The wearer of one of these confided to Richard that his gown from an Irish university made him look like a parrot. Not only that; since these foreign gowns were more suitable for the English and Irish climate, they were heavy. Unlike the American gowns, which were zipped up, prompting some more daring individuals to wear only a T-shirt underneath, theirs were open. So the miserable foreign-educated Ph.D.s had to wear a suit or sports jacket as well and had to brave the hot sun of southern California in May. It was a great relief when it was decided two years ago that a canopy would be erected over the administrators and the faculty during the commencement exercises. Too many faculty, it seemed, protesting because of the hot sun and ignoring the plight of the students and their guests, were taking breaks during the whole ceremony.

There was a certain processional order among the professors here at Leuven, he had been told. According to tradition, the theologians came first and the engineers last. Richard found this order in the procession particularly amusing. He thought to himself, the community here certainly have their priorities right: they want to build bridges to the next world – unless they have to cross the river in this world, he added, chuckling to himself.

Richard looked at the ghastly gas heaters in the church, out of place in this awe-inspiring place. However, aesthetics aside, he welcomed their presence right now as he shivered to think what it would have been like without any heating in this huge fifteenth-century Gothic church, which had been built on the remains of the former Romanesque church whose crypt under the museum of religious art could still be visited. He made a mental note to visit the museum since it contained the famous *The Last Supper* by Dirk Bouts and the fifteenth-century statue *Christ on the Cold Stone*. In the church itself, Richard had observed, was a Gothic choir rood loft dating back to the fifteenth century and the statue of the Sedes Sapientiae. This was a gorgeous church, no doubt about it, but he wondered how it was still possible to maintain such works of art in this day and age. On one of his walkabouts during his first week here he had noticed that this church was being renovated. Half of the outside was clean while the other half was still covered in the dust and grime of yesteryears, probably decades or even centuries, he concluded. In fact, he almost got lost because he had used the church as his landmark. After looking around the shops in the area, he found himself at the other end of the church, which he had mistakenly thought was another church. That end of the same church looked so clean and even architecturally different compared to the other end.

The ceremonies, including the Mass, were in Dutch, or Vlaanderen. Richard had expected this since Leuven is in the Dutch-speaking part of Belgium. He had also become acquainted with the tension between Flanders and Wallonia, the two regions which, despite the fact that they share neither language nor culture, have been artificially joined. Leuven, with about 90,000 inhabitants, is 13 kilometers from the frontier of French-speaking Wallonia to the south and 15 kilometers from bilingual Brussels to the west. It is practically in the center of Belgium, in a region noted for its hilly terrain. Richard was glad that Leuven was conveniently located for exploring the rest of Belgium and even other European countries since this university town was only an hour-and-a-half drive from the Netherlands, the Grand Duchy of Luxembourg, Germany, and France, some of which he hoped to be able to visit.

Richard did not understand a word but managed to follow the different parts of the Mass. He could not help wondering about the reform in the liturgy of the Catholic Church due to Vatican II. Prior to that momentous event, he was told that no matter where a Catholic went, the Mass was the same: the liturgy was conducted in Latin, the universal language of the Church, and the rituals were uniform. The Catholic worshipper felt at home whether in the USA, in Poland, in Spain or anywhere else in the world. It was claimed that Latin helped to ensure the catholicity of the Catholic faith. Did he feel like a stranger now since he did not know the language? Did the Mass mean anything to him since all he was able to do was to follow the movements of the congregation?

His thoughts were interrupted by the beautiful singing of the university choir. It dawned on him that here was a universal language. One did not have to understand the words to appreciate and feel the emotions being stirred up by the music. The singing lifted up his spirits, just like the Gothic spires all over the town. Are we perhaps forgetting the importance of the emotions in our practice of religion? Why can we not worship with our hearts and not just with our minds? he asked himself.

He certainly was not worshipping, he had to admit; instead, he was musing. Perhaps even amusing himself – if he were to be honest. His lack of knowledge of the language made it easier for his mind to wander.

★   ★   ★

Philip was also finding the services rather tedious. He and his mother had been invited to the same liturgical celebration taking place in the church. He was fascinated with the academic outfits and ceremonial trappings at the beginning of the ceremony. Now he was trying hard to be patient, but, boy, was it hard when he had no clue as to what was going on.

'I wish I'd brought my colouring book,' he whispered to his mother. 'And it's cold.'

A few minutes later, Philip shook her elbow for attention. 'Can I go to the bathroom, Ma?'

Aisling was getting embarrassed. The lady beside them looked at her and smiled. She smiled back. To Philip, she asked in her lowest voice possible, 'Can you hold on a little longer?'

'I'll try.'

But ten minutes later, Philip tugged at his mother's elbows again. 'I need to go, Ma.'

That was her signal. This was an emergency. When Philip resorted to this, he meant business. The trouble was she did not know where there was a toilet. The poor child, the cold had been too much for him. So up she stood with Philip in tow. Fortunately, they had taken their seats at the end of the pew so they did not have to be bothering anyone else.

As they hurriedly walked towards the door of the church,

she remembered that there was a Quick restaurant nearby. Surely there would be a toilet there. But her sense of direction not being the best, she turned left once they were outside the church. It meant a longer route for Philip, whose grasp of his mother's hand was getting tighter and tighter. He said nothing; but his face was registering some concern as he kept putting his two knees together as they walked fast.

'Can you hold on, son?'

But before Aisling could stop Philip, he had put on a sprint. Seeing that the roads were empty, Philip had crossed Fochplein, climbed up the Fons Sapientiae fountain, pulled down his trousers and joined the scholar in pouring into the pool what he had with great effort been keeping in!

It was a rare sight indeed. Passers-by stopped in their tracks, laughed merrily and pointed at Philip and the scholar doing their own thing. In the background the organ in Sint-Peters continued to play melodious music while tourists scrambled for their cameras. This was meant to take place in Brussels, not Leuven. It was simply unbelievable and yet here it was happening. A real-life *Mannequin Pis!*

Aisling was blushing to the roots. What should she do now?

However, realizing that there was nothing she could do, she joined in the laughter. In fact, she was laughing so hard that tears flowed down her cheeks.

Rescuing Philip, she hugged him.

'Aaahh...That's so much better. We can go back now, Ma,' said the much relieved boy.

★   ★   ★

The sacred ceremonies being over, Richard joined the academic community as they processed once again through the streets but this time towards the Pope's College. But the procession was only passing through the college which had been Pope Adrian's residence when he was a professor at Leuven and which had been rebuilt. It was going further to the auditorium where the conferring of honorary doctorates was to take place.

Richard was tempted to slip away for a quick cup of coffee at a nearby cafeteria. He needed to keep warm. But he decided against it since he did not know where the auditorium was. So he stuck with the crowd; it was safer that way. Besides, he wanted to experience a European conferring of such degrees. Meanwhile, the town was humming back to normality, the signs for the traffic diversion having been removed.

If it was a European experience Richard was expecting, he was not disappointed. Three eminent individuals were being honored: a medical doctor from England, a sociologist from Germany, and a bishop from Zaire. The *laudatio* and the honorees' response were in Dutch, English, German and French. Richard marvelled at the ease with which the Belgians could switch from one language to another. It was an experience that he would constantly have since shop assistants and taxi drivers in this truly European town were used to addressing their customers in any of those languages. And yet he told himself, with embarrassment and dismay, he lived in southern California with a bewildering variety of languages – he just had not bothered to take any interest in that.

There and then he resolved to do something about his lack of knowledge of other languages. His Asian colleague had always said that you lose out in your communications with others if you do not speak their language. There is something about language, she had stressed. It is not only the spoken word but also the culture, the connotations, the traditions and so on which cannot be translated. It is like listening to a joke, his colleague used to say, you miss the punchline if you have not been able to follow everything. And with a joke it is the punchline that matters. Richard was beginning to realize the truth in that observation. In his case he could not even understand the signs and notices all over Leuven.

The Rector had initiated the conferring of the doctoral degree on the medical doctor from England. Since this part of the proceedings was in English, Richard was, of course, able to follow the Rector's speech. But he became more interested in the whole idea of a university honoring someone with a doctorate. It must be a great privilege, he thought. Certainly only eminent ones received such honor. But wasn't it strange since they were already eminent and really did not need additional titles? Or was it because a university wanted to be associated with the work of such eminent individuals? But many of these universities were definitely more renowned than any of the individuals being honored. So what was the point? One thing sure, that would never be a problem for him – he was not even tenured yet. He better finish that manuscript. He doubted whether he would ever rise to such lofty heights as ...

His intellectual wanderings were interrupted by the loud clapping of the audience, who were on their feet. He thought it was for the English chap, but he discovered that the audience were showing their respect to the Zairean honoree, who was absent. The Rector had laid the cap and certificate on an empty seat.

★ ★ ★

After that incident, Aisling did not think that they would bother returning to the church. In fact, she did not think it would be a good idea to attend the conferring ceremony since understandably Philip would be bored by the lengthy speeches. She couldn't really explain all the academic goings-on to a six-year-old. Somehow academic affairs were not really family ones. Perhaps they were too formal and needed some loosening up.

So she asked her young charge what he would rather do.

'Look for a troll – with green hair,' came the quick response.

'OK, how about something to warm us up first?' she suggested. It really was cold today, and fortunately both of them were well wrapped up. But she had had to wear a dress for the occasion when she would rather have worn jeans, which she much preferred in wintertime.

There was a cosy-looking restaurant facing Sint-Peters so they headed in that direction, noticing in the meantime the seats outside. Who would be sitting out in this cold? she wondered. But then she realized that there were gas heaters above, radiating some heat on any adventurous clientele. She wasn't one of those so she chose a seat inside. Philip thought this was a great idea as he clapped his body for some warmth.

When the waiter asked them what they wished to order, she instinctively asked for tea.

Aisling and Sean were great tea-drinkers. They would have endless mugs of tea at home. It was a great way to relax and chat; and on cold days, it was particularly welcome. They would have tea before setting off on their walks and tea immediately after the walk. The warm liquid inside you was a good way of thawing you, they would say.

'Milk or lemon?' inquired the waitress.

'With milk, please.'

'And the child?'

Philip volunteered a response. 'Tea, please.'

He must need some warming up, Aisling thought, since Philip did not like the tea in Belgium. He thought it had a funny taste, remarking that it was not the same as the tea at home. Was it the water or the milk? Or the brand of tea? Aisling agreed with him. Somehow the tea in Ireland was different and really refreshing. The Continentals preferred coffee and their coffee was indeed marvellous, but she did not like drinking too much coffee. She was not yet ready to be European in that sense.

'Do you think we'll be able to get a troll today?' Philip's tone was definitely hopeful.

'I don't want you to be very disappointed if we don't find one. OK?' Aisling wanted to prepare him.

They had searched all over Dublin, Barrowtown and Kilkenny for those green-haired treasures, but without any success. They found several trolls in various costumes, all right, since they seemed to have been the fashion this year. Last year it was the Ninja turtles. But none of the trolls was good enough to end their search. There were trolls with pink hair, orange hair, red hair, blue hair. In fact, practically every colour, except the precious green. It was like looking for the

Holy Grail, she remarked with exasperation after they went in and out of toy shops in Ireland.

'We could be lucky.' There was that charming twinkle in Philip's eyes which conveyed the message that if you wanted it to remain there, you had better look hard and long for the troll – of the green-hair variety.

'We'll keep looking while we are in Belgium. Fair enough?'

Philip nodded and sipped his tea. 'I've had enough.' He was eyeing her chocolate that came with the tea. Aisling knew what he wanted.

Just as she handed him the chocolate, she saw the two ladies seated next to them. They waved at her and with a knowing smile, pointed to Philip. They were talking animatedly in French.

Aisling's French was more than adequate for her to follow the conversation.

'Oh my God,' she exclaimed to herself. 'My son has become famous!'

Evidently the two dears had witnessed the entire episode at the fountain. They had taken great delight in it as it gave a human touch to the bricks and mortar. Wasn't that young boy cute? they were saying. Just as well they had their camera ready.

Aisling froze. She had visions of her Philip being shown all over the world – and it would not be his good side! she hoped to God that none of the academics from Leuven or in Leuven had been present. She would never be able to live it down if she were shown a particular photo of Philip. It could be here or it could be at some conference somewhere else. She had a paper to give in Denmark next year. What if someone there had been here at that precise moment?

Was her imagination perhaps getting the better of her? But only a few days ago she had observed a middle-aged gentleman taking a photograph of that very statue. She saw him later doing research at the main library of the university. He must be a professor, she surmised. After all, that fountain seems to be the symbol of Leuven academia. Or somebody from Boston College, where she had been invited to teach during the summer, could have been here. Oh, my God. She started to become unsettled.

Philip noticed that Aisling was no longer enjoying her cup of tea. 'Shall we go now, Ma?' He was anxious to start their troll-hunting.

Oh, well, Aisling shrugged her shoulders, I will wait for that to happen. The ladies were right about one thing, her son was cute. So after paying the waiter, she took Philip's hand, waved at his admirers, and said, 'Where do you think those trolls are hiding?'

★   ★   ★

As prearranged, Richard met Dr. van der Riet at the entrance to the newly constructed auditorium. Milling around it were various university and civic dignitaries and several guests who had emerged from the building. There was an air of excitement as groups huddled together, presumably talking about the day's event or just catching up on the latest activities. Since Richard did not know anybody or understand a word being spoken, he kept a reasonable distance from the different groups.

It had been a good experience, he thought, but he was glad the ceremonies were over. Long speeches could be boring, especially if they were in a different language, and the other speeches had been in French, Dutch and German − which accounted for his mind wandering off.

Dr. van der Riet and he were going to the reception at Universiteitshal, which would be a nice opportunity for him to meet several people at the same time, van der Riet explained, since very rarely were they together except on occasions like these. Richard agreed. Since his arrival in Leuven he had met only Dr. van der Riet and he wanted to get to know other academics.

And yet Richard was apprehensive; he hated these socials where one talks to an individual or a group for a few minutes and then moves on − to mix around, so they say. He always got the impression when he was talking to an individual, that the eyes of that individual would be darting back and forth as if looking out for better game. He knew he wasn't an important person, but neither did he like anyone thinking that he or she was stuck with him. Whenever he joined a group he always felt that he was crashing in. Still, it was an effective way of meeting people without himself being stuck in long, boring conversations.

Inside the building Dr. van der Riet pointed out with pride the magnificent marble stairway. A great tribute to the Belgian stone quarries, he remarked. The stairway of honor, which led to the Graduation Room and the Jubilee Hall, was lined with the university choir, bursting into a stirring song once the crowd began to make its appearance. The hymns which they were singing so marvellously added to the impressive atmosphere created by the architecture of the place. Baroque pomp was visible in the university hall. There is definitely history and tradition here, Richard observed. These gorgeous buildings have character. It was an observation that he would be making several times over the more he came to know Leuven.

Several individuals had already gathered in the Jubilee Hall, most of them sipping the wine being served by immaculately dressed waiters. Dr. van der Riet cornered a rather dignified-looking gentleman, who seemed to be very much in demand.

'Professor Hausen, I introduce Dr. Gutierrez to you? He is from America and is here to do research. Professor Hausen is the Rector of Mercier University.'

'So, Dr. Gutierrez, you are here to spend a semester with us. Welcome to Leuven. When did you arrive?' The tall, elderly Rector extended his hand.

'Just a few days ago. I came via England,' Richard answered as he shook Professor Hausen's hand.

'And how is your accommodation? I presume that you are staying in the Groot Begijnhof.' Professor Hausen peered above his eyeglasses at Richard.

'Oh yes, and it's a wonderful place. Full of character and charm. And it is very comfortably furnished.'

Richard had come to know that the centuries-old Beguinage was a showpiece of academic life in Leuven. Guest professors were normally housed there and since they came from all over the world, the community in that place was indeed international. In fact, he was beginning to realize that part of the experience of spending some time in Leuven was to live there.

'Well, I hope that your time here will be fruitful,' he said as he extended both hands to sandwich Richard's, since someone else was desperately trying to catch his attention.

'Thank you,' replied Richard, at the same time accepting with his free hand the glass of white wine which one of the servers had offered him.

Dr. van der Riet had disappeared during this brief encounter between Richard and Professor Hausen. Richard, now left on his own, approached the server who was balancing expertly on his right palm a tray of tempting appetizers, some of which were actually in silver spoons. How does one eat these? he wondered. He spied someone take one of the spoons, put it into his mouth and return the empty spoon on the tray. How strange, he thought, but he did exactly the same thing. Whatever was in those spoons was absolutely delicious. The server encouraged him to have another one; but before he could help himself to it, Dr. van der Riet was back at his side.

'So you are there. I wondered where you had gone. How was your meeting with the Rector?' Dr. van der Riet had to raise his voice slightly above the din in the now crowded hall, full of chattering academics, administrators and guests. No one was paying any attention to the singers who had been orchestrated to provide background entertainment.

'Quite good, I suppose. He welcomed me to Leuven.'

'Come on. I want you to meet...' But he could not finish his sentence. Someone wanted to see Dr. van der Riet and they conversed, quite excitedly, in Dutch.

So Richard excused himself. Whatever it was the two Belgians were talking about was certainly important since both seemed very much engrossed in the conversation. An academic matter? Or an administrative detail? It couldn't be the results of the European cup? Richard often wondered what his fellow academics talked about at socials like this.

'So you are Dr. Gutierrez from the USA. I couldn't help overhearing your conversation with Professor Hausen. Oh, by the way, I'm Jennifer Sidney. No, not from Australia, but from England I always have to say that since people immediately think of Australia when they hear my last name.'

The speaker was a stunning lady who was dressed in a very fashionable long dark blue dress. Her finery enhanced her natural beauty and she had a pleasant smile.

'Hi! I'm Richard. Pleased to meet you, Jennifer. Been in Leuven long?'

Instinctively Richard wanted to compliment her on her beauty, her name, her ... But he was afraid that that might be interpreted as sexist. That was why he had brought up Leuven as a more neutral subject. But he couldn't resist admiring her.

'Mademoiselle Sidney, I see you again. How wonderful!' With that, Pierre Lamennais, a French professor of biology, kissed Jennifer's hand in great flourish while holding on to a small tray loaded with crackers and cheese with his cupped left hand. 'Come, I show you my learned colleague.' He took her by the arm and gracefully escorted her out of Richard's sight. Jennifer Sidney wasn't given much of a choice but she did manage to give Richard a parting wave.

Blast it, anyway, Richard cursed under his breath. Here he was, minding his own business, and this thing of beauty, oh yes, he may as well say it, comes into his view and introduces herself to him. And before he has had any time to exchange pleasantries with her, this damn Frenchman takes her away from him. Richard was disgusted. He felt like a child who had been offered a lollipop and had it grabbed away the minute he reached out for it. It was despicable.

*   *   *

Richard's eyes scanned the crowd hoping to catch sight of Jennifer again. After a while, he did spot her in very friendly conversation with Pierre and his group. He was tempted to join them, but decided not to. After all, he did not know her, not yet anyway. He stood where he was, sipping his white wine and smiling at whoever passed his way. He felt very much on his own since most of the guests near him were speaking in Dutch. It would have been rude to walk around listening to conversations in English, rather like shopping around for a better deal. Anyway, he was secretly hoping Jennifer would bump into him before the event was over.

But what if she never did? This was a big crowd. Would there be another chance? In an academic place like Leuven, surely they would meet once more. But he did not even know what department she belonged to. The different departments were scattered in various colleges throughout Leuven. She could even be from another university. Perhaps he should make a move. After all, that was the nature of the social; one could just crash in.

He edged his way towards the part of the hall where he had spied Jennifer. But she was nowhere in sight. The group was not there either. When he turned around, he brushed against someone. It was Dr. van der Riet.

'You have been enjoying yourself, yes? Ready to go?' asked his polite host professor.

Richard could not very well tell his host professor that he was looking for someone whom he did not really know. Nor could he say that he wanted to stay because he was determined to find Jennifer. So he answered by asking a question, 'Do you think we should go?'

Unfortunately, Dr. van der Riet replied in the affirmative.

★   ★   ★

Philip knew that today was a free day since his mother did not go to the office as usual. That was why he wanted to make good use of it; after all, he was supposed to be on holiday. And on holidays he and his ma always did something special. Today it was the hunt for his troll.

Aisling welcomed the break, too. She had been reading up on Postmodernism since they arrived and she seemed to be getting nowhere. She could not understand what these

Postmodernists were writing about: no plot, no character, nothing. Yet it was considered literature, at least by some avant-garde people. Her colleague, not one of them, had described it as '*excretum tauri*'. She found herself mired in it. Anyway, she owed it to Philip to take the day off from academic work. He had been patient so far.

'We'll start with the big stores,' she said with enthusiasm. Philip's excitement could sometimes be catching.

So they made a beeline for Inno on Diestsestraat, not far from Fochplein. But no such luck, there was nothing there. They tried another big store, G.B. Still no success. There were trolls, yes, but not the elusive green-haired one. She was beginning to blame Philip's cousin. Why, oh, why did he have to choose a green one? Just because they were Irish was no reason. In fact, she thought the troll with the orange hair was more attractive. Of course, that was the wrong word. It was not attractive, definitely not. Cuddly, perhaps? Or maybe eye-catching? How would one describe those little monsters? Aisling had to stop herself. She was getting deeper into Trolloloquay.

After they visited a number of shops and found no darling green-haired troll, she called for a break because her shoes were killing her. The cobbled streets of Leuven did not favour high heels. She suggested returning to their studio apartment so she could change into something more comfortable. They would have lunch and then start their search again.

Philip agreed. His legs were getting tired but he would not admit it in case his mother postponed the hunt. Wisely, Aisling decided that they should take the No. 2 bus which went close to their place. Their investment in an eight-journey bus-card was paying off.

★   ★   ★

Richard had come to know that the No. 2 bus passed near the Groot Begijnhof. Sometimes he took it since he could get off at the stop in Naamsestraat near the American College. He was then only a few minutes' walk downhill to the part of the

Groot Begijnhof where his apartment was located. But since it was still cold, he thought he would walk instead. Just like this morning. The cold air might help clear his mind, thus preparing him to work on his manuscript.

He told himself that he had had enough time to adjust to Leuven and he should now get down to serious work. So far he had found the place very pleasant. When he first arrived at the train station, he wondered what it would be like to spend the next five months here. Dr. van der Riet had kindly met him and brought him to his accommodation, which he immediately liked.

He had spent the next few days acquainting himself with the town, having been supplied with informative brochures by the Office for International Students about life in Leuven. So he read those. He also managed to get more information, particularly about what was on that year in Leuven, at the Tourist Information in the Stadhuis. From what he had read it was going to be an exciting semester since the Luister van Leuven/Bierfeesten, organized every five years, was going to take place this year. He read that Leuven is the beer capital of Belgium! Imagine that, a university town with that reputation. In fact, he had heard that it had become a beer town because of the students. He was wondering about the connection between academia and beer-drinking.

The town was certainly a hive of cultural events. Leuven was truly a cultural center. Lectures, concerts, folklore, open-air performances and many other activities were advertised all over the place. In fact, tonight his host professor and he were attending the concert at the Aula Maxima Pieter de Somer, and he was looking forward to that. The inhabitants of Leuven are lucky to have all these in their midst, he observed.

Richard was also very impressed with the general appearance of Leuven. Culture, history and tradition were evident no matter where one looked. The town was like an open-air museum of architecture because of its abbeys, monasteries, beguinages, university buildings. Leuven could boast of a green circle as well as of the absence of the unsightly trappings of the twentieth century. In particular,

71

Richard really appreciated the fact that the electric cables were buried rather than criss-crossing the streets. As he glanced at the buildings, he admired the Belgian initiative in refraining from using poles. Instead there were well-designed lamps from the side of the buildings. Not only were these safer for pedestrians since there were no poles to bump into, but they were aesthetically more pleasing. He shook his head in disgust as he thought of a part of Lincoln Boulevard in Los Angeles, complete with ugly poles, overhead cables and gaudy shopfronts. A big difference when the pedestrian, and not the motorist, is king of the road.

What appalled him in Leuven, however, was the cost of living. He discovered to his horror that because of the poor rate of exchange of the dollar Belgium was turning out to be very expensive for him. Necessity being the mother – this time – of explorations, he had learned to check the restaurants' *Dagschotel* for his main meal. Even better, he discovered that the Chinese and Cambodian restaurants offered the best lunch deals. He would ask for the *Studentmenu*, which was around BF 180. Compared to other restaurant prices, that was cheap. Just as well he relished Chinese food.

But what really bothered Richard was the charge he had to pay to use some of the toilets. Even in some restaurants he had to fork out nine or ten francs! In the cold weather sometimes he had to make a number of trips. It was bad enough to be out of pocket, but to be short of funds for this reason was ludicrous. So he was going to find out which toilets did not charge users.

As Richard ambled down Naamsestraat towards the Groot Begijnhof, he could still feel the festive air of the university day. But tomorrow it will be solid academic work, he promised himself. In fact, this afternoon before going to the concert he would read over what he had written.

Somehow Richard seemed to have forgotten Jennifer. Or was he merely attempting to block her out of his consciousness?

*   *   *

'Go, go, go!' Philip was ready after their hearty soup-and-rolls lunch. His mother had finished her second mug of tea.

Philip had learned that his mother didn't like to rush her tea, and to try to make a move before that special moment would have elicited the remark, 'Now, Philip, you know that we shouldn't rush our tea.' The whole thing could have spoiled his chances.

It was just as well that Philip was fond of that quick-to-prepare kind of meal since there was no way Aisling could comfortably cook any decent meals in this tiny place in Tervuursevest. One advantage it did have was the proximity of Delhaize, since this supermarket was directly opposite them. All she had to do was cross the street for their groceries. But it was a dangerous crossing as it was a dual carriageway and the traffic was always busy. Sometimes she would be tempted to follow the others who would simply time their crossing at the spot where there were flashing amber lights. But with Philip with her, she always walked to the traffic lights although these were farther up the road. This doubled the crossing time, but at least it was safer.

Aisling had changed her outfit to suit the cold weather. She did not have to be burdened by a dress and high heels this time. Besides, it would be easier to walk around the streets of Leuven in her boots in another attempt to find these trolls who seemed determined to elude them. She thought they would try the toyshops Magma and Christaensen in Dietstraat. Surely, they will have the much-sought-after green-haired trolls, she tried to console herself.

'Shall we walk or take the bus?' she asked Philip.

'The bus – in case the shops close before we get there.' It was only three in the afternoon. But she could see that Philip was not taking any chances.

So once more the O'Sheas were on the No. 2, heading in the direction of the Centrum. They immediately sought out Christaensen, the bigger toyshop. Sure enough, there it was – a troll with green hair! It was the son of the troll family. And it had arrived only that very morning.

'Wow, great!' were the comments of this six-year-old.

73

So relieved was Aisling and so pleased with the end of their search that she did not even bother looking at the price, especially since there was only one of them. She would have to buy it, cost what it may. She looked at Philip's face – yes, it was a cute, happy face.

'Happy?' she asked.

'Yes, Ma, thanks. This is the son, like me. Now I can start looking for his father!' he joyfully announced.

IV

Richard was up, bright and early, despite staying up late the previous night rereading his manuscript. Although he thought that the argumentation he had developed in his written work was consistent and strong enough, he concluded that he really needed to edit his work before attempting to write that last chapter. In this way he might even be able to see more clearly the direction that he should take for that chapter, having been advised that at times the best way forward when one is bogged down with the writing is to review what one has already done.

He was by no means a whiz at the computer, but he had learned to use it effectively since he could now directly transfer his thoughts onto the screen. In fact, it usually facilitated the task of writing. So he had ensured that his disks were with him. Before departing from the USA, he had taken the trouble of transferring all his data onto a number of disks, since he had been informed that WordPerfect, the computer program in which his manuscript had been done, was in use at Mercier University. That meant he could really work on his manuscript with the help of the computer – without the distraction of having to prepare classes, correct papers or meet with students. He was bent on making substantial progress with his manuscript this semester.

Dr. van der Riet had handed him the key to the office made available by the Head of the School. It was a facility that he appreciated. So this morning he was determined to make a solid start; after all, that was what he was here for. With energy and enthusiasm therefore he made his way to the School and climbed the wooden staircase to the office.

But Richard was in for a major disappointment. There was

no computer in the office! Not even a typewriter was in sight. Only a long wooden desk and three chairs.

He sat down and stared at the empty desk in utter disbelief. How could he do his work? Was he wrong in taking it for granted that there would be a computer? But he thought it was now so much a part of academic research that it was incredible that there would be none here. To think that he could have done his work in his own office at his university. So much depended on his having access to a computer since his manuscript was on disk. He had made a hard copy, but editing that meant practically retyping the whole thing on a typewriter. And be did not even have that.

This is darned awful, he cursed to himself. How could he finish this manuscript? Of course, books, even the most influential and important works, had been produced without all this technology. But that was not the issue, he defended himself. The fact was, his manuscript *was* on disk. It needed to be edited, it had to be finished. What should he do now?

He made up his mind to do something about the situation immediately; going down to the secretary's office in another part of the building, he made inquiries about the availability of a computer. He really hated having to make a fuss, but he could not see how else he could manage his work.

The secretary informed him that there were two computers in the library for the use of staff and students and that he was welcome to use them. Richard felt relieved. That seemed to take some pressure off him. Perhaps he had panicked too soon.

Unfortunately, that relief proved to be short-lived since he discovered that he could really use only one of the two computers. Attached to the second one was a keyboard which was very different from what he was accustomed to. The A and the Q were in different places, the M and the comma were somewhere else. Other letters and symbols were elsewhere. Initially it had seemed to have been a minor problem, but when he tried using it for an hour, he made so many mistakes that it took him half an hour correcting them. Richard saw no point in relearning a different way of touch-typing. He had always presumed that the arrangement of the letters on the keyboard was uniform throughout the world. Evidently he was mistaken because there was a Belgian arrangement. That limited him to the other computer, which at least had the usual keyboard and the WordPerfect program in English. Still, all he needed was one computer which he could utilize.

There were to be more frustrating incidents, unfortunately, as he quickly learned that the use of the library computers was limited to two hours. If no one else wanted to use it, he could continue for another two hours. But the students were also under pressure to type their papers. A number of times, just when he felt a creative burst coming on, he had to relinquish the computer to accommodate another user. He was competing with the students, who, quite understandably he felt, had equal access to it. Moreover, since the library was closed during the weekend, there was no way he could proceed with his work during those two precious days. On top of all this, the library computer had no printer. When he inquired where he could print his work, he was told that this could be done at the computer room in Erasmus House, some distance from the School. Sensing his difficulties, the librarian of the School kindly allowed him to use the printer in her office when it was not in use. But Richard felt he was imposing on people and he did not like to do that. Worse, it was really having an effect on his enthusiasm and creativity. He sorely missed the personal computer and printer back in his own office in the USA. He did not feel as free to work on his research as he would have liked to.

Richard's frustrations over the lack of computing facilities led him to make inquiries about where he could rent a computer while he was in Leuven. He wanted to make use of the time he was here for research; but he was starting to question whether it was indeed wise to have transplanted himself, particularly since he was under pressure to complete his work. To add to his problems, he did not find a computer to rent. To buy one was out of the question since things were rather expensive in Leuven.

He was beginning to wonder whether technology or the

lack of it was getting the better of his research. Perhaps this is what some philosophers like Heidegger had been warning about the shift in priorities in contemporary society, he thought. We have become so used to all these developments in technology that we take them for granted. When they are missing, we are left in utter confusion. Worse, we are frustrated. But life is more than that, these philosophers have insisted, and we are in danger of forgetting its true value. We have confused the tool with the true goal of life.

But Richard could hear himself sniggering, that's fine in theory. One could even argue for its validity in a philosophical discussion. Right now he was confronted with his inability to work on his unfinished manuscript because he had to keep reshuffling his timetable to suit the availability of that one computer that he could use in the library. If the problem of evil that he was working on in his scholarly pursuits had anything to do with being frustrated, he certainly had the experience to go with it right now. He was getting a taste of what many people feel who have been frustrated, through no fault of their own, in their efforts to develop themselves. How can one grow when one is being blocked, hindered or even being stampeded upon?

Inevitably the issue of his tenure flashed past him. His anxiety over his application for tenure was being compounded by his present frustration. If he did not complete his manuscript, he certainly would be down in the dumps. He had the best of intentions: he wanted to finish his work, so why was he being prevented from doing so? The pressure, which he was once again feeling, of getting tenure weighed so heavily on American academics that many, particularly females, were postponing having a family because the demands of rearing a child would create havoc with their chance of obtaining that much-sought-after academic prize. Richard remembered someone at another university, admittedly a research-oriented one, remarking that she was expected to produce scholarly work, not children, while waiting for tenure!

Maybe he was making too much of this. Maybe he should

just turn to alternatives. But what are they? Would anyone really understand or care about what he was going through? It seemed so petty to an outsider. But when one has a goal that has to be achieved and one is being restrained, no matter how unconsciously, it does not seem too much to complain. For in the end what mattered, as far as his case was concerned, was that his work should be finished. How was that to happen?

His mind shifted to larger concerns. Unwilling to minimize the frustration he felt, he nevertheless couldn't help but wonder at how countless others go through life in utter frustration and despair. Humans have this inbuilt desire to succeed, they want to make something out of their lives; yet for these individuals, all that life offers are insurmountable obstacles, blank walls and unfair situations. Who is responsible for this imbalance in life – or even injustice? He kept thinking of the riots in Los Angeles the previous year. They were very costly and troublesome. It was the frustration felt by so many that had erupted in violence. Why is life so frustrating? Why do many seem destined to end up beating their heads against the hardness of life?

All that week Richard was in no mood for any scholarly work. The concentration demanded by such a task would not come. Today, after merely an hour at the School's library checking references rather than actually writing, he decided to head for Sedes, one of the university restaurants in Leuven. He had now learned where students went for relatively inexpensive yet substantial meals. The Sedes was also known for providing meals from different countries. Spain was the flavor of the month.

Several students, most of whom were in pairs, were already standing in the line. Their bags and other paraphernalia, dropped on the floor, had been pushed to the sides of the hallway. Above them were signs indicating how long the wait was from where they stood till they reached the food counter. Richard was amused by this detail, but he appreciated how efficiently and quickly the line moved. The different menus of the day were prominently displayed, and although the names were in Dutch he could make out what he would have. He had learned very fast that 'kip' meant chicken.

Five minutes after Richard had joined the line, he was loading his tray with a paella and a delicious-looking red apple. He decided not to have wine or beer. Instead he would just fill his glass with the cold water available from one of the drinking fountains conveniently located in the dining hall.

After paying the cashier, he looked around the hall in search of an empty seat and spotted his fellow American, Dr. Anton Brown, whom he had met the previous week, motioning to Richard to join him at the table. Anton was Associate Professor of humanities and Chair of his department and was here at Leuven, among other things, to explore the possibility of faculty and student exchange arrangements between his university and Mercier University. Richard, keeping a firm grip on his tray as he negotiated his way past tables and tables of hungry students, was glad he would have company.

After a few pleasantries, he told Anton of his plight.

'I *certainly* know what you're talking about, man. Have I had my share of frustrations here.'

Anton then narrated how he had been experiencing a difficult time with his mail. He had arranged to have his mail forwarded in a padded envelope every week to the Department of Interdisciplinary Studies of Mercier University. For three weeks he had been wondering why his mail was not getting through as he had expected. He even rang his office in the USA to check, but his secretary confirmed that she had been sending his parcel of correspondence and other important documents dutifully. So he promptly made a number of inquiries at Mercier University, but nobody seemed to know or even care. Finally he learned that one of the secretaries in another department had been receiving them. But since they were padded envelopes, this unthinking secretary thought they were books and just put them aside!

'You'd have thought that he'd have the initiative to find out since these were coming regularly. Wouldn't you?' Without waiting for a reply, Anton continued, 'And you know, I missed important deadlines because of all this inefficiency!'

Richard could still observe the anger in Anton's eyes.

'When you're the Chair of a department, and I am, important decisions have to be made, and they had to be made without me simply because my mail was on someone's shelf. Can you believe that?'

Anton banged his fist on the table. Fortunately, the students at the next table were too busy with their unintelligible chatter to notice.

Richard appreciated the significance of this complaint. He was waiting for the decision regarding his tenure application and he was going to make sure that important letters like that did not go astray.

The Chair was definitely on a high. This must have been brewing up in his mind and Richard's remarks were the catalyst to bring it to boiling point.

'That's not the most absurd thing, you know. Let me tell you what happened to an important fax sent by the President of my university. Here she was wondering why I hadn't replied. Evidently it had been received in the Department of Interdisciplinary Studies. But for whatever reason – only a fool could give an answer, I'm certain of that, certainly not me – it was forwarded to the Academic Center. The girl there thought I was still in the States. So guess what, she sends it to me in the States by airmail! What kind of logic would drive her to do that? So, of course, my secretary, not knowing the important contents of that airmail envelope, understandably sends it with the weekly mail to me here at Leuven. It took *three* damn weeks for the damn fax to come to me! Three! It's just unbelievable. When I confronted the girl at the Academic Center about it, she just shrugged her shoulders and raised her eyebrows. Never bothered asking herself why a fax from my university would be coming to me here in Leuven – if I were still there. Nor did it cross her simple mind to send it by fax back to the sender so that at least she would know it hadn't been delivered.When I pointed out that when people send anything by fax it is urgent, she just nonchalantly, I tell you, answered that they receive several of them. Oh yes, she continued without a blush, there was another fax for you last week, but I sent it by airmail to your university in the USA.

Two weeks later I'm still waiting to find out who sent it and what it was about. Can you beat that?'

There was no stopping him. Richard kept eyeing the knife in Dr. Brown's hand. From the way he was gripping it, he meant to plunge it into someone's chest.

'From then on I always check the mail when it arrives in the staffroom. But there is this enormous woman who has been viewing me with suspicion. I've tried avoiding her, going in when I thought she wasn't in, but she seems to be in that room all the time. I sometimes get the impression that she's guarding the mail and the coffee! It really has been a running battle between us. But I won't risk a confrontation. Man, not with *her*! What d'you think of all of that?'

Richard had no answer. But he was relieved to see that Dr. Brown had downed his tools. The absurdity of the situation was making him laugh. Fortunately, Anton Brown appeared now to be in the same frame of mind. Sometimes the only way out of such a frustrating, absurd situation is to laugh it off. It was indeed unthinkable, but there was nothing they could do now. So they had a good laugh about it.

Somehow such a move helps one to cope.

★ ★ ★

There was a knock on the door of Aisling's office. Aisling stood up to open it. It was the Head of the Department of English and American Literature.

'You will be pleased to know that we will have an American visiting professor this semester, and he will be giving a course on Postmodernism,' she said with some formality, after greeting Aisling and smiling at the young scholar on the floor, once again busy with his 'words'. 'It is an undergraduate course since we do not have graduate classes in this department. I thought you might be interested in joining, correct?' The Head seemed a bit apologetic. Then she added, 'There will be some American students too. As you know, we have this Junior Year Abroad programme with a couple of American universities. This American visiting professor has written some novels in the

82

Postmodern mode. Would you be interested?'

'Certainly, and thank you for letting me know.' Aisling took her hand off the door handle. She intended to invite the Head in, but she was not given the time. 'This stuff is completely new to me. I probably need a guide through the maze. When does this course start?'

'Tomorrow morning at eleven. The class meets once a week for two hours. I do not know yet which room is available. A last-minute arrangement. But I or the secretary will let you know.'

The available information having been communicated, the Head, still rooted in the same spot at the doorway, then asked how Aisling was enjoying her stay at Leuven. Aisling did not want to burden her with the problem regarding her accommodation. Anyway, she had already seen the gentleman in charge of housing for visiting academics and he had promised to let her know when there was a vacancy in the Groot Begijnhof. Instead Aisling talked about what she had learned regarding Leuven and what she and Philip had done so far.

The Head was evidently pleased. Then, directing her gaze at Philip, she smiled rather knowingly. Aisling was thrown off guard. That smile seemed to hide something: had the news about the incident at the fountain filtered through to the Head yet? Was she getting a 'name' for herself in the department? So she tried to fish it out of her by talking about the wonderful symbol of Leuven academia. You know, that scholar at Fochplein who keeps pouring water into his head while reading a book. Yes, the Head agreed, it was a wonderful symbol, and wasn't it appropriate that it was right in the centre of the town? But no clues, no snapping of the bait. Aisling was studying the Head's face.

'I better go now,' the Head said, cutting the conversation short. 'There is still much to be done.' She then waved to Philip, who waved back (Aisling thought she detected in him a tremendous effort to control himself). 'You and the scholar have a lot in common. But you are more cute, right?'

When the Head left, Aisling had to put her hand in front of

Philip's face to stop him from laughing. She did not want the Head to think that they were laughing at her. But she herself was starting to shake with muted laughter. It was Philip's turn to place his tiny forefinger in front of Aisling's mouth.

★   ★   ★

Richard abandoned any attempts to compete for the use of that one computer in the School's library. Instead he tried reading his sources so that he could make a start with the last chapter. He had learned meanwhile that the Theology Department of the Katholieke Universiteit Leuven had an excellent library. However, books and journals could not be borrowed. Since some of the books and articles which were relevant to his work were in this library, he was spending more and more time reading there. Besides, somehow there was a serious and scholarly atmosphere in that library, and what he was in dire need of was inspiration, not frustration, if he was to make any progress.

So this morning he had planned to spend a few hours there just as he had been doing throughout the week. As usual he hooked up his coat and bag in the ante-room provided, placed his library card upright as was customary among the library-users, and on entering the reading room, searched for a bright spot where he could do a bit of serious reading. There was plenty of reading space on this floor.

After a few minutes he decided to go downstairs to check out some books. He had just taken out a few books on philosophical theology and was on his way to a quiet corner when unexpectedly he heard someone address him.

'Dr. Gutierrez, what are you doing here?' He turned around to face the speaker who had asked the question in a very soft tone so as not to disturb the others. 'Do you remember me?'

'Dr. Jennifer Sidney, imagine meeting you here!' said a very delighted Richard. To himself, he added, 'How could I forget?'

It never occurred to either of them that the question and the response were rather strange. Of course, he was in the library for one thing only – is there any other reason to be in an academic library, except to study? And what was peculiar about meeting another academic in a library? Shouldn't he or she be in such a place?

'A pleasant surprise! Care to join me for some coffee?'

The invitation was quick. Even Richard surprised himself. But this time he wanted to be more direct. He had wished to meet Jennifer again but he had not expected their paths to cross here. Now that it happened, he was not going to let this opportunity slip by. Something like *carpe diem*, he thought. Nevertheless, Richard took the precaution of looking around, just in case that French professor was lurking somewhere. When there was no sign of him, Richard breathed a sigh of relief.

'I'd be delighted. There is a nice restaurant just outside the Maria Theresia College. Would that do?'

Richard said that was fine. As far as he was concerned, the place was not as important as the chance to finally get to know Dr. Jennifer Sidney. She had created such a favorable impression on him, albeit fleetingly, that Richard was captivated. So Richard left the books he was carrying on one of the desks, rationalizing to himself that those books could continue the scholarly pursuit while he chatted with the lovely Jennifer!

★   ★   ★

Aisling had been juggling in her mind about what to do with Philip while she was attending Professor Chisholm's course on Postmodernism. She could not very well drag her young son to hear about Derrida, Lyotard and company. Fortunately, the Head of the Department had anticipated her plight. Since Aisling had been given such short notice, she knew that Aisling would have trouble finding someone to care for Philip. So she offered to leave her door ajar and keep an eye on him in Aisling's office. The two offices were opposite each other. Aisling would leave instructions to Philip to keep the door open, too, and if he needed something, to see the Head.

85

Once again, the Head gave Philip that knowing smile. Had she heard finally? Aisling was still in the dark.

Aisling felt quite nervous entering the classroom. She was, of course, used to being on the other side of the desk, but here she was going to be with the students. What would they think of her? A mature undergraduate? Or a student who was taking a long time to finish? She could not very well let on that she was a lecturer in English. In this field she was simply a complete beginner. The others might expect too much in an area about which she knew very little.

She looked around the classroom, deciding to take a seat at the back of the room. Quite a mixed group, she thought. Strange, that she should be paying attention to the composition of the class. At her university, the tendency was for her and the other lecturers simply to face the crowd of some 800 students in First Year Arts and deliver their lectures. It was up to the students to take notes or not – so long as they knew their stuff come examination time.

'Hi, everybody!' The American professor seemed to have appeared suddenly from nowhere. 'My name is Dr. Robert Chisholm, but you can call me Buzz.'

Isn't he cool? the girl who was chewing gum in front of Aisling whispered to her neighbour. Ya, this will be great, I just know it, whispered back the neighbour as she sipped from her can of Coke.

Aisling blushed. She was not used to this informality on the part of academics. But, she consoled herself, at least he was in a suit and tie. So what if the introduction was a bit out of place? It would have suited some skateboard fanatic in Venice, California, where she had learned this American professor was from. Maybe he just wanted to establish some kind of rapport with the students. She had heard that American professors were always on the lookout for effective ways of communicating with their students.

Buzz, the informal formally attired professor, faced the class. 'Now you know I've a suit and tie – there'll be no need for me to wear it again this semester. I prefer to wear my "work clothes" so don't you expect to see this suit and tie again.'

86

With that he proceeded to remove his jacket and tie, unbutton his collar and roll up his sleeves.

Some of the students applauded. A few others did not know how to react. The religiously garbed nun in the class had her head down. She was probably wondering what he would do next. Aisling and another mature student looked puzzled. Was this Postmodernism in action? Aisling asked herself. If only they would turn the heating down, that would teach him a lesson, she said to herself as she clutched her jumper to herself to keep warm.

Buzz, the informal now also informally attired professor, then asked each one in the classroom to introduce himself or herself. Aisling was quite uneasy. The next thing he'll be telling us to do is hold hands, she muttered to herself. How charismatic! What a way to start a lecture.

But when she heard the others introduce themselves, she began to be curious about their backgrounds. There were a number of American students on their Junior Year Abroad programme. Her own university was starting this programme and it would be good to know it first-hand. She listened carefully to their accents and idioms. Of course, they spoke English. But an English colleague of hers, rather haughtily, always said Americans spoke 'some sort of English'. In a film that she saw on the BBC, the Oxford don with dry humour said that some of us – he was referring to the Americans – tortured the English language more than others. Aisling suppressed a smile. These American students seemed so uninhibited. She could not imagine her students in Dublin presenting such colourful descriptions of themselves.

There were also some Belgian students who were taking English as their degree subject. Their English was quite precise and impeccable. Aisling wished her Dutch were as good. The nun and the mature student gave short introductions. The nun said she was Sister Mary Joseph of the Order of the Veiled Madonna (Aisling was sure the nun overstressed the word 'veiled') and the mature student said she was a journalist on an assignment. The American students wanted to know more, but the journalist would not be drawn out. Aisling just said she was a teacher and was doing a refresher course – a strategic move on her part.

After the introductions, the professor distributed the syllabus – quite unlike the ones Aisling used or had received as an undergraduate. This was quite detailed: dates, specific readings and page numbers were provided. Then came the volunteer sheet: each student was to present three authors from this list. A few of the American students seemed excited about this since they had studied some of the authors on the list previously. Poor Aisling. She had not heard of any of them. When the list came her way, she simply ticked off Max Apple, Robert Coover and Don DeLillo. She had no idea who these were. The assignment was to examine the short stories and novels of these writers and to identify the Postmodern features in each of them.

The professor then dismissed the class. There and then Aisling had entered a different kind of world.

★ ★ ★

'Do you come here often?' Richard initiated the conversation once they were in the comfortable lounge of the restaurant chosen by Jennifer.

It was a nice place, and it had an inviting atmosphere about it. All around them the owner's preference for wood and iron was very much in evidence. The subdued lighting created a certain intimacy inside even when it was still bright outside.

The waiter had ushered them to a corner table. From where they were seated, Richard had a view, framed by the colorful bouquets of flowers, of the square outside, which boasted of a small stage topped up by an elegant dome. Clearly this was a favorite and significant corner. Richard wondered why the waiter had chosen this special spot for them.

'No, not really, but I have been here before with Professor Lamennais,' Jennifer replied. 'Do you know him?'

'No,' lied Richard. The truth was that he had no intention of making Lamennais's acquaintance since he suspected it was that French professor who had spirited Jennifer away from

him during the reception in the Universiteitshal. He would
have liked to have said a few choice words about him. But
this was not the time to be nasty.

'Sorry I had to leave you rather abruptly the last time.
Hope you were not offended. I've been hoping we would run
into each other sometime.' Jennifer was genuinely apologetic.

This pleased Richard immensely. He was being carried
away on some kind of cloud; Jennifer had that effect on him.
Yes, the two times that they had met. And imagine she cared
about how he felt!

'Oh, no offense taken. You seem to be very popular. Why
don't we start where we left off?'

The waiter had brought the two capuccinos which Richard
had ordered.

'I was asking then how long you had been in Leuven.'

Jennifer placed aside the small packet of sweets that came
with the hot drinks. 'I've been here since the beginning of the
academic year. I'm working with Professor Lamennais on a
research project.'

Him again, Richard grumbled to himself. But it is on a
professional basis. So no point in attacking the man, after all.

'But you are in Theology and he is in Biology.' Richard
was confused. He could not remember how he got to know
their fields. Worse, he suddenly realized that his previous lie
could be exposed, St Peter-like.

Jennifer laughed. It was an endearing laugh. 'That's correct.
You see, my specialization is bio-ethics. We are co-authoring a
book on the subject. It is important that my theological
conclusions are based on solid biological data. And Professor
Lamennais is an eminent authority in the biological sciences.'

Richard did not like the emphasis on 'eminent.' It was
showing him up – an untenured, unpublished neophyte in the
academic world. And he wondered what kind of 'biology' this
Professor Lamennais was really interested in. Maybe he should
make a caustic remark about him after all. But reason prevailed.

'That sounds rather interesting,' lied Richard a second time.
It was one of the comments which he had heard some
academics utter when they do not understand what their

89

colleague is doing. 'When do you expect to finish it?' As far as Richard was concerned, the sooner, the better.

'Oh, we have just started. That is why we have been meeting regularly. You know, it is more difficult to co-author a work, especially in different disciplines.' Then suddenly Jennifer looked at Richard. 'Well, what about you? I am curious to know more about you.' There was a twinkle in those eyes.

Richard told her about himself. Not everything, of course, and certainly not the fact that he was not yet tenured or that he was not a published author – not like this god-like Professor Lamennais. Between sips, he talked about his teaching and his research project on the problem of evil.

Jennifer became really interested. As she put it, the problem of evil is a theological hot potato. It is always a challenge to anyone who wants to defend a theistic perspective.

But Richard was not really keen on discussing his work, especially since he did not want to admit that he was stuck. Such academic discourse could wait till another time. So he carefully maneuvered the discussion to learn more about Jennifer.

★   ★   ★

After that first class, Aisling opted to go to lunch in Sedes, the university restaurant located at Vlamingenstraat, rather than return to their studio apartment. So she went back to her office to pick up Philip. He had been well-behaved, she was assured by the Head. He was no trouble at all: he stayed where he had been told and concentrated on his drawing.

On seeing his mother, Philip jumped up to pack his bag.

'How was the class?' the Head wanted to know.

'Different from what I am used to. Quite interesting,' Aisling replied. This was always a tactful way of not letting people know what you really thought about it.

But the Head was persistent. 'Did you get some kind of direction?'

Good, Aisling thought, that is a helpful line of inquiry. She didn't have to describe what actually took place in the classroom.

'Definitely, I will be reading the novels of Apple, Coover and DeLillo and tracing any Postmodernist elements in their works. That should help me find out whether there are any such elements in any of the Irish poets.'

Aisling was tempted to add that she had no clue what it was she was looking for. The American students in the class seemed to know, but her pride prevented her from asking these youngsters. The professor kept saying that these elements would 'emerge' as they read the stuff. Aisling would have preferred to have been given some idea of what it was that was going to emerge. Anything could happen in this course.

Aisling thanked the Head and left with Philip. She promised to find out about childminding facilities for next week. But the Head assured her that the same arrangement could be made if she was not successful. Childminding in Leuven could be difficult, she was told.

'Well, did you miss me?' she asked Philip when they were on the street in front of the Central Library.

'A little. I was busy.'

Philip had been holding his mother's gloved hand. But when he caught sight of the pigeons, one of which pluckily alighted on the shrub in front of them, he wanted to let go. Aisling, however, held him firmly.

'No chasing of pigeons today. The Head said you were drawing pictures. Did you bring them with you?'

'They're inside my bag.'

With those words said, he stopped in the middle of Hooverplein, a pleasant rectangle lined with trees, beside the Central Library. They had already passed by the statues of people inside a basket attached to a bronze balloon, a source of fascination for young Philip.

Philip showed her a drawing he had made of the roosters and hens at Donatus Park.

'Aha, I know where I've seen them before. Very good, Philip. Did you show these to the nice lady who was minding you?' Aisling inquired.

'Yup.' The short answer was concealing something.

'And what did she say?'

'Beautiful.' Another mysterious one-word answer.

'That was good of her, wasn't it? And what's this?' She noticed another drawing inside his bag.

Philip giggled. It was a drawing of a fat woman with big eyes. 'That's your friend.'

Aisling was horrified. She could just imagine her Philip sprawled on the rug in her office, mischievously sketching out the occupant of the office opposite hers. And to think that she had kindly offered to mind him!

'Did she see this?'

'I kept it hidden. I showed her the other drawing. Not this one.'

Aisling felt tempted to scold him, but what could one do with such innocence even when it was mischievous? Resigning herself to the *fait accompli*, she extracted from Philip a promise not to do it again. This child will be the death of me yet, Aisling thought with affection. Then she and Philip had a good laugh.

★   ★   ★

Richard learned that Jennifer was a lecturer in theology at the newly created University of Bartley Green in the West Midlands of England. It had been a polytechnic but recently it and several other polytechnics and larger colleges in England had been made into universities at the stroke of a pen.

She had come to Mercier University because of Professor Lamennais. He was spending his sabbatical here and they both agreed that working on a joint project would be more feasible if they were in the same institution. The attraction of an excellent theological library in Leuven was another reason. She could make use of the resources there for her research, which secured funding from the British Council and thus enabled her to go on leave from her university for a few months.

Jennifer had impeccable academic credentials – which really

impressed Richard. Her D.Phil. was from Oxford and her dissertation had been published as a book by Oxford University Press. She was interested, as she put it, in moving up to another university, probably even Oxford or Cambridge. Somehow she felt that to make it to the top, one had to be teaching in one of those two renowned universities – giving the impression that her present university was not good enough for her. Richard detected a certain snobbishness, especially when she mentioned that in England the 'new universities' did not really have the same standing as the older ones.

Richard was fascinated with her English accent. It sounded so posh, so cultured. He enjoyed talking to her as they exchanged accounts of the differences, despite the common heritage, between life in America and life in England.

Jennifer was young, enthusiastic and ambitious. Richard liked those traits. And her enthusiasm was catching. Listening to her somehow gave him the energy to pursue his own academic interests. He even said to himself that he 'felt energized.'

They walked back to the Theology Library after their coffee break, which lasted an hour. And they agreed to meet again – for dinner the following evening at the T-Bone Restaurant.

Richard was beginning to form the opinion that Leuven was after all an ideal spot for meeting people with the same interests, especially now that he had become acquainted with Jennifer.

When Richard trekked back to his office in the School of Philosophy, he noticed a note under his door. It was from Professor van der Riet, requesting him to phone him when it was convenient. Richard wondered when Mercier University would have a VoiceMail. He had found it tremendously helpful when his own university installed it for everyone. He could retrieve messages no matter where he was and promptly reply without having to go to his office. He wondered what his host professor had in mind. What if he had not gone back to his office? How would he have known about the message? Was it urgent?

He picked up his office phone. Since he needed to get an outside line, he had to dial 11 first. Unfortunately, it was after 5:00 pm, which meant that the 'Centrale' would be closed. He had no option but to locate a public telephone or to call from his apartment.

Remembering that there was a public telephone just outside the School, he decided to call from there. So he locked his office, climbed down the wooden stairs, and crossed the courtyard of the School. He fished out his telephone card and the note on which Professor van der Riet had written down his telephone number.

'May I speak with Professor van der Riet?' Richard asked when he heard a female voice, Mrs. van der Riet probably, answering the telephone.

'Just a moment, please,' came the answer and then some words in Dutch.

'Professor van der Riet. This is Richard Gutierrez. I got your message only a few minutes ago,' Richard explained when the Professor came to the phone.

'Oh, Gutierrez. Yes, yes, I wanted to speak to you.' The Belgian academics tended to call each other by their last names. An awkward pause. 'I can't remember now what it was.'

Oh no, Richard thought, not a real absent-minded professor. He thought that that was a stereotype. He had no wish to meet such a stereotype in real life.

Since Professor van der Riet's memory seemed to be on the blink, Richard felt there was nothing he could do. At least he had returned the message. But wasn't it frustrating to be told that someone wanted to speak to you and then not to know what it was about? Should he just hang up or give Professor van der Riet more time to retrieve the information from somewhere in his brain?

'I'll be in my apartment in a few minutes' time in case you need me.'

Richard had found a more diplomatic way out of the embarrassing situation.

The following day there still had been no call from Professor van der Riet. Richard wondered whether he had missed it or whether his host professor had forgotten about it altogether. He did not want to phone him a second time, in case that would annoy the professor. One thing he had been told was that in Europe professors occupied quite a respected status that put them at some distance from non-professorial mortals. He was not yet at that level, no, since he was only an untenured assistant professor. Anyway, if it were important Dr. van der Riet would be in contact again. So he tried to put the whole matter out of his mind.

Still, he could not help being curious about it. But he had a more important thing on his mind: he was meeting Jennifer for dinner tonight. And he was looking forward to it. Should he wear his suit and tie? He had noticed that here people were much more formal than in southern California, where they tended to dress casually even when dining out. He had been told that the British also tended to be formally dressed. Anyway, the weather was still cold and his suit would keep him warm, if nothing else.

He was checking out his suit in the bedroom when the phone rang. He rushed to get to the living room before it stopped, almost knocking down one of the dining room chairs that blocked his path. It must be his professor finally.

'Gutierrez?' Sure enough, it was Professor van der Riet.

'Hello, Professor van der Riet. This is Richard Gutierrez.'

'I remember now. Come to my residence tonight at eight. I want you to meet some people.' The voice at the other end sounded authoritative.

Richard was furious. Such short notice, and he had a prior engagement with Jennifer. But he could not turn down Professor van der Riet's invitation. After all, he was van der Riet's guest.

Then he realized that he had no way of contacting Jennifer. They had arranged simply to meet in front of the restaurant at 8:00 tonight. How could he contact her? He was starting to panic. Jennifer would be rightly annoyed if he did not turn up – and that would probably end the whole thing right there and then. Anyway, he never liked making an appointment and not keeping it. He always thought that one had some kind of moral obligation. What should he do now?

It was still early in the afternoon. So he rang the Theology Department. The secretary was quite helpful; she gave Richard Jennifer's home telephone. Richard called the number immediately.

Unfortunately, there was no reply. Richard tried again, thinking he may have dialed the wrong number. Still, no reply and no answering machine either. She must be out, Richard thought.

An hour later, Richard tried the number again. Still, no answer. Richard looked at his watch. It was 3:17 pm. She could be in the Theology Library.

He rushed from his apartment to the library. So far he had enjoyed not having his car while in Leuven, but he sure wished he had it here now. While at times he disliked having an answering machine at home in southern California, he found himself insisting that it should be made available to everyone here. He could simply have left a message for Jennifer. Sometimes technology was after all a benefit – one missed it when it was not there. On the other hand, he could have been less stupid and asked Jennifer or the Theology Department for her address.

In his haste he almost forgot to take off his coat and take out his library card. But the quick-eyed and nimble library assistant, the guardian of this academic haven, blocked his way. So with apologies, he went through the routine, at the same time craning his neck for any sign of Jennifer.

Lady Luck was with him. Jennifer was in the library! Richard breathed a sigh of relief as he spotted her reading. She had positioned herself in a conspicuous place.

'Jennifer, am I glad to see you!'

'Oh, hello, Richard. You know, I was hoping you would come here. I have been trying to contact you.' She closed the journal she was reading. It was the latest issue of *Modern Theology*. Before Jennifer could continue, Richard started to explain his predicament to her. To Richard's surprise Jennifer laughed.

'You know, that was why I was trying to get in touch with you. Professor van der Riet is organizing a social evening at his residence. He rang this morning to invite me. Now I see he has invited you too.'

Amazing, the turn of events, Richard thought.

They both had a good laugh – incurring a hostile look from another reader who until now had been buried in her books at the next desk. The two then arranged to go together to Professor van der Riet's place.

Richard was glad he had not turned down the professor's invitation after all.

★   ★   ★

'Hurry, Ma! We'll miss the train,' Philip urged his mother excitedly.

'I'm rushing. Anyway, if we miss it, we'll take the next train.'

'But what about Granny? She'll be waiting for us.'

Aisling and Philip were on their way to Brussels National Airport (the name was rather confusing since it was the international airport) to meet Aisling's mother. Aisling had invited her before they left Ireland to spend a fortnight with them in Leuven. But when Aisling sized up their accommodation, she had reluctantly to tell her that the place was too small for her to stay longer than a week. They would try to get out as much as possible, and Aisling kept praying that the weather would be fine. The three of them holed up in the boxy studio apartment at Tervuursevest would not really be her mother's idea of a holiday.

After a few minutes' bus ride Aisling and Philip arrived at Leuven's railway station, which is fronted by a memorial to the soldiers who had died in the two world wars. To the right of the station were lines and lines of parked bicycles, a testimony to a favourite mode of transport here. Once inside the station itself Aisling glanced up at the timetable. They would make the 10.26 train to Brussels Nord, where they could change to the express train service to the airport. Plenty of time since Mrs Holohan's flight was not due in until midday.

'Ma, we're going back!' exclaimed Philip when he noticed that the second train was retracing their earlier journey.

Philip recognized some of the sights since he had been looking out practically the whole journey from Leuven to Brussels Nord and commenting on the various sights that sped past them.

'Not the whole way back, only part of the way,' pointed out Aisling.

'Why?'

This had become a constant word for Philip, who was forever asking the why of things, sometimes to the consternation of Aisling when she did not know the answer. But this time she did. She explained to Philip that since the intercity train to Brussels did not stop before Brussels Nord, they had to go all the way to that station to get the Airport Express. The airport was actually in Zaventem, between Leuven and Brussels.

'We could have taken the local train. That stops at Scherbeek. But the Airport Express does not always stop there. So we could be waiting there a long time.'

A long pause. Philip was taking all this in.

'But couldn't the train from Leuven could go all the way to the airport?'

'Well, to do that they would have to put special railway tracks from Leuven to Zaventem.'

'Why not do that then?' Philip made it seem like an easy solution.

'Maybe there are not many people going to the airport that way.'

'Well, there are two of us. And when Granny comes, there'll be three of us!'

And as if to lend support to the child's argument, Philip spotted the family of four who had been on the train from Leuven and were now also on the Airport Express.

'See, me, you and them four – that's six!' Philip concluded triumphantly.

They were soon at the airport terminal. First they took the escalator to the Arrivals section, where Aisling checked the

TV screen. Her mother's flight was on time, but it was not due for another hour.

'How about a glass of something and then a tour?' she asked Philip, who was looking around. The Arrivals section was starting to get rather crowded with visitors.

'Great! Maybe some hot chocolate. I'm thirsty – and cold.'

They proceeded to the stairs to the cafeteria in the Departures area. There were relatively few people inside so they had no trouble finding a nice place where they could look out and observe the planes taking off and landing.

'What will you be telling Granny?' Aisling asked the minute they sat down with their drinks.

'That I've been good and learned my words,' came the ready reply.

'Why?' This time it was Aisling's turn to be inquisitive.

'Maybe she'll have a surprise for me.' Philip raised his head to look at his mother expectantly. Philip loved surprises. He liked to see them parcelled up so he could spend time opening them.

'And will you be showing her your drawings? One in particular?' teased his mother.

Philip smiled. 'I'll think about it.'

Sometimes the young lad could be non-committal. Aisling was wondering what was going on in that young mind.

'And the incident at the fountain?'

With this Philip burst out laughing. 'Yeah, that should be good. When should I tell her?'

'Not right away. We want Granny to enjoy her holiday, remember?' teased Aisling. 'Anyway, finish up now so we can look around before her flight arrives.'

Philip drank up his hot chocolate. Aisling had already finished her cup of coffee.

Aisling and Philip spent the next three quarters of an hour traipsing around the airport terminal. They located the chapel after seeing the sign in the Departures area and went in to say their prayers. Then they browsed around the shops before returning to the Arrivals section. There was one particular souvenir in the shops that Aisling did not want Philip to see.

99

At the Arrivals section Aisling and Philip planted themselves at the exit so they could see her mother immediately. Some passengers were coming out, and Aisling looked at their duty-free bags. No, they came from New York. Wrong crowd.

A few seconds later an old lady being escorted by a Sabena representative suddenly rose from the wheelchair and hobbled out towards the waiting crowd. There was a lot of flurry as a couple stepped out from behind the barriers. They must be her family, Aisling concluded. They kissed one another on the cheeks. The new arrival and her family were shedding tears of joy. Then the man took the trolley while the woman linked the old lady. They thanked the Sabena representative and waved goodbye. That was nice, Aisling thought; airlines provide good service for unaccompanied people to travel. And whatever the story of the family was, it had a happy ending.

A lady then appeared, dressed very fashionably, with costume jewellery complementing her gorgeous frock. Her make-up looked professionally applied. She must be a model, surmised Aisling. Without warning a young fellow from the waiting crowd immediately scurried towards her, nearly hitting Aisling in his haste to be with the new arrival.

'Marta!'

'Jorge!'

'Oh, how I missed you!'

Jorge then proceeded to kiss her passionately on the lips in front of everybody. The crowd cheered. It could have been a scene from Hollywood and it helped dispel the boredom of waiting. Aisling looked down at Philip, who was watching all this.

'That's a lot of loves,' he said about the prolonged kissing.

The lovers might as well have been in a different world since they did not notice the crowd's reaction. Looking into each other's eyes and wrapped around each other, they inched their way to the car park. There was no need for words. The body language was too strong.

Next came a well-dressed middle-aged fellow. The cut of his dark blue suit was quite impressive. He paused to look around briefly but almost immediately continued walking in the direction of the Airport Express station. Aisling always thought it was sad when no one was there to meet you at the airport. Perhaps he was a Eurocrat or a businessman, she imagined. Still, it would have been nice to have been met.

The next thing that Aisling became aware of was the strong smell of whiskey. She saw a lady emerging from the customs area in some kind of embarrassed distress. She had dropped her duty-free bag which contained a bottle of whiskey. The poor lady, sympathized Aisling. Carrying all that only to lose it in the end. Fortunately, the precious liquid, or the *uisce beatha* as they sometimes call it in Ireland, did not spill out of the plastic bag so there was no mess to clean up. But it was small consolation since obviously the whole thing had to be thrown out. Which was what the unfortunate lady had to do. Meanwhile, the smell wafted all over the place.

More passengers came out. But it must still have been from the same flight. There was no one with an Aer Rianta duty-free bag. Aisling checked the screen again. Yes, the flight from Dublin had arrived. The passengers were probably still collecting their luggage.

For a while no one exited into the waiting area. Then came a trickle of passengers, a few with the duty-free bag that Aisling was hoping to see. These passengers were clearly from Dublin, not only because of their plastic bags but also because Aisling heard the familiar Irish accents.

'Granny should be out soon,' she whispered to Philip, who was closely monitoring the passengers. 'Let's see who can spot Granny first.'

Philip became even more excited. It was a game they were playing. So his eyes were fixed on the exit from where the other passengers had come. There were very few passengers, Aisling observed. The plane could not have been full.

Still no sign of Mrs Holohan. Aisling was getting anxious. Had she missed her flight? That was possible since she still had to come from Barrowtown.

'Do you think Granny is coming?'

Aisling knew that Philip sensed that something was askew. Where could her mother be? Perhaps she should try to call her home number. But that would come to nothing if her mother had already left. Should she ring her sister? She would not be there either since she and her husband were supposed to be bringing their mother to the airport. Anyway, she would just be unnecessarily worried.

★   ★   ★

Richard and Jennifer walked to Professor van der Riet's residence, a fabulous townhouse very close to the center of Leuven. Richard had passed by Jennifer's apartment – which was also in the Groot Begijnhof. He had asked her for her address, which she was delighted to give, to prevent another incident like this morning.

It was a pleasant 20-minute stroll to the residence. It was still quite cold and people were well wrapped up, some in heavy woollen coats – so unlike southern California, remarked Richard, but so similar to England, replied Jennifer. Only the umbrella was missing, she added.

When they reached Professor van der Riet's place, Richard rang the bell. Since he had been a previous visitor to the professor's home, he had no trouble finding the right townhouse. Professor van der Riet himself answered the door.

'Come in. I see you know each other.' The professor was delighted to see them both.

'Yes.' Richard was reluctant to go into details about their meeting.

'You have a beautiful place, Professor van der Riet,' joined in Jennifer. She too wanted to deflect the attention from them.

'Thank you, thank you. Yes, it is nice. My wife keeps it in good condition. Come, come, the others are in the lounge.' He placed their coats in the adjoining room.

There were about 20 people, in groups of two or three in the large lounge. Beautiful strains from Wagner softly filled the air. Richard and Jennifer were introduced to the group closest to the impressive marble fireplace. There was no open fire since the place was heated by the oil-fired radiators, but it served as a charming focal point of the room.

'Professor Malachowski, Professor Tanaka, Dr. Linden. I introduce Dr. Jennifer Sidney and Dr. Richard Gutierrez to you. I leave you now to get to know each other better.'

Professor van der Riet then went to the door since the doorbell rang again to announce other new arrivals.

As the group became better acquainted, Richard learned that Professor Malachowski was a professor of philosophy from Lublin in Poland and was particularly interested in meeting Richard since he too was writing something on the problem of evil, but from a process philosophical point of view. Dr. Tanaka, a professor of education from one of the universities in Japan, was on a flying visit as it were. He said that he was spending his sabbatical in England since he was working on a comparative study of educational systems in the world. Dr. Linden had come from the Netherlands to attend a conference being held at Leuven. She belonged to the theology faculty of one of the state universities in that country. After a while, it was not surprising that Dr. Linden and Jennifer should break away from the group to chat about common interests in theology.

Richard tried to circulate so as to meet as many individuals as possible. And it was a lively gathering, helped no doubt by the generous amounts of drink being poured by their solicitous host. Richard was impressed at how international the gathering truly was. He introduced himself to a professor from Ghana, then to another one from Sweden. An academic from Argentina joined Richard and a professor from Spain as they were conversing about their common heritage.

Most of the evening, however, Richard found himself talking to Dr. Malachowski. He found Dr. Malachowski very critical of Thomistic philosophy, the school of thought that informed his own perspective on the problem of evil. In contrast he had only a vague idea of process philosophy, which the more senior professor was very interested in. All Richard knew was that it was a contemporary movement in philosophy associated with Whitehead and Hartshorne and had been influential particularly in theology. Instead of entering into a debate about the subtleties of their respective

103

philosophical schools of thought, however, the two talked about how they approached the problem of evil.

As they discussed their specific approaches, Richard disclosed the difficulty he was experiencing in completing his work. Somehow there was an important factor missing in his scholarly research, he confided to Dr. Malachowski.

'I feel that I'm working on a solution without knowing what the real problem is,' remarked Richard after they had retreated to the corner of the spacious dining room to give themselves some room away from the others.

Richard kept swirling the contents of his brandy glass. It was particularly welcome, given the chilly temperature outside.

'That sounds strange. We philosophers are supposed to be able not only to evaluate the merits of each argument but also to clarify the issues.' The professor looked Richard in the eye. 'You are talking about the proper starting point for our philosophizing, aren't you?'

'Possibly. But I don't just mean articulating what the philosophical issues in a problem are.' Richard tucked his left hand under his right elbow. 'Take human suffering, for instance. A very concrete reality if ever there was one. I've worked on this topic for some time now and yet when I am faced with the challenge of talking to someone who's just lost a loved one, or an individual who has just been through a disaster, I'm lost for words. Surely we philosophers should be able to say something meaningful in situations like that. Maybe it's me. Maybe it's not philosophy that is at fault here.' Richard retrieved his left hand and slipped it into his trouser pocket.

'But do you expect philosophy to say something meaningful in this situation?'

'Yes, since the study of philosophy is meant to provide us with wisdom. But I sometimes get the impression that what we philosophers have become concerned with is knowledge and more knowledge.' Richard paused, not knowing how his remarks would be accepted.

'Go ahead, I'm listening,' the older professor, who took a sip from his glass of Beaujolais, was encouraging.

'We sometimes blame the sciences for accumulating all this information and math for juggling with figures and becoming too abstract in the whole process. And yet aren't we doing the same thing? I know of some philosophers who regard the problem of evil, for instance, as an intellectual puzzle. They get a lot of kicks from solving problems which are of their own making. In the end one could ask what that has to do with life.'

'Wait now. Are you talking about the problem of suffering or of philosophy as a problem?' interrupted Dr. Malachowski. 'Are these not separate issues?'

'That is precisely *the* problem. We philosophers are so fond of being clear about the issues that we start classifying reality.'

'But how can you expect to address the issues adequately if you have not clarified them? That *is* important, as you know.'

'True, but sometimes we do lose the real issue as we dissect, as it were, what we perceive to be the problem. I remember my Asian colleague once quoting Mencius, who said that what one dislikes in clever men is their tortuosity. I'm probably taking the words out of context, but I can't help seeing their relevance. And I remember being intrigued by her reference to Chuang-tzu, who disdained all the philosophical disputations carried on during his time. And we're still doing it today.'

'I'm not familiar with Chinese philosophy, but there is something in Whitehead's *Adventures of Ideas* that I was reading just this morning.' Dr. Malachowski, placing the forefinger of his left hand across his lips as if to recall the appropriate passage, knit his eyebrows. 'He was alerting us to what is lost from speculation by scholarship. He says, in speculation there is delight and discourse while in scholarship there is concentration and thoroughness. Of course, Whitehead claims that for progress both are necessary.'

'I believe that we have lost the "feel" of the problem because of all our disputations, as Chuang-tzu I suppose would put it, although I too don't know much about him except through my colleague.'

'But that is not the domain of philosophy, at least as commonly understood.'

'Exactly, we have left out an important aspect of the problem in our philosophizing.'

'And what is that?' quizzed the professor.

'The element of life. The importance of experience. The necessary connection between our thinking and our living.'

There was some laughter from another part of the house, but the two philosophers engrossed in their conversation ignored it.

'And how does that relate to the problem of suffering that you mentioned earlier on?'

'That we need a different way of describing the problem. Philosophy shouldn't attempt a solution until it has done justice to the reality of suffering. It's much too abstract to do that. At least the way philosophical thinking has become.'

'And how do you propose to do that?' inquired the Polish professor.

Before Richard had a chance to respond, a third voice joined them.

'I see you two are discussing an area of common interest.' It was Professor van der Riet with a bottle of wine in his left hand and a decanter of brandy in the other. 'I fill up your glasses first. You are not driving, yes? And I introduce you two to Dr. Fuentes from the Philippines. He is here – sent by his bishop – on sabbatical.'

Richard and Dr. Malachowski shook Dr. Fuentes's hand. Much to their delight, they realized that his field was also in philosophy.

'You know, that was what we had just been talking about,' remarked Dr. Malachowski. He then summarized what he and Richard had been discussing.

Dr. Fuentes was quickly on the scene. 'Who was it who said – I think it was Heidegger – philosophers are reducing reality to a mentally fabricated axiomatic project. I can understand your situation.' Dr. Fuentes, who was about ten years older than Richard, looked at him. 'Although my difficulty with the way philosophy generally handles the problem of evil is that it is seen too much as a theodicy. Too much attention is given to the challenge of atheism. Don't you agree?' He

106

turned his head in the direction of Dr. Malachowski, who nodded. 'And so we are expected to provide a coherent and credible resolution of how God can be defended as almighty *and* all-good when there is so much evil and suffering around us.'

Richard's face must have registered some surprise – after all, that was exactly what he was working on here in Leuven – since Dr. Fuentes quickly added, 'Oh, don't get me wrong. That is still an important issue. But you know, for us in the Philippines – and I'm sure that it is true in Latin America too, from what I have read of liberation theology there – the important question is not theodicy but idolatry.'

More laughter from another part of the room. But Dr. Fuentes continued, 'Like you, I've been wrestling with the starting point for our reflections on this important subject. But I ask myself, why do philosophers not sometimes reckon with the fact that many people continue to believe in God despite their suffering? Granted that one may need to scrutinize the reasons that these believers come up with for their continued belief, isn't it strange that we do not focus on the concept of God that lies behind their belief? Perhaps it is very different from the way philosophers have portrayed God to be and has consequently led to the so-called problem of evil. It seems to me that the existence of evil is challenging us to reformulate our descriptions of God.'

'How would you state the problem of evil then?' asked Dr. Malachowski, whose interest was aroused since his leanings towards process philosophy made him pursue a remarkably similar line of inquiry. It was good to hear somebody coming from a different background, making the same point.

'What kind of God can we continue to believe in, given the presence of so much undeserved suffering?' came Dr. Fuentes's ready reply.

The glass of orange juice which Dr. Fuentes had been drinking was now empty so he gently set it on top of the nearby drinks cabinet, thus providing himself with the opportunity to gesticulate for emphasis.

'The danger for us is that in our attempts to defend God, as

107

it were, we could be perpetuating idols, rather than the true God. Christianity is part of our Filipino culture' – with those words he pounded his breast with his fist – 'just as it is in Latin America, but our complaint is that the concept of God which we have inherited from the past is not only inadequate, but worse, it could also be responsible for supporting the structures which maintain the status quo, which in turn results in the misery, poverty and degradation of our people.' Dr. Fuentes ticked these off with his fingers.

Richard was very attentive. He wanted Dr. Fuentes and Dr. Malachowski to elaborate more on this issue, but since two others attached themselves to the group there was no opportunity to continue the conversation. After all, this was a social, not a seminar. It was just that it was so natural for the philosophers not to shed their professional gown, so to speak. But he made a mental note to contact the two philosophers again. Perhaps not all was lost with his research.

The rest of the evening Richard enjoyed chatting with the other guests. He managed to exchange a few glances with Jennifer, who was certainly quite popular with several of the guests.

*   *   *

'So there you are!' It was Mrs Holohan, dragging her suitcase. She looked hassled as she patted daughter and grandson on their shoulders.

'Granny!' shouted a delighted Philip when he recognized who had tapped him.

'Ma, where did you come from?' asked a confused Aisling.

'From Dublin, where else?' came the quick retort.

'You know what I mean. We've been waiting here since this is the exit for the passengers.' Aisling pointed to the sign above the exit.

'Don't mind that. I followed the Irish crowd. Those who seem to be in the know.'

This was Mrs Holohan's first unaccompanied trip by air and she had been anxious about it. Her stomach had been

108

doing some calisthenics, she later confessed to them. Aisling had planned the whole thing so that her mother would not be fussed: at the check-in at Dublin airport she was to tell them that she was travelling on her own and would need assistance. 'The airline staff will take care of you,' she had assured her mother. Mrs Holohan did as she had been instructed, but when Tony and Fiona were allowed to accompany her all the way to the plane, she told the airline staff that she was all right. So when they landed at Brussels airport, no one came to her assistance. That was when the hassle started. First of all, as she recounted, she understood not a word being spoken. She found the signs confusing. Then she tried to yank a trolley from the other trolleys in the line, but it would not come out. That was why she was dragging her heavy suitcase.

'But you're supposed to put in some money first,' Aisling tried to explain.

'How was I supposed to know that? Anyway, we don't do that in Dublin Airport. The trolley comes out when you pull it. Are these Eurocrats, you know these big shots, trying to make money or something out of poor widows like me? Anyway, I couldn't get any coins for these things.' There was no arguing with Mrs Holohan.

'And then what did you do?' asked Aisling as she loaded her mother's suitcase on to a trolley that Philip had spotted close by and had retrieved. 'And what's in this suitcase?'

Philip's face lit up. But Mrs Holohan ignored the last question. She always enjoyed keeping her grandson guessing.

'Well, I followed those important-looking people.' She pointed to a group of dark-suited Irish men who were probably attending a meeting connected with the European Community. 'They breezed through the blue exit – I overheard them saying that that was the proper channel for EC nationals. I went with them. So what do you think of that? One learns something new every day. No more the green channels, now the blue,' said a now beaming Mrs Holohan. That was why she had ended up in a different area from where Aisling and Philip had been waiting for her.

109

Before Aisling could say or ask anything further, Mrs Holohan continued.

'Don't look now. But d'you see that bearded scruffy fellow? That one over there. Just look at his eyes. A bit shifty, aren't they?' Mrs Holohan looked sideways at a lone figure making his exit from the Arrivals section. 'You know, he was on the plane with us. I thought he was a hijacker. So I made sure that I did not take my eyes off him. What do you think?'

Aisling felt embarrassed. 'Ma, what you need is a cup of tea. You'll feel better. Forget that fellow.' Aisling was trying to divert her mother's attention. 'And tell me the latest since we left.'

'What's a hijacker?' Philip popped the question innocently. At the mention of the word, several individuals nervously turned in their direction.

'Philip! Come on.' Aisling was getting more and more uneasy while her mother chuckled at the consternation she detected in these foreign-looking people, whose language she did not understand.

When Aisling finally managed to herd mother and son, the previous and future generations, away from the waiting area to the small cafeteria in the Arrivals section, she sat down with relief and ordered tea.

'The tea here is different, Ma,' she warned her mother, who was an expert in Irish tea-drinking.

'That's all right, alanna. I came prepared. You never know what to expect in these foreign countries.' With that she produced a box of Lyons tea, the one which contained 120 teabags. 'Just ask for boiling water.'

'Ma, we'll have that when we get to our place. Not here,' Aisling whispered to her mother, getting edgy because of her mother's exuberance.

'Any surprises for me, Granny?'

Philip had been very patient. He had sensed that earlier was not the right time for his all-important question, but when his grandmother opened her carry-on bag to provide the Lyons teabags for everyone, he noticed other things underneath the box.

'Oh, yes, here it is!'

Out came a number of green-haired trolls!

'The shops in Ireland are full of them. Just in time for St Patrick's Day. Well, what do you think?'

'Thanks, Granny. Wow, look at them!' Philip said with delight as he examined each one of them. One troll was dressed as a judge, another was made up as a medical doctor, another looked like a rock star. The others came in various guises.

'I suppose one of these could even be a father troll,' he remarked rather wistfully.

'And I brought you some Christmas pudding. And Christmas cake. Your favourites.' And she pulled out the goodies for the two to admire.

'No wonder your bag was very heavy. That was very thoughtful of you, Ma. Although you shouldn't have bothered.' Aisling beamed. She was thinking that at least they would have the comfort of home even when the studio apartment did not provide the facilities.

When the goodies were once again safely tucked inside her mother's bag, Aisling asked, 'Well, how was the widows' day out?'

'Oh, don't ask me about it,' protested Mrs Holohan, shaking both palms in front of her frowning face. But she then proceeded to narrate the disastrous outing of the widows' association.

The association, at least the active members, had decided to go to Wexford on their annual outing. And, of course, it poured on that day – what else can one expect in Ireland? Mrs Holohan added for effect. The trip to Wexford itself was enjoyable but uneventful. On the return trip the widows chatted away, exchanging stories, showing off their shopping, gasping at the prices some had paid for insignificant items and admiring those who were able to get bargains.

Suddenly someone let out a scream. 'Stop the bus!' she yelled, frightening the wits out of Mrs Keller. The poor driver had to jam on the brakes and the bus nearly skidded. Two of the widows were almost knocked off their seats, but

111

fortunately no one was injured. Katie Menaghan, the 'around 80-year-old' respected member of the executive who was rather hard of hearing, wondered what all that braking was about. Did the driver want to shorten their time here on earth? She declared that she did not care about the rest but she was in no hurry. The screaming Mrs Lyons then announced to the whole busload that they had left behind Mrs White and Mrs Robinson. (Mrs Holohan couldn't help providing a commentary by remarking that there was no stoppage in Mrs Lyons' voice, not like when she read the minutes when only every third word could be heard. Not that it mattered anyway since they were always approved.)

Katie Menaghan retorted that Mrs Lyons did not have to shout – she could hear her explanation. There was furious questioning: who was with them? who saw them last? were they not at the designated meeting place? who the hell did they think they were anyway, not turning up at the right time? There was a cacophony of widows' voices.

Two of the most radical widows insisted that they continue with their journey. It was their own fault, these two claimed. Anyway, the stranded widows were old enough to look after themselves. But the rest did not have the heart to leave the two souls behind. What if they did not have the money to get home? Then the young driver said that it was his responsibility. So back they went in the rain and the dark in search of the two wanderers.

To cut a long story short, said Mrs Holohan, the driver found them: they were enjoying a hot meal in a posh restaurant! No less. They had been late in arriving at the designated spot but they immediately accused the driver of having left early or of having conspired with the others to confuse them, etc. One of the two clouted the driver with her umbrella. The poor driver, thinking that she was suffering from the effects of the brandy, tried to hold his tongue and to get them aboard the bus without a scene! And to think that his boss had assured him this would be an easy run to Wexford. The widows wouldn't be any trouble, he had promised. Not like school teenage outings. Little did he know.

But with some persuasion the driver did get the two aboard the bus.

By then, of course, he was soaked to the skin. The youngish Mrs Moran, who was seated beside Mrs Holohan, offered the driver a towel to dry himself. She encouraged him to remove his wet shirt and wrap himself up in the towel: 'We don't want you to die of pneumonia, love.' That was when there was a sudden hush on the bus. All eyes – 'and you know what they are like,' remarked Mrs Holohan, again for effect – were on the poor driver. He was clearly embarrassed. He politely thanked Mrs Moran for the towel, but he would not remove his shirt. Can you blame him? interjected Mrs Holohan. In front of that crowd? He could be accused of indecent exposure. He had enough complaints already.

And then those two stranded widows, indeed those very two, asked what all the hurry and fuss was all about since this was supposed to be their annual outing. Mrs Holohan shook her head as she commented, 'And they were surprised why no one on the coach would talk to them!'

Aisling shook with laughter. Her mother's account of these outings and meetings was always amusing. She often wondered whether her mother did not at times make them up. But she knew some of these characters in the association, so she could well believe that these things did happen.

'Well, Ma, any more stories to tell us?' teased Aisling when they were on the train to Leuven.

'What do you mean, stories? They really happened, you know.' Mrs Holohan was quite adamant.

'Yeah, come on, Granny.' Philip loved his granny's stories even if he did not always follow everything. Mrs Holohan could be very dramatic.

'Like that time the widows went on that trip? Was it to Arklow, you said?' Aisling was hoping her mother would swallow the bait.

'Well, that was what we *had* decided on. So you would have thought everyone who signed up knew that. But no, not Mrs Robinson. You know, here we were halfway there,

113

enjoying ourselves, when from the back of the bus there was some kind of commotion. Mrs Robinson, it was. And do you know what she was doing?' She leaned forward as if divulging confidential matters. 'Telling the others that there was *nothing* in Arklow. When somebody pointed out – I forget who it was – that we could visit the pottery there, she raised her voice, you know, with a sneer, "And who wants to visit pots anyway? We see them every day!" Boisterous laughter. And that's how it started. Her friends, it's a real clique, backed her up.'

'And what did you do?'

'Nothing!'

'But shouldn't you have?'

'What? and get myself skinned by that crowd? No, thanks.'

'Well, what happened then?' Of course, Aisling knew the details from hearing it before, but she loved the way her mother told the story.

'The bus was split up. Mrs Robinson, her backers and others put pressure on the driver not to go to Arklow. But the other half shouted that that was what they had paid for – they were going to Arklow, even if they had to walk there. Wrong thing to say,' Mrs Holohan shook her head, 'since Mrs Robinson was now loving her role as leader. "Go ahead, walk there then," says she. And she looks at Mrs Price defiantly as she spat out those words.'

'And?'

'And Mrs Price, who's as deaf as a doornail, asks her neighbour, "What is Mrs Robinson mumbling about?" She had turned off her hearing aid the minute she sensed she was going to be the target of Mrs Robinson's wrath! Bully for her. And nobody, nobody would tell her. So Mrs Robinson's comments fell flat.'

'And what was the poor driver doing all this time?'

'Shaking his head and ... cursing under his breath, somebody said.'

'Can you blame him?'

'Yes, definitely.'

'Ma, I'm surprised at you. I thought you'd have pitied him.'

'Pitied him, indeed. He should have just put his foot down and said we were booked to go to Arklow. And that was it.'

'So you did go to Arklow after all.'

'No, we ended up in Dun Laoghaire.'

'That's rather a good distance away,' laughed Aisling. 'Who suggested it?'

'*Mise*. We all wanted to go shopping anyway. I said there was a nice shopping mall there, my daughter brings me there.'

'You shouldn't have dragged me into it. I'll get a bad name with your crowd.'

'They loved the suggestion. Someone shouted that there was a pier there and if anybody wanted to push anybody into the sea that was the right place. And old Mrs Price clapped and clapped. She had meanwhile turned on her hearing aid and thought that somebody had suggested that we could go swimming in the sea there!'

Aisling's sides split with laughter. She stood up suddenly.' I have to go to the toilet.'

'Oh, do be careful, alanna. Do you know what Dympna said about this going to the toilet on the train?'

'I don't, but I'm sure you'll tell me. And who's Dympna?'

'Go ahead, I see you're in a hurry. I'll tell you when you get back.'

Aisling looked at Philip. He said he was OK.

'Well, what did Dympna say?' inquired Aisling once she was seated again.

'She says that one shouldn't use the toilet on trains.'

'Now she tells me! And why not?'

'Because you get bruises all over your hips! All this swaying and moving. That's why. She showed me. She was going to Dublin for to buy a new jacket when it happened,' stated Mrs Holohan matter-of-factly.

Mrs Holohan then explained that Dympna, the friend who shared this bit of wisdom, was one of the leading lights in the widows' association. And her experiences were highly valued.

★   ★   ★

115

That evening when Richard returned to his apartment after the social in Professor van der Riet's house, he found it difficult to sleep. The conversation he had had with the other professors kept returning to his mind. After much turning and twisting, he decided that there was no point in trying to sleep. He looked at his alarm clock beside his bed. Two o'clock in the morning. Better to get up, he concluded. So after wrapping his dressing gown around himself he went to the kitchen to make some coffee.

He turned on the TV, wondering whether any interesting program was on. But after a few clicks on the remote control, he gave up. For a few minutes he tried some reading. He picked up the *Time* magazine that he had bought at the kiosk the other day. But he could not concentrate. So finally he thought that he would go out for a walk; anyway, the coffee was making him more awake. Perhaps the cold air would at least clear his mind.

He might even wait for daybreak. In Los Angeles he often entertained the desire to drive to the seafront for a walk on the beach to watch the dawning of a new day. But he was always apprehensive because of all the stories about people being attacked on the beach, particularly at that hour.

On the other hand, relatively carefree, he derived a lot of pleasure watching the sunset, which he admired regularly as he drove towards Playa del Rey. Or sometimes he would walk to an elevated place near the beach, a chosen point for plane-spotters but ideal for witnessing the close of day. The sun's fiery colors fading away as the sun slipped into the distant horizon like a gold coin into a savings box were spectacular. He always thought of the sun being tucked away for the night, just as the gold coin would be safely hidden to come out another day.

Now he wished he could also watch its coming out. Well, maybe this time.

Everything seemed peaceful in Leuven, the atmosphere lending itself to wanderings. As he quietly closed the entrance door to the apartment building behind him, he toyed with the idea of simply roaming around the Begijnhof. He looked

116

around. The Begijnhof was absolutely quiet, but it was not well lit up so he thought he would go out to the street instead. Maybe towards the town center. It was always a focal point.

First he made his way to Naamsestraat, a street that he had come to know quite well. During the day, it was busy with traffic, although the number of cars would be nothing in comparison to that in Los Angeles. The narrow streets here meant that when cars were also parked, a driver had to be extra careful not to hit them or the cyclists who seemed to be everywhere.

But tonight Naamsestraat was almost empty, the peace and quiet broken now and then only by a passing car or a staggering pedestrian. He crossed the street when he noticed one of those pedestrians who had had a drink too many approach him. Further up the street as he neared the Centrum, he heard a group of merry students who must have been celebrating or simply enjoying each other's company. It looked as if they had come from the Olde Markt. Richard smiled – student life, oh, the fun and the freedom despite all the pressures of essays and exams. Sometimes it was a luxury to live that kind of life.

The Fons Sapientiae – affectionately dubbed the Fonske by the students – was still lit up and flowing. Richard wondered whether it was left that way throughout the night as well as during the day. It certainly was an imposing statue, particularly with the brightly illuminated Stadhuis in the background.

He paused. Somehow the sight of the young scholar, Leuven's first honorary citizen, pouring water into his opened head as he read a book, beckoned to him and kept his attention. The fountain, Jef Claerhouts's creation, had been a gift of the university of Leuven to the town on the occasion of its 550th anniversary in 1975. There had been some debate regarding its significance, but the popular interpretation was that Fonske pours out wisdom: 'If the beer is out of the can, then wisdom is in the man.' Richard had passed by this place a number of times, but tonight it suddenly loomed large on his horizon. Why?

He folded his arms, hugging his coat to keep warm. Although the temperatures were not unusually low, he started feeling the cold once he stopped walking. Now he found himself directly in front of the fountain.

No doubt, the fountain represented what this university town was all about. The pursuit of knowledge. But how odd, he thought. Did the pursuit of knowledge mean reading volumes and volumes of information? Was it to be poured into one's head? Why was the open book covering the face of the scholar like a shield? From what was the scholar being shielded? Did the bent knee have any significance?

Richard kept staring at the statue in front of him. Why was he asking all these questions? Did he expect the statue to answer him or to come to life? But he could not shake off the idea that this fountain was symbolic of something. It represented what academic life was all about. All right, not everything about it. But it stood for what was essential. On the other hand, maybe he was seeing too much in it. It is funny how many times we give an interpretation to something that even its creator had not thought about. Was this the case now?

Richard sat down on the cement seat facing the fountain since he felt odd standing in front of it − he, a lonely figure before a stone creation at such an ungodly hour. There was something about its symbolic significance that kept bothering him and preventing him from moving on. Somehow he felt that it was saying something to him personally.

As he kept staring at the young scholar who remained unperturbed by this onlooker's questions, it dawned on him that there was a connection between his earlier conversation with his colleagues and his present musings. He had been concerned about the gap between the problem of evil and the philosophical way of dealing with it. Now it seemed that he was actually questioning the very idea of academic life itself, the life that he had dedicated himself to.

What was it really that he was meant to do as teacher? Pour information into his students' head? Or ram knowledge down their throat, as it were? Did students enter university merely to acquire knowledge? Or to get a degree, which many of his students still believed was the passport to well-paid jobs? Sometimes he felt that that was what was being communicated to his students in America – that education was a marketable commodity, and that was why they insisted on value for their money. But what about the pursuit of wisdom? Had academia become too stultified, too objectified? Where did inspiration come in? Questions and more questions.

Richard recalled what Martin Buber said of his philosophy, that he did not really have a philosophy but a vision, and all he wanted to do was to encourage people to open their own windows so they too could see that vision. It was an image which encouraged Richard to be a teacher. Teaching was his chance to broaden people's minds as well as his own. That was what he wanted to do; but despite excellent course evaluations by his students, he always felt hampered by expectations, probably caused by the evaluation itself, that teaching had to be marketed, analyzed and assessed just like any other product. Centuries ago, Richard recalled, the Athenian stranger in Plato's *Laws* had bemoaned the practice in Italy and Sicily of leaving the judgement of poets in the hands of the spectators. Such a practice spelled the destruction of the poets since they were in the habit of composing their poems to suit the taste of their judges. Similarly, Richard found himself pressurized into teaching according to the evaluation, designing his methods, his style, his syllabus, to ensure that he would score high in the evaluation questionnaire. His syllabus, readings (including specific pages), assignments, grading criteria were set out in great detail, leaving nothing unexplained because he did not want the risk of possible complaint. Nothing was left to the imagination. His lectures were systematic, clear and informative. He labored hard to provide study-guides. Class time was effectively used: 'every minute of it,' many of his students wrote.

But where was the excitement of discovery, the suspense of groping for the truth, the challenge of ambiguity? Did he communicate that to his students? If not, was it his fault as their teacher? He felt that he was losing the creativity and the spontaneity that mark the work of a true educator. He was afraid of being inventive because it might not be appreciated by his students, a reaction that would be noted no doubt in the evaluation, and ultimately by the administrators.

Perhaps it was his own fault, perhaps he should not have been too obsessed with the questions being asked of his students in the evaluation, but if one wanted tenure one had to tailor one's teaching to meet those expectations. He wanted to discuss his misgivings with others in the department, but as a young assistant professor he did not want to convey the idea that something was wrong with his teaching. Despite assurances that the comments rather than the percentages (both of which were fine in his case because he had learned to play by those rules) were what really mattered, he suspected, based on ample evidence, that the increasing need for quick and tangible evidence meant that the survey of percentages was a more handy way of assessing someone as a teacher.

And yet he had not been asked by the Rank and Tenure Committee for those evaluations which he had carefully filed. Had he played the wrong game after all? Had he misunderstood the whole situation?

His mind drifted to his students back in the USA. He missed them. No one in particular, but being with them in the classroom situation. There were many bright sparks among them. And their eager and lively undergraduate minds at times forced him to forget the whole darned evaluation and accompany them on their journey towards the truth, unfettered by the specific questions that would be asked of his course at the end, out of Plato's cave into the sunlight. He cared too about the not-so-bright students, whose talents lay somewhere else and whose academic efforts needed stimulating. By him, their teacher. There were hurdles to be overcome. His experience, his understanding and his skills would be much appreciated – not his concern about how his performance in the classroom would be subjected to scrutiny.

All of a sudden something startled Richard and put a momentary stop to his reflections. The fountain had been switched off. Funny, he thought. Just as he was being stimulated by the sight of the water, they had to turn the whole thing off.

The sight of the young scholar now frozen, as it were, in that pose, created a different impression on Richard. It was a cold statue now; no movement or life that the flowing water had given it. Like a human being that had ceased to open herself or himself up to the current of life – merely an object, rather than a person.

Richard was reminded of something again from Plato, of how ideas get some kind of life. For Plato ideas are static, frozen and lifeless, like that statue now in front of this twentieth-century philosopher. But just as ideas get their life and motion in a live intelligent being, so does this statue when water vivifies it. Richard asked: Have we perhaps forgotten this in academia? That the pursuit of wisdom is about life itself and not just information?

Three o'clock in the morning on the streets of Leuven. Strange how this town provoked one's mind – at such a time. He had gone for a walk to clear his mind. Now the fountain had filled it with more thoughts.

Perhaps he should move ahead. Anyway, it was getting colder. The Centrum was still bathed in the yellow light that was focused on the town hall, imposing on it a particular splendor.

But Richard's mind would not rest, even as he retraced his way back to the apartment. More questions kept surfacing. What was it that he was really searching for? Were these questions about academic life, his teaching and his academic research symptomatic of something deeper? He had come to Leuven to do scholarly work, but was he being given, unplanned and unforeseen, an opportunity to take a closer look at himself and even at life itself? He turned around to check the fountain. It was still now. There were no answers there. Would there be? he wondered.

The dawn was long in coming.

V

Jennifer was pleased with her decision to come to Leuven. She was meeting people here – the right people. This was important for her career, she told herself. The more she got to know certain individuals, especially in her field, the more she would be known. Such contacts would open up useful opportunities to further her career. She was glad to be working with Professor Lamennais; apart from the joint project, he was introducing her to other scholars who had shown considerable interest in her research. The social at Professor van der Riet's house had proved to be the kind of gathering that also opened doors to her. The Dutch professor of theology whom she met there had invited her to give a lecture at her university.

And a chance encounter with Dr Dietrich Holden, a Fulbright scholar doing research in Leuven, would surely be another golden opportunity. He and Jennifer had talked at some length about their research work and about grants and fellowships. Dr Holden, a well-accomplished scholar and an associate professor of theological studies at one of the prestigious universities in New Jersey, was engaged in a semester-long project at Leuven. He planned to write two chapters of a forthcoming book on a critique of Gerhard Ebeling's hermeneutics while at Leuven, having spent the first semester in Germany, where his research resulted in three chapters. The Fulbright award enabled him to extend his sabbatical for a year, freeing him from all the teaching and service to devote his entire time to his scholarly project. The more Jennifer listened to Dr Holden's account of the satisfaction experienced in obtaining grants and fellowships, the more Jennifer was motivated to stretch herself even more.

She wanted to excel, and she was confident of her abilities.

'It's very competitive, you know,' warned Dietrich Holden. 'Out of the hundreds of proposals submitted, very few are funded. Perhaps I was lucky, but I also sweated blood writing and rewriting – I forget how many times, I revised my proposal – to make sure it was exactly what the panel of evaluators would want.'

Jennifer merely smiled and then asked, 'Do you think I should apply for a Fulbright award?'

Having heard Jennifer's qualifications and accomplishments, Dietrich Holden was quite encouraging.

'By all means. The Fulbright works both ways: for American scholars to spend time overseas and foreign nationals to spend time in America. Hey, that's a good idea, your area of expertise would be particularly welcome in my department. And your project sounds particularly exciting. How about it then? It helps when you have an American contact. I'm sure I can arrange for my university to host you.'

'That's very kind of you.'

'Oh, no problem. Hey, we Americans need to be educated, by our British counterparts.' Dietrich had taken a real liking to this charming, intelligent and competent lady.

A flash of inspiration hit Dr Holden. Why wait until then? After all, he was anxious to impress Jennifer. He was organizing a major conference at his university in the coming fall. Many of the top theologians would be present, a wonderful opportunity for Jennifer to shine even more. There and then he issued her an invitation to present a paper on the project she was engaged in here at Leuven. And he would be glad to host her and escort her to the beauty spots of New England as well.

So the future was really looking bright for Jennifer. Leuven's academic portals were even wider than she had expected.

But tonight she was having dinner with Richard at the T-Bone Restaurant. Richard had heard that the steak there was quite special. The restaurant was a popular place, quite small though cozy. So reservations were a must. She was really looking forward to it, especially since they had postponed this dinner on account of Professor van der Riet's social two nights ago.

Richard was going to call for her and they would walk to the restaurant. She had better be sure she was warmly dressed then. She couldn't wear again the elegant green suit that she had worn to Professor van der Riet's. So she checked her wardrobe. Her new maroon trouser suit should do nicely. But which blouse would go with it? No, perhaps her beige polo neck would be better. It would also be warmer. Should she wear her pearl necklace? Slipping the polo neck inside the trouser suit, she wrapped the pearl necklace around its neck to view the entire attire and see its effect.

'Hmmm, not bad.' Then she looked at herself in the mirror. Not bad, either, if she may say so herself.

She liked Richard – he was young, handsome and articulate. His Latin looks made him a rather dashing figure. So far she had enjoyed their conversations. He had certainly been interested in getting to know her better and seemed impressed with her academic progress. But how useful would he be in her quest for academic success? Had he made a name for himself yet? He seemed shy about discussing his work. In the Theology Library she had checked the computer for any works authored by him. A blank. But surely he had some publication to his name, especially since she knew about the 'publish or perish' factor that plagued most university teachers in the United States. Maybe she'd find out tonight.

Richard arrived promptly at seven. He did not have far to go since his apartment was in the next building to Jennifer's. He too was looking forward to this dinner; it would be nice to have Jennifer's company. And to enjoy it the way the Europeans do it – complete with candlelight, flowers, wine and a great meal.

He had worn his suit, since dining out here was more formal. In Los Angeles, he sometimes wore shorts and tennis shoes. That was perfectly acceptable. Of course, the climate had a lot to do with it. Plus the rather informal lifestyle of southern California. But he was beginning to like the formality of the Belgians, at least when going out for a meal. Dressing up did add something to the occasion. As his Belgian host duly informed him, there was a difference between merely eating and dining. And tonight he was dining with Jennifer.

He pressed the doorbell that had Jennifer's name on it. There were three other doorbells for her building, all three names on them sounding foreign. Most likely also visiting scholars of different nationalities. Leuven was certainly a gathering place for academics.

Absent-mindedly, he expected some kind of response from Jennifer and a click opening the main entrance. None came, however. Then he heard some footsteps coming down the stairs. He had forgotten that here in the Begijnhof, the tenant had to open the door in person. There was none of those modern gadgets that enabled people to open the front door from several floors up.

'Hello, Richard. How nice to see you again. Won't you come in for a while?'

Jennifer looked stunning in her trouser suit. She was as attractive as the first time they met during the reception in Universiteitshal.

'How are you?' asked Richard as he stepped in. He admired the wooden carvings which decorated the inside walls of Jennifer's building. 'These are really beautiful buildings. Isn't the university of Leuven very lucky to have them?'

Jennifer agreed with him. 'Do you know that they were going to knock these down had the university of Leuven not bought them from the town? It did cost the university some money to renovate them, but it was certainly worth it, don't you think?'

She ushered Richard to her apartment on the second floor. It was neatly and very comfortably furnished, like his own, although the furniture was quite different. Richard seized upon this to make small talk, to relieve himself of some embarrassment, and started comparing their apartments. After all, this was a safe topic since neither of them had a stake in their accommodation.

125

'Well, will you have some sherry? I have dry and sweet,' offered the gracious hostess.

'Sherry. The British are fond if it, I heard. I'll have some dry, please,' replied Richard. And then with a pleasant smile, he said, 'Here, I brought you these. I hope you like them.' He kissed her on the right cheek.

'Belgian chocolates! Of course I do. They're not good for my figure, you know.'

Richard hesitated. Should he compliment her on her slim figure? He certainly did not want to be accused of making sexual advances. He always had that fear in Los Angeles because of all the legal cases he had heard about. He did not want to ruin what promised to be a truly lovely evening.

But out of the blue, Richard uttered what he would not dare to say back home: 'You look lovely, Jennifer.' He felt himself blush a little.

'Thank you, Richard,' was Jennifer's appreciative reply. Then she added, 'Won't you sit down?'

Over sherry the two talked about the social at Professor van der Riet's house. This was the first time there was the opportunity to chat about it since Professor Malachowski had walked with them back to the Begijnhof after the social. That night Richard and Jennifer had time just to bid each other goodnight. But now they had the chance to compare notes.

Both had appreciated the invitation: it facilitated their meeting other academics who were in Leuven. Richard remarked that getting to know Dr. Malachowski from Poland and Dr. Fuentes from the Philippines would be a great boost to his research. Dr. Malachowski was working on the same topic but from a different perspective, while Dr. Fuentes, at least from the brief discussion Richard had with him that evening, was expressing the same misgivings he had about the abstract approach in philosophy. He hoped to exchange views with them for a more extended time. Jennifer in turn told Richard of the invitation to the Netherlands.

'That's a great chance for you. Will you go?'

'Oh, yes. Dr. Linden – oh, she is the Dutch professor of theology – rang the next day after she had contacted her university. They said they'd be very interested. It seems that members of the department were familiar with my book.'

For some reason Jennifer never alluded to meeting Dr. Holden and his plans for her.

Richard froze. He wanted to change the topic of conversation immediately, but he forced himself to congratulate her while quietly reminding her that their reservation was for 7:30.

'Shouldn't we go?'

'Indeed, we should.'

★ ★ ★

Aisling was waiting for her mother's reaction once they reached their accommodation. Philip was mischievously grinning. He seemed to anticipate what his grandmother would say.

'Nice, clean sitting room, I must say, with those white tiles. Hmm, the kitchen's tiny though, isn't it?' observed a rather perplexed Mrs Holohan. 'Where are the bedrooms?'

'Ma, this is it.'

'You're joking, surely.' Her eyes kept searching. But all she could see was the one room.

'No.'

'You mean, you sleep right here on this cold floor?' Mrs Holohan had noticed that there were no carpets either.

Aisling stood up from one of the two dining room chairs in the studio. Philip was in the other, while Mrs Holohan had been given the one comfortable cushioned armchair positioned near the window. Aisling pulled down the bed from its upright position, which made it look like part of the shelving.

Mrs Holohan could not believe her eyes.

'You mean, you left your comfortable three-bedroomed semi-detached house for this?'

'It's only for a few months,' answered Aisling in defence. 'Anyway, I was promised better accommodation at the Begijnhof once there's a vacancy. I had hoped that would happen in time for your visit. No such luck. But don't worry,

127

we'll be out most of the time anyway. For the week that you are here.'

'I see. That's why you booked my return. I thought you wanted to be sure that I'd be gone after a week!' Mrs Holohan winked at her grandson.

'Guess where I sleep, Granny.' Philip jumped up and sidled up to his grandmother.

'Let me see. The shower! That's the only other place I can see. Right?'

'Granny, guess again.' Philip was enjoying the guessing game.

'Oh, I know. You sleep on the bed and your mother sleeps in the shower!'

With that Philip had a good laugh.

'That's where you will be sleeping – in the shower.' It was Philip's turn to tease his grandmother.

Immediately Aisling assured her mother that that was not the sleeping arrangement. Her mother would have the bed and she and Philip would sleep in the space between the door and the locker. They would use the rug which was usually in the middle of the room as their floor covering. The lady in charge of accommodation at the university had supplied them with a mattress for more comfort. There were plenty of blankets to keep them warm.

Mrs Holohan would not hear of it. No, she would be the one to sleep on the floor. She was not going to deprive them of their bed.

But after much discussion and encouragement from young Philip, who claimed it was going to be fun and an adventure for him, she relented. But she shook her head. She could not understand these academics who were prepared to put up with a change in lifestyle for the sake of what – more knowledge? Give me my own hearth and home anytime, she proclaimed, and these scholars can have their so-called academic pursuits. She looked pityingly at her daughter – and to think that she was one of those strange academics!

The three then had a really lovely cup of tea – with all the trimmings from home: the Christmas cake and some queen buns that Mrs Holohan had baked and brought with her. For

Philip and Aisling, it was like being at home again. For Mrs Holohan the company of her daughter and grandson, both of whom she had not seen for two months, brought tears of joy to her eyes. It was good to be together again — even in a cramped studio apartment in Leuven.

'To celebrate, we eat out tonight!' announced Aisling.

★   ★   ★

The next morning Aisling woke up early. She tapped Philip on the shoulder to wake him up. But he merely rolled over so she had to shake and nudge him.

'Philip, time to get up,' she whispered into his ear. 'Don't make too much noise, we don't want to wake Granny.'

But Mrs Holohan was already awake. In fact, she had been awake a long time but tried not to stir for fear of disturbing the two stretched out on the floor. She could not really see them since Aisling had left the door of the wardrobe open to give her mother some privacy.

'Well, Ma, did you have a good rest?' asked Aisling when she realized that Mrs Holohan was actually awake.

'Thank God for small mercies. At least, we are not camping. Not like that poor unfortunate family in Dublin who were turfed out of their house and are now out in the rain.'

Aisling interpreted that to mean no as an answer.

'Good morning, Granny,' came a voice from behind the door of the wardrobe.

'Did I hear something?' Mrs Holohan pretended not to know who it was.

Philip rolled over so his grandmother could see him.

'Well, did you sleep well?'

'A bit.'

'A bit! I could hear you snoring the whole night through.'

Philip giggled and crawled over to his grandmother to give her a kiss. 'Granny, I don't snore.'

'Breakfast, anyone?' Aisling interrupted.

Aisling had already put on her dressing gown while this

129

conversation was going on and gone to the kitchenette to take out the oranges from the fridge. She then took out the cornflakes and the milk.

Meanwhile Mrs Holohan and Philip tidied up the place. Philip showed his grandmother how to tie up the bedding and to tilt the bed back to the wall. Then they folded the blankets and placed them neatly inside the wardrobe. They placed the mattress behind the armchair and against the wall.

'We'll spend the day in Brussels. We'll go by train. Is that OK?' announced Aisling as she handed Philip freshly squeezed orange juice.

'What time's the train?' asked Mrs Holohan while she poured warm milk into her bowl of cornflakes.

'I think, there's one every twenty minutes.

'As frequently as that? Imagine that. And to think that there are only four trains to Kilkenny during the day.'

'Don't forget the extra one on Friday!' added Aisling.

Mrs Holohan was becoming impressed with Continental travelling until she was informed that, unlike in Ireland, senior citizens here did not get free travel, merely a reduction.

'You know, Tessa was saying that it wasn't fair for senior citizens to be getting free travel in Ireland. Wait till she gets to be my age. And that is *not* very far off. We'll see what she'll say then.' Then a note of concern marked her next question. 'This EC thing, they're not going to take away our free travel, are they? We were told that they want everything to be the same in Europe.'

Mrs Holohan really appreciated her free travel. Although she used it mainly for going to Dublin to visit her daughter and grandson, she would miss it terribly if that small concession to the senior citizens of Ireland were to be taken away.

'I don't know, Ma. Anyway, don't worry about it. Brussels is waiting for us right now.'

'Yes, the very place. Will you bring me to this EC headquarters so I can tell them to leave the senior citizens of Ireland alone? We've managed without them. We don't want them ruining our lives. And if they don't listen to me, I'm going to organize the widows' association. They'll *listen to us*,' warned Mrs Holohan.

Aisling fixed her eyes on her mother. Was she serious? She could not imagine her at the head of a widows' delegation to Brussels. On the other hand, why not? Perhaps after that Arklow-becoming-Dun Laoghaire outing she had turned radical.

★   ★   ★

Jennifer enjoyed the evening out with Richard. Everything went well and he was most certainly pleasant company. The meal at the T-Bone Restaurant in Tiensestraat turned out to be, as was to be expected from what Richard had heard, definitely superb. She knew that Belgians regard dining out as a special occasion and therefore restaurants make an extra effort to make sure everything goes well. She and Richard were definitely delighted with their choice of a restaurant for that evening.

Every single table in the restaurant had been occupied. At one end of the room there was a family of five. She surmised that it was some kind of a celebration meal since everyone, including the small daughter of four, was all dressed up. At another part of the restaurant, there was a group of three: a boy probably five or six years old, his lovely-looking mother and an older lady. From their accents, she was sure they were from Ireland. They seemed to be a close family. But she wondered to herself where the father of the boy was. The young boy, who looked cute in his dickie bow, had requested Richard to take a photograph of them. Richard was only too glad to oblige. At another table there was a young couple who were obviously in love since they had eyes only for each other. They were holding hands. So mesmerized were they that the meal itself seemed to have been an intrusion.

The memory of the young lovers made Jennifer pause. She had looked forward to Richard's company, had enjoyed the dinner and conversation, and now – she found herself wanting to be with him again.

It can't be, she pleaded with her emotions. She couldn't be falling in love again. She had promised herself that that would not happen – ever. Her career came first.

But her feelings now were strong. And every time she closed her eyes Richard's smiling face came into view. She was even hoping that Richard would call so she could hear his voice again. He had kissed her lightly on the cheeks when he gave her the chocolates and then again when he said goodnight as they parted at the entrance door. Did he feel the same way about her? He had seemed genuinely interested in her and had said that he hoped they would see each other again.

Why was she feeling this way? It was disturbing her peace of mind. She thought that she had gone beyond such feelings after so many years. She had made such progress in her academic career and she was not going to let her feelings ruin all that. It had been very difficult but she had succeeded in forgetting what had happened to her. She had managed to throw herself into her studies, achieving excellence and gaining control of her life again.

Until now. She was beginning to have the same kind of emotional feelings that she felt then. No, she won't let that happen. Not at this stage. Not when her work was beginning to attract attention. She did not want to be unfair to Richard either. She was here to work on her project and to meet people, not to fall in love.

And yet she felt so vulnerable. Suddenly the years of putting up defence mechanisms were proving to be ineffective. It was funny how years of work could simply vanish. On the outside, she was known to be a very competent and sociable person, with a strong and secure personality. But right now she felt weak. Crumbling even. All she wanted was to be with Richard. Even to be held by him.

Maybe he did not feel that way. Maybe it was all on her side. Maybe Richard did like her company and even sought it but that was all there was to it. No romantic connections. It would be odd if she, the strong personality, felt that way and her feelings were not reciprocated. No, she would have to put up her guard again. She would not let Richard know how she

132

felt for him. These are just momentary feelings, she assured herself. They will go away. They will fade with the memory of the evening. She wouldn't repeat her mistake.

Jennifer had been listening to a recording of the Birmingham Symphony Orchestra playing Mozart, a particularly apt piece for such a wondrous evening. The clear night sky put the full moon on show. She blamed the music and the evening for her feelings. So she stood up and moved towards her tape recorder to turn it off and to shut the window. She had brought the tape recorder with her and some tapes of classical music since she liked to listen to it for relaxation. She found that it put her in a mood to study. But tonight it was not to be the case. It was putting her in a mood for love. Study was becoming an effort. She could not concentrate.

This is a bad sign, she told herself. She was now sure that falling in love was not for her. Especially if it was distracting her from real work.

★   ★   ★

It had been an enjoyable evening, Richard told himself. Jennifer was wonderful company. The restaurant had the right kind of atmosphere for a truly relaxing evening. And he needed that. His mind had been too preoccupied with so much questioning that he wanted to switch off and enjoy the pleasures of life.

The other guests at the restaurant too added to the homely and even romantic atmosphere, something that he really appreciated. He was amused that the small Irish boy had asked him to take their photographs. He had a very attractive mother. When she thanked Richard for acceding to her son's innocent request, she gave him and Jennifer a captivating smile. Her husband must be a lucky man to have such a charming wife. And the lovers at the other table. Richard had noticed that they hardly touched their meal.

Jennifer's conversation tended to focus on her work and on her career, and she was genuinely interested in his career. But somehow she was hiding something about her life, while he himself was not keen on talking about his career. He could not put his finger on anything in particular but he got the feeling that there was a wall between them every time one or the other topic came up. He knew why he did not really want to talk about his career. But why was she reluctant to open up about herself? And yet when their talk touched on other things, she was quite open and ready with her comments. The conversation flowed freely.

A pleasant companion. Anyway, why should she be interested in him? He really had nothing to offer her. Certainly in comparison to what she had already achieved in her career he did not have much of a chance.

Why was he having these thoughts? He should be thinking about his research. Like Jennifer. Why could he not focus on his work? If he did, perhaps he would get that tenure that he needed. Why couldn't he be more like Jennifer?

He liked her a lot. And he was full of admiration for her.

*   *   *

Aisling, Philip and Mrs Holohan took the bus to the station at Martelarenplein. Along the way, Aisling pointed out a few landmarks in the centre of Leuven which Mrs Holohan had missed the previous evening, since the taxi had gone via the ring road which encircles Leuven.

This time Mrs Holohan managed to see the Centrum and the main shopping street of Bondgenotenlaan, which was the route of the No. 2 bus. Mrs Holohan kept looking out of the window trying to take everything in, admiring Bondgenotenlaan, a street with dwarf trees and a Paris-boulevard perspective with a lot of Dutch chain stores. A showcase of the prosperity of the nineteenth century, this street connected the town centre to the station.

In a matter of minutes, however, the bus stopped at their first destination today: the railway station.

Aisling purchased their tickets and checked the platform for the train to Brussels. Fortunately they had missed the rush hour for commuters to Brussels and although there was still a good crowd milling around, she was confident that they would be able to get three seats together.

No sooner had they reached the platform than the intercity train to Brussels arrived – on time. And that is normal, explained Aisling to her bemused mother, who often had to guess what time the train from and to Barrowtown would leave or arrive.

Aisling had come to admire the railway system in Belgium. Not only was it punctual and frequent, it was a very convenient way to see places. She had earlier entertained the idea of renting a car while they were in Leuven so that she could take Philip to see many of the important places until she discovered the convenience and the comfort of weekend train travel in Belgium. And it was relatively inexpensive too. So far she and Philip had managed to visit Bruges, Ghent and Antwerp, charming cities that she hoped to bring her mother to. But today she thought they would go only as far as Brussels since it would be a good way for her mother to adjust to this 'foreign country'. Anyway, she knew that her mother was bent on visiting this 'so-called capital of the European Community' which was having an impact on their daily lives. She also wanted to be able to tell her widow friends where these Irish Eurocrats were spending the money taken from the poor widows of Ireland!

In 20 minutes the three found themselves at Brussels Centraal station, a huge terminal. Inside, near the main entrance, was parked an immaculately clean old-style car, which glistened in the bright lights of the station. But the car was actually a shop for Belgian waffles.

'Do you want to try it, Ma?'

'Ya, go ahead, Granny,' egged on Philip. 'It's simply delicious!'

He had come to like the stuff and every time they were on an excursion, he asked for it. Philip was becoming very adventurous in his taste for food.

'Oh, I don't know.' Mrs Holohan was rather hesitant. 'Maybe I'll just have a bit of yours, Philip.'

135

Aisling asked for two waffles and handed one to Philip.

'We'll go over there for some hot drinks. Some central heating inside us before we leave the station.' She led the way to the nearby café.

Mrs Holohan said she would have coffee. After all, she was on the Continent now. When Aisling asked whether she would have expresso, adding that her mother may as well go all the way and be Continental, Mrs Holohan said that Aisling should take it easy.

'One step at a time. I don't want to die on the Continent,' came the quick reply.

Two regular coffees then and one hot chocolate, she ordered. Philip would have preferred a cold drink but his mother reminded him that he would find it colder when they left the station.

'OK, then. Granny, over here, free biscuits come with the coffee.' Philip volunteered the information. 'You don't have to ask for them. They always give them to you ... Also, with the hot chocolate,' he added with a smile. The nice lady took the hint.

'Well, what do you think of the Belgian waffle, Ma?' inquired Aisling after Mrs Holohan had finished the sampler she had from Philip.

'At least you can eat it.'

It was a typical Irish compliment – positive but vague. Aisling laughed.

'By the way, how was the parish cake sale?'

'Oh, very well. Father Murray was very pleased. Broad smile all over him. You know, like the one he has when the bingo hall is packed and he rubs his hands in glee.'

'Did you do any baking for this good cause then?'

'Of course, and my tarts were a great hit, so Mrs Connolly tells me. No, not the one, God help her, who's not right. But the one married to Bill who lives next to Mrs Reilly. They sold like hot cakes, too. Poor Mrs Byrne. No one bought her gooseberry and apple jam.'

'She usually makes good ones, doesn't she?' Aisling jumped to Mrs Byrne's defence.

'Well, this year's gooseberries were not out yet!'

'And?'

'It struck me that her gooseberries must have been from last year. It must have struck the others, too. Poor Mrs Byrne. Maybe she can sell them off next year if the harvest is better. And no one would notice the difference!'

'Do you remember Mrs Shelley?' Mrs Holohan was off again, not waiting for any prompting this time.

'Mrs Shelley? I don't know a Mrs Shelley.'

'Ah, you do,' corrected Mrs Holohan, forgetting that Aisling left Barrowtown several years ago to study at the university and then to live in Dublin. 'You know, she lives near Mrs Reilly.'

'That's very helpful, Ma. Who's Mrs Reilly?'

'The eighty-year-old widow who's always asking for Mills and Boon novels. The "romance ones" says she to me.' Mrs Holohan mimicked her friend, sending Aisling and Philip into an uproar.

'Now, which one is that, Mrs Reilly or Mrs Shelley?'

'I can't get anywhere with you. I'm just after telling you, that's Mrs Reilly.'

'Well, what about Mrs Shelley then?'

'She won the Lotto! And a great win it was, too. Half a million. That's not to be sneezed at.'

'Wow. That was something. What's she going to do with all that money?'

'Buy plots in the graveyard.'

'What?' Aisling stared at her mother in disbelief.

'Buy plots in the graveyard,' repeated her mother, emphasizing each word to make sure Aisling caught it.

'Here, pull the other one, Ma.'

'I'm serious. That's exactly what she did. She said that it's impossible to get one now. You have to be dead to get one.'

'Well, that makes sense – I mean that you have to be dead.'

'She wants to be sure that her whole family are buried together, not scattered all over. There's a headstone without a name. You can see it for yourself.'

Aisling bit her lower lip. She was tempted to ask: what if

they were cremated? They would have to be scattered, but that would have been pushing it a bit.

Mrs Holohan continued. 'So she bought one for herself and her husband, and one each for the families of all her children. Now we'll all be together, says she with pride and joy.'

When the three were refreshed and warmed up, they headed for the Grand-Place. It was a mere ten minutes' walk from the station. Aisling read out the information on the square from the guidebook.

'In 1695, the bombardment of the Grand-Place by the French troops left only the Town Hall standing. Reconstruction was begun immediately, and the result is one of the most beautiful squares in the world. Every façade is different, the whole in perfect harmony. The square consists of the Town Hall in flamboyant Gothic style, the Maison du Roi and the various guild houses with their ornate gilt and lavishly decorated Dutch baroque style façades.'

'What does that mean?' interrupted Philip.

There were too many 'funny words' for him so Aisling abandoned the whole idea of reading from the guidebook. She translated all the information into more intelligible language for her son.

'There's a flower market here every day,' Aisling added for the benefit of her mother, who adored flowers. 'And every Sunday morning there is a bird market. When it is floodlit at night, this whole place is an unforgettable sight. But you know what? The most colourful of all, so I'm told, is the living chessboard. The chess pieces are actually human beings in medieval costumes. And the carpet of flowers which covers the square every other August. Ma, you'd really love it.'

Mrs Holohan stood at the square in awe, transfixed by the grandeur that surrounded her. It was indeed an impressive sight.

From there they walked in the direction of a notable Brussels monument. This was the first time Aisling and Philip were going to see it. Aisling had read about it and the legend surrounding it, but she wanted to wait until her mother was with them to take Philip.

There were some tourists at the scene, taking photographs. From where he was Philip could not see what they were staring at as they gripped the iron bars that surrounded something. They looked amused. Cameras clicked away.

But as the small crowd dispersed, Philip saw what all the amusement was about. He turned red – red as a beetroot! And it did not escape Mrs Holohan's notice. And then unexpectedly Philip roared with laughter, confusing Mrs Holohan further.

'What's wrong with him?' asked a very puzzled Mrs Holohan. 'And what's wrong with you?' she added when she noticed that Aisling was laughing just as uncontrollably as Philip.

It was exactly the reaction Aisling had expected from Philip when he saw the *Mannequin Pis* for the first time – the bronze statue by Jerome Duquesnoy symbolizing the irreverence of the *bruxellois*.

The sight of the young lad passing water into the fountain reminded Philip of that fateful day in Leuven. Aisling, between giggles, explained to her mother what had happened. It was Mrs Holohan's turn to burst out laughing – to the amusement of the group that was beginning to gather around. Mrs Holohan kept imagining her grandson in place of the statue doing exactly the same thing.

'Did they see me do it, Ma?'

Philip was convinced that it was him. Aisling had to tell him of the legend of the boy who went missing. When finally his father found him, he was doing exactly what the statue was doing.

'Oh, it happened many, many years ago, Philip. And now, you know what they do? They dress him up in different costumes. I believe it's quite a sight. That's why it has become famous.'

'Are you really sure, Ma?' persisted a doubtful Philip. He was not convinced. But he kept chuckling to himself.

Aisling informed her mother that in Leuven the students had wanted a *Manneken-Pis* instead of the statue of Justus Lipsius who graces Bondgenotenlaan.

139

'Well,' remarked Mrs Holohan, 'they've a good reason now to put one up!' She looked in the direction of her grandson.

Aisling admitted that she had been planning it ever since she read about it in one of the books she had consulted on Belgium. Philip said it was really funny. Aisling detected from the tone of his voice that Philip was scheming something.

'What are you thinking of, son?'

'Nothing,' came the evasive answer.

Mrs Holohan saw that this time Philip was gaining the upper hand. Aisling had her day, but Philip would have his.

'I'm hungry,' remarked Philip.

Aisling suggested lunch in a nearby Chinese restaurant which she had spotted from the square. They could have the *Dagschotel* since it included hot soup. After all, the day was still cold.

Since there was no objection, they headed that way. Suddenly Philip started gripping his mother's hand and twisting his legs. The cold must have got to him. He looked up at his mother and a silent communication took place.

Oh, my God, not here, thought Aisling. There was no place to go. What should I do? She looked around. They were right at the centre of the square. From the look on Philip's face, she did not think they would make it in time to the restaurant. She'll just have to pull down his trousers right here and now.

Just as she was about to do it – and getting red from embarrassment – Philip let out a good laugh. Then he straightened his legs and walked confidently ahead, leaving behind a bemused Aisling.

'He got you well and good this time,' said Mrs Holohan. 'One all.'

Aisling chased Philip, who shrieked with delight.

Mrs Holohan said to herself that she always knew she had a cute grandson. Like mother, like son. After all, what can one expect? Aisling was quite cute herself when she was Philip's age. Even younger. Mrs Holohan remembered quite well an incident when Aisling was only four years old.

Aisling wanted to be taken to the shops, but she was very busy with the housework and told young Aisling to play in her bedroom instead. They were living in a bungalow, with fields at the back. After a good ten minutes and no sound was coming from the toddler's bedroom, she became suspicious. The place being unusually quiet, she checked to see what was going on.

No Aisling to be seen! She called – no answer. Then she noticed that the bedroom window was open. She looked out. No, there was no sign of Aisling. She was beginning to panic. What could have happened to her?

Straightaway, she took out the bicycle from the garage and pedalled furiously in the direction of the shops. Where could the child be? She could hear her own heart pounding.

Then she noticed a lady with her groceries coming from the shops. Had she seen a young girl of four, by any chance? Yes, she was running as fast as her tiny legs could carry her, she was told. No, she was in no danger now. Mrs Cleary was with her. Good, Mrs Holohan said with relief, but wait till I get her.

But when she reached Mrs Cleary and Aisling, the rescuer-friend said immediately, 'Oh, don't touch her, she is only an aul' slob.'

Aisling always remembered those words. Mrs Cleary's description of her hurt, but she was grateful for Mrs Cleary's defence of her, Aisling told her mother much later. But from then on Mrs Holohan knew that her daughter had a mind of her own and was capable of taking care of herself.

And she was glad that her daughter had that ability. With Sean's death, she had been concerned as to how Aisling would cope with raising their infant son on her own and pursuing a career. She was amazed at how she could balance the two. She had offered to bring up the infant Philip so that Aisling would manage to continue with her career. Aisling was really devastated when Sean had that terrible accident. But she said that she owed it to Sean to be a mother to their son and to be a good one at that. Aisling and Sean had had dreams about Philip's future. Against their will, those dreams were about to be shattered by an untimely death. But she would not let that happen. Aisling always said that Sean would have wanted her to get on with life. She wanted to perpetuate Sean's memory by bringing up what their love had created.

That ideal had demanded a lot from her daughter. But she admired Aisling's courage and determination. Above all, she wondered at her equanimity amidst the trials and tribulations of life. Between juggling schedules in her domestic and professional life and coping with pangs of loneliness, Aisling nevertheless had succeeded in raising Philip almost singlehandedly.

She had also become a lot closer to both of them, not only because they visited her frequently but also because she understood what her daughter was going through. She had felt that pain and loss when Aisling's father died. She wondered whether she would have had the same courage as Aisling if her husband had died as tragically and as untimely as Sean. People always said that misfortunes brought people together. This was certainly their case. She was learning much about life from her daughter's attitude. She was grateful that all her years of caring for the young Aisling were indeed bearing fruit. And Philip and Aisling were very close, supporting each other. She could also see that Philip was becoming very much like her own daughter.

★   ★   ★

The attendance at the Liberation Theology seminar taking place at the American College was large. The presenter tonight was a Brazilian Ph.D. student. As he surveyed the packed hall, Dr. Fuentes noticed that there was a large contingent of students from Africa, Asia and Latin America. This was not surprising since this form of theology was very much associated with those places insofar as it arose out of the experiences of oppressed, exploited and dehumanized peoples. The history of those continents was full of them. As grassroots Christians as well as some academics and pastors reflected on their Christian faith, they asked – critically – how their concrete negative experiences would enable them to make sense of their Christianity. What was their task as Christians

142

who were confronted by widespread poverty and institutionalized misery?

It was a giant task, often misunderstood even by those who should be expected to understand. So whom would such a gathering attract? Dr. Fuentes continued looking around because he suspected that those would be there who were already committed to facing such a challenge. What about those who needed to hear the message of liberation theology?

From where he was seated he spotted Richard Gutierrez, whom he had met at the social in Professor van der Riet's house. He wondered whether the young Hispanic-American philosopher would see a link between his scholarly activity and the topic of the seminar. Professor Malachowski was there, too. In fact, Dr. Fuentes was not surprised since he was aware of the eminent professor's interests. Yet liberation theology did not seem to have taken root in Eastern Europe.

Dr. Fuentes had a specific question prodding him on: was there really something he would learn from his stay at Leuven? This seminar was at least a start.

★   ★   ★

'Well, are we going to have that lunch?' asked Mrs Holohan when she caught up with the other two.

Philip was still laughing at the idea of having succeeded in pulling his mother's leg.

Outside the entrance to the restaurant the menu was clearly displayed on the front of a wooden figure. There was nothing 'Chineesy' about the figure, who looked more like a European character from the Middle Ages.

'Chicken and sweetcorn soup. That should do the trick since we all like it. And that should keep us warm. Let's see what else comes with it. Hmm. Sweet and sour pork, or lemon chicken or beef and broccoli. Well, what do ye think, folks?'

Aisling was grateful that restaurants in Belgium had their menu also in English; she would not have managed otherwise. Everyone took up her suggestion that they just go in and make up their minds when inside. The cold weather made the idea of soup particularly welcoming.

After lunch, the party of three continued with their exploration of the area around the square. Philip was fascinated with the display of fish in the various stalls in front of the restaurants. It was particularly eye-catching and imaginative. The artistically arranged fruits and vegetables that accompanied the various fishes and sea–products were worth a photograph. Which is what they did, of course. Mrs Holohan remarked that the huge staring eyes and tail of the fish would scare any decent Irish diner!

Mrs Holohan was curious as to whether they put all that work into arranging their display, only to take them down every night. Aisling said she did not know, but she could find out. Mrs Holohan, however, pulled her back. 'D'you want them to think we're tourists?'

So they did not bother and instead continued admiring the fine display, meant to trap the hungry visitor. After that they explored the elegant shops nearby as well as the not-so-elegant ones. Both Mrs Holohan and Aisling liked browsing around.

After they had gone in and out of several shops Philip said that it would be a pity if Granny did not have the chance to taste those wonderful Belgian chocolates, especially the ones that his mother really liked. Mrs Holohan agreed. Philip offered to lead the way to the Neuhausen shop that he remembered from their last visit.

The day out in Brussels was enjoyable for everyone despite a minor disappointment. Later in the afternoon they had made a short trip to see the Europark, a miniature Europe showing off miniature replicas of the important buildings in Europe, like the Eiffel Tower and so on. A tour of it would be quite educational for Philip, Aisling had suggested. And her mother could even say, without of course revealing that it was at the Europark, that she had seen the Eiffel Tower on this trip to the Continent. 'Europe at a glance like', Mrs Holohan remarked.

Unfortunately, the park was closed and was not scheduled to reopen until later that month. Not ones to be put off by this hiccup, they did manage to see some things through the holes in the walls that other disappointed sightseers must have made. Aisling, however, saved the day. She surmised that it would be even more wonderful to see it all from the Atomium. And sure enough, they did get a splendid view from way up there. In fact, they could see all of Brussels. Philip was really fascinated with the architecture of the tower. Huge balls, he exclaimed, all stuck together.

They did not get back to Leuven until late that night. After saying goodnight and thanking them for a lovely day, the exhausted Mrs Holohan sighed, 'Oh, the life of a tourist' and immediately fell asleep.

The following morning during breakfast Aisling informed them that they would stay in Leuven that day. There were so many interesting sights which she thought her mother would be interested in seeing. But for a couple of hours in the afternoon she would have to leave the two of them together since she had to attend a class.

'Are you going to class here? I thought you were finished with all that stuff once you got all them degrees.'

Mrs Holohan could not understand any of this. After all, Aisling had been teaching for a few years now. Why should she still be sitting and listening to someone else teach her?

'Well, one is never finished learning – you taught me that, Ma, remember?' replied Aisling.

'I meant learning about life; one is never through with it. I didn't mean all that education. What are you going to do with all that, anyway? You have a job. So where's that going to class here leading to?' Mrs Holohan was not about to give up easily.

'It's hard to explain, Ma. But it's part of my job. I have to keep up. There are always new things to learn about. That's why I have to continue reading all those books and attending classes.'

'You mean, you'll never be finished?' She looked at her daughter, who was trying to enjoy her cup of tea.

'You can say that, I suppose.'

'And what will you do with all that knowledge?'

'I pass it on to my students – and to Philip.' Aisling smiled at Philip, who was eating his cereal but listening to all this with keen interest.

'And then what?'

'And then maybe we'll understand more about life, about ourselves and about everything.'

'But you don't get that from reading books or spending so much time in libraries. Getting on with life is where we can learn a lot.'

Mrs Holohan caught herself. Aisling had done exactly that. But that was also what she could not understand. Aisling was a very down-to-earth person who met life's challenges squarely. And yet she was also studious. She could read for hours with terrific concentration. But the minute she put her books down she faced life as if it were the only thing that mattered. Aisling was not the kind of academic who shut herself up. Mrs Holohan always liked that in her even as a child, but she supposed that Philip had also something to do with it now.

Aisling turned to Philip, who had finished his breakfast.

'Will you be good and not make any trouble for your granny while I'm in class, Philip?'

'Am I not always good, Ma?'

Philip was looking for reassurance. He approached his mother for a hug. Aisling held him tight and tousled his hair.

'Of course you are. But you'll be extra good, won't you?'

'All right.' After a pregnant pause, he muttered, 'And I promise not to draw any pictures.'

With that Aisling and Philip had a terrific laugh. Aisling had to explain to her mother what had happened when she was in class the first week and Philip was being minded by her host professor.

'You'll have to show me those pictures, Philip. So I'll know her if I meet her.'

This time Philip's face dropped. 'Oh, Granny, you won't tell, will you?'

'Not if you do what I ask you to do today. Is that a deal?'

146

'Granny, you know I don't like deals. But you win. This time.' Then with a large grin on his face, he continued, 'Remember that time when I played a trick on you, Granny?'

'Let me see, which one? I seem to remember several of them.'

'That time when I stayed with you for the night. I told you that I still wet the bed. So you got a plastic sheet to cover the bed. Then I laughed because I had fooled you. Remember?'

'You little divil!' said Mrs Holohan with affection. 'What about this one? You went to the toilet on your own to pass water, with your dodo in your mouth. Remember what happened?'

'Oh, yeah, you called me and when I answered, the dodo fell out of my mouth into the bowl!'

'I can see it's going to be one of those days. Recalling tricks played on people. So long as you don't play tricks on each other today,' Aisling warned the two.

Philip was indeed a source of much amusement, thought Mrs Holohan. She remembered the time when the three of them were in church in Dundrum. Philip was probably only three-and-a-half then. When the collection basket was being passed around, Philip took a look at the contents and picked out the biggest coin! And then said thank you to the embarrassed collector. Philip had thought that it was like sweets being passed around and that he could help himself to them. Another time when she rang from Barrowtown Philip had picked up the phone. When she asked him whether his mother was home, he nodded his head! She thought he had gone quiet and had to repeat the question. Yes, Philip had definitely brought much consolation to them.

But Mrs Holohan could not help feeling concerned. The boy was growing up without a father. She belonged to the generation which always regarded children as growing up in the care of both parents. Aisling was doing her best to provide Philip with everything that he needed. But something is missing, Mrs Holohan thought. Especially since he is a boy. A boy needs a lot of things that only a father can give. You know, even just to talk about things. Father to son, that kind of stuff.

147

What will happen when he grows up? She kept looking at her grandson, who was now getting ready to go out after helping his mother clear the table. He is getting taller, she observed.

★   ★   ★

The symposium in the Theology Department of Mercier University had been organized in honor of one of the professors who was retiring. The topic chosen, being the title of her last book, was one that marked her academic work as a Professor of Systematic Theology: 'Images of God.'

It was a topic that Richard was particularly interested in since it touched on philosophy of religion, his own area of specialization. Aside from professional reasons he had another reason for wanting to attend, a personal one. He knew that Jennifer had been invited to comment. Although her specialized field was in theological ethics, the Chair of Theology had felt that the scholar from England would bring a fresh perspective to the subject matter. Jennifer's academic excellence was indeed gaining a lot of recognition.

The Kleine Aula of the Maria Theresia College, where the conference was taking place, was filling up when Richard arrived. It was going to be well attended. Richard noticed two professors from the School of Philosophy in the second row. Smiling at them, he gave a slight nod of recognition. He decided not to join them, however. They would probably be talking in Dutch to each other anyway. One of the things that was beginning to irritate Richard in Leuven was when the people he was talking to would suddenly turn to each other and converse in Dutch. It was only to be expected, but he sometimes felt he was in the way.

More people arrived. Some came in groups of two or three. Richard always thought that when going to functions like this it was better to go with someone. Otherwise one was left twiddling one's thumbs or pretending to read. He would have liked to have come with Jennifer. That would not be true today, of course, since she was one of the speakers. But it would have been nice to have someone to converse with. Since no one came to sit beside him, he could not turn to

148

anyone for some conversation. He would have to pass the time by himself.

He could watch the attendees, which is exactly what he proceeded to do. Viewing the gathering crowd, he sometimes wondered what kind of people came to functions like this. Academics, students, that was to be expected. But he had noticed some individuals who did not look like academics.

Then he checked himself. What did an academic look like anyway? A foolish question. But those people in front were too well-dressed. The lady in the third seat, for instance. That must be a rather expensive attire she had on. And that group of fellows to his right. They did not look like students either. He had come to form an image of Leuven students from having practically all his meals in the university Almas and the Sedes. There was something different about that group. And yet he did not know what it was.

So who cared, really? At least, it was helping to pass the time, he defended himself. He looked about the hall. It seemed to have been renovated recently, Richard noticed. Given the fact that the building was quite old, like most of the buildings here, this lecture hall looked modern. The comfortable seats were tiered. A good idea since it gave everyone a good view of the podium and panelists. Okay, what else was there to observe?

Richard looked at his watch. The symposium was scheduled for three o'clock. It was now five past three. Nothing unusual there, he told himself. He had been informed that academic practice in Europe allowed professors to be up to 15 minutes late. And that was understood by everyone. So since classes obviously couldn't start without the professor and since the professor would usually be about 15 minutes late, students would themselves sometimes come late. So it was a vicious circle. Why not just schedule the class for 15 minutes later? Richard could not understand this European academic practice. He did hear that professors finished on time or even earlier, however. Professors were really masters here. Would that that were true in his own university in southern California!

The panelists were starting to take their seats. The Chairman of the Theology Department moved towards the podium and adjusted the microphone. Richard took a second look at the panel. There was no sign of Jennifer. Where was she? Had something happened to her? Was there a change in the panel? He glanced at the program he had picked up at the registration table. Her name was on it.

The speaker spoke first in Dutch. Richard could not understand what she was saying but he did catch the name of Jennifer. I wish I knew Dutch, he said to himself. I really must do something about my lack of knowledge of languages, he promised himself.

'Ladies and Gentlemen,' the speaker was now translating what she had said earlier, probably for the benefit of non-Dutch speakers like himself.

Richard looked around. The audience was international in composition, and the printed program was in English and Dutch. I doubt whether they'll be speaking in Dutch and then repeating the same thing in English, he thought to himself. That would be too boring for those who were bilingual.

'Welcome to this symposium in honor of our esteemed colleague, Professor Dr. Ursula Scholz. As you know, we are marking her retirement from our university with a symposium on a topic that is dear to her heart. We had invited three prominent theologians to speak on that topic. Unfortunately, Dr. Jennifer Sidney from England has been taken ill and so she will not be able to join us.'

Richard felt his stomach tensing. What happened to her? He wanted to run to her apartment. But he could not do that right now without drawing attention to himself. Was it the meal they had two days ago? But it had not affected him. She looked fine when they parted that evening. Nor did she mention anything about not being able to participate in this symposium. In fact, she talked a lot about the comments she was going to make. He had helped to clarify an issue here and there with his probing questions – at least that was what she told him in the restaurant. So what happened? He had meant

150

to call her yesterday, but couldn't. She had not called him either.

Richard was very much distracted during the main speaker's lecture. Only disjointed sentences kept parading in front of him: '... the limitations of human language ...' 'language games and all that ...' 'preserving the transcendence of God ...' 'the main point is ...'

Yes, what was the main point? Richard knew he was being unjust to the speaker. He just felt that she was going on and on. On the other hand, he was not really listening. His mind kept drifting back and forth. He was concerned about Jennifer, and being stuck in this lecture hall was the last thing he wanted. Normally the topic would have been of interest to him. But not now. Definitely not now.

But why not? We spend all our time pursuing interesting and significant ideas, he thought. And yet when it comes to brass reality, they are bankrupt. Why? If they are really important enough to capture our professional lives, why do they seem hollow and irrelevant when we are faced with a concrete situation? Like now. Are our academic pursuits merely a luxury of a more leisurely kind of life? As Aristotle seems to imply? Can we really afford to have that?

Richard knew that he was not being fair. He was expecting a particular issue that was being discussed by the speaker to satisfy a more general dissatisfaction on his part. No aspect of life can do that. As a philosopher, he should have known it. And yet he could not rid himself of the idea that his instincts were correct. There was a gap between life and the pursuit of academia. And there really should be none. While the two may not be exactly the same, the gap should not be so great either. After all, what was the point in having all that knowledge if it did not make any difference to the kind of life that we lived?

Jennifer ... what was the matter with her? This would have been a good opportunity for her academic prospects, a wonderful chance.

Richard's eyes roamed around. Yes, various impressive-looking academics, a few of them looking rather like odd characters, others from the look of it obviously resting on their laurels (or cushions, to be more exact, as he sarcastically thought of tenure). And then there were the graduate students, all appearing enthusiastic, wanting to soak everything up. You could spot the difference, he told himself. The graduate students were those who were furiously scribbling down notes, trying to catch every pearl that dropped from the masters' lips. The professors were those who were laid back. They knew it all or pretended to know. He was being sarcastic again. What was happening to him?

I don't believe this, he thought. Did he hear the first commentator say that she had had many discussions with the professor being honored about the books that Professor Dr. Ursula Scholz had *not* read? What kind of compliment was that? Or was it meant to be a compliment? Did this kind of thing go on in European academia?

But the remark elicited laughter from the audience. So it must be, concluded Richard. The speaker then went on to say that this time the honoree would have to listen to her ideas since she could not very well walk out of the symposium in her honor! That was a clever tactic, Richard thought. And well received, judging from the reaction of the honored professor and the audience.

After the first commentator's talk, the chairman called for a short break. Good, thought Richard. This is my chance to slip out. So he fetched his coat. He would need it to brave the cold winds outside. Leuven was still cold at this time of the year.

He noticed that a few others were doing the same thing. Did it mean that they were not returning either? He did not like going off halfway through the symposium. It was always a disappointment or even downright rudeness to the organizers and speakers when the second half would attract only half the original audience. One was never sure whether those who left really had other commitments or whether they were simply bored or frustrated.

At least he had a genuine reason this time. Jennifer.

It took him only ten minutes walking rather briskly to

Jennifer's apartment. The cold wind, as well as his anxiety, kept him going. He hoped that Jennifer was all right, after all.

He rang the bell when he arrived at the entrance to her apartment. Then he waited for Jennifer to come down. No answer. So he rang again. Still none. He was perplexed. Where could she be? She could not be in the library since it had been announced that she was ill.

Richard hovered about the place for a while, wondering whether Jennifer would open the window to look out. That would be unthinkable, given the cold air. Still, he hoped that there would be some sign of her. Should he call out her name? That would be rather impolite, he told himself. Maybe the bell was not working; he had no way of knowing. But she may not like the idea of being called from the street below. This was not going to be a scene from *Romeo and Juliet*. What should he do now?

Just when he was about to leave, someone came in his direction. The new arrival took out a key and opened the main entrance. Richard politely asked whether he could come in, and introduced himself. After being allowed in, Richard thanked him and then bolted up the stairs to Jennifer's apartment.

'Jennifer, are you there? This is Richard.'

No reply. Richard knocked louder. If she was in the bedroom, she wouldn't have heard his first knock, he rationalized.

This time a voice came from inside. 'Just a minute.'

After a while, Jennifer opened the door. She looked pale. 'Richard, what are you doing here?'

Richard explained his reason for coming. He wanted to know how she was. He entered the apartment without waiting to be invited in.

'Thank you for your concern, Richard. I am fine.'

But Richard did not believe her. She did not look fine, she had not attended the symposium in which she was scheduled to speak, she had not answered the doorbell. How could she claim that she was fine?'

'Really, I am.'

153

Richard persisted.

'I thought we were friends, Jennifer. Was it something you ate? Tell me, maybe I can sue the restaurant,' he said jokingly.

'No.'

'Did you catch something, a bug? I believe that there's much of that going around with this kind of weather.'

'No. And Richard, thank you for your concern.'

With that she stood up. A sure sign that she wanted him to leave. Richard was not to be daunted, however. He stood his ground.

'Jennifer, please tell me. Was it something I said or did? I'd rather you told me.' He held his hand to touch hers.

'Don't do that! How dare you!' Jennifer was getting hysterical.

Richard was really shocked. His face betrayed disbelief at the turn of events. He was not going to do anything. He had extended his hand in simple friendship. One could not expect it to have been any more than that. He did not see anything wrong in what he did. He certainly hoped that it was not interpreted as a sexual advance. Why did Jennifer react like that? And yet she seemed to have been receptive when he kissed her on the cheeks when they went out for a meal.

'Jennifer, I'm sorry. I did not mean ...' The embarrassed Richard rose to leave.

He was about to open the door when unexpectedly he heard Jennifer. Strangely, this time her voice was more calm and reassuring.

'Don't go yet, Richard,' pleaded Jennifer. 'I am very sorry about my reaction. I hope you'll forgive me. Please sit down. There is something I want to tell you.'

★   ★   ★

Leuven is really fascinating, Mrs Holohan kept saying to Aisling as they visited various places. Aisling suggested that they see the place on foot; it was the best way to savour the atmosphere since Leuven is a walking-and-viewing kind of town. And to feel the cobblestones, commented Mrs Holohan.

Fortunately, her daughter had advised her to bring a pair of comfortable shoes. Not those fashionable high heels, she was warned. They'll be useless since they would have to do a lot of walking. Given all the warnings she got about shoes when her daughter called her in Barrowtown, Mrs Holohan checked whether she was being invited to an agricultural place. Well, there is a bit of that, explained Aisling, on the outskirts of Leuven. But she would need the comfortable shoes for all that sightseeing that she was going to do. Mrs Holohan was glad she had heeded Aisling's suggestion. Those cobblestones were pretty, but they surely made their hard presence felt.

They spent the morning visiting the churches. Aisling wanted to impress her mother, who was very religious. Mass was part of her daily routine. Here, she was told, she had a choice of several churches. In fact, although nearby Mechelen was really the spiritual centre, Leuven boasted of a lot of Catholic churches.

And the liturgy here was just as varied. If she wanted Gregorian chant, they could go to the eleven o'clock Sunday Mass at St Quinten's Church nearby. Of the original Romanesque church of St Quinten's, only the tower-base remained, while the church was rebuilt in Gothic style in 1450. On the other hand, if her mother wanted a quickie, since Gregorian Masses tended to be rather prolonged, they could go to the five o'clock Sunday afternoon Mass at Sint-Pieters Kerk in the centre of Leuven.

They could also try St Michael's Church in Naamsestraat, a Baroque building designed and built by the Jesuit Willem Hesius between 1650 and 1670. It had a fantastic façade, richly decorated to make an impression on the Catholics who might otherwise be lured by the Reformation. Aisling and Philip had never been inside it since it seemed to be under renovation, but she had seen a priest outside on a Sunday morning greeting people.

The 10.30 liturgy at the American College was in English. Aisling was sure of that! And they serve refreshments afterwards, Philip added. He thought it was rather cool. In the Begijnhof's early-Gothic parish church, the Sint-Jan-de-Doper

Kerk, there was also a community Mass. It was in Dutch, however. Philip added that the priest would tell them to gather around the altar. So there was no point in selecting a seat since you had to give it up anyway. Philip was thinking of how they would choose their seats in Dublin: not too near the door because of the draught or too near the altar. In fact, they always went to the same side of the church.

Or if Mrs Holohan cared for a church that was really going to be in the news, they could go to the church where Damian the Leper was buried. That was St Anthony's Chapel at Pater Damiaanplein, just a few blocks away. In fact, the Pope was going to go there next year when Damian would be canonized. Wouldn't she like that? To be there even before the Pope? And then to recognize it later on TV because surely when they cover the Pope's visit of Leuven, they would show that church. And she could tell her friends, 'I was there!' and give all the details that only a first-hand report could give.

Aisling finished up by saying that they could indeed go 'church-bashing' that morning. Mrs Holohan replied that Aisling was showing off. Did she really visit all those churches or did she read about them? Was she really going to all those Masses in Leuven? Philip jumped to his mother's defence. Oh, yes, they had been to all of them. And he wouldn't tell a fib, would he? He looked to his mother for some expression of appreciation for what he did. He got it as Aisling touched her lips with her finger and then pressed the finger on Philip's lips.

Just to make sure that her mother did not have any doubt, they would visit all those churches. They started with the church in the Begijnhof. Then they went to St Quinten's on Naamsestraat. Mrs Holohan could not make out the seats. They had very high backs and very low seats. Philip demonstrated how they were used. A sure sign that they had been here before, said a relieved Mrs Holohan. Along the way to the Centrum, Aisling pointed out a few colleges belonging to the university of Leuven, Leuven's Catholic University.

'What do you mean, belonging to the Catholic University? Is it not like Trinity or UCD? Is there no main campus?'

'No, Ma. In fact, the Catholic University is comprised of

156

different colleges all over the town. There is even one at Kortrijk several miles away. It is not like Trinity or UCD, where most of the buildings are on the same campus.'

Aisling tried to explain the background and the set-up of the Catholic University. Mercier University made use of some of their facilities but was another university.

Mrs Holohan had interesting comments on the fine buildings that they managed to see. They could not go into the American College chapel because it was not open. But they did visit Sint-Pieter's. After all, it was right in the centre. They went around to admire its rather odd architecture, the different parts having been built at different times. One end resembled Notre Dame of Paris, the clean end. The other end was still black from centuries of soot and grime. They had to enter it from a side entrance. So this is where they have the quickie Mass, Mrs Holohan remarked.

'Have you had enough of churches, Ma?' Aisling asked after they had visited a few of them.

'Say yes, Granny,' whispered Philip, who was not fully enjoying all this going in and out of cold churches.

Mrs Holohan did not let Philip's side down. So she said that it was too much to take in at the one time. Philip blew his granny a flying kiss.

'I'll have to leave the two of you after lunch. Remember I have to go to class?'

For lunch, they would just have a sandwich in the apartment since they were going for an Indonesian meal that evening, a rijsttafel.

'A what? Oh, I don't know about that,' said a dubious Mrs Holohan. 'Can we not just go Chinese? At least you know what you are eating.'

'We'll see. I was hoping you would be more adventurous while you were on the Continent. Let's see, there's Vietnamese, Cambodian, Greek, Turkish, Moroccan – '

'That's enough,' interrupted Mrs Holohan. 'I want to be able to eat my dinner.'

Like her generation of Irish, Mrs Holohan went for good, solid meals, none of these spicy foreign dishes. Her one concession was Chinese. Surprisingly, she really came to like it so much that when they were out, she would ask for it. In fact, she and her friend in Barrowtown would have a Chinese meal regularly. She had also come to enjoy the meals that she had prepared with sauces, the ones that you buy from a supermarket, like sweet and sour. She had also become an expert in barbecued spare ribs. She had been given this secret recipe by an Asian acquaintance. Her friends really loved it and begged her for the recipe. But she would not divulge the ingredients.

After lunch, the three made their way on foot to Donatus park at Vlamingenstraat. Part of the park was actually the outside moat of the town rampart which had been filled in; a few towers in sandstone and iron sandstone had survived. The park, laid out in English landscape style, got its name from the burnt-down St Donatus's college.

Aisling showed her mother the statue of Abraham, seemingly guarding the entrance to the park.

'More religion for you here, Ma,' she said teasingly. 'It'll make you feel at home.' Then she added, 'And oh, by the way, the Vikings were defeated here in Leuven in a great battle in 891! Remember Clontarf?'

Religion and the Vikings – what more could one ask for to link Leuven with Ireland?

Aisling suggested that while she was at class in a nearby building, grandmother and grandson could walk around and see, perhaps even entertain, the animals there. She would be away for only a couple of hours. If the two got bored or cold they could go to a nearby cafeteria, which she pointed out so they would not miss one another.

'Come, Granny, I'll show you the flamingos,' urged Philip after his mother kissed him goodbye.

From where they were standing they could see the animal enclosure in the park. Aisling waited until they reached it before heading in the opposite direction.

The park looked a bit cheerless, the trees bereft of leaves. It would have looked dead except for the fact that it was sunny. There was also some life in the form of pedestrians and visitors like themselves. Not too many at this time of the year. Those walking were moving briskly to keep warm.

'Look, Granny. See, I told you about the flamingos.' Philip was very excited. He liked watching them. 'Do you know how they sleep?'

'Don't tell me. They close their eyes, right?'

Philip laughed heartily. Granny was joking surely. 'They bury their heads. Inside their wings. And they stand on one leg.'

He tried to imitate them. He nearly lost his balance and his grandmother had to spring into action to stop him from falling.

'Well, I'll try again.'

Suddenly, one of the flamingos did oblige them by taking the posture described by its young admirer.

'He heard me,' whispered Philip. 'Now, we'll see.'

The couple of hours passed by very quickly. When Aisling returned, she found grandmother and grandson still poised in front of the railings of the enclosure, almost in the same spot where she last saw them. As she approached them, without their noticing her, she could see that her mother was enjoying Philip's explanation of things. And her mother was genuinely absorbed in what he was demonstrating to her. She wondered what in fact Philip could be saying, in his own way, that would make much sense to her mother.

It is funny, thought Aisling. The first few years of life our parents nurture us and teach us about life. And there is so much we can learn from them. Despite all her academic education, Aisling knew that she had a lot to be grateful to her mother for. It was an education that was shaped in the harshness of life. Not bookish knowledge but maturity that was tested by 'the slings and arrows of outrageous fortune'. It was her mother who taught her about coping with sorrow and loss when Sean died.

And yet, a time comes when the sons and daughters teach their parents about life too. Not based on experience or accumulated wisdom, but enthusiasm and even hope. Sometimes the bliss of ignorance. The joys of risk and

159

adventure. It was Philip who taught her hope. Not in so many words. Not even through example. Just by being there. Just by expecting her to be his mother and all that that word implied.

Philip depended on her. He needed her to carry on, single-handedly if necessary. He required her to face the future. That was a real lesson she learned from the infant child. And she was not expected to forget it even when other demands were made on her. When he was a baby, he would sometimes smile and stretch out his arms and legs. The message was obvious: 'Feed me' or 'Change me' or simply 'Love me'.

Now that he was growing up, there was the added pleasure of communication. Many a time, she laughed at his view on things. At his choice of words. Once when she was delayed picking him up at Granny's, he said to her mother that by the looks of things, he was being left with her. And would that be a problem, Granny? She chuckled since she did not know where he was picking up these phrases.

She admired his innocence. To young Philip life was uncomplicated. As a baby, every time he woke up he did so with a smile and then that characteristic look-around, conveying the idea of 'well, what did I miss while I was asleep?'

Yes, she was learning about life from the six-year-old who was now trying to explain to his granny how the chicken, the flamingos and the pigeons could all live together in the same enclosure.

'There's Ma!' shouted Philip once he caught sight of Aisling. 'Granny and I have been watching the animals.'

He wanted to brief his mother on the afternoon's event once Aisling was within earshot.

'And Philip has been explaining to me what they do. And even showing me how they sleep.' Mrs Holohan winked at her grandson.

There was no need to ask how they had got on. It was obvious that things had gone well. Mrs Holohan adored her grandson and Philip enjoyed her company (and her cooking, since he was fond of her apple tarts, puddings and cakes).

160

'Well, how was your class?' inquired Mrs Holohan.

'OK. I'll have to tell you another time.'

Aisling did not think that Postmodernism and the antics of this American professor would be the most appropriate topic of conversation right now.

'We'll have to get back to the apartment now so we can be ready for dinner. Have you made up your mind where you want to go?'

'Chinese!' said grandmother and grandson in unison.

Aisling wondered at the united response. The two had joined forces.

★　　★　　★

Richard had turned around from the door when Jennifer called to him. He had not really wanted to leave, but he was hurt and bewildered. And he did not want to aggravate matters by continuing to stay. But he could not understand the sudden twist in his relationship with Jennifer. She had seemed angry. Now she was begging him to stay.

His curiosity got the better of him. He did care about Jennifer, but he also craved for an explanation. So he decided to retrace his steps but cautiously chose the armchair a few feet away from where Jennifer was sitting.

Jennifer started, more composed now than a few minutes ago. More like the Jennifer that he had come to know and like.

'I'm sure you're wondering what happened. Believe it or not, I was taken by surprise myself at my rude manners to you. Again I *am* sorry. I think I can explain. I don't mean to justify my action. I know I shouldn't have done it.'

Jennifer was being too apologetic, Richard thought. But he said nothing because he could see that someone like Jennifer needed to come to grips first with their initial shock by repeating their apology. It would have been rude of him to ask her to come to the point immediately.

'I want ... to tell you something that I ... I haven't been able to tell anyone else. It's been ... such a long time.'

The usually articulate Jennifer was groping for words and struggling with her emotions. She was fighting to keep her composure, very much like a teacher who had been shown to be wrong by one of the students.

This time Richard spoke – slowly.

'That's okay, Jennifer. Go ahead if you want to talk about it.'

He tried to be reassuring without making the same mistake of physically reaching out to her.

'Thanks, Richard.'

Jennifer smiled at him, but then averted her eyes. Richard could see that she was hurt and pained.

'Years ago when I was an undergraduate in Oxford, I got to know a fellow student. We were in the same year. He was reading biology while I was reading theology. We loved our studies passionately and we spent a lot of time poring over our books. He used to discuss the latest issues in his field while I would comment on their theological significance. He was a member of the university rowing club. I would accompany him on his practice session. He would talk about their strategy for beating our old rivals, Cambridge. I had become very interested in that sport because of him. He would join me when I attended theology seminars. He was beginning to see that there had been developments in theology that had a relevance to his field.'

Richard could now understand the connection between what Jennifer was saying and her present interest in bio-ethics. He wondered how it had developed. But he did not want to interrupt Jennifer.

'We enjoyed discussing our academic interests. And that brought us quite close to each other. We also shared the same interest in classical music. We went to many concerts and performances. We even talked about going to the Salzburg Festival because of our love of Mozart's music.'

Jennifer's eyes started getting misty. But she was holding back her tears. Richard knew she was gauging his reaction. She reminded him of himself when he was in the classroom, how he would watch his students to see whether their interest was flagging.

162

'It's always great when one shares a common interest, isn't it?' Richard threw in his comment. He was about to ask whether they did manage to get to the Salzburg Festival. But he checked himself. It could be the very incident that would unlock the tears which were being held back.

'Yes, indeed. And we had fantastic plans about the future. I wanted to be an academic, he was going to do research for some medical firm. Both of us got firsts in our degree. So it was expected that we would proceed to work for a postgraduate degree. At some stage we would get married ...'

Jennifer paused. This time her tears refused to be held back.

'I'm sorry, Richard. I am being very emotional,' she said as she dried her eyes with a soft tissue.

'If it will make you feel better, I can lend you an ear.'

Richard pretended to remove his ear and give it to her. It was corny, he knew, but Jennifer managed a weak smile.

'Our plans never materialized. At least, not the ones we had made together. I did go on to get my doctorate. But he ... discovered ... and it was too late to do anything about it ... that he had cancer.'

With that, the tears welled up and then streamed down her cheeks. There was no fighting them back.

'Jennifer, I'm sorry, really sorry.'

Richard felt very helpless. What could he do? What should he do? He could not find the right words of comfort. Damn it, once again he was faced with the problem he had been experiencing.

This time Jennifer made the move towards him, seeking comfort on his shoulders. She sobbed uncontrollably while Richard simply put his arms around her. He could not find words, but at least he could provide his presence. And that seemed to be appreciated and welcomed. For a few minutes no word escaped their lips – just the awareness of each other. The awareness of helplessness and yet the awareness of the comfort of the other.

Then Jennifer continued. She wanted to tell her story. She thought that she owed Richard an explanation. After all, Richard had been a wonderful companion in the little time

163

that they had spent together. She also needed to unburden herself.

'It was our first year of postgraduate study.' Once more, a composed Jennifer. 'He rang me up to say that he'd just received the results of his medical tests. I knew from his voice that something was wrong. So I offered to go up to his flat. He said no, he wanted to be on his own. But I wouldn't budge. I said that we'd been together on many things. We would be on this. So I told him to expect me within ten minutes.

'When he told me, I was stunned. Truly devastated. He was given only four months to live. I couldn't believe it. At such a young age. At such a juncture in our lives. I felt angry, confused, depressed – all at the same time.

'The four months passed very quickly. I was in agony watching him deteriorate. I buried myself in my books. When he died, I refused to talk about it. I put all my energies into my academic work, hoping that it would make me forget about the past. And it did. My dissertation was accepted, I got my title, and my research started to attract attention. I lived for my profession. I wanted to be the best in my field.

'And I thought I had overcome my grief. My loss. I had recovered by hiding behind my books.'

And then Jennifer said something that made Richard sit up, 'Just like that scholar at the Fons Sapientiae.'

'You never told me your friend's name, Jennifer,' Richard cautiously asked.

Jennifer looked at him. A shaft of sunlight found its way to Jennifer's face, highlighting it.

'It was ... Richard.'

It was Richard's turn to be taken aback. What a coincidence! He looked at Jennifer. Hers had been the face and the personality that had given him enthusiasm for academia. Hers was now the face that was human, it was in pain. It had been hiding behind the academic mask. He had admired her social graces and her intelligent conversations. Now he was hearing a different story, so unexpectedly.

Was his own name the connection with Jennifer's interest in him? Had Jennifer shown a liking for him only because of the name? Was he expected to fill Jennifer's friend's shoes? He was not willing to do that. Had he been merely used?

On the other hand, why had Jennifer reacted so strangely when he touched her a while ago? Why this withdrawal from the academic event that mattered a lot to her? Richard's mind was befuddled. He had been allowed into Jennifer's private life – but that was not the full story. At least, as far as he was concerned. He needed to know more. He wanted to be told where he fitted in.

He was hurting a bit, but he did not want to prejudge the situation. His budding friendship with Jennifer mattered to him. He wanted to give it a chance. So putting his feelings aside, he smiled.

'That's an interesting coincidence. On the other hand, it is quite a common name. Still, you probably didn't think you would be meeting someone in Leuven with a name like Richard. Hans, maybe, or Jan or...' Richard was trying to make light of the similarity in names.

'It is more than that, Richard,' confessed Jennifer.

Rather abruptly Jennifer rose.

'Would you like something? I'm going to make some tea. I can make some coffee, too, if you prefer. I know you Americans drink a lot of it.'

'Too much, it seems. And they keep telling us different messages about it. First, they said that coffee is bad for us because of the caffeine. So, the decaffeinated version. Then they said that that's actually worse than the regular one. I don't know what to believe now. I must admit I enjoy my coffee, particularly those blended ones. There's a nice coffee place in Santa Monica, famous for its exotic blends, a few miles from where I live. Needless to say, I frequent it.'

'Unfortunately, I don't have those. Only instant. You see, I don't drink the stuff. Will instant do you this time?'

'I'll have tea with you instead. The way you British have it, with milk. At home I prefer iced tea as it is cooling in warm southern California. Here ...' and, as his gaze shifted toward the outside window of Jennifer's apartment, he could imagine the cold temperature outside, 'I've taken to drinking a lot of hot drinks.'

It was small talk. But it was making them feel more at ease with each other.

Richard, however, kept wondering whether Jennifer would tell him what that 'more' meant. It was very strange how before today they had found their conversation spontaneous; there had been a certain naturalness, even an attraction, between them. It is probably easier to talk when one is not personally involved, he decided. But once Jennifer's personal life entered the arena, there had been some embarrassment. Perhaps it was only on his side, given the kind of person he was. Despite being considered friendly and amicable and easy to talk to, he always was a little uncomfortable when others started unburdening themselves. Nor did he find it easy to share his own feelings with others. So this diversionary talk regarding drink was quite welcome.

And yet he wanted Jennifer to continue. But he would not probe. He would let the initiative come from her. One thing he did want to return was the spontaneity of their conversation.

Jennifer brought the cups and saucers, milk and sugar on a small tray to the sitting room. Richard had offered to help, but she said she could manage. She returned to the kitchen to fetch the teapot while Richard arranged the cups and saucers on the small table in front of them.

While pouring the tea, she commented on the apartments.

'It's convenient to have these furnished apartments, isn't it? It makes one feel a little bit more at home.'

Richard agreed, adding that what he particularly appreciated was being able to watch CNN International and the British channels for the news since unfortunately his knowledge of Dutch was non-existent. The cable system was also truly European since in addition they could get German, Spanish, French channels. He bemoaned his lack of knowledge of languages. He did have some Latin because that was required since his dissertation was on medieval philosophy, but what good was that to him in everyday life?

The heating system was working well, and the comfort of the apartment was some contrast to the cold outside. It made one feel like staying in most of the time these days, Richard remarked, as he waited for Jennifer to resume their previous conversation.

It was her story and there was no point in intruding into her affairs.

Jennifer did want to talk. She needed to talk. To Richard, about Richard. The Richard in front of her. It was now time to face the present.

'It has been a long struggle trying to forget Richard. But I thought I had overcome all that. Until you came along.'

Richard blushed a little. He was not sure about the full significance of that statement.

'As you know, I came to Leuven to work on a joint project and to meet other scholars. When we met at that reception, I was struck by your name. Even then it didn't bring up the past. And so I felt quite comfortable making your acquaintance. I enjoyed our conversations, I liked your company. You brought a certain freshness. And I really appreciated that.'

Jennifer turned her head away a little. She did not want to risk facing Richard directly. Then she spoke softly.

'The last two days I came to realize that you meant much more to me. They have been difficult days. What had happened in the past was once again beginning to happen. Please understand me. I cannot go through that again. It has taken me such a long time to forget Richard. I have been so confused that it has been impossible to concentrate on my research. My energy is gone, my work has suffered. That is why I could not really go to the symposium and do myself justice. Especially since I knew you would be there. And I do not want to be unfair to you.'

Richard swallowed hard. There was that embarrassing silence again. In some ways everything was starting to click. He had felt something for Jennifer, admired her greatly. He liked her company a lot and cared a good deal for her. He even admitted to himself that it would mean something to know how she felt about him. Now he was hearing that she had strong feelings for him too.

This was the first time it was happening to him. Graduate work took so much of his time that he had not really socialized much – he wanted to complete his studies first. Meeting Jennifer, however, was an experience.

'Jennifer,' Richard started, clearing his throat, 'it's hard for me to talk about these matters. I'm so unused to expressing my sentiments. Perhaps we can blame it on all this rationality that I'm supposed to be cultivating as a philosopher.'

He began to fiddle with his watch, loosening it around his wrist.

'It really has been a pleasure getting to know you. You know how I enjoy your company. And I really admire you. You are articulate, scholarly and confident.'

Richard's tone of voice grew softer.

'Please don't blame yourself for your feelings. I appreciate your candor. I feel the same for you – as you must have guessed. I care a lot about you. I suppose these things happen. Perhaps Leuven has this effect on her visiting scholars. It is such a fascinating town.'

Richard made a sweeping gesture with his left arm as if to encompass the whole of Leuven with that movement.

Meanwhile from a short distance away, they could hear church bells ringing.

'I do hope we can continue being friends since I do value your friendship. As I said, I appreciate your frankness. You're not being unfair to me. Perhaps we can continue being *good* friends. I don't know where that will lead us but maybe we can help each other that way.'

Richard then spoke with genuine concern in his voice.

'But you owe it to yourself not to let yourself and Richard down. You are too much of a good scholar to let that happen.'

Richard leaned back on his chair. 'On the other hand, perhaps we academics, at least some of us, including myself,

168

should also learn to face life and not just hide behind our academic pursuits. It would be doing the right thing for the wrong reason. I mean, academic work to cover up.'

He caught himself just then. 'Am I beginning to sound like a teacher conducting a seminar?'

Jennifer laughed. A real heart-warming laughter. It sounded good. She knew exactly what Richard meant.

'Richard, you don't know how much this means to me. I'm glad that we've been able to talk about this. You're right. It'll be difficult and will take time, but I should learn to face life again and not just my books. Or better still, maybe I should put into practice what I've been learning from my books, especially about facing life.'

Richard relaxed a bit. Somehow the embarrassment was gone. But for how long? He had learned something about Jennifer, something that he had not anticipated. But more than that there was something about the present situation that in some way touched upon his own anxieties, yet he was unsure what it was. Whatever it was, however, it had something to do with him and with his stay at Leuven.

How long would it take him to find out? he asked himself, as he and Jennifer talked about other matters while finishing their cup of tea.

*   *   *

Mrs Holohan was worried that her visit was taking Philip away from his school exercises. Since Philip loved doing his schoolwork, she thought this would be unfair.

On the other hand, she was not at all too concerned about Aisling having to take time off from her books. 'It'll do you a lot of good,' she promised Aisling, 'to take your beloved mother around and for once not to be buried in all this research. What's this you are doing anyway? Post ... Postmod? Postmodernism?' The only post Aisling should be worried about was what the postman brought (or in her case, what the postman did not bring, meaning her widow's pension). God knows, she added, going off on a tangent, widows were getting only a pittance. And the government was so niggardly about it, their increases were so minimal that it wasn't worth talking about (and yet it was a hot topic and the only one that had occupied their undivided attention for three hours at their recent widows' association meeting!).

At the mention of government, Aisling couldn't resist asking which government wasn't in her mother's favour. Mrs Holohan, like so many of her friends, was a strong Fianna Fáil supporter.

'Oh, they're all the same,' she replied vociferously. 'Once they're in government, they forget us poor widows.'

To which Aisling answered that it was not at all like her mother to criticize the political party of her parents and grandparents.

'Well, what about you, eh? What party do you support?'

'Sometimes Fine Gael, sometimes Fianna Fáil, at other times Labour. At the moment, I am leaning towards ... Sinn Féin.' Aisling was waiting for her mother's reaction. Sure enough, it came.

'What?' Mrs Holohan did not put a tooth in it. 'Didn't I teach you right from wrong? Where's your loyalty? What's got into you?' Mrs Holohan was concerned about where she had gone amiss in educating her daughter.

'Come on, Ma, I'm just pulling your leg. Of course, I always vote for the right person.'

'And who would that be, tell me?'

'Whoever is the right candidate come election time, of course.'

Mrs Holohan shook her head. This young generation did not seem to appreciate party loyalty. Not like her generation. Her people always voted Fianna Fáil. Now that is the only party that can form a real government, she said proudly. All the others have to depend on a coalition.

'Enough of this politics. We have a lot to do today,' said Aisling, trying to bring the brewing debate to a close . . . .

Politics and religion were two topics that elicited much comment from her mother. She and her sister used to dig up one of these two topics at home every time they thought their mother got too interested in what they were up to. In fact,

170

when they were teenagers, they cunningly planned strategies on how to divert their mother's attention whenever they came home after a date.

Once they teamed up when her sister came home late from a date.

'Do you know whom I met tonight?' her sister announced almost as soon as she got in. 'Father Buckley and ...!' There was a glint in her eyes.

Their mother guessed what was coming next. 'Don't you be spying on priests, I'm telling you,' she warned them. 'And don't be spreading scandal,' she immediately added.

At this point Aisling jumped to her sister's defence. 'But that's true,' Aisling swore, 'I've seen them together. When was it again?'

She was finding it difficult to remember, so her sister prompted her. 'Last Wednesday, you were telling me, remember?' Sisterly love would not let the other one down.

'That's right.'

'You know, what I heard tonight was that Father Buckley is really on the way out. He's just waiting for his mother to die before he leaves the priesthood. He doesn't want to break his mother's heart by going just now. So what do you think of that?' She nudged Aisling as if to continue.

Her sister was fond of embellishing a story. She was not sure she herself liked the direction their 'legitimate' excuse was taking. Sometimes her sister went that little bit too far. Fortunately, she did not have to continue rescuing her sister since Mrs Holohan swiftly gave them a good lecture on respect for the clergy, God's representatives here on earth.

The lateness of the hour was soon forgotten, including her sister's return from her date. Since she and her sister shared a room, Aisling knew she did not have to inquire how the date went. Her sister would volunteer that information and would keep her up half the night anyway.

Aisling smiled as she recalled those years. They were fun. And she admired her mother's courage and determination. When they were younger, they always thought they got the better of their mother in incidents like that one. Little did they know that their mother saw through them but let them have their way so long as they came to no harm. 'Didn't I raise two fine girls?' she said to them several times. It was their mother's way of expressing her satisfaction at 'the way they turned out'. She was very proud of them and derived a lot of pleasure from learning about their achievements, even when she did not always understand what it was 'these lassies were going on about'. Aisling and her sister went to university while their mother did not. She belonged to the generation which understood that a mother's place was in the home. She was proud of her role; she wanted to be a mother – and she was a good mother.

It must have been challenging for their mother, Aisling thought. Their father died when they were just teenagers. Luckily he had had the foresight to join the new pension plan introduced into the firm where he worked. So at least that helped them financially. But bringing up two young girls in a fast-changing Ireland must have been tough. Not just emotionally as their mother had to cope with her husband's loss. Nor physically as she tried to keep house, teenagers and herself together ('sometimes it would take a saint to keep ye on the straight and narrow path,' she would teasingly remind her teenage girls). But more importantly, Aisling wondered, how have the changing attitudes in Ireland affected her mother?

It must really be confusing for her mother's generation when suddenly, after years of being taught one way, your daughters would come back from university with very different ideas. Strange ideas, it must have seemed. Even challenging ones that required infinite patience on the part of the older generation so used to doing things and believing in a certain way. Patience that stopped them from simply telling the young ones that they were undoubtedly wrong. The young, on the other hand, did not always have that patience with their elders. And Aisling knew. She was one of those young ones, and as a university student she often impatiently cried out that Ireland needed to come out of the Middle Ages. That unless attitudes changed, there would be no development in her beloved country. And she meant more than just all the debate about artificial contraception that raged in conservative Ireland. At that time one politician even said that all the blame could be put on television, namely the newly established RTE. He claimed that before television 'there was no sex in Ireland'. Now it was going on all the time! No, Aisling meant more than that. Attitudes die hard and it would be a struggle to change attitudes.

At that time, she was out to change attitudes in Ireland. But now she was beginning to care about how the older generation was being affected. My God, she thought to herself, am I getting old? Why am I taking their side?

She glanced at young Philip dressing himself. No, I'm not old ... yet. But here is another generation. And it's a generation in Ireland that is fast becoming truly European. How will my generation cope with that? She consoled herself, well, at least she was making a headstart by being here in Leuven. She was experiencing the life of a Continental European ...

'Don't worry about Philip, Ma,' she replied to her mother's concern about taking Philip away from his school exercises. 'Being here and seeing all these places is a wonderful opportunity. It'll be good for his education. After all, he's now a European.'

With that assurance from Aisling, Mrs Holohan rose and asked, 'Well, what are we waiting for? I'm ready to hit ... what was that foreign-sounding name again?'

'Bruges, Granny!' volunteered Philip.

'Yeah, that one,' she said.

VI

Richard could not keep Jennifer out of his mind. So much had happened in so short a time. And she was occupying his thoughts in a very different way. Not Jennifer the person. Instead it was what she meant to him now that she had unexpectedly revealed her feelings for him. So unusual too, he thought. Still, he felt wonderful being told about how strongly someone felt for him, and this was certainly doing a lot for his ego.

Maybe he was reading too much into this. Perhaps he was really flattering himself. After all, he could not ignore the possibility that Jennifer felt this way for him only because he had reawakened her dormant feelings for Richard, the other Richard. What was he to do now? He had felt something for Jennifer. Definitely. But what kind of feelings were those? Strange how when someone is confronted by someone else's plight, one is inevitably drawn towards one's own. Does one see a reflection of oneself in others?

But what was it about himself that he was seeing in Jennifer? He was attracted to her – he had already admitted that. He also admired her. He had envied her passion for her work. It was becoming more obvious to him that there was a huge difference between the two of them. She was quite accomplished, whereas he still had a long climb up the academic ladder. In fact, he had been finding it difficult to continue with his research.

Right now he could not even concentrate. He had wanted to do some writing this morning in his apartment. But an hour later the blank page in front of him was still staring at him. Contrary to what he had expected, his stay in Leuven was not giving him the kind of inspiration he had wished for.

He did not want to blame the place, just the turn of events and the circumstances, including his own questioning mind. And there was something about yesterday's conversation with Jennifer that bugged him.

Instead of forcing himself to write, he decided to go for a walk. It was a mild day, inviting him to see what nature had to offer to him in Leuven. So he put on his coat, looked for his scarf but changed his mind. He did not think he would need his scarf today. He had become attached to it, and had used it all the time ever since he first set foot in Leuven. But today looked different. It was not spring yet, but there was a rise in the temperature as if an early indication of things to come.

This time he thought he would go in the direction of the Spanish quarter of the Begijnhof instead of heading for the Centrum. Then maybe from there he would ... why make any plans? He would just go where his legs would take him, so to speak. After all he was out for a stroll. And there should be some unpredictability about it, he reasoned.

As he stepped out, Richard realized how much he liked the Groot Begijnhof, which had been restored by the university of Leuven in 1962, since it had largely retained its seventeenth-century look. He could feel its history as the surroundings embraced him.

This Begijnhof was founded in the thirteenth century outside the city walls of the time. The oldest houses dated from the sixteenth century, when the original houses were replaced by brick structures. He had been informed that the houses, with their typical arched doorways leading onto narrow cobbled streets, were generally named after a saint or a Biblical event. In the seventeenth century approximately 300 Begijns lived here. In fact, there were more if one included the mothers, aunts and nieces who lived with them. Many of the Begijns looked after foster children, whom they taught to read, write and sew.

Richard had read that the Begijns or Beguines were women who lived a religious life but did not make perpetual vows. Moreover, they kept their property and supported themselves.

The beguine movement, very strong throughout the Low Countries, was based on the old values of purity and sobriety. In the Middle Ages because many men had died in the crusades or other military adventures, several women were left only with the choice between the religious life or marriage beneath their station. Since they did not want to follow a strict religious regime, they opted to devote themselves to God but without completely surrendering their freedom. So no convent walls shut them out from the world and no eternal vows bound them. They were certainly not nuns. But they were more than just laity. There was something about their independence that made them objects of suspicion to a male-dominated Church. They were suspected of heresy even after they had been accepted by Pope Honorius III in 1216. Was this a triumph of women's emancipation? Richard had heard that the Beguine movement was highly regarded by today's feminist theologians.

Richard had reached the Spanish quarter when he heard a voice call out to him: 'Good morning, Dr. Gutierrez. Do you remember me?'

'Well, of course, Professor Malachowski. It's great to see you again. Do you have your accommodation around here?'

'Yes, the university got us one of those fabulous houses right here in the Begijnhof.' His house was in Middenstraat, timber-framed and with clay walls. 'And you?'

'I'm staying in one of the apartments in the building beside Schappenstraat.'

Richard's apartment was near the gatehouse which the French Republic had demolished in 1798 so as to connect the beguinage with the town. Only the frame of the gate remained.

'Isn't this a magnificent location? So peaceful. It certainly encourages one to be reflective, doesn't it? When I go for a walk inside the compound, I try to imagine what it was like for the Beguines to live here. They must have spent a lot of their time in quiet meditation. This place seems to have been built for that purpose. But tell me, are you going anywhere in particular?'

'Not really, I wanted to clear my mind. I thought the air would help. I was trying to do some writing on my manuscript, but I'm afraid that nothing would come. I've made no progress since our last conversation.'

'Well, why don't you join me then? I'm out for some exercise. A habit, and a good one at that, which I formed when I was in America a few years ago. Why don't you take up where we left off the last time?'

Richard hesitated. He had not come out for an academic seminar. In fact, it was the last thing he had intended. Anyway, he was more concerned about what was happening to him personally than he was with his research.

But his respect for the professor got the better of him. He did want to talk to him again about his manuscript, but at some future day when he was more prepared. This was like being put on the spot and being asked to don his academic hat. But he had been asked, so he may as well talk about it. This time he did not rehash his difficulty about finishing his manuscript on the problem of evil. Instead, without his knowing it, he found himself telling the professor what happened that evening after the social when he went for a late night/early morning stroll to the center of Leuven. He repeated to this learned man the questions which buzzed in his mind about academic life.

'You know, Richard – shall I call you that? – it seems that you're grappling with a much wider problem about what we academics do. To outsiders, our job is teaching, and that's easy enough to understand since they can see us inside the classroom in front of our students. Others will probably accept that we also engage in research, although that is less tangible.'

The professor smiled knowingly as they turned around since they had come to a dead end.

'I'm sure you will have met people who are really bothered about what all this research means since until there is some published work there doesn't seem to be much evidence. Particularly in philosophy. Even some administrators don't see that. They always want the finished product, so to speak.'

This time it was Richard's turn to smile, nervously, as his Dean's words reverberated in his mind.

'And then there are the cynics. Confronted with the published work, they appear shocked. Astonished.' And Professor Malachowski became rather dramatic. 'You mean after all that time, money and effort, *this* is the result? they utter in dismay. Like the conclusion that reason is so limited that we could not possibly describe reality in its entirety. I remember talking to somebody in America who said that he could have told me that for nothing! Needless to say, he was the kind of gentleman who was results-oriented, as you put it over there. But what's it really that we do as academics? Academia is not just a profession. It is a way of life, but what is it really? Is that the real question you're asking, Richard?'

The Polish professor and Richard had been treading the cobbled walks of the Spanish quarter. Richard couldn't help feeling that it was very much like the Lyceum of Aristotle. The Peripatos and all that. It was as if the professor were Aristotle and he one of the students walking around the Lyceum, debating, questioning, criticizing, in search of the truth. It was Greek philosophy being relived or maybe restaged. Just as well they were not moving in a circle. That would have been too much for the professor's results-oriented acquaintance. It would have invited the comment that that was what philosophers did – talk in circles. Their dialogues never came to any hard conclusions.

'Part of it, I think, Professor. In some ways I wish I really knew. Somehow it has something to do with not losing touch with concrete life.' Richard noticed that the professor did not suggest that he call him by his first name. The hierarchy was clearly established. Was that the case in ancient Athens?

'I remember from our previous conversation about your difficulty. Despite all the research and the writing that you had done on your topic, you always felt that you have no convincing answers to give when faced by the reality of evil. Is that right?'

'Correct.'

'Now you seem to be saying that academic life, particularly

the scholarly part of it, is moving you away from what you regard as concrete life to something that is of importance only to a few. Do you believe that we've lost the true purpose of the academic task? You know, when you made the distinction between wisdom and knowledge.'

'Do you think that there is some truth in that, Professor?'

A good strategy. When a philosopher asks you a question, ask another one. That shifts the burden. He never liked it though when he was asking the question and a student would retort by putting up another question. It always sounded as if the student was biding for time. A cheap shot, but sometimes it worked.

The professor welcomed the question. In fact, it led him to a pet topic of his.

'Definitely. In his *Adventures of Ideas* Alfred North Whitehead makes that very same point. He makes a distinction between speculation and scholarship.'

Richard smiled as he recalled the professor having referred to it before.

Professor Malachowski continued. 'Speculation, he says, is what makes you wonder at the world around you. It's characterized by delight and enthusiasm for the concreteness of life. Scholarship on the other hand demands concentration. Scholarly work requires us to be thorough, to be exact as to what's correct and what's not correct, to be consistent. Whitehead claims that Plato speculated. He had great insights into reality but he was not a systematizer. There is a passage in that book which says that if one converted Plato into a respectable professor by providing him with a coherent system, he would find that Plato is most inconsistent. I'm paraphrasing, of course. For progress, we need both, Whitehead tells us.'

'Would Whitehead say that the pursuit of wisdom is what speculation is all about while the acquisition of knowledge is what scholarship is all about?'

'I suppose he would.'

'Why do we need both?'

'Because we need to develop our insights, to strengthen

179

them. But we also need to keep our feet on the ground. Otherwise we could be talking about theories that have no bearing on concrete life – there's that phrase again.'

'I'm beginning to think, Professor, that I'm not ready for the second part. I don't want to lose the first.'

Richard was not expecting the professor's answer.

'On the contrary, Richard, perhaps you have gone beyond that distinction. Without knowing it, you may have understood what Whitehead really meant.'

The professor and Richard continued with their conversation as they walked further in the direction of the sports grounds of the university of Leuven. They walked past the Faculty Club, previously the infirmary of the Begijnhof but now a splendid restaurant where people dined in style, and past the Begijnhof Congreshotel. They went through the tunnel under busy Tervuursevest, a refuge from the danger and roar of the traffic.

After a few minutes they found themselves in the well-used sports grounds. The huge building to their right had a large swimming pool and an indoor basketball court. To their left was a cafeteria which served not only the sports enthusiasts but the general public as well. There was something about the clientele which showed that somehow they were all connected with university life. But as they both concluded, it would be hard to find someone in Leuven who had nothing to do directly or indirectly with the academic institutions here.

As they drew close to the running fields, they passed by the tennis courts. There was only one brave twosome playing tennis. On the other hand, there were a good few individuals running around the tracks, all trying to keep fit. It probably was early in the season for serious training.

Their conversation surprisingly turned to Chicago. It must have been the previous cold weather, although as Professor Malachowski pointed out that was nothing compared to what he had experienced in that large American city. He felt very much at home there because it was as cold as Poland in the winter! Richard had studied there so he knew what the professor meant. They talked about the beautiful walk along

Lake Shore, commented on the performance of the Cubs, described the impressive downtown with the world's tallest building and reminisced about events in Chicago. It was a relaxing conversation as they exchanged experiences.

On the way back, they decided to look inside the gymnasium. There was a basketball game going on. The teams were not professional ones, but it was still an exciting game. There was a lot of cheering as the two teams tried to outdo each other. But there was also a lot of friendly rivalry. Richard was enjoying himself, possibly because there was a lot of spontaneity in the game. The teams were under no pressure to excel, they were playing for fun. And he and the professor shared in that pleasure.

Richard couldn't help comparing it to the basketball games he used to watch back home. The statistics were blinding as figures were presented on what the average scoring was for each player, the number of rebounds, assists, etc. Even an enjoyable game had become a science. The spontaneity was lost in the quest for excellence. Do we always have to be the best? he wondered. But best at what? He was reminded of what the professor had told him about Whitehead's distinction between speculation and scholarship. Even in sports, the need for development, refinement and perfection robbed the occasion of pleasure. The spirit of competitiveness took over.

As Richard continued with his musings, uninterrupted by the professor, who was thoroughly enjoying the game, it dawned on him what Jennifer meant to him. She represented a side of academia that he was now questioning. She was constantly striving for excellence. And she was succeeding. Her scholarly reputation was certainly growing and met with a lot of admiration, including Richard's. But her devotion to such excellence had ignored life itself: the challenges, the simple joys, the ordinary results. Her life was too focused on one aspect. And now it was starting to shatter.

No, Richard was looking for more. He wanted to be able to face life itself. And life itself was not always demanding of a particular kind of excellence. Jennifer's kind of inspiration was not what he was looking for.

Back in his apartment Richard pondered on his leisurely walk with the professor from Poland. It had turned out to be somewhat of an eye-opener although the professor probably had not intended it to be. He had merely introduced the topic of Richard's research as a way of sparking off the conversation. He wanted to continue where they had left off. After all, it was very natural for two academics to discuss their scholarly work, particularly in this case since they were interested in the same area. They were even working on the same problem but from different perspectives. But their exchange led them to talk about life itself. The professor unsuspectingly left the door ajar for Richard to explore the topic himself. In the professor there was no gap between life and his academic pursuits. He naturally went from one to the other.

But what really made the conversation with Dr. Malachowski of particular significance for Richard was his discovery of what had led the professor to study the problem of evil in depth. It was not merely scholarly interest. Nor did he, unlike Richard, stumble into the topic as it were. No. Dr. Malachowski had an intriguing story to tell.

The Polish professor was the son of two victims of the concentration camp in Majdanek in Poland. His story moved and probed Richard's mind as the professor narrated how he had had to struggle to survive after his parents died in that camp. But it was the professor's reason for turning to philosophy that goaded Richard even more. Having survived such a tragedy and grown up with that painful memory, Dr. Malachowski had searched for answers to the question of why such an evil situation could possibly exist. It was so atrocious that it baffled any rational explanation. The professor needed to find some answers; he was not merely juggling intellectual puzzles. His academic pursuit was rooted in existential concerns.

What was also interesting was that, despite offers to more prestigious positions in other universities, Professor Malachowski chose to stay in Lublin. His reason was that he wanted to be as close as possible to the source of his philosophizing. He regularly visited the Majdanek camp, which was only a few miles from his university. For him that was *the situation* that spurred on his philosophizing. It was the *font* which fed his craving for answers.

The professor had made a passing reference to the Fons Sapientiae in the center of Leuven. Funny, how that landmark symbolized so many things and communicated various messages to the visiting academics. Dr. Malachowski had remarked that the statue partially represented his own journey. Where the scholar was reading a book, possibly for answers, he was turning to intellectual activity for answers. But unlike the scholar who was pouring water from the outside, he was very much immersed in the problem from within.

His search for answers came from a personal experience of a bitter kind of existence. That was why the Majdanek camp was more than a symbol, it was reality. The ashes which he regularly saw were those of his parents and of thousands of others. It was not like the water in the Fons Sapientiae, which symbolized knowledge. Truth stared him in the face as he meditated on the events which led to the death of his parents. As he wandered about the camp, a routine that he religiously followed, looking in distress at the piles of shoes of the former inmates, as he dodged the wire fence that had trapped his parents and several others in a pitiful existence, as he imagined the bitterness and the frustration that reduced humans to mere skeletons, he often asked why, why did such evil things happen? Why was suffering perpetuated by evil people?

Amidst all this, the professor had sensed an abiding faith even among those who suffered intensely. While others felt, and felt strongly that God had abandoned them, there were many others who persisted in their religious faith. Perhaps they needed to cling to something. One had to have some hope; otherwise one was lost completely. In the sea of fear, of shadows, and misery, one had to have a plank. No matter what. For if not, one would sink to the bottom. Faith in God was one such plank. But what Dr. Malachowski could not understand was why they would cling to God. Were those who rejected God not right in abandoning God? After all, that was what this so-called all-good and almighty God had done.

One with inferior qualities would not allow that to happen. So why were they turning to God? Why had his parents persisted in praying to God?

He toyed with a psychological answer. Maybe it could all be described and explained by psychology. He did not doubt that, since all human reactions can somehow be explained. But there was something more. He turned to religion, starting with the Book of Job. The character Job was wrestling with the same problem. Job dismissed many of the answers his tradition had to offer him. Dr. Malachowski found that book sharpening the question he was asking: who is this God that a suffering people are dealing with? Job supplied an answer: a mysterious God whose ways are not our ways.

But Dr. Malachowski asked for more. Surely more could be said about this God. It did not make sense to be endowed with an intellect and to be left wandering about in murkiness when it came to this crucial question. That was when he turned to philosophy. Not because he was confident he would get an answer, but because philosophy, at least the philosophers he had come to know, challenged him to dig deeper.

But philosophy let him down. He read Augustine, Aquinas, von Hügel voraciously. In the professor's view they presented a God that was causing all the problems he was having. A God who should have been able to do something about the situation because this God had all the power. A God who should have cared about what was going on because this God was all-benevolent. It did not match. Such a God needed to be defended against the charge of atheists. But he did not believe such a God should be defended. So Dr. Malachowski abandoned the task of looking for a defense of God. A God who had to be defended in the face of suffering must not be a caring God. Why should he care about such a God? The answer presented by the philosophers he read seemed irrelevant in the face of his experience of suffering – of his parents' and countless others' tragic lives.

That was why he listened to and was very sympathetic to Richard. This young philosopher sensed what he had long been searching for. He wished he could offer a convincing answer. But that was why he was in Leuven. He would not allow philosophy to let him down. Maybe there was another kind of philosophy, born out of concrete experiences like his. He had met one of the professors from Mercier University when he gave a talk at his university in Lublin. This professor, a specialist in process philosophy, invited him over to Leuven so that he could study the philosophy of Whitehead. Dr. Malachowski was not optimistic. But he was willing to give it a try. After all, it would give him a chance to follow up on his personal–academic pursuit.

And that was what really impressed Richard. Academic work should not be an escape route as had been the case with Jennifer, he thought. It is not merely a profession which one could put aside after a day's work. As Dr. Malachowski put it, it *is* a way of life. Or it should be. Not in the sense that there is nothing else that one does, but talk and write as a scholar. That would be obnoxious. But one's academic work should come from one's experiences.

That was what was missing in his own research work. It was meant to be scholarly – but should it be divorced from daily life? That was the big difference between Dr. Malachowski's work and his, although both of them were working on the same topic. On the other hand, perhaps his peers would dismiss Dr. Malachowski's work as not scholarly enough. Richard doubted whether it would bother the senior professor, who had after all already established himself in the field of the philosophy of religion. For him the present work was a culmination of his search for truth, probably a different kind of *opus magnum* that he would be more proud of.

But could he, Richard, an untenured assistant professor, afford to change his approach to his research? And yet could he afford to be dishonest with himself since he really was bogged down with the so-called academic research that he was doing? He knew that he had to prove his scholarship. What should he do?

★　　★　　★

185

The day in Bruges was pronounced a huge success by Mrs Holohan as she settled herself in the comfortable seat on their return train journey. She was beginning to enjoy the idea of hopping in and out of trains. A far cry, she said, from the service operated by Iarnród Éireann. You could thank your lucky stars if the train left only five minutes late, assuming there was a train. Aisling insisted that it was not that bad. 'No,' countered Mrs Holohan, 'not if you don't have to take a train.' She did concede that it was great to have free travel in Ireland, even if it meant tolerating sometimes the kind of service that the Belgians would be up in arms about. Grudgingly, she admitted that there had been improvements in the Irish service.

'So you'd an enjoyable day, Ma.' Aisling wanted to divert her mother's interest from the trains to the day itself.

'Definitely.'

'And what did you like best about Bruges?'

'The church!' prompted young Philip, who knew of his grandmother's affair with those, as he put it, 'huge buildings that were sometimes dark and scary and had candles all over the place.'

'Yes, that was something. Imagine it had a relic of the Precious Blood. Tell me this, Aisling, and tell me no more – you with all this learning. Is it really true that that church has the blood of our Saviour?'

Mrs Holohan was referring to the Basilica of the Holy Blood and was really in awe over the Relic of the Holy Blood which is alleged to have been kept there since the twelfth century.

'Well, that's what they claim. It says here on the guide.'

'Don't mind the half of it. Is it really true?'

'How would I know, Ma? It says here that the procession of the Holy Blood is the major traditional religious event in Bruges. Let me read it to you. "The shrine containing the Holy Blood, which was brought back from the Second Crusade by Thierry d'Alsace in 1150 is carried in a solemn procession re-enacting the principal scenes from the Old and New Testaments."' Aisling was waiting for Philip to ask her

186

what that meant. But he said nothing so she continued. ' "It takes place at three o'clock in the afternoon on Ascension Day every year." Thousands come to that. So there must be some truth to it.'

'Imagine that, all that religion. That reminds me. Did I tell you about Sister Patricia Josephine's book? She had this book signing at the bookstore. It was in the local paper. Signs all over the place. To let people know, like.'

Unexpectedly she started to laugh.

'Trouble was, they got to know about it and the bookstore lost business that day!' she continued.

'What do you mean? A book signing is supposed to bring in business for the bookstore, Ma.'

'Ah, but not in this case. People passed by, all right, and looked in but would not go in.'

'That's not very funny. And why not?'

'They were afraid that they would be cornered. She would talk the hind legs off a dog, you know! They would not be able then to do their shopping or nip over to the pub!'

'Ma, I'm surprised at the whole lot of you. Poor Sister. And she taught me, you know. I think I'll buy her book, just for that.'

'Go ahead, and waste your money, alanna. Even Mrs Donnelly would not do that. And she's very religious, you know. Goes to Mass every day and receives communion. Confession every Saturday night, keeping Father Healey awake in the confessional box. For God's sake, that woman has no sins to tell.'

Aisling had to grin. She did remember Mrs Donnelly since her mother had previously described her as the one who would not receive from the lay ministers. She would rather 'step over the legs to cross over to the other side where the priest was distributing communion'.

'Well, what did you like about Bruges, Philip?' Mrs Holohan turned to her grandson to see what had captivated him.

'The canals! I *loved* the trip we took. I wanted to put my hand in the water, but Ma would not let me.'

Bruges is indeed one of Europe's loveliest cities, best experienced on foot and on the canal. In the Middle Ages, Bruges was an international port linked to the sea by the Zwin. Aisling was grateful that on this second visit the season had started. Otherwise, Philip would have been disappointed again. The first time they came here, which was late February, there were no canal cruises. Philip had looked longingly at all the boats just swaying idly in the water.

The three of them had visited the Beguinage that had been founded in 1245. It was quite different from the one in Leuven. Here tiny white houses surround a graceful lawn with tall trees and with yellow daffodils just popping out of the ground as if heralding the arrival of spring. The premises were now occupied by Benedictine nuns whose vestments dated back to the original fifteenth-century design. To Mrs Holohan's disappointment they were not allowed to visit the nuns.

From there they had gone to the Canal of Love, since Philip had expressed a wish to see the swans and the ducks again. It was also a famous beauty spot that Aisling wanted to show her mother.

But Mrs Holohan was very much more taken up with the nearby shops which displayed the lace industry in Bruges, renowned throughout the world for its bobbin lace. The craft developed from the habit of Bruges women of hemming their clothes with lace so as to protect them from wear. Years ago a young student who had visited this place had brought Mrs Holohan a piece of such lace. She found it so artistic that she framed it. Now she was able to watch how it was done. In fact, it was a real task to drag her out of the shops which sold the products of the laceworkers. Full of admiration, she had bought an expensive piece which she intended to frame and hang in her sitting room so that she would always be reminded of her trip here. She also bought a few small ones to distribute to her friends – so that they would believe her that she had indeed been in this wonderful place. She would extol its beauty and charm at the widows' meeting. Maybe, just maybe, the executive members would decide that it was about time that the widows became more adventurous and not limit their annual outings to St Anne's Park in Raheny or to resorts in Wexford – or to Dun Laoghaire or Arklow, added Aisling for good measure. They should look farther. After all, they were now Europeans. Bruges would be a delightful place for her crowd.

Bruges indeed had both the charm of a medieval place, with its old but well-preserved buildings, nooks and narrow streets, and the attractions of modern shops – for those uppity ones, among her crowd, declared Mrs Holohan. In fact, Mrs Holohan was sure that shopping in Bruges would also be a pulling point.

She was worried though about old Mrs Reilly. How would she manage with her walking stick, hobbling about the place? She could go on the canal cruise, volunteered Philip, and then she could go on the horse-drawn carriage. Philip was not going to let that slip through. He had suggested taking it but his suggestion had not been taken up. Oh, well, he could try again.

'Philip, you *are* a genius, did you know that?' said Mrs Holohan to the beaming six-year-old. 'Of course, we can take care of Mrs Reilly that way.'

They had spent a couple of hours around the Markt. After all, that seems to be the focal point of any Belgian city or town and where all the activities and notable buildings are concentrated. They marvelled at the thirteenth-century halls to the south of the Markt. They looked up for a long time at the belfry, dominating the place and made famous by its octagonal tower, 83 metres high, with a magnificent carillon. Mrs Holohan had refused the invitation to go to the top for a breathtaking view of the city and the surrounding region. Close to it is the town hall, which goes back to 1376 and is the oldest commemorative town hall in Belgium. Like the town hall of Leuven, its façade is adorned with statues and bas-reliefs depicting Biblical and historical scenes.

And they did go in that horse-drawn carriage since, according to Philip, Granny would have to know what it was like so she could tell Mrs Reilly about it. The tactics of this cute lad.

189

The train journey home seemed short. They almost missed the station in Leuven because they were so engrossed in their conversation and in recalling the day's events in Bruges. It was only when Philip recognized the same family who had joined the train in Leuven and who were now getting off that it dawned on Aisling that they too should be getting off. They were up like a shot. Mrs Holohan said that she did not want to be left behind in case this train was going to some foreign place. There was no danger of that, however, since all they had to do was to grab their few parcels and step off the train. Nor was there any need to walk up the train carriages, unlike getting off in Barrowtown, where the train driver tells them to do so 'so that they would be aligned with the platform'!

★　　★　　★

Mrs Holohan's week-long visit passed by very quickly. It had been a fabulous trip, she said, but she would need another holiday to recover from it. Not only did she manage to see Leuven, Brussels, Bruges, but she was even taken to Antwerp since her daughter informed her that it was the European cultural capital that year. A lot of things would be going on there and they could see all the preparations being made. Aisling had also insisted on taking her to Mechelen, a short train journey from Leuven, since for centuries it was the religious centre of Belgium and the residence of the primate of Belgium. Besides, the town was world-famous for its carillon bells. Bell-ringers practically everywhere in the world had received their training at Mechelen. Maybe including the bell-ringers at St Patrick's Cathedral in Dublin. When Aisling caught herself sounding out Edgar Allan Poe's *The Bells*, her mother and son joined in unison, she's off again!

Aisling had planned to take her to Paris, but Mrs Holohan decided to draw the line. 'After all, I'm no longer a spring chicken. And you know what they say, once I see Paris no one can hold me down on the farm.' This remark made Aisling laugh. Poor Philip did not understand. He could not see the connection, especially since his granny did not have a

190

farm. Maybe another time, promised Mrs Holohan. That gave Aisling hope. Maybe her mother had been bitten by the travel bug. Perhaps she'd give up all this talk about her pushing up the daisies soon. She was grateful that her mother was in good health – never had to go to hospital, very active in the community and the church. This European trip would give her even more zest. Indeed, maybe the next time, Paris, Amsterdam, Rome – who knows, maybe there would be no holding her back.

It would be nice if her mother got the opportunities for travel that she herself was enjoying. To some extent her generation was luckier. And they owed much of that to the previous generations of Irish people who worked hard to make sure her generation and the next would have ample opportunity to live a fuller kind of existence.

★   ★   ★

As Richard rounded the corner into Naamsestraat on his way to his apartment at the Begijnhof, he bumped into a rather distressed Dr. Anton Brown.

'Hi, Anton. What's up?'

'A lot of trouble, that's what all this tenure business is all about,' replied Dr. Brown, with obvious anger.

Richard seized up. Oh, no. His own situation loomed large again. 'But I thought you had tenure. You're the Chair of your department, so what's the problem?'

'Come on, let's have something to drink. I need to cool off anyway.'

Anton and Richard then retreated to a nearby bar for some beer. Evidently, Dr. Anton had received a communication from his President alerting him to a possible lawsuit regarding the denial of tenure to a member of his department. Unfortunately, he was implicated. Yet it was not a case where a faculty who had been denied tenure would sue the department and the university. That he could handle, he said, because there would be a 'paper trail', such was the necessity of providing solid evidence against someone whose application for tenure had been denied. So as Chair he was not being asked to defend the negative decision. Rather, he was 'being sucked into the whole damn thing,' as he put it.

Richard failed to understand the situation. 'In what way? Anyway, aren't you protected by tenure?'

'That's what one expects. But what's stupid about this case is that my tenure – you know, what's supposed to protect me – is what is being contested!'

'That's ridiculous,' protested Richard as he thought of his own plight.

Anton then explained that the colleague who was suing the university was comparing her own case with Anton, who had received tenure the year before, and was claiming that her academic record was equal to, if not better than, Anton's but that she had been denied tenure because she was a woman. This meant that Anton would be in the spotlight as the court examined the two cases. It would investigate the quality and number of his publications, his standing among his peers, his record of successful grant applications and so on.

'They'll be raking over the whole thing. For what? Because I got tenure – isn't that rather stupid?'

Richard could not believe his ears. Tenure was becoming a messy business, even when one got it.

And yet, mulling over Dr. Anton Brown's predicament, Richard surprisingly felt a surge of hope. While proceeding towards his apartment, he realized that perhaps all might not be lost in his case. Fine, his scholarly work may not be up to par – given the present expectations of his university. But his teaching was above average, at least as far as the student evaluations were concerned. And Anton's situation reminded him of at least two colleagues in the university who did get tenure based on their commendable showing in teaching. Richard felt that his case was comparable to theirs. If they got tenure, he couldn't see why he would be denied it.

On the academic scales, someone's unhappy weight, paradoxically, tipped over someone else's.

★   ★   ★

The parting at Brussels National Airport was difficult. Aisling's mother always had a tearful goodbye even when she and Philip were just returning to Dublin after spending the weekend with her in Barrowtown. When they arrived at the airport, Aisling looked for the Aer Lingus check-in desk. At it turned out, it was a Sabena check-in because the Belgian national airline was responsible for Aer Lingus services.

The check-in assistant was very friendly. When she realized that Mrs Holohan was travelling on her own, she offered to have her escorted by one of their staff. Mrs Holohan thanked her and said that she would very much like to avail of the kind service. They were told to go to the hospitality desk half an hour before her departure. In the meantime they were free to explore the place.

Which is what they did. Philip kept showing his granny where they had been when they were waiting for her flight to arrive a week ago. He showed her the lounge where they had kept a lookout for her plane. Philip, however, was not as enthusiastic as before, obviously saddened that his granny was leaving. The situation got worse when he said to his granny that he would miss her. Mrs Holohan's tears came flowing down her cheeks. Aisling's eyes got misty. Departures are never easy, she thought. So different from arrivals. Expectation gives way to anticipated loss. Laughter is replaced by tears. And yet one has to go on.

It was time to say goodbye. The young girl who was accompanying Mrs Holohan seemed competent and friendly. It was reassuring to know that her mother would be taken care of before, during and, hopefully this time, after the flight. There were instructions to ring her the minute she arrived in Dublin, where her sister and her husband were supposed to be meeting their mother. Then it occurred to them that probably Mrs Holohan would be in Dublin before they got to their apartment in Leuven. In which case it would be Mrs Holohan who would be worried if there was no answer from Aisling. So Aisling said to scrap that original plan. Instead, her mother should ring when they got home to Barrowtown. Both of them could stop worrying then since by that time Aisling and Philip would be home too.

More tears flowed as they kissed each other goodbye. Philip gave his granny a long hug – enough to cause her to cry even more. Aisling said that they were creating a scene at the national airport of the European capital. She joked that there could be some journalists around who would capture the moment in print or photography. And imagine that, it would be splashed all over the papers – wouldn't that be a disgrace to their country?

The Sabena girl patiently waited as all this was taking place. She was probably used to it all. She told Mrs Holohan to have her passport and her boarding card ready in case they were needed and then helped her through passport control and the security check.

The Brussels airport terminal had glass panes separating the Departures area, which is on the ground floor, from the check-in area. And so friends and family could still look down and follow the movements of the departing passengers. Aisling and Philip were anxious to know how Mrs Holohan was getting on, so they circled the place and looked down into the Departures area, where they could see the Sabena girl and Mrs Holohan enter the duty-free shop. They planted themselves in the spot where they would be able to see them when they emerged, no matter from which checkout counter.

'There's Granny and the lady!' announced Philip. 'Do you think they can see us?'

'I don't know. I hope so,' replied Aisling.

Right on cue, the girl paused just before they went any further to the gates. She scanned the panes, saw them and said something to Mrs Holohan.

'Granny sees us!' said Philip as he waved furiously. 'Goodbye, Granny!'

And he kept throwing her kisses. The girl smiled. Somehow she knew that the dutiful lady and her young son would be up there trying to catch a last glimpse of their grandmother. That was why she stopped. And she knew that her charge would appreciate that last moment which somehow made all the difference.

She was right – there was a pleasant smile from her charge as she waved to her family perched in the visitors' lounge above. It made her job a little easier when people showed care – even the small matter of waiting until it was no longer possible to see the departing passenger. She too waved at the two above. So Philip threw her a kiss – which made everyone smile even more. 'He's starting young, isn't he?' remarked the proud grandmother to her rather attractive escort.

After a few minutes the Sabena girl returned. Her instinct made her glance up. Sure enough, the two were still there, hoping for some reassurance that everything was fine. So she gave them a thumbs-up. Aisling waved her thanks to her. Then the Sabena girl blew Philip a kiss. It was Philip's turn to be surprised. He blushed, smiled and blew her two kisses. Even departures can be a little bit more pleasant, after all.

When Aisling and Philip returned to their studio apartment, they noticed a note waiting for them. It was from the housing manager of the university informing Aisling of the availability of a one-bedroomed furnished apartment in the Begijnhof.

Aisling did not know whether she should be delighted or not. Of all the rotten luck that it should come now rather than last week when it would have been much more welcome. Her mother's stay would have been a lot more comfortable. But as she glanced around the place she realized that any apartment would be more comfortable than this one.

So Aisling studied the note with more care. It said that the apartment would be available the following day and that they could move in at any time in the afternoon after it had been cleaned. The rent was much higher than she had expected but it included electricity and heating, both of which had made their present studio rather expensive.

'So what do you think?' Aisling was soliciting her son's opinion.

'Why are we moving?' was the inevitable question.

'It's a bigger place and you'll have more room to play.'

'Will there be anyone to play with?'

'Yes, I think so.' Although Aisling was not really definite about it. 'Are you game then?'

Philip said he was ready. After all, he had only his schoolbag to pack.

'Well, what about all our other things?'

'Now, that would be a problem,' giggled Philip. 'But I'll help,' he promised.

Later that evening Mrs Holohan rang to reassure Aisling that she had arrived safely. She spent about 15 minutes thanking them in so many ways for the wonderful holiday that she had. Aisling sensed that she missed them so she stayed on the phone as long as her mother wanted to talk. But she jokingly informed her mother that at the rate she was going and the expensive long chat she was having on the phone it would be cheaper for her to book another flight to Brussels. Then she told her mother about the new accommodation.

'That settles it,' joked Mrs Holohan back, 'I'm definitely booking my flight tomorrow! And you won't be able to do any of that studying that you're supposed to be doing there.'

Mrs Holohan told them that the flight to Dublin had been smooth. And that girl, yes, that one that her young grandchild threw a kiss to, was very helpful.

'And do you know what she said about you, Philip?'

Aisling repeated what Granny had said on the phone. Philip then shared the phone with his mother.

'No, what did she say, Gran?'

'That you are a handsome fellow. That's what she said! That's God's honest truth.'

'I'm glad I blew her two more kisses!'

'What's this?' asked Mrs Holohan.

Aisling informed her mother of what had transpired between the Sabena girl and the young fellow after she was gone. Imagine that, was her mother's comment.

As had been meticulously arranged, Aisling's sister and brother-in-law had met her at the airport. They would whisk her right away to Barrowtown to avoid the evening traffic, she was told. But they stopped at Kilkea and to Mrs Holohan's pleasant surprise she was treated to dinner at Kilkea Castle. Kilkea Castle, no less. She assured them that she could get used to all this lavish treatment – between Belgium and Ireland, it would not be a bad life after all. If only they would extend the free travel to include the Continent!

Everything was fine at home since Aisling's brother-in-law had checked on the house every day. And her next-door neighbours had made sure that it was fine at night too. The kind of good relationships that had been built up over the years. The kind that you did not want to lose by moving out.

It had been a wonderful holiday, but it was also nice to come home to her own place, where there would be a nice welcome for Aisling and for Philip when they returned to Ireland, and for anyone whom Aisling might want to introduce to her!

The next day Aisling phoned the university housing manager and found out that they could pick up the keys from the reception office of the Begijnhof. After getting the keys, Aisling and Philip spent the morning packing. Then they called for a taxi, which came in about ten minutes just as they were bringing the cases and boxes down. It was drizzling a bit, but not hard enough to wet their things.

Philip's eyes popped when he saw their new apartment. Wow! it was big! It had a very big bed – almost like his own in Dublin. He really liked the rope which functioned as a bannister for the stairs to their apartment. Cool, he said. Not only did he have his own bed here, there was also a desk where he could colour his books. This was more like home. He even had his own table and a small lamp beside his bed. The bathroom had a bath, not just a shower. He liked that too. Now he could 'splish, splash' again. A shower is OK where there is a bath too. The last place only had a shower. And you couldn't blow bubbles or sail your boat in a shower.

The ceiling here was different. It was not white but had lots of brown wood with green paint in between. The doors were pinkish with green lines while the windows had lots of panes of glass and wooden shutters, which could be shut and locked with little wooden ladybirds. The doors folded just like the windows he had seen in Maeve's doll's house. Maeve was his friend in school. Philip thought she'd like it here too.

There were lots of nooks for playing hide-and-seek. He was especially taken up with the fireplace – it had no fire! Instead there were dinner plates at the back, which his mother had warned him to be careful about. It was very wide and would suit Santa Claus better than their own fireplace in Dublin, which was rather black from lighting fires. It must really ruin Santa's suit. Yet Santa's suit never looked black. Magic cleans it for him though, Philip had decided, since every time he saw Santa he was always wearing a clean red suit.

Philip was able to join the play school for the children staying at the Begijnhof. In Aisling's view, this was an excellent opportunity for him to socialize. Philip quickly made friends with an American boy of the same age, called R.J., who showed him how to do high fives with their joined palms. At the play school the children shared their toys and had parties. Aisling knew that this would give her the opportunity to watch Philip in action with all his new pals. Each day he came out elated, having learned a new game or new phrase. Some of the children were English-speaking; others spoke French, Spanish or German, so Philip had the opportunity to learn greetings or rhymes in these languages. One day, he greeted her with ¡Ola! and then another time he answered *Danke* when she handed him something. Amazing how the language difference does not impede a child's willingness to play and learn, she thought. This experience was really making Philip a true European. Aisling truly believed he was learning more than he would have had he stayed at home.

Cable TV in Belgium was also quite European. Philip liked the familiar BBC children's programme best of all. No RTE, however. His curiosity sometimes made him switch over to the French, German and even Dutch channels. Also he learned how to make things, or dance, or sing a few notes from watching the programmes; and he was quite quick to pick up these things. If there were magic tricks he would practise them in front of the mirror before showing them to his ma.

The latest trick involved cotton buds. When he asked for them, his mother wanted to know what they were for. 'I'll show you,' was the immediate reply. The trick was to turn nine cotton buds into ten without cutting any of them. Aisling knew the trick, it was a familiar one. But she pretended to be puzzled, much to Philip's delight. Anyway, Aisling sensed that Philip really wanted to demonstrate how to do it. But she prolonged his excitement by trying various manoeuvres. 'Cold, cold, freezing,' commented Philip. Eventually, Aisling gave up. Philip promptly arranged the nine cotton buds to spell TEN. 'Clever!' was Aisling's encouraging remark.

Philip was attending the play school every day so there was no need to be making arrangements for him whenever she went to the office, the library or class. She would miss his company, but Aisling knew Philip was learning more in the playgroup. Besides, it meant that she had more time to research. Over the years she had learned to adjust her academic work schedule to fit Philip's: while he slept she researched or prepared her classes. The time in Leuven was really welcome as she had more time to read her sources without having to worry about preparing lectures as well. She was glad of the opportunity to attend the course on Postmodernism not just for the subject matter but also because it gave her a chance to observe another style of teaching and the other members of the class. It was such a long time since she was in an undergraduate class. She was learning again what it was like to be a member of a class.

*   *   *

'Gutierrez?' inquired the anxious voice at the other end.

'Yes, this is Richard Gutierrez ... Oh, hello, Professor van der Riet. I –' Before he could continue, however, van der Riet cut him short. Richard suspected something was wrong.

'I have been trying to locate Dr. Tanaka. You remember him? The Japanese professor at my house?'

199

'I was talking to him only for a few minutes at the social, and I haven't seen him since then. Is something wrong?'

'Yes, yes. I got a very urgent message for him. From Japan.' Van der Riet would not disclose anything more, however.

After Richard had replaced the receiver, he kept thinking about the call, which puzzled him a lot. Why would van der Riet contact him since he hardly knew the Japanese professor? He had merely exchanged a few words with him. Was it bad news from Japan? Whatever it was, it seemed highly important.

Richard looked for his coat. He would roam around the Begijnhof just in case he caught sight of Dr. Tanaka. He was not even sure he would recognize him. Maybe he could pass by the Begijnhof office to find out where his apartment was. But on checking his watch he concluded that the office would now be closed for the day. So that would not get him anywhere.

But Professor van der Riet should know his address in Leuven, Richard thought. And yet the professor had called Richard. There was something fishy about the whole thing.

Richard had no luck locating Dr. Tanaka. Unable to think of anything else he could do to help, he put the whole thing out of his mind. Instead he headed for the library of the School of Philosophy, where he spent a few hours, reading a lot and taking copious notes. It had been a fruitful few hours, he told himself. Time to return to his apartment now, he decided after he glanced at his watch.

So he gathered his things, neatly stacked the books he had been consulting for the staff to reshelve, and got up. He checked out a couple of the books which he thought he might be able to read that night after watching the English news on TV. After putting on his coat, which had been hanging on the rack just inside the door to the library, and collecting his bag, which had to be left in compartmentalized shelves, he bade goodbye to the librarians.

He walked in the direction of the Begijnhof. There was definitely a change in the weather. Gone was the biting cold of a few weeks ago. In fact, the restaurants had started to put chairs and tables out for their customers. Signs of times to come, he concluded. He had heard of Europeans spending a lot of time chatting, discussing, arguing in outdoor cafés. He knew that philosophers like Sartre used to do that. Perhaps he would experience that way of life here.

As he turned his key to open the entrance door to his apartment, he noticed for the first time that there had been a change of name over one of the doorbells. He had not made the acquaintance of the previous occupant so he did not think he would get to know the new one either. The Begijnhof served as the housing for visiting scholars, so people came and went. He walked up the stairs to his apartment.

As he was about to open his own door, he heard some voices down at the entrance to the building. He was about to go inside his own apartment, when it dawned on him that the voices were not totally unfamiliar. It was their Irish accent. But he did not know any Irish people. Curiosity made him come down. He saw a mother and a young boy bringing in their bags of groceries. It was Aisling and Philip.

'Here, let me help you,' he offered.

'Thank you. It's a bit difficult when one has only a pair of hands,' said Aisling. 'But he's a great help,' she added, smiling at Philip.

'I wish I were bigger. Then I could carry all of them for you, Ma.'

Aisling tossed his hair.

'Well, you have some help now. My name is Richard.'

Philip's eyes widened with recognition. 'You took our photograph at the restaurant!' he said excitedly.

Richard recognized them immediately. That was why the voices sounded rather familiar. He never thought he would meet them again. Yet unknown to him they had been neighbors for a while.

VII

Spring had definitely arrived. The cold, sometimes biting, winds were long since gone. Everywhere there was new life sprouting – out of the ground as well as from seemingly dead branches and twigs. Leuven was turning green, ready to shed off all the burden of the gray winter months. True, it had not been a bad winter. Snow this year had fallen only on a couple of days and even then it was a mere sprinkling, lasting on the ground for only about an hour. Right now the flowers, impatiently peeping out, were anxious to display their best colors. The birds which had made the park their home were once again chirping, alerting passers-by to the oncoming beauty of the months ahead. Lovers did not want to be left out either, as more and more of them strolled, leisurely enjoying each other and the slightly warmer weather.

In some ways nature in spring is like Leuven itself coming to life after the night before when everything had been closed. There would be some stirrings, tentative at first as if the town were still coming to terms with the day. It could be the garbage collectors making their rounds. Then there would be the early risers moving hurriedly in different directions, a few at first then growing larger and larger in numbers. Then shops would raise their shutters. An odd shopkeeper might even appear, pulling out a couple of shelves or sweeping the front part of the shop. Traffic would initially be light but as the minutes ticked by, more and more cars would fill the narrow streets. Then, of course, the bicycles, the schoolbuses and the students. Only after a while does Leuven really come to life. The town would be waking up just as nature now was in the process of coming back to life.

There is always something vibrant about waking up,

whether it is nature, Leuven or in general. It always signals a fresh start. Like the dawn of a new day. It makes one want to look forward rather than backwards. As if it is cajoling you into thinking that whatever happened in the past, there is yet another chance. Perhaps life is but a series of such beginnings. And we make it cumbersome when we burden it with the ever increasing weight of the past. Waking up, the beginning of spring, a town facing a new day stir up anticipation. Each gives one some hope. Maybe that is how we are meant to live – and nature provides numerous examples.

Nothing, however, is a surer sign of the onset of spring in Leuven than the opening up of the outdoor cafés in the Olde Markt. Passers-by can readily observe the restaurateurs there swishing away the canvas used to cover the stacked-up chairs and tables which will soon deck the place. Restaurants in the vicinity compete with one another in offering the best and most convivial atmosphere. And at the far end of the Old Markt, from inside the portals of Trinity College, a grammar school connected with the university of Leuven, one has an excellent photographic view of the entire square as it readies itself for the arrival of the new season.

As they toured the square in the afternoon Richard pointed out to Aisling that, judging by the youthful look of some of the occupants of these chairs and tables, it must be a favorite watering hole of university students, who could spend hours at these tables, their conversation of course helped by the beer that seemed to flow endlessly. After all, Leuven is the beer capital of Belgium. Right now they were standing in what is truly regarded as the longest bar in Belgium.

The link between the beer and the university seemed to be rooted in history; Richard had learned that historians found out that the students and professors in sixteenth-century Leuven each got through an average of 520 liters of beer per year when the rest of the citizens had to be content with 270 liters each. Some of these precious liters were obviously sold at these university bars to ordinary people, a practice that resulted in endless cases of dispute with the town council.

'This outdoor café is really a way of life here, isn't it?'

203

remarked Richard when they managed to find an empty table with three chairs, after scouring the place for over ten minutes. The fine day seemed to have brought the whole population out. Richard had spotted the place only because he happened to have been near the occupants when they got ready to move out. They were probably visitors since the townsfolk would hardly be leaving so early.

'Yes, and isn't it great? I really like this. After the winter, it's fantastic to be out – just to be out, enjoying the fine weather. We can't have this, you know, in Ireland. One restaurant tried to have it in the country. One summer the owner thought he would bring in the Continental way to the folks back home. "After all," he loudly proclaimed, "Ireland is now in the European Community." So he put out a number of seats. It was very popular and it was a big hit. For a day. That summer we had only one fine day.'

Aisling took to laughing. Philip joined in. Aisling then explained to Richard what had happened.

'The sun parasols he had added, for effect he said, soon became umbrellas. He was ruined, the poor man. One of the wisecracks said that if the Almighty God had really wanted the country to be European, he would not have placed the Irish Sea to keep the Continent away! She added that the owner should have brought the Continental weather really, and not just the parasols. He was unlucky. In good humour he donated his chairs and tables to the school, which was only too glad to get them and use them for indoor gatherings. He consoled himself, saying it was for a good cause. He was thanked publicly in church. And you know, the next summer was a gorgeous one. That's the trouble with the Irish climate. It is *so* unpredictable.'

Richard shared in the laughter. He had heard that the Irish talk a lot about the weather.

'And you know, we in Los Angeles, have the fine weather. But we don't seem to take advantage of it in this way. There is a bit of it in Santa Monica, near where I live. The Third Street Promenade. But it's nothing compared to this.' And he waved his hand in a wide sweep to take in the entire scene.

The waiter interrupted them for their orders. Aisling asked for ice cream. Philip requested the same thing, but was quite specific, 'the one with chocolate on top'. Richard said he would have a beer. Just the right thing, he said, for this weather and this place ...

Being neighbors meant that Richard and Aisling got to see each other plenty of times. Since the time he helped them with their groceries, they saw a lot of each other. Philip was thrilled to have Richard as a neighbor. He would first ask Richard whether he was finished with his studying and invite him to kick ball in the nearby yard. Philip seemed to have the knack of coming to see him only when Richard had done a lot of reading and needed a break anyway. Perhaps it was from having an academic for a mother that the young child knew there were times when he should not disturb someone who was studying.

Richard was getting fond of Philip. The fact that the young fellow was looking up to him probably enhanced his ego. But there was a genuine bonding that was gradually taking place. And it was Philip who would suggest that the three of them could go out together or do things together. Aisling was reluctant as she did not want to impose on Richard, but Richard really wanted it to happen that way. He enjoyed the company of mother and son, feeling very much at home in their midst even when they were doing nothing special.

Last week they had attended the performance of the university choir, held at the Aula Maxima, a half-circular temple-like auditorium with a box ceiling, rather austere like a pantheon. The auditorium had a remarkable wooden construction, the oak pillars supporting the domed roof hidden behind clear straight neoclassical shafts covered in white plaster. Aisling and Richard had been thrilled with the singing but Philip enjoyed the silly antics of the students introducing the music even more.

Most of the time, however, they went for a stroll. The conversations Aisling and Richard had during those times naturally brought out their past as they talked about so many things. And that was what really brought Richard close to Aisling. Aisling was very natural; she did not want to pretend or aim to be someone else. She had a very balanced temperament. Most of all she was a good conversationalist. She listened, she contributed and she encouraged. And from her he learned the beauty of going for long leisurely walks with pleasant company.

And Leuven in springtime provided the perfect environment. The walks, the parks, the gardens have indeed much to offer to nature-lovers. And for Richard it was wonderful to feel nature under his feet, to trample on the soil, to hear the crunch of twigs, to be rooted in the ground, to brush against the leaves of overhanging branches. How he missed this in Los Angeles, where most of the time when he was going from one place to another it was the floor of the car under him or the cement walk that prevented him from being in touch with nature.

Arenberg Campus, a beautiful and idyllic setting for such walks, became their favorite haunt. The central point of this green campus is Arenberg Castle, where the lords of Leuven had lived: the de Croys from 1446 on and the Arenbergs from 1635 to World War I. Around 1520 the castle had been given its late-Gothic contours, but over the centuries its constant renovations ranged from a neo-Gothic bay to a Postmodern touch. Not surprisingly, the Architecture Department of the university of Leuven found its home here. The river Dijle, which had given power to many a mill in years gone by, passed beside it, and then along wooded lands, continuing on a windy course past the tennis courts and sports centre with its racing tracks.

With the coming of the fine weather it was another excuse for the three of them to observe the daffodils, narcissi, pansies come to bloom at Arenberg Campus. Philip always wanted to see the old watermill and the ducks, which were residents in the area. Aisling joked that given the frequency of their walks, they could monitor the budding of nature.

Sometimes they headed for the Park instead, where one could visit what was originally a Romanesque church standing at the highest point, flanked by the monastery with its cloisters and by the abbot's quarters, which are joined to the rest of the building by a terraced garden and a flight of steps. On its grounds is also a guest house which stands slightly lower in a walled ceremonial square. There is even a farm with baroque volutes, a coach house, stable and barn in a courtyard with a water-trough. The well-preserved complex draws visitors, particularly on a Sunday afternoon when one can be escorted by the Abbot himself around the interior of the buildings.

During their walks, while Philip ran ahead, sometimes chasing the birds or butterflies, Richard and Aisling would converse. About anything. About their work, world affairs, about their countries. Aisling talked about the class she was auditing, and about the American professor and students. Her witty comments and perspective on the differences between the American students and her own Irish students amused Richard. But mostly they touched on life. The challenges of life and their attitudes towards it. Aisling would bring up literary passages to illustrate her point. It was amazing how she could quote verbatim from poems and plays. She said it came from having to teach them so many times. But Richard suspected that it was more. Aisling really loved literature, not merely as an academic discipline but because it talked to her of life. For her, poets and playwrights captured in words many of the things she was experiencing. Even now as they walked around the grounds of Arenberg, she would cite passages from Hopkins, Frost, Hardy and Wordsworth as they marveled at the beauty in nature.

And yet Aisling was not a romantic. Her love of life was tempered at the anvil of hardship. The loss of her husband, the difficulties of raising Philip on her own, the challenge of a career – life must not have been easy on her. And it was this closeness with life that Richard really admired in Aisling. She was not driven by an ambition to be the best. She knew her strengths and weaknesses. She saw life as a gift to be nurtured, not tortured. Not excelling to the point of forgetting the wonder and simple pleasures of life. And that was why she liked poetry, because poets were very much in touch with the concreteness of life. But she also acknowledged that she was learning a lot from her own son. She learned from trying to see life at his level – a perspective on life that adults sometimes forgot. The wonder, the enthusiasm, the spontaneity. Above all, simplicity. It is amazing, she said, how adults make life, for various reasons, some of which are admittedly good, more complicated than is necessary.

Richard recalled the first evening he had dinner with Aisling and Philip. It was a particularly cozy evening for him, being with a family. After all, he had been living the life of a bachelor for a long time. Not the kind of person who liked socializing on a big scale, he much preferred a small intimate group where people would talk with him rather than breeze through empty platitudes the way many flit around in those socials. Aisling had invited Richard to have dinner with them that Sunday evening. They could have early dinner and have time for a chat before watching the Eurovision on TV.

Unsure as to what the Eurovision meant, Richard was about to ask Aisling when Philip, thinking that Richard might be saying no to the invitation, piped up.

'And my mother bakes a nice cake, coffee-walnut-brandy gateau. Simply delicious! You'd love it.'

'Well, how can I refuse then? I'd love to come.' Richard winked at Philip.

'Good, good,' Philip clapped his hands for added effect.

After thanking Aisling for the invitation, he said that he would be looking forward to enjoying their company on Sunday – and to the coffee-walnut-brandy gateau, of course. He asked whether he should bring something but was told no, only yourself.

Richard was indeed looking forward to that evening as he hoped that he would get to know Aisling better. He chuckled at the idea that right from the beginning young Philip seemed to be on his side. He found genuine warmth and openness in Aisling and Philip.

He recalled the first time he saw them at the T-Bone Restaurant when he and Jennifer were dining. He could not help admire the closeness of the Irish family near their table. It had turned out to be Philip, Aisling and her mother. It had just been a brief glimpse of the family. And he would have forgotten all about it if he had not met Aisling and Philip again. He learned that Aisling's mother had just been visiting them. And he found out about Sean when Philip blurted out that his father had died in a car crash when he was a baby.

Getting to know Aisling and Philip made Richard think of family life. He himself came from a wonderful family. His parents were still alive and living in Chicago. His brother had had a bad marriage and was now involved in a bitter divorce case. His brother's unfortunate experience had soured any plans Richard had of marriage. That was why, among other things including his own graduate studies and new career, he had put it out of his mind. But his parents were happy together and they had provided his brother and him a real home. Could it be that such family life was in the past? that his generation had to accept what they in America are now calling 'dysfunctional families'? If he ever got married, he wanted a marriage like his parents'. It was by no means ideal. But they were together and they stuck together. And they aged wonderfully together.

But on one occasion when he was flying from Chicago back to Los Angeles, his seat was next to a seven-year-old girl who was travelling on her own. Between sobs she told him that she had just been with her father for a week. Now she was returning to her mother, who had married someone else. The court had decided that her mother had the primary care of her – a mouthful for a seven-year-old to say and a bitter pill for her to swallow. She kept saying that it was not right. Her place was with her mother and real father, who were thousands of miles apart. Every time she had to do this, and she had to do it regularly, her heart was torn between them.

Richard sympathized with her. This unhappy situation was really psychologically damaging to children. It did not provide them with stability nor security, so important in the early years of growing up. On the other hand, what could one do when adults really could no longer get along, sometimes even to the point of violence? It would be just as harmful to

209

preserve the marital arrangement. Back in the USA they were talking of family values. A return to tradition. Would that stabilize society? The American dream seemed to have included a husband, a wife and two kids. And of course, their own house, and maybe a dog. When they talked of family values, did these people have this picture of a family? But the world was changing and the word 'family' was also changing. What about single-parent families? Or single-gender families? What was more important, to retain the notion of the traditional family or to emphasize the values which the traditional family sought to preserve: like loyalty, respect, sharing, and so on? Was it the structure or was it the practice that supported that structure? Could we afford to lose those values and yet be open to other forms of family structure?

In his case he had to admit that he wanted the home atmosphere that he had experienced with his parents and which was now becoming rare in America. And that was why he was drawn into the warmth and unsophisticatedness of Aisling and Philip. Those two meant a lot to each other. Even a casual observer could see that.

And he had come to like being invited for a cup of tea. He had even developed a liking for the way the Irish drink their tea. It was refreshing to knock on the door and be asked in for a 'quick cuppa'. Sometimes he declined because he was rushing, but the openness in the invitation appealed to him. It was a sharing, a genuine openness. The tea was at times merely a symbol or an opener.

But he was equally aware of the hard practical realities of conmen, violent strangers and even untrustworthy friends – all of whom did not deserve to be welcomed into one's home. But, he wondered, are we not missing something, an important something in our lives, when we have to think before we can invite people in for a cup of tea?

That was why he was looking forward to spending the evening with Aisling and Philip. Richard hoped that they would not be disappointed with his company. But they seemed to like him. Their meetings and conversations had been natural and spontaneous. Most of all, he was made to feel at home with them.

While he had enjoyed Jennifer's company tremendously, it was now becoming clear that indeed it was as an academic that he had related to her. Until that afternoon in her apartment. Jennifer was a very competent person in her field, but sometimes that kind of competence limited a person or hid another dimension. Richard did care about Jennifer and they had parted that evening as good friends. And he did not want to lose touch with her. It is amazing, he reflected, how people can enter one's life and leave a mark there – unexpectedly and differently, as was the case with him in Jennifer's life. Her story was a real revelation to him. And he had become part of that story, but it was meant to continue in a different direction. At least for now. It was not so much that he wanted the crossing of their paths to be regarded as important, but he really was concerned about Jennifer. She deserved more from life. Jennifer had been an inspiration to him, and he was grateful, but it was an inspiration that prodded him to look for something else.

Aisling and Philip were providing him with a different kind of inspiration, one that had been far from his plans, but was now opening up new vistas. He wanted to show his appreciation by bringing a present, but he had been told to bring 'just himself'. A funny expression, he commented as he reflected on its significance. Normally when he was invited by colleagues it was to a 'pot luck party'. One was expected, and sometimes specifically asked, to bring something. He also liked that tradition. It reminded him of the significance of the first Thanksgiving dinner. People pooled their resources together. It brought out the idea of sharing, of commonality, of partaking of one another's bounty. But the invitation to bring 'just himself' had another significance. To him, it seemed that his presence was more important than the things he brought. There was sharing too, but of a different kind, one that conveyed that what they had was also his, as their guest. And it made the guest important. Better still, it made him one of them.

Richard was surprised by his thoughts. A simple invitation. And yet it had stimulated him. He doubted whether many of his fellow philosophers would have much time for that kind of musing. On the other hand, maybe these philosophers did not really pay much attention to unraveling the significance of many down-to-earth practices and traditions. Why did they always assume that sophisticated and abstract reasoning is high-level philosophizing? Why did they presume that the complex and the important meant the same thing?

He decided to bring flowers to Aisling and a train set to Philip. Both were delighted with his presents, although he did not immediately catch the Irish significance in Aisling's remark. After she had thanked him and said that they were very beautiful, she had added that he 'should not have bothered.' She said, thinking that Richard might have understood it literally, that it was an Irish expression to show appreciation! Language, it was fraught with cultural nuances. But Philip's reaction transcended any cultural divide. There was no need to translate his sense of gratitude: his eyes widened, he said, '*Go raibh maith agat*' and he gave Richard a peck on the cheek and asked him to help him set it up.

Aisling had prepared a splendid meal. For appetizer she had cut and sliced the melon and then, using a colored cocktail stick, had curved a slice of orange with a red cherry on top and set it in the middle of the melon. The main course was mango chicken served with rice and green vegetables. It was meant to be mango, but Aisling confessed that she substituted peaches since she had not been able to get mangos. And Philip was right: Aisling's gateau specialty was simply delicious. One thing that she had come to appreciate in the apartment in the Begijnhof, Aisling told Richard, was that it was very comfortably furnished, unlike the studio apartment in Tervuursevest. Here they were able to prepare their own meals since the kitchen had everything that she needed. Richard laughed because, despite having had that all along, he still had his meals either at the various Chinese restaurants in Leuven or at the university student restaurants.

Over dinner they talked about being in Leuven, about America and about Ireland. Aisling had never been in America although they had relations in Boston and New York. She added that probably every Irish family had a relation in one of those two cities. She was looking forward to the conference in Boston that she was participating in. Richard for his part had never been in Ireland. But he had heard so much of it from friends and colleagues, many of whom claimed to have Irish roots. Maybe he had roots there too! He said that his university's Study Abroad Programs Office was investigating the possibility of holding a summer school there like the ones they had in Cambridge, Madrid and Florence. He was hoping that if it did materialize he would be able to teach there.

'Will you visit us then, Richard? I can show you all my toys.' The invitation from Philip was prompt and sincere.

'I'd love to, Philip, but a lot depends on so many things.'

'Like what?' It was Philip again following up his question.

'Whether I'll continue to be a teacher. What about you? What are you going to be when you grow up?'

'I'm going to be a farmer,' Philip replied as he tucked into his mother's cake.

'A farmer?'

'Yes, with a big farm and a tractor.'

Aisling laughed. 'I don't know where he got that idea. But he had been saying that for the past year.'

Their conversation covered so many things. Small matters. After all, it was a social occasion. What mattered most was the togetherness. It was a togetherness that was laying a foundation for a valuable friendship.

They watched the Eurovision, which brought Ireland very much into Richard's attention since it was taking place in Cork. Different Continental TV stations were covering the event, but they chose the BBC since they would all be able to follow the commentaries. Aisling explained that the Eurovision was an annual song contest in which songs representing various European countries would be competing. The judges were panels stationed in each of the countries represented. These panels would assign points to each song, except to the song of their own country. Whichever country garnered the highest number of points won and had the right to host the competition the following year. It was in Cork

213

this year because the Irish song had been the winner the previous year. The host country, as Ireland was doing now, would use the event to showcase its country. It was good for tourism for that country but it was also an opportunity for bringing Europe close.

From what he could see on the TV, Richard could understand why he had been hearing that Ireland was indeed a beautiful and fascinating country. Watching it in the midst of a warm Irish family made him understand it even more. He got a glimpse of vast green fields sprawled all over the country and the lakes that dotted it. The significant monuments of Ireland's past and the throbbing challenges of her present paraded before him.

Most of the songs of the contest were good and catchy. And it was an exciting contest. He had thought he would merely be a spectator. But Aisling's enthusiasm and Philip's sound effects as the votes were tallied found him rooting for Ireland. And it was not because he was trying to be respectful of his hosts, it was because in some mysterious fashion he was beginning to feel that Ireland was tugging at him.

Yes, it had been a truly enjoyable evening. And it was not the glittery type, nor a large social. It was at a home that opened its doors and hearts to him.

... This afternoon, as Aisling and Philip spooned their ice cream and Richard drank his ice-cold beer, they were prepared to let the world pass by. Or rather to let the beauty of a sunlit world penetrate their being. The warm rays of the welcome sun caressed their bodies. It was pleasant to be touched by nature. And it was nice to be here at this very moment, enjoying each other's company.

Philip was engrossed with his ice cream, saying very little, as if wanting the adults to converse. Excusing himself, he asked his mother whether he could just go over to where a group of Chileans were playing some folk music, promising to stay where they could see him. Aisling allowed him on condition that he did not stay long. Another promise. So when he was moving towards the musicians, he kept looking

214

back to be sure that he could still be seen.

Richard wondered about Philip. He was only six years old, but he seemed to have a sense about life that other children of his age did not. Was Philip going over to watch the musicians or did he really want the two of them just to be together?

An incident in the church at the Begijnhof drifted back to Richard's mind. Several weeks after Aisling and Philip had moved into their apartment and after they and Richard had got to know one another a little better, it became routine for them to attend the Sunday Mass in the Begijnhof together. That particular Sunday when the celebrant asked them to hold hands during the singing of the *Our Father*, Philip happened to be between Aisling and Richard. So he linked them on both sides. But there was something in the boy's countenance that expressed satisfaction with this arrangement. Aisling was paying attention to the celebration, but Philip raised his head very slightly towards Richard and smiled – very briefly but meaningfully. After that Mass, the churchgoer next to them complimented them in English on their well-behaved and good-looking son. Aisling thanked the lady and blushed a little. Richard did not know what to say. Philip gave that meaningful smile again.

From where they were seated, they had a good view of Philip. A small crowd had started to circle the musicians, but both of them knew he would be safe. They could hear the haunting music of the Chileans as they strummed their guitars, much to Aisling's and Richard's delight. For Richard it was probably his Hispanic background that tuned in to this kind of music. Aisling generally liked folk music because for her it spoke from the heart, it brought out certain emotions that kept one in touch with life. Richard commented that there was something too about this kind of music that enveloped and permeated you rather than deafened you. At this both of them laughed as they made other remarks on the contemporary music enjoyed by their students and by partygoers.

★   ★   ★

The British Midlands plane which had departed from Brussels for Birmingham International Airport was taxiing towards the terminal. Inside, Jennifer was putting away the novel which she had tried to read during the flight. But her eyes would not focus on the words. Most of the time her mind just kept drifting away.

She had not been able to concentrate much since leaving Leuven that afternoon with mixed feelings. She had not expected the turn of events, the primary thing she had planned on doing while in Leuven being to work on the joint project with Professor Lamennais. Leuven was meant to be an intellectual adventure; instead, it pulled at her heartstrings. The schedule she had given herself should have led to at least a first draft of the book which she and the eminent French professor were co-authoring. That did not materialize. Perhaps it was just as well that Professor Lamennais had pulled out of the project first – some administrative problems in his university back in France which needed his attention immediately, she was told. She would have to deal with the matter of her grant from the British Council at some stage. At least, Professor Lamennais's 'emergency' saved her the trouble of having to explain to him that her heart was not in the project any more.

And yet it was not really her feelings for Richard that occupied her even if it had been Richard who had stirred those feelings in the first place. No, she and Richard had talked things over. Their parting had been very friendly, and both had hoped that some day they would meet again.

Rather it was what she had learned unexpectedly about herself while in Leuven. And yet she had to admit that all along she knew about it. But sometimes, she realized, we repress something in our unconsciousness or subconsciousness, only to have something trigger it off and catapult it to the surface. And then we are forced to confront it. Jennifer had always suspected that all the energy and drive she had been directing to her academic work had been a diversion from other matters in her life – like accepting the death of Richard. She had wanted to block it out of her consciousness and the only way she knew was to hurl herself headlong into her academic work. And it worked because she did forget.

216

Or did she? Was it not merely postponing the inevitable? As it happened, that was exactly the case because she met the other Richard in Leuven.

After Richard had left her apartment, following their talk, she found herself bursting out into tears. Unexpectedly, because their conversation had been quite pleasant. They had talked about life, not about their academic work. They had touched on a topic that for long she had refused to acknowledge openly. And perhaps that was the reason for this different kind of outburst on her part. What she had been holding back for so long refused to be reined back. What had surfaced would no longer be kept down.

And this time she had made no effort to restrain the floods of tears. For they were not tears of weakness. They were forceful reminders of an important fact of human life. That we have to face up to the ups and downs. That we cannot afford to ignore the demands of life itself. That we cannot shield ourselves from its persistent tug, not only at our mind but also at our heart.

Paradoxically, it was at that moment of apparent weakness that she had learned something about her strength. She had wanted to cry because now she cared about the challenge of life, not just about her career. It was when her face was covered in tears that she realized how life had been struggling to unlock itself to her.

As she emerged from the plane and headed towards the baggage collection point in the terminal, it dawned on her that the last time she had walked here it was in the opposite direction, to work on a project in bio-ethics. Now on her return she knew that she would have to explore a more demanding project – *bios* itself. It would be a lifelong one.

★   ★   ★

'Come in, the door's open,' Dr. Miguel Fuentes called out.

'Excuse me, Father Fuentes, but are you very busy? I can come back another time.'

'That's all right, Jose, I can always go back to this reading

217

later. To tell you the truth, I wasn't concentrating anyway.' Dr. Fuentes had been reading a rather thick philosophy book. '*Pasok*,' he motioned to the young student.

Jose Mananzan, a Filipino seminarian belonging to a religious order, entered the room but remained standing until he was invited to sit down in the chair nearest the window which, since the room was on the top floor of the College of the Holy Spirit, provided Dr. Fuentes with a magnificent view of Leuven. Since he was an early riser he sometimes watched from this window the arrival of the day, having been awakened gently by the sun's early rays as they penetrated the pane and softly lit up the room.

'*O, ano kumusta?* How are you finding your studies at Leuven? Quite different from the Philippines, I bet.'

'*Opo*, and it's rather cold here. It's not too bad now *pero noong winter* I don't know how many layers of clothes I put on. Somebody told me *parang Santa Klaus daw ako* – minus the beard!'

The two compatriots laughed.

'I was wondering whether you had any news from the Philippines,' said Jose, to explain his visit.

Dr. Fuentes was only too glad to share whatever news he had received about their home country with the young student. Since he was in constant contact with his bishop, who had sent him to Leuven for his sabbatical, and since his own seminary students kept him up to date with news clippings, he was aware of what was going on in the Philippines. Regularly he would call long distance to several individuals there to check on specific details whenever the news coverage was not sufficient.

It was obvious where Father Fuentes's mind and heart were. It was with great reluctance that he had agreed to come to Leuven. Having struggled with his promise of obedience to his bishop, who had been concerned about him, he had consented to his directive to leave the Philippines only at the last minute. Bishop Pedro de los Reyes was worried that Father Fuentes's deep passion for his native country was making him lose the proper balance, thereby rendering him less effective in his ministry with future priests. Father Fuentes's strong stand against the military during the Marcos regime had made him a target of those whom he denounced in the classroom and in the pulpit. His political activities against the US military bases in the Philippines were leading him to adopt an anti-foreign stance. So the bishop's solution was to send the seminary professor of philosophy to Europe. The bishop, who had studied in the Catholic University of Louvain before the separation between the Flemish and the French constituents of the university took place, thought that Father Fuentes would benefit intellectually and emotionally from being immersed in the traditions of this academic town. There he might drink from its fountain of wisdom.

Father Fuentes, however, did not want to uproot himself even if only for a few months. He believed that his place was in the Philippines, his mission was to the Filipino people. So he thought it was a waste of his time and unnecessary diocesan expense to send him abroad.

Some 20 years ago this bishop's predecessor, a rather authoritarian individual, had summoned him too because he wanted to send the neopresbyter to Rome to do his doctorate, but Father Fuentes explained that he preferred instead to study in the Philippines, since he wanted to write his thesis on Filipino philosophy.

'But you are wasting your talents. You are very gifted, you have a bright future in the Church. I want you to go to Rome.'

'Thank you, your Grace. But whatever gift I have I want to use it to serve the Philippines.'

'But you can do that better if you go to Rome. You'll be getting your doctorate from the Gregorianum, you'll be known in the most important ecclesiastical circles. In that way, you'll rise quickly.' The bishop obviously was recalling his own elevation to the bishopric.

'Your Grace, I really would like to study Filipino philosophy. I cannot do that in Rome or anywhere else for that matter.'

'But there is no Filipino philosophy! And who's going to

notice your work? Look at what you have studied in the seminary — good solid Thomistic philosophy. *Philosophia perennis.* That is what we need. That is why you have been studying Latin. You have been prepared for *Roma aeterna.* Forget this nationalistic sentimentalism. We belong to a universal church. We should be concerned about eternal truths, those which cut across cultures. Besides, if you want to be taken seriously as a professor and as a future candidate in the Church hierarchy you need to study in Rome. You are wasting your time studying Filipino superstitious beliefs. Look to Europe. That is where true culture is. That is where you will meet important people. That is where your talents will be appreciated. I have decided.'

The young, idealistic and patriotic Father Fuentes could not believe his ears. His bishop was a Filipino. Yet he was extolling the virtues of foreign lands and downgrading his own culture. Obviously all the hopes that the Filipino clergy had pinned on this bishop had been wasted. Because he was one of them, the Filipino priests had thought that they had a champion in him in their struggle to make the Catholic Church in the Philippines more aware of the plight of their people. They had been miserably wrong. Father Fuentes wondered whether it had been the bishop's long stay in Rome that had alienated him and made him unappreciative of his native land.

As he faced the bishop Father Fuentes vowed that he would not let that happen to him. How could a foreign education equip him to work with his people here in his own country? Why were many, including bishops it seemed, succumbing to what could only be a heresy that the West was best?

But what could he do? He had promised obedience to this very man. Father Fuentes wanted to fight back, his blood starting to boil at this insult to his country by one of its own people. He was tempted to hurl insults at this power-hungry cleric and accuse him of reneging on his own people.

He resisted the temptation. That would make matters worse, he knew. Fight authority and authority will wield its power. He desperately wanted to contradict the bishop. But show someone in power that he is wrong and the powerful will waste no time in putting his foot down. Refuse in strong terms and one will be compelled.

He would bide his time instead. So Father Fuentes pretended that he was a bamboo, rather than a narra tree. He would stay rooted in the ground of his convictions, but would bend with the strong wind and let the typhoon pass by. When heavy rains lash down on it and forceful winds beat against it, the bamboo tree remains firm while being pliant. The recently ordained priest would accept the compromise that he could still pursue his interests while in Rome, although he feared that his work would turn out to be an academic study divorced from the concrete experiences of his people. He wanted and needed to be immersed in them for only then would his work have credibility. The daily lives, the traditions, the struggles of the Filipino people were the fountain from which he wanted to be nourished. For what he wanted to do, losing touch was the worst thing that could happen. But for the moment the horizon was being darkened by this dreadful typhoon. Father Fuentes thought it better to weather it out.

And like all typhoons, this one passed by – and died down. With some help. Father Fuentes was wondering whether it was from Providence that a week after their 'conversation' the bishop had a fatal heart attack. The bamboo immediately snapped back into place. It had bent as the gale-force wind blew, but it was not broken. Since it was only the bishop who had raised the issue of his going to Rome, Father Fuentes was sure that that was the end of the matter. He promptly registered at the University of Sto. Tomas before a successor could be appointed. In record time he had produced some pioneering work on Filipino philosophy, based on folklore, beliefs and practices. He did not care about academic honors or recognition although it did gain him a doctorate. All he had wanted was the opportunity to study the values and traditions of his people. Nor did he have any ambition to rise in the ecclesiastical ranks. His passion, his enthusiasm, his love was for his country. So when he was asked to teach in the seminary, he was overjoyed since he would be able to share his passion with and motivate the future 'workers in God's vineyard' – in God's ricefield, really.

And he was happy planting seeds, the true seeds that over the years sprouted in the muddy, murky but fertile fields of the Philippines.

Until Bishop de los Reyes's secretary phoned him to say that his Grace wanted to see him the next day at his palace. When the bishop informed Father Fuentes of his plan for him, the professor rehashed once more, this time with the benefit of maturity, his reasons for wanting to remain rooted in the Philippines. But this bishop reminded him that he was the bishop after all and knew what was best for him. Father Fuentes, again made painfully conscious of his promise of obedience, nevertheless wondered how this time he could ward off what appeared to him to be an anointed dragonfly.

Perhaps he would be a bamboo once more, even if much older, since sometimes the swish of the bamboo leaves frightens the dragonfly. But this was no mere dragonfly; this was a gusty wind. So maybe he would bend again in the face of the gathering storm. Maybe it would pass by again. Like the last time.

However, there was no such storm. Nor did Providence intervene this time. So Father Fuentes wondered whether the bamboo had bent too soon before there was really a gale. Or maybe he himself had mellowed with the passage of time since he did not put up too much of a protest. He did try delaying tactics, but the bishop's superefficient priest-secretary, who had an eye (both eyes, to be more exact) on the next episcopal vacancy had ensured his departure.

So after all the years, an episcopal gust managed to blow Father Fuentes into Europe – not to Rome but to Leuven, the alma mater of Bishop de los Reyes. This was why he was now in the College of the Holy Spirit, chatting with Jose.

★   ★   ★

Richard had just tuned in to the BBC World Service for the latest news from abroad. As usual after he had turned on the radio, he sat back with only half his attention given to the news broadcast since he would normally pick up a newspaper to scan its headlines at the same time.

But this time he did not bother with any other distraction. There was a major scandal in academia in Japan. Richard immediately increased the volume since he did not wish to miss any of the details. An academic scandal is rare, he thought – and in Japan! This must really be major.

And indeed it was since it involved one of the most prominent professors in Japan. The reporter had mentioned the name of the highly respected university, but to Richard's ears the Japanese name of the university sounded too foreign to catch. Apparently, so the reporter said, for the first time a Japanese professor was being sued by a member of his department for sexual harassment.

Another voice came on the air. Someone was being interviewed. Bringing up such a case in Japan is so difficult – it was the interpreter speaking – because traditions, which are largely male-oriented, are almost impossible to break down. The legal system is also such that one is bound to lose the case or at least face insurmountable barriers if a female academic tries to accuse a male colleague of rape or any kind of sexual advances. So the norm, explained the interpreter, is not to do anything.

Back to the English-speaking reporter. This was why this particular case was making the headlines. The female academic alleged that her professor had made several advances to her and threatened that she would not be promoted if she did not give in to his wishes. She also claimed that he had done the same thing to her sister, who had had to leave her job. As news of the allegation caught the attention of the public a number of graduate students summoned the courage to make the same accusation.

The difficulty was that the accused professor was a very prominent one whose reputation as Chair of the biggest department had attracted large grants to his university. If the university were to take any action, there was a great risk that it would also lose a sizeable amount of donations. That was why many people in Japan were wondering what these female academics and graduate students would gain from this publicity since the case was loaded against them.

Richard stiffened. This seems to be worldwide, after all. Academic life no matter where is affected by this, he said to himself as he recalled several cases back in the USA.

The reporter continued. This particular situation seemed initially to have been solved, Japanese-style. The eminent professor resigned from his position and sought refuge in a Buddhist temple in Kyoto. So the university did not have to take any action.

Richard could not believe his ears. What did that mean? Was the professor absolved from any responsibility? Were the accusations well-founded or not?

Initially solved, the reporter stressed, since the scandal refused to lie down, as it were, with the Buddhist monks. The temple kept getting a number of letters condemning the professor's conduct. So he had had to leave the temple. The last that was heard of him was that he had gone to Europe. He was now wanted back.

The professor's name was Dr. Tanaka.

★   ★   ★

'Do you want to join me for a walk? I need to get out since I have been incarcerated in this room since this morning.'

Father Fuentes invited Jose Mananzan after he had communicated the latest goings-on in the Philippines. He had actually welcomed Jose's intrusion since he missed his country, which he had left a few months ago. It was some comfort that here in Leuven there were students from his native country. He had sought them out because the cultural shock, initially at least, had been a real obstacle to his adjustment to life in Leuven. Being with Filipinos helped cushion him.

'Yes, I would like to, but I have to fetch my coat. Otherwise I'll be shivering.'

'Why don't I meet you at the parlor then? I must not forget my own coat too.'

The two of them had a laugh over this. It was already springtime in Leuven and the temperatures were really not that low. Yet these two individuals from the tropics did not want to take any chances.

A few minutes later, Father Fuentes and Jose Mananzan were striding out of the College of the Holy Spirit into Naamsestraat. The sun was shining brightly, the temperatures had risen a bit, and there was a buzz around the place.

They looked at each other.

'We don't really need this, do we?' Father Fuentes pointed to his coat.

Jose Mananzan agreed and offered to leave both coats in the parlor. They could pick them up when they returned.

While Jose was away, Father Fuentes looked ahead towards the town center, which was bathed in sunlight. There was no doubt that the gloom of winter was behind them. He felt like one of those individuals in Plato's cave, emerging from the rather dark corridors of the college into the sunlit world. There was a lot of activity in the center as people were happy just to be out, celebrating the freedom that the sun brought with it.

Why? Had they been trapped? Father Fuentes wondered. It is sometimes an awful feeling to be forced to stay inside. He knew from experience since the cold air of the previous weeks was enough to stop him from venturing out. But can one be trapped, not just by the weather, but in other ways?

Just then Jose reappeared. That put a momentary stop to his musings.

'Well, any particular direction?' asked Father Fuentes.

'*Kayo pô ang bahala,*' deferred the young seminarian to his elder.

'*O sigue, punta tayo sa* center. There seems to be some life there.'

Sure enough, the gorgeous spring day had enticed the people to congregate at the outdoor cafés or to stroll along the streets window-shopping. No one was really in a hurry; people were ambling along, and even the traffic slowed down, patiently waiting for pedestrians crossing at different points.

225

Refreshment spots were doing brisk business. Ice cream was definitely the popular choice among the strollers while beer, of different kinds, as well as coffee, was prominent on the tables of the cafés. One could detect a hum in the air, a cheerful welcome to the fine weather.

'Do you like Leuven, Jose?' inquired Father Fuentes.

'Very much so, I am really grateful that I have the opportunity to study here. The university has so much to offer, its traditions, its learning, its –'

'And yet you hope to return to the Philippines afterwards?' There was a tone of sarcasm in the priest's voice.

'Definitely, I want to share with the people I'll be serving what I have learned here.'

Father Fuentes couldn't help but smile. History was reversing itself. Here was a seminarian who wanted to serve his country yet was studying abroad, doing the opposite to what he had done. So he disclosed to Jose his own situation, his patriotic ideals when he was a young priest, his brush with ecclesiastical authority, his views about studying outside the country if one wanted to serve the people in the Philippines.

'Why did you come then, Father Fuentes, if I may ask?'

'Good question. Ultimately because my bishop wanted me to. He said being steeped in the atmosphere of Leuven would do me a lot of good.'

'Was that a sufficient reason? I mean, what about your ideals?'

Father Fuentes looked straight at the young seminarian.

'As sufficient a reason as there is, young man. Wait until your turn comes.' Then he chortled. 'I wonder if I had stamped my foot and said no, what would have happened.'

Jose smiled. 'Our novice master used to say that of the vows we would take, celibacy would be difficult when we were young, poverty when we were middle-aged and obedience when we were old.'

'Let me see, where do you fit?'

Neither, however, was able to pursue the question any further since they were distracted by the visitors clicking away at the Fons Sapientiae. The symbol of Leuven's academia had become the center of attention of a group of American tourists.

'What do you think of it, Father?' inquired Jose, turning in the direction of the fountain.

'Do you want my honest opinion, Jose? I think it represents what I have come to detest in academia. Look at how that scholar is immersed in the book. That is not what education is all about. That is why I resisted being sent to study abroad – because it means being buried in books, some of which have no relevance to our concerns in the Philippines. Don't get me wrong. Some books are important. Those written by our people, including those written in their blood.'

Knowing that he was being carried away by his feelings, Father Fuentes glanced at the young seminarian.

'I'm sorry, I shouldn't be poisoning your mind. It's just that ...'

To Father Fuentes's surprise, Jose offered a challenging response.

'That's okay, Father. I've thought about this a long time since that statue somehow is frequently on my mind. I have wondered about it and what it's saying to me. To my situation here at Leuven. To my being educated for the Philippines here in a Western milieu.'

This time it was the younger Filipino who was expressing his views.

'I would agree with you if one only looked at the book. But, look, Father, at what he's doing. He's reading a book, true. And pouring water. Sometimes beer.' He laughed as he added those words.

'But he's standing up, not sitting down. And he has his legs at two different levels. To me he's firmly rooted in the ground. That's the real source of his education, the book merely expresses what has been derived from the true source. It is the ground we stand in that matters – no matter where we are. In the Philippines, in India, in Africa, or here in Leuven.

'My fellow students come from all over the world, Father, not just from Belgium. I've learned a lot from my interactions with them. Yes, for what I hope to do in the Philippines. I've one foot, just like the right one of the scholar, firmly stuck in Philippine soil. I intend to leave it there. I've not left it even if I have lifted the other foot, as he does with his left, to tread on Leuven's soil.

'With both feet on the ground, I want to explore what others have learned and written in their books. After all, they have their valuable experiences to share and that's what I find them doing when I read their books. That scholar is not in an ivory tower. It's out here in the open, where we are, where the people are, here in a busy junction of Leuven. Out here in the sun, not in the darkness of the cave. In our midst.'

Father Fuentes looked at the young seminarian in astonishment. Jose had the same passion he had shown several years ago in front of his bishop. He had no reason to doubt Jose's sincerity about serving his country. Yet he was expressing a different view, one that startled Father Fuentes.

Here in the center of Leuven, the now older Father Fuentes was listening to another Filipino, not extolling the glories of European culture as his previous bishop had done, but challenging him to rethink what he had long believed in, prompting him to see things differently, not to be trapped ...

Father Fuentes put a fatherly hand on Jose's shoulder, one generation resting on the next.

'Thank you, you've given me something to think about. Maybe my bishop knew you would be here,' he joked.

★   ★   ★

'Richard could mind me – no problem there, right, Ma?'

Aisling was consulting her young son. She wanted to attend the lecture being given by Professor Lyotard at the Institute of Philosophy of the university of Leuven. It was on Postmodernism and she wanted to hear first-hand the views of one of the most well-known exponents of this trend in literature, but she was concerned about childminding arrangements for Philip. It seems, however, that Philip himself was not bothered by the situation. In fact, she got the distinct impression that she was being strongly encouraged to go – and not for any academic reason on Philip's part.

'But it wouldn't be fair asking him, he might want to go himself,' Aisling commented.

'He might, then again he might not.' Philip was not put off easily. Then he added, 'I'll ask him, he won't say no.'

'What makes you think that?'

'Hmm. I just know.'

'And what will you say to him?'

'I need someone nice to take care of me!'

'Philip!' Somehow Aisling didn't like the sound of it.

'Only while you're away.'

'That's better. But on second thought, I think I'll ask him myself.'

When Aisling approached Richard, he assured her it was no problem. He had not intended to go to the lecture anyway since it was in French. And looking after Philip would be a pleasure.

'See, I told you, he'd say yes.'

Aisling's colour changed.

'Were you very sure then?' Richard asked.

'A nice man would say yes.'

Richard exchanged glances with Aisling as if to say, how can one beat that logic?

So it was arranged. That Saturday during the two hours that Aisling would be engaged in academic matters, Richard and Philip would pursue their own interests. Philip had added, 'The men will be together!' Since there was a small fair at the Centrum, Richard suggested spending the time there. Unless, of course, young Philip had other plans. No, he had answered, he just wanted to be with Richard.

Richard was both amused and troubled by Philip's answer. He was thrilled to see that Philip liked him – and even proud of him the way he was holding his hand most of the time when they were roaming around the streets of Leuven. Philip sometimes led the way when his childish interests took him to the jugglers on the street or when his curious eyes spotted something more intriguing than what they were presently

229

looking at. Aisling had warned Richard that he would be worn out before the two hours were up because Philip could be a bundle of activity and would literally pull him from one attraction to another.

But Richard was also bothered – Philip put a lot of trust in him. And Richard couldn't help thinking about the innocence of children and how adults could prey on it. Just wanting to be with Richard meant that Philip felt secure with him. How a child's world is demolished, he thought, when adults take away, sometimes violently, that sense of security.

The two hours passed by. Since they had arranged to meet Aisling at the Fonske, they moved towards it. But Aisling beat them to the meeting place. She was anxious to know how the 'two men' had got on.

VIII

The news Richard had been waiting for was due today. So he had gone to the School of Philosophy to pick up his mail before the concierge could disappear with it.

The last time Richard felt nervous about his mail was when he was wondering about the outcome of his application to do research at this university. He had opened the envelope which bore the seal of Mercier University with some trepidation. Fortunately, it was good news then, his application was successful. He hoped it would be the same with today's mail. This was a more important one since it would contain the news about his application for tenure.

He had submitted his application packet last fall, a rather thin one. As was requested, he had written a narrative addressing his teaching, scholarship and service, the three aspects of his work which would be evaluated by his department, his Chair, his Dean, and the Rank and Tenure Committee composed of tenured full professors.

He was known to be a very good teacher, in fact quite popular among the students. Since peer evaluation had begun to feature in his university his classes had been visited by two of his colleagues.

One of them gave him the impression that there was nothing to be concerned about. Since this faculty member was by all accounts an effective teacher he felt reassured by her comment.

The other one was quite vague. When he pressed him for suggestions, he merely said: better preparation, more use of audio-visual aids and more handouts. All rather general and to some extent even ludicrous suggestions. Did he want him to be showing slides, videos, and playing CDs in a philosophy class? Was he meant to entertain the students?

231

Richard was not really convinced. In fact, he was rather suspicious of colleagues evaluating other colleagues when they themselves needed to be evaluated! Who evaluates the evaluators? Should their report have any significance just because they were given the task of evaluating, particularly when there were no guidelines on how to evaluate? 'See what he is like as a teacher,' was all that was said to this colleague. Just because he has experience does not necessarily mean that he can be a reliable evaluator. Some experience is *bad* experience and should not be shared. He remembered something from William James to the effect that having experience is not the main thing, it is what you do with that experience that counts.

Besides, Richard had some reservations about using too many audio-visual aids in teaching. He had gone to a conference on Teaching Philosophy where one of the speakers demonstrated the use of such aids in teaching an introductory philosophy class. The speaker had been funded generously to put together some kind of philosophy syllabus which would be taught using this highly sophisticated technology: filmstrips, newspaper clippings, sound, lights, etc. The idea was to show the students that they were bombarded with all these opinions, comments and vague generalities and that true philosophizing goes beyond that.

The theory was fine since it showed the relevance and the concreteness of philosophy, Richard felt, but he couldn't help but wonder whether it was not more of a show than real teaching.

Perhaps he was too young and inexperienced to appreciate what this very experienced professor who was providing them with this fantastic methodology was sharing with them. But how long could one keep that up? he wondered. It may interest the students for a while, but even that which is interesting becomes boring when it is kept up at that level.

That is why he did not really understand nor appreciate his colleague's suggestions. And yet that report would be part of his file, to be taken into account by all those who would be evaluating his application. Still, he was hopeful since all along he had been getting rather positive and even flattering student evaluations. The only snag was that this rather vague colleague-evaluator pointed out that popularity among the students was no guarantee of effective teaching – whatever that means, Richard had muttered to himself after that faculty's comment.

His real fear was his scholarship. He recalled what he had written down by way of a report on his scholarship in the last six years. Very skimpy. A mere three book reviews. The rest was a report on what he had been working on – for the last three years, the Dean had pointed out to him, without any obvious progress. Still, he thought that the award of the research fellowship might straighten that dismal record out.

To his horror he realized that he had not accomplished anything on paper either in the last couple of months that he had been here. He had learned a lot. But what was required were 'tangible results' of his scholarship. That was what all those evaluating his application would be looking for. His stomach was in a knot. There really was pressure to 'publish or perish'.

Richard's thoughts went over his service. He had been conscientious in attending departmental meetings and had done whatever he had been asked to do by his Chair. But when he thought about it he had been asked to do little except to be in charge of ordering books for the library philosophy collection. It was really a matter of simply circulating slips and cards on new books among his departmental colleagues and collecting their order cards for forwarding to the acquisitions librarian. Hardly a great record for service, he felt. He had asked to be on committees. But he was told that he should spend more time on making progress with his scholarship. So no committee work, no service. It was a vicious circle. On the other hand, he was really being given plenty of scope to pursue his research. Was it too late?

Richard rehearsed some of his misgivings about the whole process. Maybe he was rationalizing, steeling himself up in case the news was bad. It was easy to blame the system when things did not go your way. So maybe he was not being fair.

Still, like his friend in another university with whom he shared some of his academic experiences, he had always found it difficult to comment on his colleagues' performance whenever anyone else was up for evaluation: first year, second year, then application for advancement to tenure and/or promotion to a higher rank.

His friend did not make things easy for Richard when he told him that at his university colleagues were generally critical of the person being evaluated. That person would of course be absent and all discussion was confidential. But it was amazing the kind of comments that would be made. His friend remembered one in particular about somebody's scholarship not being considered up to par because that colleague had dared to write an article and had not cited the evaluator who was an expert in that field. The topic of the disputed article was the existence of other minds!

Richard always felt uneasy about judging someone else's performance. Who was he to make a judgement? If only the others felt that way about his own performance. But there was no chance of that, he reminded himself as he bit his tongue. In fact, one colleague had warned him that in her department a colleague's reticence at their meetings was interpreted as showing that person's inability to make insightful and perceptive observations. Richard shook his head in disbelief when he heard that. Fortunately, it was not his own department. But these people were debating someone's career, not an academic issue. He really felt annoyed that some academics could make such facetious comments.

Maybe it was just as well that he was not on a committee, particularly the Rank and Tenure Committee, whose responsibility was really onerous. He wondered whether any of them agonized over the idea of having to recommend that somebody's application for tenure or promotion be turned down. On the other hand, he could see the need for such a committee. It was important to ensure that certain standards were maintained throughout the university. Anyway, it was common practice in American universities. Such an entrenched tradition could hardly be uprooted, no matter what he felt or said. After all, he was an untenured assistant professor. Would he remain that way? That was what this mail was going to tell him.

And there it was, the airmail envelope he had been waiting for. It came from his university. It was just as well that it had been sent by airmail rather than by fax, he said to himself, recalling sarcastically Anton Brown's unbelievable experience with fax being sent to him and how the girl in the Academic Center would send it back to the professor's university by airmail while the professor was here in Leuven. He noted that the letter came from the Vice-President for Academic Affairs on whose shoulders rested the important task of communicating the outcome of the faculty member's application.

Richard took the envelope, slipped it inside his jacket and walked off. He did not even bother checking whether there was any other mail for him. He was anxious to find out the content of this one. But he would not open the envelope here since there were other people around who had come for their coffee, this small room being actually the place where the School's staff could spend their coffee break. He always felt out of place here because all the discussion was in Dutch. Which was perfectly understandable, given the fact that he was in a Dutch-speaking university. Before leaving, however, he did say hello to the two persons who had entered the room.

Richard decided to head for the Erasmus restaurant close by. Perhaps he could have coffee. But when he saw that there were several students already taking up their position for a morning session of open-air deep philosophical discussions at the outdoor part of the restaurant, he changed his mind. Particularly since he recognized one of the students who was a Ph.D. candidate and writing a thesis on Leibniz. He merely waved at the future Leibniz scholar. He was apprehensive, that was rather obvious. And yet he would not open the envelope immediately to put an end to his agony. Was he testing his patience? Or was he postponing whatever reaction he would have when he did open the envelope? Is there ever a good time for such news? Or a good place?

Without realizing it he found himself in Donatus Park. It was a municipal park but because it was almost completely surrounded by buildings belonging to the university of Leuven, it was to all intents and purposes a university park. One could see that from all the students who were lying out in the sun today. This park was also starting to come to life. The trees which lined the street were putting on a spurt of growth. Only a few weeks ago they were still bare. Last week the first signs of greenery appeared, hesitantly as if the new leaves were checking to see whether indeed it was time for them to grace the scenery. Very much like the first animals sent out by Noah after the flood. A rather apt comparison, Richard thought, since opposite him was the theology library. He wondered whether Jennifer, if she had not returned to England, would be there, buried in her research.

But today, the leaves were definitely out. They must have decided that it was indeed time to come out, that spring had sprung, as he had heard Aisling put it.

Jennifer and Aisling. How similar their lives were, yet how different they were. Both had experienced the loss of a loved one yet how different their reaction had been. And their reaction told him a lot about their personalities and their attitude towards their academic work.

His mind went back to the conversation he had had with Jennifer in her apartment. Had it made any difference to the way she thrust herself into academic work? He had thought of writing her a letter but decided not to in case it would be misinterpreted. Still, he hoped that sometime their paths would cross again. The times he had spent with her, a brief period come to think of it, opened his eyes to a number of things about himself. Once again he admitted that to some extent she had been an inspiration, like a Muse, to his creative work. He did not want, however, to adopt her initial attitude – how did she put it? – of hiding behind her books, like the scholar at the Fons Sapientiae.

Aisling was just as much of a scholar as Jennifer was. But her enthusiasm for literature was not an escape from the frailties of life. Nor a shield from the 'slings and arrows of outrageous fortune.' He admired Aisling, but differently from Jennifer. She too had been like a Muse, her Gaelic name implying that role, inspiring him and showing him that there was more to life than was dreamt of in his philosophy. He smiled as he became aware that Shakespeare was becoming alive to him in Aisling's conversations. Aisling kept life alive in her pursuit of scholarship. That was what he really liked.

What if there was something more? Was he beginning to feel love for Aisling? He really craved for her company now. But was he ready for any commitments? When he did not know what his future was — which he was holding right here in front of him.

Slowly he slipped his forefinger between the flap and the envelope. He was trembling, he was nervous. Finally, the letter opened up. He read its contents — and he groaned. He had been denied tenure.

$$\star \quad \star \quad \star$$

'Isn't Richard a nice man, Ma?' Philip looked up at his mother, who was cosily seated in the armchair reading.

He had been drawing some pictures on bond paper while sitting at the study desk. He always liked it when his mother let him use the desk. It made him feel like a grown-up. Besides, it was a lot easier to manoeuvre his pencil when he was in an upright position rather than sprawled on the floor. That was fine when he was little but now he wanted to do his work the way adults do.

'I suppose he is.' Aisling's reply was non-committal.

Besides, she knew that Philip's question was a leading one. Her young son had become good at asking in a certain way that pre-empted the reply he wanted. But she put down the book, sensing that there was more to it than a casual remark from Philip.

'You know, he's good fun.'

'Like your friends at school? Maeve, for instance, or Ian?' This time it was her turn to put Philip on the spot.

'Sort of.'

'What do you mean, sort of?'

Aisling was not content with the reply. Was she needling him? Now she realized where Philip was getting all this knack of following up the question.

'He minded me, 'member? I had a terrific time. He's good at kicking the ball. He tickles me. He beats me at running. And ... and he is fantastic at the bullfight!' That seemed to clinch it for him.

Richard and Philip liked pretending one was the bull and the other the bullfighter. Richard had never seen a real bullfight and Philip was only one year old when he was taken to a bullfight that time her family went on holiday to the Costa del Sol. So it was all imagination, plus of course what they saw on television. But the two seemed to enjoy swinging a towel or any large cloth and then snorting and rubbing the ground with one foot.

'Oh, I see.'

Her reply must have sounded disappointing since Philip set down his pencil and edged over to her side. He put his arms around his mother and kissed her.

'What was that for?' inquired a delighted Aisling.

'Nothing ... isn't it nice when Richard brings you flowers?'

Aisling blushed a little. Unfortunately, to Aisling's disgust it did not escape her little divil-of-a-son's notice.

'Ma, you're blushing!' Philip's uncalled-for observation made the situation worse.

'I'm not!' protested Aisling to no avail, more colour creeping into her cheeks.

'You are, you are,' said a delighted Philip.

'You are being bold now, do you know that?'

'You like him. The way he likes you.'

'What made you say that?'

There was no way Philip was allowing her to wriggle out of the situation. So she might as well confront it by asking Philip the question. To her surprise Philip had a ready answer.

'He brings you flowers. So he must like you. And ... and he kissed you.'

Aisling's colour became a deeper red. The trouble with her

Irish complexion, Aisling thought, was that it could never hide a blush. She was getting warmer with embarrassment. Richard had kissed her a couple of times. But it was a harmless, a friendly sort of way on the cheeks when saying goodbye. And that was all there was. They were becoming good friends, nothing more. But this little fellow was becoming too interested, too much so for his age. She must put a stop to it this very minute.

'But I also kiss you and you kiss me. So what does that mean? And you kiss Granny and your aunt and your uncle. And even when you are not asked for a kiss. Remember?'

This time she thought she had Philip. She was referring to the kiss he blew to the Sabena girl. And the one that nearly knocked down the poor parish priest! Her mother's parish priest had been visiting them on that occasion when they were in Barrowtown for the Christmas holidays. He had not seen Philip for two years so he wanted to say hello to him. Aisling had gone to the kitchen to call Philip, who was playing with his toy cars. She had prompted him on what to do, telling him that the priest was a holy man and that he should ask him for his blessing. Instead when Philip entered the room he immediately gave the elderly parish priest a kiss – on the lips! The parish priest jumped up from fright. He was not used to this treatment, after all. Normally kids would simply say hello to him, at a distance. To relieve the embarrassment they all laughed together. And Philip never forgot the incident. That was why it was his turn to blush now when he was reminded of it. Maybe she was being unfair to him, thought Aisling.

'See, see.' Philip was quick on the draw. 'You kiss me because you love me, and I kiss you because I love you. And that's why I kiss Granny, Auntie and Uncle. So that means Richard loves you too! Doesn't he?'

This time it was Aisling's turn to be sorry. She was in deep water.

'Enough of this nonsense. I'll tell you what we'll do. The shops are still open,' she remarked, checking her watch. It was only three in the afternoon. 'Why don't you and I look for other trolls?'

She was not prepared for Philip's answer. She had expected him to jump at the invite.

'I've enough. We don't have to look for others any more.'

'But I thought you wanted to complete the troll family.'

'I did. But Granny brought a few, 'member?' And he pointed to the grotesque-looking individuals lined up on one of the shelves. 'And one of them can be the daddy troll,' he added rather suggestively. 'Maybe Richard can play ball with me. Will I check?'

'You know you shouldn't be disturbing him when he's studying.'

'I know, but he *could* be finished. Like you are.'

'He's probably not back from the School.'

Aisling was doing her best to restrain Philip. But not convincingly since she agreed that it was not a bad idea after all.

She had come to appreciate Richard's company. The times when they went for walks were times that she really enjoyed. She felt at ease in Richard's company. She had not felt that way for a very long time, not since Sean. Their conversations helped them to get to know each other better as they shared one another's experiences.

Not all of their conversations were profound. But sometimes there is a certain depth in shallow talk, she realized. It can bond people, create a context, usher in other factors. That was one thing she really appreciated about her Irish heritage. All this so-called small talk, even about the weather. She recalled the number of times she and Sean had gone for long walks in Marlay Park or at the Phoenix Park. How they treasured those moments. How they brought them closer to each other.

And funnily enough Richard was doing exactly the same thing now. But she did not want to regard Richard as another Sean. It would be unfair. Yet she had to admit that her warm feelings were coming back. And Philip was right, Richard was fun to be with. There were times when she longed for his company. But she was in no rush to enter into any relationships. She needed a friend, she could offer friendship.

And Richard seemed to appreciate that and to enjoy her company.

'Will I check?'

'If you like. But he's probably not in yet. We'd have heard him.'

His mother's permission was all Philip needed. So he stood up immediately and strode out of their apartment, leaving the front door open, as he had been instructed right from the beginning. He knocked on Richard's door as was his custom whenever he wanted to see Richard. There was no reply. He tried again. Still no reply.

A rather downcast Philip retraced his steps. Where could Richard be?

★   ★   ★

Richard was angry. With himself, with the decision. And yet he was half expecting it. There had been some warnings along the way. Still, when the news came, it was a big blow. His world had suddenly collapsed. He had hoped, against hope it turned out, that the award of the research fellowship would swing it in his favor. His good record as a teacher had not carried the weight he thought it would. And yet it seemed to have done the trick for a couple of his colleagues with whom he thought he could compare his case. He sympathized with Anton Brown, who had to return to the USA to defend his own success with tenure. But damn it, if the two at his own university got it in the past, why did the authorities refuse to give it to him? His colleagues were right. The university was really placing the emphasis on research.

But what was he to do now? He certainly had no enthusiasm to read a book, and definitely none to plow furrows of scholarly work. The letter said that according to university regulations he was entitled to a terminal contract for one year. The Vice-President for Academic Affairs said that he hoped that the year would give him a chance to look for another job.

But Richard did not feel like returning to his university.

241

How could he, knowing that his colleagues were aware that he had been denied tenure? There could be some tension too. His friend in the Business School had suffered the same fate two years ago. He stayed for that one year, but there was ill feeling all around. How could one really stay in a place that had rejected one?

Richard kept staring ahead of him. It was a blank stare. Unfocused. But that was exactly the way he was now. One minute he had a job, an identity. Now he felt he had been stripped of that identity.

And he had to worry about money. He had not yet fully paid back the loans he took out when he went to graduate school. He certainly would not be able to pay them back now. He had thought of buying a condominium in Los Angeles. Now he was somewhat relieved that the then inflated prices of property in Los Angeles prevented him from doing so. He would have had to sell it anyway since, deprived of his job, there was no way he could afford a mortgage. He was sweating although it was not a particularly warm day. It was cold sweat. He was panicking. Look for another teaching job in philosophy? He knew the odds were against him. In fact, he was in a worse situation now since he had been denied tenure, compared to the time he applied for a position right after finishing his doctorate. That question would surely come up at the interview, presuming he would even get to that stage.

When he had landed a job after submitting several applications, he thought he was very lucky indeed. Many of his fellow philosophy graduates were not. The job market was simply limited. One of his friends was still driving a taxi. A really educated taxi driver, his friend bitterly described himself. That could be his fate. And it would be worse since he had had the chance to stay at the job. He blew it. Was it all his fault?

He wished Lonergan University had been a teaching university or college. Perhaps he would have gotten tenure. Times had changed in his university. He knew that scholarship was being given a lot of importance. But fresh from graduate work, he believed he had a contribution to make to the

242

development of his field. Then he seemed to be stuck. And he was still stuck – as far as that part of his learning experience was concerned.

Leuven was providing him with the kind of environment he valued more, but not the kind that he needed. Perhaps it would have been too late anyway. Even if he had completed his manuscript at the end of his stay here, he would still not have made it. The evaluation of his work was done in the fall and early spring.

There was no point in blaming anyone but himself. That was why he was angry. It just had not come together for him.

Richard checked his watch. It was past lunchtime. But he was not hungry. How could he be, given the circumstances? He had been at the park for hours, fixed to the one place.

His mind was confused, his future looked bleak. His facial muscles tightened, betraying the worries he had, as he thought of applying for another job and going to the meetings of the American Philosophical Association.

Six years ago he assiduously checked the *Jobs for Philosophers*, published by the association. He was told that for one job opening there were 100 to 200 applicants. Still he went through the listing trying to match his specialized field with the requirements of the job. He got one interview after submitting his resumé to several departments. He had not expected to get the job, but he did. That was why he regarded himself lucky. The thought of having to go through all the job-hunting at the 'cattle-market', which was what these placement sessions at the APA's conventions had come to be known, sickened him. The frustration, the low morale, the endless search among the job-seekers.

But what choice did he have?

*   *   *

Richard had lost track of the time. When it started to get cooler in the park, he decided to go for a walk in search of some kind of an answer to his plight. He had gone to Arenberg, where he kept walking aimlessly, trying to come to grips with his emotions. His anger had turned to frustration, then to melancholy.

After a while, he did not even know what he was feeling. In fact, he felt simply empty. He stared at the ducks swimming in the small pond, the small ones following the mother. Without a care in the world. He thought of Philip and his smile whenever the ducks would approach him for a feed. Both boy and ducks seemed to have no cares at all. He wished he could be like them. But he couldn't. He had to worry about his future.

He thought of Aisling. What would she say to him? What would they talk about now? He had told her about his situation, and she had wished him the best. He could have used more of that Irish luck that he had heard so much about. But Aisling did not have all the luck either, having been through a tough time herself. She had coped. She had lifted herself up. Maybe he could learn something from her.

Yet he would not go back to the Begijnhof since he lacked the courage to tell her the bad news. So he continued walking without a definite goal. But the more he did so the more he thought of Aisling. He was starting to treasure her friendship. Was this news going to bring it to an end? Even their growing friendship was being threatened by this development. The bad news was beginning to sink in. It was not just being denied tenure. It was all the consequences that he had to face.

He stooped to remove the stone that had lodged itself in his right shoe. It was hurting him – just like this news. Righting himself up, he stared at the fields ahead of him.

And what about his parents? They will be very disappointed when they hear about it. All along they had supported him through thick and thin. He thought that he had given them reason to be proud of him when he became an assistant professor. Now he had to tell them that that was no longer true. He wished he could say that it would not bother them. He loved his parents and they loved him. But parents are also human, he thought. They can take pride in their children, but they can also be disappointed. And rightly so. After all, there is a part of them in their children.

When he was a kid his father and mother smiled with him, wept with him and laughed with him. He had desperately tried to repay them. And he had started to do that, even hoping somehow to help them financially, although they always assured him that what mattered most was that he cared for them. He did, but how could he concretely help them since he was on the brink of being jobless? At his age he could not expect his parents to still support him. Especially when his parents were not particularly well-off themselves.

They were entitled to their retirement. When he got the job, that was the situation. And he wanted to ease them into a more leisurely kind of life after all the sacrifices they had made for him. He wanted to share with them what he had, but now he was going to be reduced to nothing. And as his friend told him, the abhorrence of poverty is not just that you do not have anything, it robs you of the ability to share.

That was when it really hit him. And hit him hard. Thinking of financial trouble made him realize what could lie in front of him. Joblessness led to poverty. Worse, it could lead to alienation.

Before, when one was jobless, one could say that it was probably the fault of the jobless person. That was no longer the case. Jobs were not there. And even if they were there, one's training could lead to frustration. Could he work as a waiter? Or washing cars? He would be told that he was overqualified. And he would be.

The trouble with getting all these qualifications was that if you did not get the right job, you could be left complaining as to why you had wasted all that time and money to end up in such a job. He had nothing against waiting at table or washing cars. In fact, as a graduate student, he did exactly those things to try to earn enough to survive. But he did not need a Ph.D. – he could have done them several years ago and spared himself and his parents a lot of money and effort.

Now he was beginning to understand an aspect of 'senioritis.' His students, in their last semester, would often be afflicted by it. Often the faculty, including himself, would brush it off as an annual malady affecting the seniors, who were presumed not to want to study any more because of their impending graduation. Or probably they had had enough of papers, exams and professors! But was it more? Once a student talked to him of her anxiety over her future. Somehow in the first three years, she admitted, one was cushioned by the knowledge that there was another year ahead. But what about life after graduation – when there was no job in prospect? Nor graduate school or anything. The openness of the future frightened her. And while fretting over the oncoming year, while desperately sending their resumés to often uncaring employers, while spending a considerable time haunting career offices, they were expected to turn in their papers on time, read stacks of seemingly irrelevant texts and prepare for exams. No wonder there is such a thing as 'senioritis!'

Meanwhile some kind of mist descended on the place, wrapping itself around Richard. He buttoned his coat, and quickened his pace a bit. Two students, chasing one another, passed him by. In the distance, he could hear the engine of a car being started.

His thoughts would not leave him. What was bothering him now was that he had heard that some of the homeless in Santa Monica had once had excellent jobs. But what had happened? Was that what was in store for him? A number of times he had driven to Santa Monica because he liked the place. However, the number of homeless people in the park, on benches, near the beach troubled him. What pricked his conscience most was when he saw an old lady carting her pathetic-looking possessions around. Nobody, especially in one's old age, should be reduced to that. There must be a better alternative. And when he recalled the faces of the homeless in Santa Monica, he kept telling himself that there was a time when every single one of them had been a cute baby. Every single one of them should have had a better future. What had happened?

He had had these thoughts before. Yes, that was when he was thinking about the problem of evil that he was supposed to be working on. Then it was an academic problem

246

challenging him as a philosopher. Now he was caught up in it. It was no longer a theoretical issue, it was reality. It was a hole that he was fast sinking into.

He looked at the river that divided the two parts of Arenberg. The swiftly moving water looked so inviting.

*   *   *

Philip wanted to know the time. He was playing with his train, which Richard had given to him for a present.

'The time? Time to go to bed, young fellow.'

That was not what he meant. And of course Aisling knew that. Philip had been waiting up for Richard. And at eight o'clock there was still no sign of him. Aisling explained to Philip that Richard was probably still getting some work done. She said that sometimes when they were studying, what they were thinking about would become so interesting that it would be a pity simply to stop.

'It gets hold of you and you forget the time. You get pulled by your thoughts. Like your train set as it keeps going around and around. You cannot just stop. You could forget it the next time.'

'Like when I'm playing?'

'That's right.' Aisling thought she had found the apt analogy. Her Philip was a quick learner.

'Pity for me to stop now and go to bed then.' He smiled ever so innocently.

Aisling could have kicked herself. She had been outsmarted by this six-year-old. He had turned the tables on her, using the very same example she had given him. What a move! She may as well admit it.

'Well, wise fellow. You may have another few minutes.'

But Aisling knew that Philip was not really enjoying his train. She could see his ears prick up the two times when the main door to the apartment opened. But it was the other tenants in the building. One of them passed by their apartment. And Philip thought it was Richard. He even made a slight move to get up until the footfalls showed that the

247

person was going to the floor above them. She could read the disappointment on Philip's face.

After an hour there was still no sign of Richard. Philip had to go to bed. He was trying not to show his disappointment as he kissed her goodnight.

'Will you read me a story, Ma?'

'Certainly,' said Aisling, trying to cheer him up. 'OK, what will it be?' as she and Philip got up and headed for the bedroom.

It had become a routine for mother and son so she was surprised that he had asked her to do it. Was this the young boy's way of coping with disappointment?

*   *   *

It was rather late when Richard finally returned to his apartment. He looked at his watch. It was eleven o'clock. He had not been aware of how late it had become since with spring came the long evenings. At nine it was still bright. In the middle of the summer it would still be bright even at eleven.

Richard noticed that the light in Aisling's apartment was still on. She was probably still doing her research. It was very quiet so Philip must be in bed. At this time he would be, he told himself.

He wondered whether he should call, not wanting to burden Aisling with his bad news. But he desperately needed someone to talk to. So he knocked on her door softly so as not to awaken Philip since the bedroom in Aisling's apartment was just opposite their front door.

Aisling opened the door.

'Hi, I know it's late. Can I come in still?'

The look on Richard's face betrayed what he had gone through the past several hours. Aisling knew.

'Come in, Philip's in bed.'

They went to the large sitting room.

'I'll make a pot of tea. I won't be a minute. Do sit down.'

When she came back with the tea, Richard unburdened himself. Aisling listened, listened with care and affection.

248

Just then the bedroom door swung open. It was Philip in his pyjamas. He rubbed his eyes to take away the sleep.

'Richard, you're back!' and with that he flew straight into his lap.

★   ★   ★

Had Richard checked his mail more carefully he would have seen another airmail envelope addressed to him. By coincidence it had arrived on the same day that his bad news reached him. Given the arrangement of the distribution of the mail in the School, it was brought by the concierge that afternoon to Richard's office. Richard had no reason to go to his office after learning the outcome of his application. So two days elapsed before he did go up to check whether there was any mail or messages for him.

The airmail letter also came from a university in the USA. It was from his friend, Dr. Raúl Sanchez, who was a member of Ethnic Studies at one of the universities in the Bay area. He and Richard had got to know each other quite well more through personal contact than because of any common academic interests.

Dr. Sanchez was in the social sciences. His interest was not just in the academic discipline but also, and in fact more so, in the political arena. He lived his politics, breathed it and survived in it. Moreover, he felt a strong obligation to serve the community, particularly ethnic minorities in the US whom he believed had suffered a lot of discrimination.

Dr. Sanchez believed that to rectify the imbalance there was a need to take serious account of this historical factor (none of this 'cosmetic exercise' trying to hire people merely to reflect the changing face of the population) when assessing the qualifications of applicants for a job. He was a strong defender of affirmative action. Against those who claimed that because affirmative action favored a particular group, namely the minorities, and that a more equitable way was to open the job to everyone regardless of gender, race, religion and age, he argued that one could not expect minorities to compete on an

249

equal basis since they were products of discriminatory policies in the first place. How could you suddenly be expected to compete on an equal basis when there was no equality in the first place? Equal competition assumes – wrongly, Dr. Sanchez pointed out – that people can shed off years and even decades of unequal treatment. That was why he was very critical of certain tests which were influential in enabling students to enter into higher education. Those tests were biased in favor of white, male and privileged students. What chance then had those who did not fit that category?

He fought for academia to be more multiculturally diverse. Look, he argued, America has become multicultural. It has always been, right from its beginning. And yet our university education is still predominantly male, white and privileged. Look at our faculty, check out our administrators, examine our curriculum, he demanded. What will you find? The obvious fact that many still think universities do not have to face the multicultural, multi-ethnic reality factor.

Dr. Sanchez was making strong demands. He knew the climate was right for them. There was a growing awareness of this since recently some universities had in fact come out with affirmative action policies. But he suspected that, despite what was said on paper, the reality was not yet what it should be. One of his research projects was to survey all the American universities and colleges in order to provide statistics and factual information. He was also interested in examining the policies and the mission statements of these institutions because he maintained that these are what really guide the actual action. Or if they don't, one can have recourse to those guidelines.

In one case in his own university, an Asian-American was given tenure before she finished her Ph.D. She did get her degree in the fall semester prior to her tenure becoming effective. But it was not a popular decision among some of the faculty, even among one or two minority faculty. The usual policy was to hire somebody who had a Ph.D. or was at least on the verge of getting one. This was not the case with the Asian-American individual. The objectors claimed that to give tenure to such a one, when everyone else was expected to be bound by the university practice, was not only to disregard the practice but to discriminate against the others. What kind of justice was this? You cannot rectify an injustice by another injustice, cried out the opponents of this decision. They suspected that the only reason why this person got tenure was that she was a minority. They cited a case in the university where the tenure-track faculty did not pass the second-year evaluation since he did not complete the Ph.D. dissertation during that time. Was the university making exceptions for minorities, they angrily asked?

It was a hot issue, but Dr. Sanchez who was then the Chair of his department fought hard for the Asian-American member of his department. To lose her – and he confidently pointed out that she would be snapped up by other institutions – would be to make a dent in the progress already made by the university towards showing that it cared about the injustice done to racial minorities. And it should not be forgotten that she was a woman, which meant that it was a double-kill to racial and gender inequalities. But the opposition would not be silenced. Perhaps if she were also a lesbian and a Jew, they sarcastically protested, it would be a quadruple victory then.

It certainly was causing an uproar.

It was only a partial victory for Dr. Sanchez: his Asian-American colleague was given tenure while her promotion to the rank of associate professor was delayed. The champion of minority faculty was convinced that more work in this area needed to be done. By some accounts, however, it was a brilliant compromise on the part of the administration since it was still in line with accepted practice in that university where advancement to tenure and promotion in rank were separate. But the critics alleged that fear of being accused of racial discrimination and any possible backlash was behind the decision. From the perspective of the administration the move was tangible evidence of their support for affirmative action. And what about gays and lesbians? Let's see what the administrators will do then, announced these begrudgers.

And so it went on and on – and is still going on in these controversial times in American academia.

The letter from Dr. Sanchez to Richard was a letter of support. He had heard from the grapevine that he had been denied tenure. Richard was puzzled since all this was supposed to be confidential, especially since his university was in southern California while Dr. Sanchez was in northern California. It must be all this networking, he shrugged. Anyway that was not what was important at the moment. Dr. Sanchez had offered to muster support among ethnic faculty and students to put pressure on Richard's university to reconsider the decision. The loss of the Hispanic philosopher would be detrimental to Lonergan University and would erode the credibility of that university. It would damage the morale of the student body and do away with their role models.

Richard could just imagine the situation. He had read in *The Times Higher Education Supplement,* two copies of which the bookstore right in the middle of Leuven near the Fons Sapientiae stocked every week, that some Chicano students and faculty at California College of Los Angeles had gone on hunger strike in protest at the impending closure of Chicano Studies there. He could not imagine himself doing that. He was not a politically minded person, unlike Dr. Sanchez, nor did he want to be hoisted on the political pole of his fellow minorities. He did appreciate Dr. Sanchez's show of support, but he was not sure whether it was really support for him or for his race.

This was where Richard and Dr. Sanchez differed. Despite coming from the same ethnic background, their outlook and approach varied. Richard was proud of his ethnic background and ashamed that he did not speak Spanish; but he was determined to remedy the latter. At least until the bad news arrived, since now he did not know what he was going to do. But he wanted to make it on merit – even if the standards were dictated by white, male, privileged groups.

He would have been reluctant to accept the job at his university solely on the basis of his color (although someone did try to convince him that that was the case in the first place.) He was convinced that affirmative action, at least as it was aggressively practised, was not only an injustice to his white colleagues but also to people of color who were trying to make it on merit. He had always pointed out that any appointment based on that factor would not win any respect. It would deflect from the achievements of people of color since there would always be that nagging suspicion that they had made it only because of the concessions made to the color of their skin.

That was why Richard had opposed, to the surprise of white colleagues and the disgust of his fellow minorities who branded him a traitor, the introduction of Ethnic Studies in his university for political reasons. He had argued, not from a position of strength since he was merely an untenured assistant professor who had only been a few years in the university at that time, that if the university wanted to introduce Ethnic Studies it should be for academic reasons. Only then would it be able to stand up to the demands and standards of other academic departments.

At that public meeting he was booed by a small group at the corner of the hall. After the meeting, one of those booers lambasted Richard for being uninformed: he had been brainwashed by the privileged majority. Richard resented the personal attack because he thought that he had argued on the basis of what he believed in. He was particularly peeved on this point. The meeting had been hastily called after the Los Angeles riots following the announcement of the not-guilty verdict on the policemen involved in the Rodney King incident. Several concerned students wanted the university to take action, insisting that 'business should not go on as usual.' Richard was full of admiration for the initiative and concern of these students, including their request for a public meeting to air their views.

It was a very good idea until the clamor for Ethnic Studies came from a small group of students backed by a couple of faculty and staff members. Richard had been taken aback by this turn. Yet he could see the logic. There was a need to face the issues which had been the cause of such a violent reaction.

There was a lot of frustration due to discrimination. The disturbances, as these students observed, were an outburst of that frustration. Richard knew there was a lot of truth in that. He also accepted that as a university they had a responsibility to tackle such issues and to educate people about them. He had always felt the need for courses which would address those very points, not just for minorities but for every student of his university. And come to think of it, also for faculty and staff, including himself. The students were making a good case. He was about to add his support when he suddenly realized that there was a different agenda, not from what the students were saying but from what was being demanded.

That was when he balked. And then spoke his piece about academic standards. At the last moment, he decided not to reveal what he was really thinking about. Which was that a few individuals were capitalizing on the incident to press demands that they had been making in vain for a long time. He was becoming suspicious that these individuals were riding on the misfortunes of the victims of the riots to push for their own demands. How was having a large department of Ethnic Studies really going to help those whose shops had been burned down, those who had been attacked or even killed, or those who through no fault of their own felt trapped in their poverty in Los Angeles? While he accepted, and accepted wholeheartedly, that making people aware would ultimately make a difference, as the students were saying, he could not see how the creation of a large and strong Ethnic Studies Department would be the solution.

Perhaps he was one of those who really needed to be educated about these matters – as his colleague vociferously put it. But all he could see were professors in fancy cars, drawing their salaries for teaching and doing research, or becoming well-paid administrators! He acknowledged that he was one of them, but at least he was not teaching courses which allegedly were meant to alleviate the misery and poverty of those discriminated against. He had a high regard for many of his colleagues and students who did spend some time in the community helping out. But that was due to their

254

sense of community. It was pointed out to him that minority professors, like minority sportspersons, politicians, all those who had 'made it', were role models for the minority students as it showed them what they could achieve. But he wondered. Those who had made it had become privileged and those who were not so lucky were still down in the gutter.

And yet, he knew full well that there were many who did use their good fortune to help those who were not so lucky: they were in organizations designed to help the not-so-fortunate.

Maybe he was a traitor to his people. Maybe he had really turned his back on them. Maybe he should be more aware of his ethnicity in terms of the history, the unfortunate history, of his people. Was it not time that he looked for his roots, not in genealogical terms but in social terms? Where was his social consciousness? He was getting confused about the whole thing, starting to feel guilty for not fighting for the rights of his people.

But he could not ignore his other suspicions.

As he relived that incident during the public meeting he wondered whether that had been a factor in his being denied tenure. Anyone before tenure is careful about statements he or she makes. Perhaps he should have kept his mouth shut. To his horror he discovered that the faculty member who had made that cutting remark was a member of the Rank and Tenure Committee.

But he shook his head. He was looking for scapegoats. He was not surprised by the decision, but still it hurt a lot. And it was really hurting him emotionally. And he knew it would also hurt him in other ways.

Richard put down Dr. Sanchez's letter, which he had been holding in his hands while his thoughts carried him away. He would reply to him right now, thanking for his support. But no, he did not want Dr. Sanchez to take any action ...

Richard paused. He had his ideals, but the reality, his reality, his desperate plight. . . Should he compromise what he really believed in? He needed that job badly; there was not much by way of an alternative.

255

So he put down his pen. He needed time to think. It was amazing how academia could also be a political issue.

★   ★   ★

'Richard, what will you do now?' Aisling and Richard were out on their usual afternoon stroll. It was really a marvelous spring day. Arenberg was draped in natural beauty, full of colors, vibrant, even dazzling. A few students were playing football on the fields. Philip had gone over to watch the game while Richard and Aisling ambled along beside the playing field.

'I don't know. It's really hard to tell. I don't even know whether I should tell my host professor. It really doesn't matter as far as the fellowship is concerned. I mean, there was no stipulation that I need to return to my university. It was, of course, expected that I'd finish my manuscript. But all they want from me here is a report of what I've done.'

'Is there anything we can do to help you? You've been very good to us, to Philip especially. You know that he looks up to you.'

Richard smiled. He put up his right hand to shield himself from the strong sunlight. 'Do you think it would make any difference to him if he knew that I've been denied tenure?'

Aisling smiled – it was a lovely natural smile that accentuated her natural feminine beauty. Richard looked at her with affection as he admired her beauty, one that came from within, that bespoke the goodness of her soul.

Richard stretched out his hand to caress her cheek. A loving touch. A response to the goodness he was facing. Aisling's short brown hair brushed against his palm as she slightly tilted her head to respond to his gentle touch.

It was a beautiful moment in a picturesque setting. And everything about it was as natural as the water that flowed nearby, the wind that rustled the leaves, and the sun that warmed their skins. It was a moment that no photograph could have captured. For it was tender and real.

But Philip did capture it. He had turned around just at the

right time. And he smiled. But he said nothing. Nor did he approach them. His place was where he was. Their place was where they were.

'It would *not* make a slight bit of difference. He wouldn't even know what tenure means.' She laughed. 'Nor would I really since the Irish university system is quite different. We don't really talk of tenure ... it must be a tough time for you,' said Aisling, trying to change the subject.

'It is. How does one react to it?'

'Well, I am not a psychologist ...'

'A shrink, we'd say in America. Quick, get me my shrink on the phone. I need some – what do they say? – self-reinforcement.' He laughed at his own joke.

Aisling joined in the laughter.

'They say, laughter is good medicine. That's one of the sections in the *Reader's Digest*. I used to read that stuff when I was an undergraduate,' remarked Richard. 'Some of the jokes were really good. But it doesn't solve anything.'

'Doesn't it? Perhaps we don't give common sense too much credit. But a smile or a laugh can ease tension. It relaxes our muscles. You're right that it doesn't solve the problem. But it does change us. Sometimes I find that it does enable me to see the same unsolved problem from a different perspective.'

'And is that how you cope with misery, frustration and in my case now, joblessness?'

Richard hoped it did not come out as a cynical remark since he did not really mean it that way. He looked at Aisling's face. No, she still had that lovely smile.

'No, not completely; can you imagine a world where people are smiling or laughing all the time?' She laughed heartily. 'Think how tiring that would be, physically as well as aesthetically. I wouldn't like everyone to be grinning at me the whole time. I'd think they were loony or that something was wrong with me!'

This time it was Richard's turn to laugh. He could imagine what such a world would look like – all those mouths stretched sideways. No, he could not take that either. He pictured the world to be full of people with frozen smiles, like

257

those in dance troupes, or chorus girls. That would be awful indeed. But Aisling meant something else.

'So you're saying that a smile or a laugh has not only a physical but also an emotional effect on the person,' Richard concluded, quickly stepping back to avoid crushing the snail crossing his path.

'Even more than that. It reflects a certain attitude. An attitude that refuses to let the situation get the upper hand. It shows an inner strength. An Asian friend once told me about the way the poor and oppressed in Korea deal with their plight. The *minjung*, he said. It's a Korean word taken from the Chinese language. He said the *minjung*, who are oppressed, act out their situation in order that they can laugh at the oppressors. They can't fight them, they don't have the resources. So they ridicule their oppressors through dances, songs and plays.

'I don't think he meant me to do the same. Can you imagine if every time I've been put down, I laughed at those who've done it to me? It would just lead to more of the same. Laughing at someone's face, which is what the *minjung* do, is not necessarily the point here.

'But I've often thought about it. There's something to it if you laugh at the situation, not the perpetrator. It means you've transcended the absurdity of the situation. You've not allowed it to overcome you. And that's difficult.

'Have you ever noticed the inner strength of a child who manages to smile despite the tears?' Aisling laughed as she thought of how she had witnessed it in Philip, who right now was engrossed in watching the game.

'But it still doesn't solve the problem. You can't solve injustice or suffering by a mere smile or laughter. Isn't that rather too simplistic?' objected Richard.

'No, you won't. In answer to your first point. And it would be simplistic to think otherwise. But we've to start somewhere. And I think attitudes, changing our attitudes, is an important first step.'

'You know, that reminds me of Confucius. I don't know much about him, but your Asian friend's reference to ... what was it again?'

'*Minjung.*'

'Yes, the reference to *minjung* made me think of Confucius, especially after you talked about changing attitudes. But let me say this first. A student of mine who was taking Asian philosophy with my colleague said that reading Confucius's *Analects* with all those bits of wisdom or sayings, was like reading a thousand fortune cookies!'

Aisling laughed.

'Anyway, Confucius – at least this is what my student told me – is supposed to have said that if you wanted a clean street you have to clean your own front yard first. And if every householder did that we'd have a clean street.'

'That's a very down-to-earth way of putting it, I must say. I must remember that the next time I eat a Chinese cookie! Yes, I agree that our own individual attitudes do matter. But you were saying something about social justice.'

Two birds, chirping continuously, suddenly flew away as they approached them.

'Yes, as you know, I've been working on the problem of evil. Or maybe I should say now, *had* been working. I'm not sure I can face that work again. What about the hunger in the world, the social injustices, the inequalities? Would changing attitudes really work?'

'No, not if you put it that way. Shouldn't we rather ask what causes these problems? The poverty and the injustice all around us, and we have plenty of that in Ireland too, comes from people's greed, bias, or ignorance.

'I once read a book by Herder Camara that made me think. Camara couldn't be accused of being abstract or theoretical. In fact, he lived with the poor in Brazil. But in his *The Spiral of Violence*, where he rejects the use of violence, he talks of cultural revolution prior to structural revolution. If you changed the structures of society without first changing radically your attitude, your cultural outlook, as I think he puts it, what you'll have is a mere reversal of roles. The oppressed becomes the oppressor. To obviate that, both need a change in attitude.'

'I thought your field was poetry?' interjected Richard.

Aisling smiled. 'Isn't poetry, beautiful poetry, one way of

changing one's attitude to life? Poets have a way of unlocking the beauty of nature but also of voicing a protest.'

'I know what you're saying, and I understand your point. But I still don't see the connection between what you've been talking about, referring to cultural revolution and poetry ... Wait now, maybe there is. From what you're saying about poetry. You mean that it changes the heart?'

'And the mind and the soul. And to top it all, it could change one's life.'

'I can't imagine going around reading poetry. It'd be just as ridiculous as going around with a frozen smile. Can you imagine, if I said, I need a dose of poetry? Don't mind me, I am being facetious.'

'Actually you're not. It *would be* facetious to put it that way.'

Richard could see that Aisling was just as adept at turning the tables on him for Aisling continued, 'Isn't it better than saying, let me have a drink, or I'll pop in some tension-relieving tablet? Come to think of it, Confucius did talk of music soothing the nerves.'

'Not the kind of music my next-door neighbor likes!'

They had a good laugh.

'How did we get to this?' they both asked at the same time, surprised at how the conversation had developed that afternoon.

'It all started with a smile, your smile,' Richard said as he caressed her cheeks again.

For the first time Richard held Aisling's hand. It was a gentle expression of how he felt for her, a symbol of the closeness that was developing. She did not resist; she felt the same way.

Then both called out to Philip, who was content to let the adults have some privacy.

IX

For days before the Beer Festival there was a real buzz and bustle in Leuven. There was no mistaking the kind of festival it was since signs all over the place had been sponsored by the various breweries, the most prominent being Stella Artois, Leuven's very own and the largest.

Leuven became a brewers' town in the fifteenth century. One can still sniff this historical fact to this day although only one big producer has survived – Interbrew, better known as Stella, which has become its trademark. Previously the town had tried to produce wine in the Middle Ages but it failed to win the tastebuds of Erasmus, who called it *Vilica* or peasants' wine, nor even of the people of Leuven, who sold a lot of it in Antwerp and bought German and French wine instead! Leuven's future definitely lay with beer, for which the necessary grain was produced on the Brabant plateau.

Many restaurants and cafés had last-minute make-overs with paint, new umbrellas, sun-screens and a touch-up of attractive color here and there. The last of the flags was hoisted. Even the Fonske, which had been closed for some time, was again filled with water and the cordons which had screened it for a few weeks were removed. Apparently the inside had been treated for algae and the capstones re-cemented. Philip was relieved that it was once again on show. He was beginning to form the opinion that the closing, temporary it turned out, had something to do with what he had done a few months ago. The town center was decorated with historical flags for the event. It was going to be the venue for 'continuous activities'.

One feature during these last few days before the festival was that there was a noticeable increase in outsiders.

261

Apparently many academic conferences had been arranged for the few days directly preceding the festival – no doubt, with the added incentive that those attending the conference could stay for the beer festival: a one-in-five-years attraction was not to be missed, even by those whose usual concerns were in another kind of world! Nor was the opportunity to loosen one's tongue with the 300 varieties of beer to be ignored by those who otherwise needed no such help with articulating their views. Indeed, some who had come to drink from Leuven's academic fountain did not need to wait for the start of the festival before sampling Leuven's other offering.

The festival's flyer, in four languages, promised the visitors, academic and otherwise, art and culture, conviviality and, what else, beer. Leuven was celebrating all the traditions which it cherished. Once again the spotlight was on Leuven's historical past, this year's choice of a theme being Burgundy. After all, the foundations of present-day Leuven had been in Burgundy in the fifteenth century, as can still be seen in its town hall, Sint-Peter's Kerk, the university of Leuven ... and in the beer. Burgundian means lavish, elegant and abundant living, as true in the fifteenth century as it is in present-day Leuven.

The festivities would commence with the crowning of the Beer King, who would rule for the four-day festival. There would be 'continuous neighborhood animation,' a phrase that amused Richard. Numerous attractions would submerge Leuven in the Burgundian ambience; there was to be a 'historical pageantry' procession which would mark the important centuries in the history of Leuven. It would be like reading chapters of its history, only much more colorful and interesting. The organizers expected approximately 2,000 participants at this procession, almost 300 horses and several floats – a real spectacle. There were to be re-enactments of historical scenes in Leuven's life at designated spots. Finally, bringing the celebrations to a close would be a festival market 'Dirk Bouts'.

Mgr Ladeuzeplein was cordoned off, thus displacing the regular Friday market. At this square is the Grote Markt, which had been damaged during World War I. But it rose from the debris and ashes, more beautiful than ever. Most of the buildings surrounding the square were reconstructed following the historical originals, each of them having been drawn by the architect L. Govaerts between 1921 and 1922. Many of these buildings have restaurants downstairs, including an Irish pub!

The University Library at one end, complete with the tower and the carillon which provides sweet music which can be heard throughout Leuven, looms over the square. This immense building is Leuven's most spectacular monument, where the names of generous donors, mostly American academic institutions, are immortalized on hundreds of commemorative stones in the outside walls. Richard discovered that stopping by Leuven to check the name of their college and university was a fascination among American tourists. Reactions would vary depending on what they found or did not find. Richard had noticed that his own university's name was not featured there. The original library had been destroyed at the outset of World War I and the present one had been built by Whitney Warren in the Dutch Renaissance style.

Now, as part of the preparation for the Beer Festival, fronting the University Library were rows of seating on two sides of the square. On the third side, closest to the library, a semblance of castle gates had been erected. The fourth side was for those who would remain standing during the performance. Everybody knew from posters throughout the town that the construction going on was for the jousting tournament, an exciting reconstruction of the favorite pastime of the knights and noblemen from the Burgundian period. Philip was very excited since he had never been to one. And the idea of knights on horseback fighting with lances or swords captivated him. Without hesitation he announced that he would like to be taken to it.

Aisling was relieved to learn that the Beer Festival was more than what the name implied. She had imagined it to be no more than a *beer* festival, an excuse for the townsfolk and

263

visitors alike to get drunk. It was not to be that, despite the amount of beer being drunk. In fact, surprisingly, they had not met, so far, any riotous, drunk crowds. Just merriment, entertainment, for children and the old, for individuals and families, for citizens and visitors. And she really relished the idea of making history alive. Philip could immerse himself in all the pageantry.

As the threesome roamed the streets of Leuven imbibing the atmosphere, they passed by Domus, a tavern renowned far and wide. Its charm lies not only in its proximity to Leuven's historical town hall, but also in its timeless, rustic interior, with massive wooden beams and rafters adding to its pleasant, warm atmosphere. Its own brewery is connected directly with the tavern's taps via a pipeline, making it unique in Belgium. The Domus beer, Richard explained – from what he had read, he insisted – is available throughout the year, but the tavern also provides seasonal beers: Dubbel Domus Honingbier (with honey), Honing Kriekbier (with honey and cherries), Meibok, Leuvens Witbier, Fonske and Bugel.

Going through the inner courtyard of the Domus and maneuvering past the merry diners, they found themselves in Munstraat, where from the thirteenth century coins had been minted by order of the Duke. Richard's claim to know this place quite well was based on his frequent visits to the Chinese and Cambodian restaurants in the area. These days the restaurateurs were bringing their cooking outside, adding a spicy aroma to the festive air.

Philip's eyes were wide open the whole time. He wanted to take everything in – there were so many things to see and so much to do. Aisling teased him that if he did not blink now and then, his eyes would bulge and no longer fit his sockets!

'But I could miss something,' he protested.

'We can take turns then. If we see anything interesting, we'll definitely let you know,' Aisling assured him.

Philip was right, Aisling conceded. The whole festival was a magnificent spectacle and the people of Leuven must have put a lot of time and effort into preparing for it. The details were unbelievable. One couldn't help but relive history. And in some ways, although the beer was definitely a part of Leuven's history, it was not the most important thing. There were the promised parades, street performances and lots of music and food – and kegs of beer to wash it down.

Philip really enjoyed the jousting. Richard enjoyed it even more. It was completely new to him, although as he recalled there is a similar performance somewhere in southern California. Aisling said that it reminded her of the English tournaments. As it turned out, the performers were actually from England. When the emcee spoke in Dutch – with a strong English accent – there was a roar of approval from the crowd.

Later that afternoon Richard put Philip on his shoulder when they were watching the parade. That gave the young fellow an excellent view, an advantage that made him tell Aisling what he could see. In his excitement, he did not realize that he was keeping up some kind of commentary as each float and group of costumed people came on the scene.

One float did keep him quiet, but only for a few minutes. Towards the tail of the parade was a float in honor of the university. They had to symbolize it with, yes, the famous Fonske.

'Ma, look! There's the statue!'

And then he started to laugh, to the astonishment of those around them. So Aisling suggested that they move elsewhere. Philip climbed down Richard's back and suppressed his laughter by pressing his hand against his mouth.

Richard was amused at Philip's reaction to the float depicting the Fonske. But Aisling would not betray the family secret. That earned her Philip's gratitude.

The evenings were just as delightful as the days, even more so since they were more relaxing. They could choose where they wanted to sit down – for the entire evening if they wished – entertained by various groups of minstrels. Philip relished the chance of being allowed to stay up with the adults. And there were many children about the place, just as appreciative as Philip was of the privilege of sharing in the festivities even at night. One advantage that Aisling, Philip

265

and Richard had was that they did not have to travel far to return to their apartments – and no parking problems either. All they had to do was to walk a few blocks since the Groot Begijnhof was near the town center.

'Isn't it great to be surrounded by all this history and culture?' remarked Richard.

'And to sit back and be able to absorb it all,' added Aisling, who was enjoying the whole atmosphere.

They had decided that evening to sit at the small square in front of the Pope's College. At the center of the green square was a canopy where the various musicians were taking turns performing – 'continuous animation,' said Richard, quoting from the flyers.

It had been difficult to get any table or chair since once people did manage to get themselves seated they were usually there for the evening. But the open-eyed Philip had spotted some folks getting ready to move around, to check out the other spots of entertainment. In fact, the threesome had done that the previous evening. At that time they just wanted to amble along. But tonight was for relaxing – for letting the world, the Burgundian world, pass them by.

There's something about a festival, thought Richard to himself. It enables people to enjoy life, to celebrate life. And it bonds people. He could see families and friends coming together. He could hear people being introduced to one another. Much laughter, much talking. A celebration such as this one gives the community relief from the drudgery of daily routine, it lifts them from a miserable situation. The comic, the outlandish, the once-in-five-years happening have a place in life. For the meaningfulness of life can sometimes be read and appreciated – like the sense of a sentence – only when life is punctuated by such events.

But this was not the time for such philosophical thoughts. This was the time for relaxation. So he asked Aisling for a dance. And Aisling obliged, particularly since the music was her favorite – a waltz.

And they danced and celebrated their togetherness.

But the second time round, their dancing suddenly came to

a halt as there was a commotion. The music had stopped and several individuals started to converge on the spot where the musicians had been. Aisling's first thought was for Philip, whom they had left at the table in clear view until now. He had stayed behind to watch them dance – and to guard their table, as he valiantly put it.

'Philip!' shouted Aisling to try to catch his attention.

There was no response. And he was nowhere in sight. The crowd had blocked Richard's and Aisling's view. They raced towards the seat where they had parked Philip. But he was not there. Not wanting to risk losing her, Richard grasped Aisling's hand tightly as they tried to wade through the growing crowd. They both desperately checked the children who were being closely clasped by anxious parents. Still no sign of Philip. The fortunate thing was that it was not a big unruly crowd, so there was no fear of being crushed. But anxiety was starting to show on Aisling's face.

Apparently someone had fainted, and as people went to his help, a small crowd started to gather. Then it grew and grew. Other groups started to move away, not knowing what was happening and not wanting to be in the thick of it.

*　　*　　*

Professor Malachowski was spending his last evening in Leuven, enjoying a sumptuous meal in the company of Professor van der Riet. Tomorrow he would be taking the train to Aachen, from where he would be switching to the train for Bonn since he had an invitation to speak in the afternoon to the Philosophy Department of the university there. He then planned to spend a few weeks in Germany, afterwards a week in Liechtenstein, before returning to his native Poland.

'So, Piotr, would you say it was a fruitful stay in Leuven for you?' inquired Professor van der Riet.

'I believe so, in fact more than I had expected,' came the reply.

'You mean, you have become a convert to process thought,' teased his Belgian host professor.

'Not so fast, André,' Professor Malachowski teased back. 'You are not out to win converts, are you?'

The two eminent professors laughed heartily. Professor Malachowski had come to Leuven specifically to research on process philosophy, in which Professor van der Riet was a recognized expert.

'I must confess, I find it fascinating. But there are still a number of issues, and I mean a good number, about which I would have to quarrel with you process people. One of these days I will record my objections in print. Perhaps you and I can dialogue further.'

Professor Malachowski then proceeded to elaborate on the real reason why he believed that his stay had exceeded his expectations. As he reminded his Belgian counterpart, his search for an adequate philosophy to make sense of a life that had been marred yet nurtured by the bitter experiences of the past had led him to Leuven to read up on process thought. But what he was beginning to appreciate, in his advanced years, was that the search itself, *the process* – Professor Malachowski couldn't resist the pun – was the more important thing.

Unknown to Richard, with whom he had had a number of conversations following their walk, the younger academic's questions had sparked off a new inquiry for the senior professor. Professor Malachowski was beginning to turn to the question rather than to the answer. He wondered whether the questions we ask about life should not remain as questions. They should continue to unsettle us and not dry up because we have become comfortable with 'the truth.'

Maybe, he thought, that is what is wrong with human nature. Or, maybe that is the truth about human nature. From one point of view, we have been condemned to be seekers after an elusive truth. From another point of view, that it is our privilege. For we can ask, we can wonder. We can journey. And the quest for the answer becomes the answer itself.

Leuven had been a welcome oasis in that journey – which he now believed would go on and on.

★ ★ ★

The man who had fainted had now recovered. A common sigh of relief escaped from the lips of the crowd. Then all of a sudden, there was a hush, like the pause between the movements of an orchestral piece.

Unaware of the stillness of the moment, an anxious Aisling kept calling out to Philip. Richard joined in. The two voices rang out loud and clear, as if they were the singers leading a chorus of voices. A few moment later Aisling and Richard could hear Philip's name being echoed by others.

They then realized that the crowd that had come to the aid of the man who had fainted now found themselves with another task. When they discovered that a small boy was missing, they called out in unison. The call got louder and louder: 'Philip, Philip!'

Poor Philip must have got confused with the gathering crowd when the commotion first started. When some individuals congregated towards the center, while others moved away from them, he became disoriented. Sensing trouble ahead and not wanting to be squashed in the middle, he followed the family near where he had been sitting. They had quickly gathered their belongings to head for a safer place.

Now hearing his name, Philip stopped in his tracks and turned around. When the people near him realized that he was the missing boy, they parted a way for him. This path continued through the crowd until a much relieved Philip found himself facing his mother and Richard.

Aisling embraced him, glad to be reunited with her son. Richard smiled. Philip extended his arm to include him in their embrace. The togetherness was meant for the three of them.

The crowd clapped. It was a real-life spectacle. There had been a hitch in the festivities, a few moments of anxiousness, but now a happy ending. And good nature was showing its best. People offered to buy them a drink to celebrate. But the restaurateur from whom they had ordered their drinks would not hear of it – the family were his guests. They were indeed his welcome guests. So he insisted on another round of complimentary drinks for the couple – and anything that Philip wanted.

It was an evening – a festival – the three of them would never forget.

★   ★   ★

It was such a pleasant day. Aisling felt the urge not to waste it by staying indoors. In Ireland, she thought, if the weather is as good as this – and usually you can count the days on the one hand when that is so – people rush out in case they miss God's bounty. When nature beams, it would be a sin not to show your gratitude! And you can't do that from the inside of an apartment. And today nature was clearly beckoning her.

Aisling, however, kept resisting nature's temptation as she attempted to do some studying since Philip was still at school. Inside her apartment it was nice and quiet, normally ideal for serious reading. But this afternoon she was wrestling with the Postmodern authors, desperately trying to understand them. She was baffled by their no-plot, no-characterization, no-systemization works. These authors were being successful in ensuring that readers would not pigeonhole or categorize them. Nor understand them, it seemed. It was a real struggle of the mind.

But what was really distracting Aisling was the student who lived in the apartment across the street. Aisling's sitting room faced the street and so she had a clear view of the building opposite theirs. The student was combining her love of study (or was it a need to study since exams were coming?) and her love of the sun. There was nothing wrong with that, of course. It was quite a common sight to see students sunbathing and studying. But this particular student was perched on the window sill of her third-floor apartment! The sight of her precarious position made Aisling nervous. As if this were not enough, this student started to swing her leg, the one that was dangling. The other leg she had managed to prop up against the window frame.

For goodness sake, exclaimed Aisling, what if she sneezed or something? She could fall, yes, to the street below her. And Aisling would be a witness to it all. Aisling had no stomach for blood. But it was no business of hers to call out to her to be careful. Besides, the rather acrobatic student was oblivious of the agony she was causing Aisling.

Aisling decided that she would not face the street. But it was useless. Every time a car passed by she would involuntarily check whether the student was still there. Yes, she was. Perched like a parrot.

Then someone called out to the girl. Aisling rushed to the window without thinking. Surely the girl would come off the window sill now. Any right-minded person would, she claimed. But no – and to add to Aisling's horror, the student merely put down her book to talk to her friend three floors below, where the solid ground was. She remained where she was. With only her left leg resting on the window frame to keep her from disaster.

Aisling shook her head. How could this young girl be so lackadaisical about her situation? Had she not heard of the law of gravity? Whatever she and her friend on the street were talking about in Dutch, it must have been interesting since they were conversing excitedly. The disco last night? Something in the offing? The exams perhaps?

Aisling had heard that examination time here was something to be excited about. Not that it was any less in her own university. But in the Belgian system, there are no requirements about getting into university, not like the points system in Ireland which makes secondary school students doing their Leaving Certificate Examination particularly anxious in case they do not make it to university. Here, she was told, any student could go to the university. Screening takes place only after their first year. But then comes the chop: more than half of them would fail. Those who make it are the academically able students, those who don't have to find alternatives. Thus, their first-year university studies are really important.

Is that what these two were talking about? No, it must be something else, she concluded when she looked up from the book she was reading. The person below was hidden from her view, but Aisling, who had been checking the situation every five minutes, detected a rather rapturous smile on the girl's face.

Then came an unexpected break in the conversation. Good, Aisling thought, she must be alighting finally. She breathed a sigh of relief. Perhaps now she could concentrate.

But she was mistaken. The girl had called a halt to the conversation because she wanted to turn around. Yes, to turn around. She pointed to her dangling leg as if to say, 'Well, that one's done enough, I need to have the other leg done just as much.' She did not want to have an uneven tan, it appeared. My God, youth. And these are Europe's finest and brightest, Aisling observed. The girl did put down her book beside her, and executed expertly, obviously an expertise that came from doing this regularly, the whole process of turning around. All she did was to hold on to the window shutter above her and twirl around like a suspended doll. This time it was the other leg that was dangling on to the street while the tanned leg rested on the other side of the window frame. What a feat! And meanwhile the conversation had resumed at the same pace.

That was when Aisling gave up. There was no point. She had been reading the same paragraph about five times. And she still had no clue what it was all about. So she weighed up her situation: there was this indecipherable book, there was this distraction of a student ... And there was this very inviting beautiful day. A pity to waste it, she rationalized.

Just as she was about to get up from her desk, she heard a knock on her door. It was Richard.

'Am I bothering you? It's such a nice day. I thought it'd be nice to go for a walk. Can I tempt you?'

Aisling laughed heartily. She recounted to him what had

been happening. Richard shared in the laugher while looking in the direction of the street.

'Did you say, one student?' he asked teasingly.

With that Aisling moved towards the window. She could not believe her eyes. The student's roommate had decided to join her in this precarious situation. She had perched herself on the other window sill of their apartment.

'Let's go, Richard. And let's go quickly!'

Richard suggested walking to Tervuursevest, where there was a tree-lined long park like an island dividing the two sides of the traffic. Aisling knew the place since it was close to the studio apartment where she and Philip had stayed during their first two months in Leuven.

The park was much more beautiful now with the tall trees covered in leaves. Aisling and Philip had frequented that park. But at that time, the trees were bare, and although leafless trees have their own rugged beauty, the new growth in the trees was much more pleasant to see. She tried to describe the images which were conjured up in her mind as she watched nature awakening. And she talked of the wealth of imagery in Robert Frost's poem *The Birches* and quoted Hopkins's remarks about the grandeur in creation.

'You seem to see beauty everywhere, Aisling, even in bare trees.'

'Because it's there, isn't it? It's difficult to see it now since the trees have their leaves. And it's the leaves that give the trees their beauty in the spring. But in the winter, when the cold weather makes you wrap yourself up, nature unveils the beauty of the trunks and of the branches of the trees. It's as if Mother Nature wants to remind us that the leaves, the externals, aren't the only thing about nature that can be admired. The inner beauty that's hidden in the spring and summer and autumn comes out on its own in the winter. We don't always see it. And even when it's really there we don't always appreciate it.'

Richard could see Aisling's point. Somehow their conversation was going back to what they had talked about regarding people's attitudes, perspective and perception.

'Were you always as idealistic as this?'

'Yes and no.'

'That sounds like a real philosophical answer,' teased Richard. 'We philosophers are always making distinctions. That's why we keep answering yes and no to most questions.'

'Or because you philosophers can't make up your mind,' Aisling teased back.

'Touché.'

'Yes. Sean and I were always talking about our dreams and how we would live life to the full. Not materially. We could never do that with a teacher's salary. But we both thought life was a gift, that we were so lucky, that it would be ungrateful not to appreciate what God had given us.'

Aisling looked at the trees forming an honor guard, as it were.

'It was easy to be idealistic when things appeared rosy. But Sean was also realistic. Like the wayfarer in Padraic Pearse's poem, he also was aware that the beauty of the world can make us sad because this beauty will pass. He was fully conscious too of the evil and the suffering around. He used to say that living life to the full didn't mean living it up. He meant not letting the disappointments, the difficulties and the dark side of life cloud the goodness that was everywhere in nature. And he used to quote the Latin saying, *Dum spiro, spero*. He also maintained that living life to the full meant doing our share to bring out that beauty by working to correct the injustice, to lessen the suffering. That's why above all else he wanted to teach. He firmly believed in the power of education to change people's attitudes. And his enthusiasm was catching.'

Aisling looked up at the blue sky above, dotted with a few cotton-like clouds.

'No, I wasn't always idealistic. When Sean died, I couldn't understand how his philosophy of life could be the right one. After all, he was a victim of the cruelty of life.'

She was fighting hard to hold back the tears.

'I'm sorry. I didn't mean our conversation to lead to this.' Richard put a comforting arm around Aisling's shoulder.

274

'It's all right,' smiled Aisling.

It was a smile amidst the tears. It was a strength that was breaking out of the grief.

And Richard remembered what Aisling had earlier said about the admiration she had for a child who managed to smile while tears flowed down its cheeks ...

Indeed, Aisling had been through a testing time. Her idealism was not coming from lofty speculation. It was rooted in the experience of life; it was a response to the challenges of life. And there is a big difference between someone who proclaims the ideals culled from books and someone who has undergone the ups and downs of life, who has gone through the crucible of life. Aisling had been through that.

Sean's death had really torn her apart. She wanted to give up, she felt abandoned. Worse, she felt led on by life only to be dropped. What goodness had her Sean been talking about? She even lost her faith in God, the God that her Catholic upbringing had instilled in her. She could not continue to believe in a God who was described as a caring father, a concerned shepherd, the way the Irish nuns used to tell them at school. Her reality showed a God, if there was one, who was a tyrant, who delighted in punishing people, in laughing at them. She identified with Santiago in Ernest Hemingway's *The Old Man and the Sea* and with Kino in John Steinbeck's *The Pearl*. The experience of both characters was of a God who initially gave them hope, only to dash them down, who seemed to make fun of the human individual's valiant efforts. What she was going through reminded her of Thomas Hardy's 'Vast Imbecility' who 'framed us in jest, and left us now to hazardry', of the capricious gods Gloucester was describing, for whom humans were like flies to boys, killing them for sport, of the vengeful god depicted in Thomas Hardy's poem *Hap*, who mockingly calls to the 'suffering thing': 'Know that thy sorrow is my ecstasy,/ That thy love's loss is my hate's profiting!' She was embittered and she had a good reason to be so.

She found it difficult being on her own. The nights were

lonely, the evenings were long and dark, and the days were fraught with hardships. Many times she was mistaken for an unmarried mother, and she experienced the prejudice, the hatred and the narrowness of people's minds directed against such women even though she was not one herself. Many tried to take advantage of her the way they take advantage of widows, and helpless individuals. She was seen as easy prey by some men who thought that she was a lonely widow in need of protection and consolation, *their* protection and consolation, since they believed that they were God's gift to such women. She was the victim of those who judged her unaccompanied status before they asked what her true situation was.

She fought back, but she realized that she needed to fight herself. She knew that simply fighting back in rage and bitterness was not going to end the misery and frustration that she was experiencing. She was being hurt by others, and she was helping them hurt her even more by being bitter and angry. She was ignoring what she and Sean had talked about so many times. She was doing Sean's memory an injustice, thwarting whatever he had been living for. She was contributing to the seeming absurdity of life.

But Sean had made sure she would not forget. The young life that had been the result of his and her love kept reminding her of Sean's ideals, talked about in good times but now being tested in bad ones. She could hear Sean's words over and over again. And the infant whom she was cradling and who depended entirely on her wanted her to sail on. He seemed to be saying, 'Think of me and not just of you.'

... 'No, I wasn't always idealistic. And I don't think I'm always idealistic. But it seems to me that we have to make an effort to be idealistic. For if we don't, we lose so much of what life and nature have to offer us.'

'You said, you lost your faith.'

'Yes, I stopped going to Mass. And in Ireland, that's a big sin. And I don't mean from a Catholic religious point of view. It's a social sin. Missing Mass is socially unacceptable.

276

You might call it the result of years of conservative Catholicism, but that simply is the reality. It's changing now, of course. I didn't see any point. It was not just the ritual that had become meaningless to me. It was the very idea of paying homage to a God who couldn't care less about me. Why should I care about that God?'

'And what brought about the change? Was there a sudden conversion, like being knocked down from a horse?' Richard was trying to introduce a lighter note.

'Philip.'

'Philip? You mean he suddenly spoke and told you to shape up?'

'Yes!'

Aisling could not resist returning the tease, particularly when she knew that Richard was not expecting that answer.

'He got up and spoke in a loud voice. No, seriously, it was not as spectacular as that. But have you ever thought of the power of the helplessness of a baby?'

Richard shook his head. So Aisling continued.

'In your books that's probably a contradiction. But have you ever seen how the helplessness of a baby will get the undivided attention of everybody? I always tell the students during one of my lectures that I would bet that no matter how interesting somebody's lecture may be, if somebody brought a helpless baby into the lecture hall, everyone's attention would be directed to that cooing baby. There's power in that. It's a different kind of power. It doesn't dominate, it attracts. It doesn't threaten, it influences.'

'You must forgive me, but I don't see the connection between that and God.'

'I don't blame you. That was why I said that it wasn't a spectacular realization. It took a long time. Perhaps it was just as well. When things move more slowly, they've more time to sink in, to get imbedded. The whole thing made me wonder what made me blame God. Well, I had been taught that God could do everything. So God could have prevented the accident. But the accident still happened. But what if God were like the helpless infant, like Philip a few years ago?'

'God, a helpless infant? And to think that I've been defending God's almighty power in my research!'

'But it doesn't make God any less powerful. Only that it's a different kind of power.'

'You mean, God like a helpless baby attracts, influences, doesn't dominate or threaten.'

'I think so – you're the philosopher. Let me say it in my unphilosophical way. We tend to make God a scapegoat for many of the ills around us. That was what I was doing, blaming God for taking Sean away from me. But it wasn't God who did that, it was the drunken driver.'

'In philosophy, we could still say that ultimately the responsibility could be traced back to God since from God, who is omnipotent, flows all power, couldn't we?'

'In your philosophy perhaps. And in your understanding of power. Let me try to explain it. I'm not sure whether this would make much philosophical sense to you. But as a mother responding to my baby's needs, I realized that often it is up to me to fulfil that need. I have that responsibility. And it's a responsibility that I've come to cherish. It seems to me that God allots the responsibility to make this world more liveable for you and me and for everyone else. God doesn't monopolize that responsibility. Whenever I saw the helpless Philip in front of me ... don't misunderstand me, don't think I would be thinking of this when he needed a quick nappy change or when he was shivering from a high temperature, but I would think of it as he slept soundly in my arms ... I was grateful for having had that responsibility. But I could just have ignored my responsibility. In fact, I could have even thumped him or psychologically abused him. Sadly, there is much of that around. So it works both ways. When we don't live up to our responsibility, we can't blame God for the results. We should blame our irresponsibility.'

'And how does that tie in with the way you described power?'

'That God, because God has chosen to share the responsibility, appeals to us to exercise that responsibility. God doesn't force us. Just as a helpless baby does not and cannot. But when a baby looks up to you, you know through those teary eyes or smiling face, the baby is exerting an influence on you. The baby wants you to do something.'

'Doesn't that make God weak?'

'Is someone weak who enables you to do something? Is a teacher less powerful for inspiring others to accomplish more? Is a poet or an artist any less effective than a tyrant? Is a Muse irrelevant?'

'Answered like a good teacher. Answer a question with another question.'

'Don't we help our students think better that way?'

'I should really answer that with another question ... but yes, you're right. Where does that leave us?'

'That God works through us. And God is as effective or as powerful, in the sense that I have described it, as we allow God to be. It really took me a while to realize this. It was only when I started to appreciate the love that surrounded me, my family's, my friends' and most of all, Philip's.'

'And Sean's.' There was a tinge of envy in Richard's voice. Sean had indeed been very lucky to have had Aisling.

Aisling smiled. This time it was she who reached out to pat Richard's face.

'God was showing me goodness and care in the people I love. It was through them that I could feel God's compassion, as they wept with me over Sean's loss, rejoiced with me when Philip took his first step, felt hurt when I was victimized. God is in people, God is in nature.'

'Sometimes that's hard to believe.'

'It is, that's why we need to look. That's why I am still struggling to live by that — how did you put it? — idealism. And that's why, as teachers, we need to unveil the beauty that surrounds us and show it to our charges.... And speaking of charges, we'd better pick Philip up. Otherwise, he'll be like that forgotten child in the ad.'

Aisling was referring to the ad for a particular brand of floor cleaner which showed the mother who was using the rival brand unable to finish her work in time to pick up her child after school.

*   *   *

After walking Aisling and Philip back to their apartment, Richard excused himself, saying that he was going to his office in the School of Philosophy to check any messages for him. When he reached the office, however, he found none.

So Richard then seated himself, thinking that perhaps he should do some writing. But his thoughts kept tumbling all over his mind, and he just could not get a handle on them. He kept recalling his conversations with Aisling. Somehow they were guiding him, but how he did not know.

Without being conscious of it, Aisling was in fact talking about his research topic, but very differently from the way he had approached it. Richard was reminded of his long talk and other conversations with Professor Malachowski. Like Aisling, the Polish professor was speaking from experience, not from the comfort of academic discourse. Richard himself had previously faulted his own approach for being too theoretical and not experience-based. The irony of it all was that now he himself was experiencing the anxiety, the frustration and the agony of having been denied tenure. Was this experience going to lead somewhere? Was there a lesson he could learn from this unwelcome and unwanted experience? Would he have the strength to cope with it? He was not Aisling, he was not Professor Malachowski. What inner resources did he have?

Several minutes ticked by before it occurred to Richard that Aisling's reference to the power of the smile and of laughter was much more than the obvious. She meant transcendence. Now what did that really mean?

Richard did not think he would get the answer holing himself up inside the office. Just as he did not get any answer or hint of an answer as he swiveled around in his office at Lonergan University. At that time he kept staring at his unfinished manuscript. He had looked out to watch the sorority ritual that was then taking place just outside his office. Since his office was on the ground floor, he could look directly at the girls. The office he was using here at the School was on the top floor. It provided him with a very good view of the yard below. So he decided to look down.

A few students had gathered. There seemed to be some kind

of discussion. One of them appeared to be expounding a philosophical point. Richard wondered whether Aristotle's Lyceum was like this. Open-air philosophizing rather than in a lecture hall or a classroom. Discussion rather than mere information.

The flowers that hung from the covered walk connecting one building to another looked like ripening grapes. It was so different here compared to the campus of his own university. In some ways the School of Philosophy, comprised of neo-Gothic buildings, was a miniature university. The classrooms, the administrative offices, the library, the professors' offices surrounded this courtyard that he was looking down into from his office.

Strange, how differently things looked from a third-floor office. The height gave him a different perspective. A new environment showed him another dimension. Meeting various people exposed him to different stories. A new approach might illumine an age-old problem.

⋆　　⋆　　⋆

As an undergraduate in Ireland, Aisling always maintained that when the gardeners started mowing the grass, one knew that exams would be just around the corner. When the second cutting came, then you knew – or should know – that exams *were* on top of you. It was time to panic.

Her recollections brought on a smile. Outside her apartment she could hear the grass being cut. It was only the first cutting. Still, she was glad she had no exams, particularly in Postmodernism!

But she knew what that meant. That their time in Leuven was fast coming to a close. She had to be back at her university in time to do the correction of all those exam scripts. Hundreds of them.

She would have to talk it over with Philip. She was really glad that they had come to Leuven. She had been able to do a lot of reading, she had seen several places, she had met some academics. It was, she hoped, a useful and educational experience too for Philip, who had picked up a few phrases in the other European languages. He had broadened his horizons.

But their stay turned out to be quite different in many ways from what she had expected. She was grateful to the Head of the Department for arranging for her to sit in on the course of the American professor. It was an unexpected bonus as it gave her an introduction to all this Postmodernism that she had been hearing about. In addition to assembling the information that would enable her to work on her article, she had counted on, and indeed enjoyed, having the leisure to just read books that she had been unable to open due to her teaching commitments.

Moreover, being on the Continent gave her easy access to other European countries that she had long wanted to visit. She also managed to revisit Paris. The excellent train connections to the Low Countries meant that she and Philip could simply take the fast intercity trains to visit places in the Netherlands and Luxembourg and yet be back in their place that night, thus saving on accommodation expenses.

She was thrilled finally to be able to experience the much-talked-about Keukenhof. That huge, famous flower garden park was simply gorgeous. Indeed springtime was the best season to have been so close to it, she kept saying to Philip while they toured the rows and rows of tulips of all colours and the splendid plots of spring flowers. She wrote her mother that it would be an ideal trip for her and her friends, and everyone for that matter. She must have sounded so enthused about the visit that Mrs Holohan threatened to take the next flight to Amsterdam if she did not stop. But Keukenhof really deserved its reputation.

She had thought that she and Philip would be spending most of the time in Leuven. But the proximity of historical Belgian places meant that they were able to visit not only Bruges, Brussels, Antwerp, but also Ghent, Waterloo, Mechelen, Liege, Namur and even German-speaking Eupen, where Philip was able finally to hear some of the German phrases he had been picking up at playschool. They had gone there during the carnival which takes place from Thursday to

Shrove Tuesday, culminating in *Rosenmontag* – a pageant of costumed groups, decorated floats and brass bands throughout the town, preceded by the Carnival Prince, who flung sweets at the delighted spectators.

She had not anticipated the Belgian spring festivities nor the Beer Festival. She discovered that there were colourful festivals here even during Lent! Philip was watching history come alive since the participants, whether in Eupen, Mechelen or Leuven, were dressed up in costumes representing various periods of their history. She would have loads of stories to tell – and encouraging comments to make to her academic colleagues.

But what made their stay really unexpectedly significant was meeting Richard. And yet it had been furthest from her mind, meeting someone like him here. She had come here hoping to appreciate her European heritage; now she was also being drawn further. Perhaps Erasmus now had to seek further fields. More global.

Aisling looked at Philip, sprawled on the floor, playing with his train set. He must have grown a couple of inches since they left Ireland – she knew that for a fact from the trousers that they had brought with them. But Philip had grown too in another way. He talked a lot about Richard. She smiled as she recalled how keen Philip had been initially to complete his collection of the troll family. She was glad that he had outgrown that. And she knew that completing the collection was merely a symptom of what her young son was really looking for. It would be difficult talking to Philip about having to say goodbye to Richard.

Aisling turned her gaze away. What about her own feelings? Richard and she had talked about their friendship and their growing closeness, but neither wanted to make any commitment yet. She liked Richard. A lot. More than she cared to admit. She would truly miss his company. She had enjoyed those long nature walks and endless conversations together. But they were from two cultures, comparable but recognizably different. Richard had never set his foot in Ireland, nor she in America. For either one it would mean uprooting and re-rooting in a different world. Here in Leuven

283

it was something else. Both of them were guests here, neither was on home territory.

She wondered whether they had been drawn together because they were both away from home. Summer romances which blossom at language schools in different countries were not uncommon. Even conference romances. Were there semester romances? Did they lead to anything? She thought about the many scholars who passed through Leuven's academic portals. Did any of their paths not only cross here at Leuven but merge after Leuven?

What about Sean? She had kept up his memory in her heart, in her mind and in their son. Was it time to let go?

No, she dreaded that word. It was the wrong one anyway. Letting go implied that one had been imprisoned, as it were. As if one were clinging on to something that wanted to escape.

It was never like that. She wanted Sean to live on; she was not imprisoning his memory. Nor did she feel that her bond to Sean was keeping her back since she wanted it that way. She always felt that their love transcended the inevitability of death and that death was not meant to be a parting of ways for them. That was why she did not like the phrase 'letting go'. A time would come when Philip too would want to live his own life. That was natural, that was inevitable, that was right. But she hoped that it would not be a matter of 'letting go' because she never wanted to imprison him, to clip his wings.

And Sean? If not a letting go, what would it be now that she had met Richard? How did one perpetuate a loved one in someone else? Should she?

The future is very open, she concluded. Just as their stay in Leuven had surprises, their future will have its twists and turns. Who knows what is to come?

EPILOGUE

The Aer Lingus flight from Brussels to Dublin was quite smooth, no turbulence. Philip kept looking out of the window, fascinated by the clouds, which to him looked like a carpet of white cotton balls. But now and then he would steal a glance at his mother's face. She had tried very hard to hide her emotions, but the parting with Richard at Brussels National Airport had not been easy for anyone. She and Philip spoke very little before and during the flight, afraid somehow that the slightest hint would reveal what they were really feeling. She spent the time flicking through the pages of the in-flight *Cara* magazine.

A little more than an hour after they were up in the air they heard the flight attendant announcing that they were now landing at Dublin Airport. Aisling smiled at Philip and checked his seat belt. She stroked his head and held his hand and waited for the familiar sight of the Dublin air terminal. Then she brushed her hair and re-applied some lipstick.

As they went through immigration, she and Philip joined the queue for EC nationals, who only had to show their maroon-coloured European passports. In front of Aisling and Philip was a rather big lady who was going past the official without showing any identification.

'I suppose you have an Irish passport, ma'am,' inquired the young official.

'Don't I look Irish, young fellow?' came the quick retort.

'You do, ma'am. But you still have to have your passport. That's the rule.'

'I've been Irish before you were in your nappies, rules or no rules.' The young immigration official, whom the lady thought was still wet behind the ears, turned red with embarrassment. The queue was getting longer.

The lady then whispered to him, but loud enough for everyone to hear, 'Actually I'm Russian!'

It was all good humour and the whole group had a good laugh. She did have an Irish passport, which saved the official any legal difficulties. The queue moved very quickly from then on.

Aisling headed for the long row of baggage trolleys. Recalling her mother's experience with those gadgets, she sighed with relief that the Dublin Airport authorities provided this free facility. In Brussels she was 'nearly killed' trying to carry their three huge suitcases from the Airport Express, along the platform, up the escalator and then to the check-in. There were no trolleys in sight. If Richard had not been there, she and Philip would never have managed. Somehow, Brussels, despite being the EC capital, had not caught up with the fact that travellers arriving by Airport Express had a lot of baggage and needed trolleys at the platform.

While waiting for their luggage, Aisling overheard another conversation taking place. This time it was between an elderly man and woman. Aisling had noticed the man standing on his own for quite a while.

'I thought you'd been kidnapped,' he said when the woman, presumably his wife, joined him.

She had been at the Ladies, and must have been taking her time.

'For goodness sake, Ian, who in God's name would have me?'

With that Ian put his arms around her for an answer.

Aisling smiled. Yes, indeed she was back in Ireland. It was refreshing to hear the wit and the quick retort. It was nice to be home again.

Outside in the waiting lounge of the Arrivals section, Mrs Holohan, Tony and Fiona Burns kept looking out for them. This part of Dublin Airport, unlike the Departures area above, was always the scene of laughter, smiles, cheerful conversation as well as tears or shrieks of joy as visitors, friends, and particularly the returning Irish would be received into outstretched arms. Here the visitor or the returning emigré would have his or her first taste of the traditional *Céad míle fáilte*. Somehow it was like being welcomed into the cosiness and warmth of the Irish open fireplace as family, friends and visitors embraced one another.

'Granny!'

Philip's voice rang out as he spotted his grandmother in the crowd. There was no holding him back. People clapped as they saw him race towards Mrs Holohan.

'We're back!' he announced with glee, as if people did not know already.

Behind him came Aisling, pushing the trolley with their huge suitcases piled on top of it. Fiona rushed to embrace Aisling, nearly toppling over the trolley in the process, such was her eagerness to greet her sister. Philip was holding his grandmother's hand and going a mile a minute with his chatter. After giving his sister-in-law a hug, Tony took charge of the trolley. He said he did not mind 'doing the donkey' so that the two sisters could carry on with 'whatever it was they were yapping about'.

'Don't mind him, Aisling. Now tell me everything,' pleaded Fiona.

'Tell you what? Didn't I tell you everything in my letters?'

'Oh, come on. There's something you're not saying – about this Richard.'

Aisling's face turned into a nice pink colour. 'There is *nothing* to tell, I'm telling you.'

Aisling was rather defensive. She glanced at her mother. Both she and Philip had stopped in their tracks. Fortunately, Tony was out of earshot and did not see her embarrassment.

Aisling would not be drawn out. And young Philip was being very conspiratorial.

But Philip's face was clearly the picture of hope and anticipation.

★   ★   ★

It was the day after Richard had said goodbye to Aisling and Philip. He missed them terribly. He had spent yesterday visiting the many places in Leuven that the three of them had

287

frequented, hoping somehow that the memories would ease the pain and longing that he felt.

Today his walk brought him in front of the Fons Sapientiae. It was indeed a symbol of academic Leuven. But like every other symbol, its meaning was different for various individuals. It had a different impact on the individuals who visited this university town. This semester it could well symbolize the transformation in the lives of some of the people he had come to know. He stared at the statue for a long time, recalling what had happened to these individuals.

Leuven is truly a crossroad, he reflected. It had been in the past, for commerce and trade. It still is. But Leuven is also an academic crossroad where scholars from around the world converge for conferences or for research. And as these academics interact, they ferry back with them new knowledge, fresh inspiration.

But sometimes, they change direction. They take another road. Because Leuven pointed another path to them. Because the people they met in Leuven transformed their lives. Because events took an unexpected turn.

His musings brought back memories of his conversation with Aisling on this very point, which naturally led to their discussion of Robert Frost's *The Road Not Taken*. They had talked about decision-making in life and the consequences they had to accept. Wasn't life full of challenges?

Aisling had also cited lines from William Butler Yeats's *The Choice*. Richard couldn't remember the exact lines, but he was struck by the appropriateness of the poem regarding some of the academics he had met here. Yeats describes how the intellect is forced to choose between perfection of one's life or perfection of one's work and how one has to sacrifice one for the other. Jennifer had veered towards perfection of her work. Strangely enough, both Professor Malachowski and Aisling seemed to be able for both kinds of perfection. Even more surprising was their ability to enrich one with the other. Richard regretted that he didn't have the opportunity of getting to know Dr. Fuentes. Strange, how one could be in the same location yet not meet again. He did hear that Dr. Fuentes was suddenly recalled to the Philippines.

As Richard kept staring at the fountain, he marveled at Aisling's reference to this fountain. She said that it could well be the fountain Arethuse mentioned in John Milton's *Lycidas* where the Muses played. Yes, it was a very apt reference for after all scholars came here for inspiration, to find the Muse that would stimulate them. And he himself found different Muses, not the ones he had imagined, but Muses that inspired and changed him far more than he could ever have envisioned. Aisling had also articulated succinctly his own reflections on this fountain that memorable night. She quoted lines from John Keats's *Ode on a Grecian Urn*: 'Thou, silent form, dost tease out of thought / As doth eternity: Cold Pastoral!'

Passing by several photocopying places, Richard noticed that they had gone a lot quieter. It was a big change, seeing that during the semester photocopying was big business in Leuven. Given the amount that was being done in all the shops, there was a real need for the reproduction of books, manuscripts, theses and so on. In fact, this semester yet another photocopying place had opened on Naamsestraat. Was this a technological development of what Leuven used to do? Thanks to the university of Leuven, which bought books and produced copies, Leuven became the printing center of the Low Countries in the fifteenth century. A printed book soon cost a student five times less than a manuscript. Now Richard was hearing that in Leuven a photocopy of a book was cheaper than the book itself! He smiled on recalling his conversation with Aisling. She had wondered whether this was a sign of the postmodern world: the image of the image of reality, reproduction replacing production. He had responded that Plato had to some extent anticipated this development: here was the situation thrice removed from reality! Plato should not have been too harsh with the poets: he had attacked the wrong crowd.

Richard forced himself to go to the library. Noticing that the one computer he could use was available, he sat in front of it. The students had finished all their written work so he knew he had no competition. He could stay at it the whole day.

Then unexpectedly, as his reflections turned to his own stay at Leuven, his career and his future, lines from Yeats's poem *The Circus Animals' Desertion* kept echoing in his mind:

> I sought a theme and sought for it in vain,
> I sought it daily for six weeks or so.
> Maybe at last, being but a broken man,
> I must be satisfied with my heart . . .
>
> . . . Now that my ladder's gone,
> I must lie down where all the ladders start,
> In the foul rag-and-bone shop of the heart.

He stared outside. The cherry blossoms he had closely monitored in the previous months, from tiny bud to full bloom, were now gone. Instead the trees were covered in leaves. Leuven had taken on a summer look. Nature had bedecked herself. So many things had changed.

Then he started typing:

Richard Gutierrez had just retrieved his mail from the mail center of his university. As he scrutinized the contents of his rather stuffed mailbox, he noticed among the usual flyers, book catalogues, internal mail, the particular letter he had been waiting for.

'I do hope it's good news,' he muttered with some anxiety as he hurriedly tore the side of the airmail envelope which bore the seal of Mercier University in Leuven, Belgium. Richard had lifted the envelope from the rest of his mail and there and then proceeded to read its contents, ignoring the young undergraduate whose path to her own mailbox he was thoughtlessly blocking.

He had applied for a research fellowship at the renowned university in Belgium in the belief that it would provide him with the opportunity to finish his manuscript on the problem of evil, a scholarly endeavor that he had been working on for three years. Unfortunately, it had become somewhat of a Damocles's sword. Every time he was asked about it he would reply that he was writing the last chapter. He found himself giving that answer repetitively. And it was starting to sound unconvincing even to himself.

As time sped by, he was also becoming painfully aware that his Dean was not really impressed. At his recent annual speech marking the beginning of the academic year, the Dean had remarked quite emphatically, 'When somebody tells me that he or she is working on something, that's fine.' Then with a rather serious countenance he had added, 'But a time should come when that same individual comes to me and says, it's finished. That's when I am really impressed.' Richard did not feel that the remark (or was it a veiled threat?) was directly aimed at him since there were others in his college who were in the same boat, so to speak. Like him, his fellow academics were bumping into all sorts of obstacles. As they set out to sail in the sea of scholarship, prodded on by the administrators, they kept floundering and just could not land.

Richard paused. He thought, I wonder whether this would be regarded as scholarly work by the Dean. He smiled. All that was now changed. It had become a merely academic question for him.

ACKNOWLEDGEMENTS

Marc Derez, *Town and Gown* (Lannoo/Universitaire Pers Leuven, 1991); *Belgium: Historic Cities* (Dutch Tourist Office and the Office for the Promotion of Tourism of the Frenchspeaking Community of Belgium, Brussels); *What's On in Leuven 1993?* (Tourist Office Leuven); publications of the Katholieke Universiteit Leuven; Helen Darbishire (ed.), *The Poetical Works of John Milton* (OUP, 1960); Gerald Sanders *et al.* (eds.), *Chief Modern Poets of Britain and America*, 5th ed. (Macmillan, 1970); W. Jackson Bate and David Perkins, *British and American Poets: Chaucer to the Present* (Harcourt Brace Jovanovich Publishers, 1986); various academics, students and many others in countries around the world; the staff at The Book Guild Publishers.